THE
PRINCE
OF NEITHER HERE
NOR THERE

ALSO BY SEÁN CULLEN

Hamish X and the Cheese Pirates

Hamish X and the Hollow Mountain

Hamish X Goes to Providence, Rhode Island

THE
PRINCE
OF NEITHER HERE
NOR THERE

SEÁN CULLEN

PUFFIN
CANADA

PUFFIN CANADA

Published by the Penguin Group

Penguin Group (Canada), 90 Eglinton Avenue East, Suite 700,
Toronto, Ontario, Canada M4P 2Y3 (a division of Pearson Canada Inc.)

Penguin Group (USA) Inc., 375 Hudson Street, New York, New York 10014, U.S.A.
Penguin Books Ltd, 80 Strand, London WC2R 0RL, England
Penguin Ireland, 25 St Stephen's Green, Dublin 2, Ireland
(a division of Penguin Books Ltd)
Penguin Group (Australia), 250 Camberwell Road, Camberwell,
Victoria 3124, Australia (a division of Pearson Australia Group Pty Ltd)
Penguin Books India Pvt Ltd, 11 Community Centre, Panchsheel Park,
New Delhi – 110 017, India
Penguin Group (NZ), 67 Apollo Drive, Rosedale, North Shore 0745,
Auckland, New Zealand (a division of Pearson New Zealand Ltd)
Penguin Books (South Africa) (Pty) Ltd, 24 Sturdee Avenue, Rosebank, Johannesburg
2196, South Africa

Penguin Books Ltd, Registered Offices: 80 Strand, London WC2R 0RL, England

First published 2009

1 2 3 4 5 6 7 8 9 10 (WEB)

Copyright © The Orb Incorporated, 2009

Manufactured in Canada

LIBRARY AND ARCHIVES CANADA CATALOGUING IN PUBLICATION

Cullen, Seán, 1965–
The prince of neither here nor there / Seán Cullen.

ISBN 978-0-14-317120-1

I. Title.

PS8605.U4255P75 2009   jC813'.6   C2009-902351-2

Visit the Penguin Group (Canada) website at **www.penguin.ca**

Special and corporate bulk purchase rates available; please see
www.penguin.ca/corporatesales or call 1-800-810-3104, ext. 477 or 474

This book is for my Brendan,
who is too small to understand
how much I love him,
and for Kimberley, who is larger
and might have an inkling
of how much I love her.

An Introductory Note
from the Narrator

Hello, Person. Welcome to the book. I have been chosen
to be your narrator for as long as this story lasts. I can't
help pointing out that you are especially lucky. I am the
best.

Narration is a serious business to be taken seriously by
serious people. Fortunately for you, I am an extremely
serious person. I rarely smile and I am very careful about
personal hygiene. Not that people who are clean don't
smile ... I am however very clean and I rarely do smile.

As always in the books I narrate, there are numerous
footnotes, those little tiny numbers throughout the
text that direct a reader to the corresponding number
at the bottom of the page where an explanation of a
difficult term or perhaps a clarification of a plot point
will be found. Be sure to read these footnotes. I take a
lot of time preparing them and, indeed, I was given
several awards for best footnoting at the Institute for
Advanced Narration in Helsinki, Finland.[1] I also received the

---

1 Good. You read this footnote. I think we're going to get along
   just fine.

Footnoter of the Year Award three years in a row. The award comes with a tiny trophy that I have placed on a tiny shelf just below and to one side of the large shelf where I keep my large trophies.

The beginning of a series of books is always a momentous time. We are about to embark on a journey together into realms unknown. We will meet characters of many stripes.[2] We will delve into dark places and find great joy and sorrow. Therefore, I suggest that you examine your intentions and be sure you are ready to make the commitment to finish this tale once you have started.[3]

I always take precautions when starting a new story. I make sure I have plenty of hand lotion to keep my fingertips moist as I peck away at my keyboard. It wouldn't do to get chapped tips! With each keystroke, the pain would become more and more intense, and unconsciously I would tend to make the story more and more bitter. I also try to have several extra pairs of fresh underpants handy. When I get involved in my writing I often lose track of time. In addition,

---

[2] By "characters of many stripes" I do not mean that the people will literally be striped. I mean that they will be quite different from one another. If this were to be a story about a group of zebras, then, most certainly, the characters involved would have a stripy tendency.

[3] In ancient China, during the Han Dynasty, anyone who started reading a book but didn't finish it was thrown in prison and had to stay there for as long as it took for the warden to read the book in question. One would always hope that the warden was a speed-reader.

I have a specially designed chair that massages my lower back at the touch of a button.

Perhaps you have enjoyed some of my earlier work. I narrated Langar the Electric Donkey: Parts One Through Seventeen.[4] I also won several awards for my narration of The Secret Life of Soap, a work of non-fiction that was praised as "a foamy and delightful odyssey through the life of a bar of soap" by The New York Times Book Review. Most recently, I narrated the very popular Hamish X series, which received several accolades, including Best Use of Cheese and Pirates. My point is that I know what I'm doing, so you can relax and just enjoy the book you are about to read.

The Prince of Neither Here Nor There is the first in a series of books about a boy named Brendan who doesn't realize his true nature. Certainly, sometimes we are all confused about who we are. For several days last month I was convinced I was a little French girl named Collette, but that was after a sharp blow to the head I received during a bank robbery.[5] The boy in The Prince of Neither Here Nor There, Brendan, finds himself caught in a struggle between

---

[4] *Langar the Electric Donkey* is now sadly out of print in the English language but is still available in Albanian at fine Albanian bookstores in Albania. It is also available on amazon.alb.

[5] I was not robbing the bank! Get that thought out of your mind. I was waiting in line to obtain a money order when bank robbers entered the establishment. I objected to their butting in front of me in line and was pistol-whipped for my pains. Pistol-whipping is painful but never as painful as being shot with a pistol. I suggest that you try to avoid both options if at all possible.

two worlds as he tries to find out where he fits into both. During the course of the story he will face strange and unknown dangers, discover new and amazing powers, and meet friends and family he never knew existed. I don't want to give too much away so I'll leave it at that. Suffice it to say that you will like this story: it will be exciting and fun! So keep reading!

This is also a story about Faeries. Not Fairies. There's a big difference, and it isn't just that one is spelled with an "e." Fairies are ineffectual little things that flit about in children's stories, shoot magic dust into people's faces, and dress up in flower petals and all that hooey. Insipid little things! No. No. No! The Faeries we will be dealing with are something different altogether! They are a noble race, an ancient race, often marvellous and magical but just as often deadly and dangerous. I hope you are up to this. If not, put down this book and back away carefully.

If you haven't backed away, I assume that you are going to continue reading. Good! You're just the sort of reader I admire. Let's get down to it! How shall I start? Hmmmm. I know. How about a prologue? Sounds like a plan ...

Now, let's begin. Since this is technically a Faerie Tale we should start with a suitable phrase. Are there any four words more filled with excitement and anticipation than ...

Once upon a time ...

Prologue

... A storm lashed Saint Bartholomew's Orphanage as though intent on peeling the slate roof away to gain entry to the old red-brick building on Liberty Street.[6] St. Bart's stoically withstood the howl of the wind and the torrents of rain as it had for over a century. Water gushed from its leaky gutters, pooling in the asphalt courtyard and overflowing the sewer grate, creating a small lake at the bottom of the cracked stone steps leading up to the front door. In the flashes of lightning the slate roof tiles glistened like molten lead traced with silver. The building seemed to cringe as the thunder rolled across the purple night sky.[7]

---

[6] Saint Bartholomew lived in the first century AD. He was flayed alive in Armenia. This had an adverse effect on Armenian tourism for several centuries afterward.

[7] I know what you're thinking: how original! A dark and stormy night! I would love to change the weather and the time to suit you but the story didn't start on a sunny day in June with birds a-twitter, flowers swaying in a gentle breeze, and a pony wearing a hat while nibbling a carrot. What you must understand is that so many stories begin on dark and stormy nights because great events often inspire nature to frame them in a suitably dramatic way. I am a narrator. I tell the tale as it happened, and if the coincidence of the dramatic weather is too predictable for you, I apologize.

St. Bart's had begun its life as the chapel of Toronto Central Prison in the late nineteenth century.[8] The prison, now long since demolished, was located on what was then the outskirts of the young city of Toronto. Farther west, along the waterfront, was the small affluent village of Parkdale, home to the rich burghers[9] who could afford to be away from the soot and train yards of the growing metropolis. The prison was built on land that was surrounded by warehouses, rail yards, and the pungent hog slaughter yards that gave Toronto its nickname "Hogtown."[10]

When it was built, the prison was hardly in a coveted location. No respectable person would want to live next to a slaughter yard on a rail line. But the reek of pig manure and the clatter of freight trains were thought to be a fitting addition to the misery of those incarcerated for their crimes. Decades later the prison was shut down as the city swelled westward to encompass its grounds. The only

---

[8] When I say nineteenth century, I mean the hundred years between AD 1799 and 1899, that is to say the eighteen-hundreds. It's confusing to call the eighteen-hundreds the nineteenth century as they have 18s instead of 19s in them, but that is the way these things are done. So ... get off my back.

[9] *Burgher* is another word for citizen, not to be confused with *burger*, a delicious patty of beef on a bun. I wouldn't want you to think huge sentient hamburgers were wandering the streets of Toronto. That would be weird.

[10] There are other theories as to how Toronto got its nickname. Some say it's because the city hogs all the resources in the country of Canada. Some say that the residents have gluttonous eating habits. Another theory is that the city was built on a mound of bacon that went bad on the journey over with the first colonists from England. I don't subscribe to that last one ... although the soil *is* quite salty.

vestige of the correctional facility was the grimy chapel and the name of the road that ran before it, Liberty Street.

The chapel escaped destruction only because a Catholic charity that cared for orphans was willing to take on the task of renovating the building for their needs. The nuns of St. Bartholomew raised the money from wealthy, guilty Catholics to turn the chapel into a dormitory for children made bereft of parents by accident or neglect. Their young charges slept in rows of cots by night and learned their letters by day in a schoolroom overlooking the bleak asphalt playground that had once been the convicts' exercise yard.

St. Bart's had endured much over the decades, but slowly the district around it slid further into decline. Industry moved to cheaper locations outside the city, and the orphanage gradually crumbled despite the sisters' best efforts. St. Bart's was teetering on the brink of a precipice of debt.

On this night, the sisters convened in the kitchen after all the children were tucked safely in bed. They were discussing the future of their enterprise. A tray of biscuits and pots of tea on the table were largely ignored.

"Bleak!" Sister Anna Grace announced. Spread before her on the table's scarred surface were the orphanage's ledgers, displaying an alarming amount of red ink.[11] "We are in a very desperate situation, sisters. Our creditors have been quite patient with us up to now, but we can't hope to

---

[11] Red is a colour that often signifies danger. In the case of accounting, red ink is used to write records of debt, whereas black ink shows positive cash flow or profit. So, weirdly, the colour black is positive for once in its existence.

rely on their patience much longer. They will not wait forever to be paid."

"Why shouldn't they wait?" Sister Hildegard grumped, her normally sour expression deepening, lips twisting, and nose wrinkling as if the air itself offended her. "We do the Lord's work here!"

"Indeed, Sister Hildegard." Sister Cecilia, the Mother Superior, raised a hand in gentle entreaty. She was tired and had no stomach for Sister Hildegard's belligerence, even when it was aimed at others. "We must thank them for their generosity. They have done so much for us up to now, extending our lines of credit and donating all they can, but one must remember that they have families of their own and businesses to run. They have been kind, but we must face the possibility that St. Bartholomew's may be forced to close its doors."

The announcement silenced the nuns. For a long moment the kitchen was filled with the sound of rain lashing against the windows and water dripping from the leaking roof into a metal bucket placed in the middle of the table. Sister Cecilia looked at each of the sisters in turn, her watery blue eyes taking in the defeat on her colleagues' faces. She sighed inwardly. Motivating the staff was becoming more and more difficult. The sisters worked so hard in the face of so many difficulties. And who was going to shore up her own flagging spirits? No, she chastised herself. *You are the Mother Superior! No time for self-pity.*

"Sisters," she said, masking her worry with a smile, "let us not be so downcast. We still have a little time. I suggest we all get some rest and perhaps the Lord will send us some inspiration. Say an extra prayer tonight. Remember: miracles do happen. The Lord will provide."

"Sister." The heavy male voice made all the nuns startle. They turned toward the doorway and saw Finbar, the groundskeeper and general handyman, looming there, his flat woollen cap in his thick, scarred fingers. Finbar had served in his post for many years, coming to work at St. Bart's after his sentence at the old prison was finished. His large ruddy face and pale blue eyes spoke of his Irish origins, and broken veins on his florid cheeks spoke of his fondness for whisky, a failing that the sisters chose to overlook. He had a full head of thick white hair. He was tall and solid, filling the doorframe with shoulders that were still wide and sturdy despite the fact that he was well into middle age. A career as a petty thief and housebreaker had landed him in jail many times. When the Toronto Central Prison finally closed in 1915, the then Mother Superior, despite the other sisters' objections, had decided to take a chance on him. Finbar had been with them ever since. He was good with his hands and could fix almost anything. He also seemed to have a soft spot for the young children, teaching those who were so inclined woodworking and basic mechanics in his workshop across the yard. In a nightly ritual, he informed the sisters, "The windows is all latched and the shutters closed. If there be nothin' else, it's me for bed."

"Thank you, Finbar. Good night."

The big man nodded and clomped off to the cellar, where his bed was nestled in a cozy nook, up against the warmth of the ancient furnace.

"As I was saying, sisters, a fervent prayer would not be out of place tonight," Sister Cecilia suggested with a confidence she didn't really feel.

"Humph," huffed Hildegard, pushing her chair back

from the table. "It's a miracle we're hoping for, is it? Well, they're few and far between these days. And the Lord didn't have a mortgage."[12] With that, Hildegard tramped out of the kitchen. Sister Cecilia and Sister Anna Grace listened to the tread of Hildegard's feet on the stairs as she ascended to the nuns' sleeping quarters on the third floor beneath the rafters.

"I'm sorry, Mother Superior. I wish the news was better, but we're just running out of money."

"I know, my dear," Sister Cecilia said. "Don't worry. You've done an excellent job. There's only so much any of us can do. Never mind Sister Hildegard. No one likes to hear bad news. You gather up your things and go to bed now. Those children will be up early tomorrow as they are every morning. You need your rest."

Sister Anna Grace gathered up her ledger books. "What about you, Mother Superior? You should get some sleep. You look tired."

"Oh, I'm fine, dear. One always looks tired when one gets to be my age," Sister Cecilia said with a rueful sigh. "I'll just clear away these tea things and I'll be right up."

Left alone in the kitchen, Sister Cecilia cleared away the remnants of the sisters' meeting. Placing pot and cups, creamer and sugar bowl, and crumb-laden plates onto the tray, she carried it to the counter and set it down by the

---

12 *Mortgage*: The term originates from the French word meaning "dead pledge." It is an agreement that stands until a payment is missed or the pledgor dies. Now it means the debt owed to a bank or other financial organization when one wishes to buy a house. Usually one does die before managing to pay off one's mortgage, but that's beside the point.

sink. The window over the kitchen sink gave her a view of the rain-lashed waste ground across Liberty Street and farther on to the lights of cars crawling along the expressway. The grey bulk of the buildings that made up the Exhibition Grounds rose in a dark silhouette, backlit by flashes of lightning. In years past the great lake beyond had spread out as far as the eye could see, but the concrete span of the highway now blocked it from view.

"Not that I could see that far these days," Sister Cecilia mumbled ruefully to herself. She was getting old. Her seventieth birthday was approaching, and in the damp early mornings she felt every year in her bones, the dull ache lingering longer and longer into the daylight hours.

SISTER CECILIA HAD BEEN BORN Aislin Callahan in the County of Cork, Ireland, far across a sea of water and years. She'd gone to teachers' college and graduated high in her class, applying for missionary work overseas and dreaming of a posting in remote African climes or South American jungles. She was shocked and slightly disheartened to find herself appointed as a teacher in Canada at the orphanage of St. Bartholomew's in the burgeoning city of Toronto.

She'd found herself shuddering west along King Street in a rackety red and yellow streetcar, crushed against the window by a grimy worker who was eating an enormous sandwich. Past warehouses, past a hospital, past some small shops, she watched the city go by. She was so engrossed she almost missed her stop. If she hadn't asked the driver to alert her when Strachan Avenue came up, she would have ridden to the end of the line.

"Strachan," the streetcar driver announced, drawling the name over the loudspeaker, missing the "ch" in the middle completely and saying it "Straaaaawn." By the exasperated tone of his voice, he must have had to repeat himself to get Sister Cecilia's attention. Flustered, the nun hauled her suitcase out from under the seat and made her way through the car and stepped down onto the street. The doors clattered shut and the streetcar pulled away.

Sister Cecilia stood on the side of the road looking around in bewilderment. She fished out of her pocket the directions she had written down on a scrap of paper. Before she could even look at them, a gust of wind plucked the paper from her hand and sent it sailing high into the air.

"Oh, Sweet Jesus, Mary, and Joseph!" Sister Cecilia shouted. She watched the scrap of paper disappear over the roof of a house.

"Strong language from a nun." The deep voice startled her. She spun around to see a tall man in overalls and a flat cap. His blue eyes were smiling.

"Oh, yes. Well … I lost my directions."

The man nodded slowly. He swept the hat off his head, revealing dark hair heavily salted with grey. "Aye. That can certainly happen."

"You're Irish?" Sister Cecilia asked.

"I am." He smiled again. Before she could ask more, he picked up her suitcase. "What're ye lookin' fer? Reckon I can guide ya."

Sister Cecilia bit her lip. A strange man, albeit someone from the home country, was holding everything she owned. He could just walk away and leave her there with nothing in this strange new city.

"Don't worry," the man said. "I'll not walk off with yer valuables, Sister. We bog-trotters[13] have to stick together." He grinned again.

Sister Cecilia couldn't help smiling back. "Saint Bartholomew's Orphanage. Do you know it?"

The man nodded once. "Well, isn't that a happy turn of events. Amn't I goin' that very way meself." He turned and headed south down Strachan toward the lake. Sister Cecilia had to trot to catch up with him.

They walked down the road, passing crumbling brick warehouses. The road was pot-holed and rough. Trucks passing by kicked up clouds of dust.

"Are you sure this is the way?" Sister Cecilia asked.

"Have no fear," the man rumbled. "I wouldn't steer ye wrong." A foul stench filled the sister's nostrils. Noticing the look on her face, he chuckled. "Aye, the pigs are being slaughtered over yonder today. It's a fine neighbourhood. This way!"

A wide swath of waste ground stretched away to their left. Brick warehouses rose on the right. "Liberty Street. Aptly named. All the lads fresh out of prison would walk this road on their first day of liberty.

---

[13] *Bog-trotter* is a nickname for Irish people that started out as an insult, referring to the boggy nature of the Irish countryside. It is truly impossible to trot on a bog. You will sink into it no matter how lightly you trot. Given that Finbar is Irish, his use of *bog-trotter* is a good example of how a people can reclaim a word that is meant to be insulting and, in doing so, take away the bad connotation. There's a lesson for you: if someone insults you, start using the insult as a nickname and confuse your detractor. I now call myself Iguana-face Gingerbeard Flatbottom for exactly that reason.

Mind you, most would be returning in a paddy wagon[14] in short order."

"There's a prison?" Sister Cecilia's voice was tinged with alarm.

"Was. The worst characters ended up in Toronto Central Prison. Murderers. Thieves. Arsonists. Evil fellows all." He turned his head and winked at her. "Don't worry. The prison's long been closed. The blackguards are all gone. Well, most of 'em, anyway." He chuckled again. Sister Cecilia suddenly regretted wandering off with this strange man.

"Here we are," the man said. "St. Bart's. Safe and sound." They stood in front of a decrepit building besieged by scrubby grass and a brick wall that rose just above their heads. A wooden gate stood closed, and beside it was a faded sign that announced in fading letters SAINT BARTHOLOMEW'S ORPHANAGE AND CATHOLIC MISSION.

Her guide pushed the gate open and stepped through. She followed quickly after him, entering a cobbled courtyard with forlorn swings creaking in the breeze. Ivy grew, shaggy and untended, on all the walls. Here and there

---

[14] The "paddy wagon" originated in New York City and was a nickname for an armoured police wagon employed to transport criminals. Calling the Irish "Paddies" is a play on the Irish name Patrick, so calling the police wagon a paddy wagon is a bit insulting, insinuating that all criminals were Irish. The Irish immigrants to New York did get involved in a lot of criminal activity due to the fact that they were extremely poor and had little choice if they wanted to survive. Eventually, they realized that if *they* drove the paddy wagon they would get a regular paycheque and medical benefits, which led to a huge influx of Irish into the police force.

weeds had poked through the paving stones. A vegetable garden struggled to survive in the corner.

"I think the Mother Superior's office is this way." The man hefted her suitcase and went to a stout wooden door. She followed him into the building.

The interior was a great deal more welcoming. They were in an entry hall with hardwood floors and threadbare carpets. The smell of wood polish filled the air. Children's voices, raised in song, drifted down the hallway. Sister Cecilia recognized the hymn: "Hail Queen of Heaven, the Ocean Star." She smiled. The song had been a favourite of her mother's and she always felt better when she heard it. The man led her up a set of wide wooden stairs and they came to a closed door. The man set her bag down and rapped twice on the door.

"Enter," came a clear female voice. The man opened the door and stood aside, sketching a courtly bow and indicating that the sister should enter.

Stepping into the office of the Mother Superior, Sister Cecilia found herself in a cramped room full of filing cabinets crowded around a huge oak desk. The nun wore an old-fashioned habit with a cowl that covered her whole head save for her wrinkled face.

Sister Cecilia swallowed and mustered her courage. "Sister Cecilia reporting for duties here at St. Bartholomew's," she stammered. "I was told to report to Sister St. Martin."

The old woman stared at her severely for a long, uncomfortable moment before saying, "I am Sister St. Martin. I'm sure you'd rather be somewhere more exotic, my dear, but make no mistake, there are young souls to save everywhere, even in the heart of the most civilized places in the world ... perhaps more so!" The severe nun looked past Sister Cecilia to where her guide filled the doorway. "Finbar, take her to the attic room. She can share with Sister Teresa."

Sister Cecilia frowned as she turned to the man. "You work here? Why didn't you say so?"

Finbar chuckled, tugging the bill of his hat in a mock salute. "Never asked, did ya?" He picked up her bag and went off down the hall. Sister Cecilia made to join him, but the Mother Superior stopped her with a word. "Sister."

Sister Cecilia faced the Mother Superior. The older woman smiled, transforming her stern face in an instant. "We welcome you here. There are so many children who need help and so few hands to turn to the work. We get some angry and desperate young people to take care of. Patience and kindness work wonders. Finbar is a good example. He was a prisoner here when there actually was a prison." Sister Cecilia's eyes went wide. "I trust him completely. We took him in when he couldn't find any work and he's been a loyal friend and excellent worker ever since. Patience and kindness: remember those two words and you'll do well here. Now go and settle in. I'll see you at dinner."

PATIENCE AND KINDNESS. Sister Cecilia had taken those words to heart. For years, she had taught and counselled the young children who came through St. Bart's, and eventually she herself rose to the position of Mother Superior. She worked hard and long, battling to keep the orphanage alive, but now, perhaps, they had reached the end. Sister Cecilia leaned against the counter, her heart heavy, listening to the rain. After a moment of silent prayer, she opened her eyes.

"I'm sorry, Sister St. Martin," she said to the empty kitchen and the rain on the window. "I'm sorry that everything will end this way. But the Lord has a plan for each of us in his wisdom. We must trust in him." She sighed heavily, placing the tea things into the sink. She turned the faucet and carefully commenced washing each cup and saucer.

Outside the window, huddled under the eaves, two small figures, one burdened with a squirming, wrapped bundle, peered in at the woman as she went about her chores.

"What's she doing?"

"Rubbing a cup. Be quiet."

"What a strange thing to do."

"They are an odd folk. We must be wary."

"Ooh. He's getting heavy, this little baggage."

"Shhh. She'll hear you!"

"It ain't my fault it won't sit still!"

"Just be quiet, will you?"

"Uh-oh. Do you smell that? I think he's soiled himself!"

"Be careful! Don't …"

"EW! What a filthy little baggage!"

"Just don't …"

"Uh-oh! I dropped it."

The sound of a baby crying cut through the drumming of the rain. Sister Cecilia's head jerked upright and, for a second, she thought she saw two small faces peering into the rain-streaked window. She blinked and looked again but they were gone. She could have imagined it, but she hadn't imagined the sound of the baby crying. Years of comforting frightened children had honed her ears to pick up that sound. A baby was out there in the terrible storm. She immediately dropped the clean cup back into the soapy dishwater with a plop and went to the kitchen door.

"*There. I've got him again, the little nipper!*"

"*Drop him and let's go. We've done what himself asked us to do.*"

"*Drop it? Fith! I only just picked it up again!*"

"*Just drop it and scamper!*"

Sister Cecilia opened the heavy wooden door and stepped out into the rain. In the darkness she thought she saw a flicker of movement at the corner of the small vegetable garden. The tomato plants rustled briefly.

"Perhaps my ears were playing tricks on me," she muttered. "Maybe it was just the rain on the roof." She was about to close the door when she saw the bundle on the ground.

It glowed softly in the darkness, catching the light streaming from the open door and transforming it into a pale blue-green glimmer like the luminescent dial of the clock on her bedside table. Sister Cecilia stared in wonder at the object, frozen by its beauty. The cry of a baby jerked her out of her stupor. The bundle began to wriggle.

"What am I doing, standing here like a fool?" She crossed the garden in an instant, wading through icy puddles and bending to take the wriggling bundle in her arms.

It was indeed a baby, wrapped in cloth swaddling that, for all its simplicity, was exquisitely woven out of a thread the nun had never seen the like of before. The weft of the cloth repelled the rainwater, making the droplets bead and run off without soaking in. Its surface bore a repeating pattern of minute, intricately entwined leaves and vines so beautifully articulated that they seemed to be alive. Sister Cecilia ran her fingers over the fabric, her eyes wide. With trembling fingers, she reached up and pulled away a fold of cloth to reveal a tiny round face.

The baby had a thick head of wavy, wheaten hair that formed a golden comma in the middle of its forehead. Round cheeks, flushed from the chill rain, framed a tiny pointed nose. The mouth was a perfect little red bow. The most arresting feature, though, were the child's eyes. They were slightly almond shaped and a most unusual greenish blue with flecks of gold. Though the baby had been crying, as soon as it saw Sister Cecilia's face, it left off its whimpering and looked up at her, beaming a most beatific[15] smile that melted the old woman's heart.

"What's this?" Finbar's voice rumbled close to the sister's ear.

"A baby," Sister Cecilia said, flustered. She hadn't heard the Irishman approach. He stood looking down at the bundle in her arms. He raised a giant hand and with one calloused finger chucked the little baby under the chin. The baby gurgled with pleasure.

"Hmmm," rumbled Finbar. "Curious thing. A child left on a doorstep on a stormy night." He raised his pale blue eyes and scanned the rain-swept yard. "Uncanny."

"Surely it's just another child cast off by some poor soul at their wit's end."

---

[15] *Beatific* is a word that means heavenly or saintly. I didn't just forget how to spell *beautiful*. Give me more credit than that!

The little baby gurgled happily and gripped the sister's finger in its tiny fist. Her heart melted.

"Let's get it in out of the rain," Sister Cecilia said suddenly.

"Are ye certain ye want to do that?"

Sister Cecilia looked up into the heavy face of the groundskeeper. Something dark in the ordinarily cheerful face made her pause. "Why ever wouldn't we?"

Finbar frowned and shrugged. "Strange turn of events, this. A baby left in the dark of a storm. Puts me in mind o' stories o' the Fair Folk me ma told us to frighten us i' the winter nights."

"Oh, Finbar," the sister said with a chuckle, "I wouldn't have thought you so superstitious."

Finbar's eyes narrowed. He opened his mouth to speak but decided against it.

"What is it, Finbar?"

Finbar's eyes became wary. "Not a thing. Those stories come from a grain o' truth, Sister." Finbar squinted at the dark rain. "You're from the old country, you should know better. Some might say I ain't so much superstitious as respectful of the Fair Folk. No good ever come o' mixin' in their plans. I heard tales of folks that were disappeared, lost in fairy mounds, shot by elf bolts, or even lumbered with the raising of a changeling child that had evil effect on all around it."[16] He paused and looked at the little face. "And I've heard tell of children being led away by Fair

---

[16] *Changelings*, according to folklore, are fairy children left in place of a human child by mischievous sprites. They notoriously end up turning into wizened, sickly, ill-tempered creatures that cause no end of trouble for their unwitting Human parents.

Folk and kept for their amusement, forgetting all that they once knew."

Sister Cecilia crossed herself. She had heard such tales too in her childhood in Ireland. She looked down at the beautiful little face framed in the cloth. The child had a radiant smile, showing a pair of perfect white teeth in its upper and lower gums. The sister's heart melted again. "I can't see this little one causing us anything but joy, Finbar. And with the dire state of our finances, it might be a welcome diversion to our sisters here. I must prepare a cot. Hold the child for a moment." She gave the bundle over to the gruff Irishman, who grunted in surprise, and scuttled off down the hall.

Looking down into the eyes of the little baby, Finbar shook his head ruefully. "Ye may have charmed the Mother Superior. But I'm another kettle of fish altogether." The baby stopped gurgling and looked up at Finbar. Finbar grinned back in spite of himself. "Still, yer a sweet little bundle, no doubt about it." His eyes narrowed. "What's this?" He dug a large finger into the swaddling, revealing a thin gold chain with a pendant hanging from it. The pendant was circular with spidery lettering delicately carved around the edge. The weight and the lustre of the object suggested that the gold was real. Finbar's eyes opened wide. He read the word aloud. "Breandan."

He stared out into the rainy night. He suddenly had the feeling that eyes were out there watching him. The hairs on the back of his neck stood up. There was tingling across his shoulders.

"I know yer there," he called into the empty courtyard. There was no answer but the wind and rain. "I know yer there somewhere. I can feel it. What mischief are ye about?"

Crouched in shadow of the courtyard's brick wall, two small figures held a whispered conversation.

"He can't know we're here."

"Does he see us?"

"Impossible! ... I think."

"Has he been given the Sight?"

"I think not. It would be plain if he had the Sight."

"Something strange then.... We should be off. Our deed is done."

"The child will be safe."

"Aye. For a while. For a while."

The leaves of the tomato plants rustled. Finbar stared a moment longer but saw nothing more. He carefully closed the door and turned the bolt.

"I'll hold on to this," Finbar whispered. He lifted the chain from the baby's neck, letting the medallion spin on the end as he examined it in a flash of lightning. "It may prove very useful indeed."

When he got to the kitchen, the sister was standing at the sink, now brimming with soapy water and steaming gently.

"Let's warm up the little one." Finbar handed the child over to the Mother Superior. The child had fought free of the wrappings and was clutching at the woman's chin with one fist. A smile lit his tiny face.

"It's a boy, Finbar." The sister laughed. "A lively one too."

Finbar came and looked down at the little creature, who immediately turned his beautiful eyes upward to look into Finbar's own.

"He's a fine-looking child, he is. What's this? Looks like a burn." Finbar traced a crusted scab on the boy's left breast. The bloody blemish marred the otherwise perfect ivory of the babe's skin. Finbar had seen such a mark on the hide of sheep when he was a boy. "Someone's branded the little tyke."

"Oh dear," Sister Cecilia cried. She took the baby from Finbar and plunged him into the soapy water. Gently, she took a cloth and sponged away the caked blood to reveal a wound in the shape of a spiral.

"Who would do such a thing to a child?" Sister Cecilia demanded in outrage.

"A Ward," Finbar breathed softly.

"What did you say?"

Finbar frowned. "Not a thing, Sister. Aye, there are all manner of bad folk in the world," he said softly, peering at the revealed mark. "He don't seem to be in any pain, though, do he? He's a hardy little chap. Aren't ya, little fella?" He pinched a chubby cheek in his calloused fingers and the baby gurgled happily.

Finbar held out a little finger and the baby clutched it tight. "Hello, young Breandan."

"Breandan?"

"In the old tongue Breandan means 'prince.'"

"Does it indeed? Well, it's a good enough name, I think. Breandan it is. Oh, he shall certainly be a prince in this house when all the sisters lay their eyes on his sweet little face. Hold him a moment while I prepare a bottle for him." The sister held the baby out for Finbar to take in his huge hands, then she began shuffling around the kitchen, happily absorbed in her task. Finbar held the boy up, dripping, until they were eye to eye. He stared into the child's face. The baby, sensing the mood of the man, became sombre and still.

"*Fáilte, Breandan,*" Finbar said softly in Gaelic and then repeated in English. "Welcome, My Prince."

The medallion lay heavy in Finbar's vest pocket. "It'll be our little secret, awright?"

Out in the waste ground beyond the walls of St. Bart's, the rain and wind flattened the tall grass. Two tiny figures scampered up to an empty oil drum that had been tipped onto its side and left to rust. A dark figure sat cross-legged on the drum, silhouetted by the lightning flashes. The rain poured down onto his bowed head, streaming from the tips of his white tresses. The small figures cowered on their knees at the foot of the oil drum, waiting on the figure to speak.

"*Is it done?*" The dark figure's voice was cold, like a door flung open on a field newly rimed with frost: beautiful but cold.

"*Done, Highness. Done. It's done.*"

"*Completely done. No doubt.*"

"*Were you seen?*"

"*No! NO! NO!*" the two little creatures squeaked insistently. "*Not seen! Not seen at all.*"

"*Are you certain?*"

"*Uh …*"

"*YES?*"

"*There was one who sensed us. He didn't see us but he felt our presence.*"

The dark figure was utterly still for a moment, water dripping from his chin. Finally, he spoke. "*Very well. I release you from service. Go now. Get out of my sight.*"

"*Gladly. Oh, gladly, Your Highness!*" Squeaking, the little creatures fell over each other, darting through the grass in their eagerness to be away. Like twin comets, they leapt into the air and streaked off between the raindrops.

The figure waited until they were gone and then unfolded from its position, stepping lightly down onto the wet grass. Lightning flashed above, illuminating briefly the stark, angular lines of a male face, not quite human, with dark molten eyes of black fire.

"*I have done what I could, love,*" the dark figure announced to the empty field, his voice choked with grief. "*He is safe for a while.*" He raised one hand skyward and beckoned. In answer, a jagged finger of lightning scorched through the air toward his outstretched hand. If the human eye were capable of registering such speeds, a person watching would have marvelled to see pale fingers grasp the lightning like a rope. The lightning retreated into the sky, yanking the dark figure along with it.

PART 1

Awakening

Another Note
from the Narrator

Ha! What a prologue! Really whets the appetite, doesn't it? A good prologue is the soup before the meat, don't you agree? Maybe a salad. An appetizer? You know what I mean!

Let me caution you: the next part of the story takes place several years later, fourteen years later, in fact. The jump forward in time is a common device in storytelling that allows us to skip over some, if not dreary, certainly time-consuming and unexciting bits. I could have detailed each of the ensuing years, days, hours, minutes, and seconds in excruciating detail but what would be the point? You'd get bored by the time the child got potty-trained and we'd never get to the really interesting parts. Besides, can you imagine the size of such a tome?[17] All of Siberia would be utterly deforested just to print the first run of the book! You don't want to be responsible for such a vast amount of

---

[17] *Tome* is another word for book. I could have used *volume* or *manuscript* or *hardback* or *codex* but I like tome. It comes from the ancient Mayan practice of writing on tomatoes. Unfortunately, all the great literary works of the Mayans are now just dusty ketchup.

soil erosion. I knew of one narrator, a friend from the Institute, who wrote the life of Winston Churchill starting with the point where his father met his mother at a card party until the great man's death. Every single instant was chronicled! The manuscript was so large that the writer in question ended up abandoning any hope of mailing it to an editor and lived in the huge stack of paper instead. Sadly, the book burned down one night and he was forced to move into a small pamphlet. Sad. Sad but irrelevant.

So. Fourteen years have passed. The little boy is now in that dangerous and sinister place called "high school" with all its inherent perils. We join him in the most terrifying of all predicaments—the horror known as ... gym class!

MURDERBALL

Why? Why me? Brendan crouched in the middle of the gymnasium floor as Chester Dallaire wound up for the killing blow. *I'm a good person. I'm kind to animals. I even tolerate my sister! So why me?*

He had known it was going to be a bad day when he woke up with a giant, red, glistening pimple at the junction of his eyebrows. Pimples were a constant worry for him. Clustered at the corner of his mouth or at the side of his nose, they were a common occurrence. This pimple, however, was different: it was a harbinger of doom. He had tried to squeeze it but that had only made it redder and angrier. He knew then, as he left the house, this day was going to be a bad one.

"Ches-ter! Ches-ter! Ches-ter!" the crowd of students at the edge of the floor chanted. They were all excited and eager for the kill. There is nothing a crowd enjoys more than not being the one who is about to get clobbered.

Chester Dallaire was really savouring the moment, allowing Brendan to contemplate his fate at great length. Chester Dallaire was the largest boy in grade nine at Robertson Davies Academy. Chester truly was a misfit in RDA. Usually, jocks are the norm and nerds are the minority in high school. RDA, however, was a small school that recruited academically gifted students from all over the city. In essence, one could call RDA a school of nerds where Chester was the odd man out. Physically more mature than the other students, Chester had the beginnings of a moustache, and the rumour ran that he had a tattoo of a crouching panther on his back. No one had ever seen this tattoo as Chester rarely took off his shirt and scrupulously avoided bathing. He tossed the ball playfully in the air and leered at Brendan, who trembled in terror, waiting for the blow to fall.

Brendan was on the exact opposite end of the spectrum, physically. Where Chester was already well on the way to adulthood, Brendan's body was still teetering on the edge of adolescence. He was thin and gawky. He had to wear thick glasses if he didn't want to run into walls and furniture. As an added bonus, he wore braces on his crooked teeth. Yes, indeed. Brendan had definitely won the Teenage Affliction Lottery.

He pushed his glasses up onto his nose. *Why do we even play this stupid game, anyway!* Brendan thought miserably. *Who, besides Chester, even likes it?*

"CHES-TER! CHES-TER! CHES-TER!"

Murderball[18] is a game that is ideal for bullies. Why bother picking on the weaker kids in the schoolyard when you can just whack them in the head with a ball during gym class? Every gym teacher on the planet fails to see

---

[18] Murderball (also known as Dodgeball): Before becoming the modern pastime enjoyed (or dreaded) by students the world over, Murderball was devised as a means of executing criminals in seventeenth-century Germany. Murderers were sentenced to be pelted with rubber balls until they were dead. However, the murderers became very adept at dodging the balls and so the modern sport of Murderball was born.

how humiliating and often painful it is to let these bullies have their way. Gym teachers the world over believe that Murderball is a great way to instill character in their young charges and allow the kids to blow off some steam.[19] Most schoolkids would rather leave their steam where it is and live without the giant purple welts on their backs.

"CHES-TER! CHES-TER! CHES-TER!"

Murderball is a game for sadists[20] and masochists.[21] Chester definitely fell into the former category, while Brendan liked to think of himself as neutral. How he'd ended up lasting to this point in the game he couldn't quite understand. Maybe his desire to avoid being the recipient of a smack from Chester Dallaire had infused him with some hitherto unknown agility.

Usually, Brendan could barely avoid tripping over his own feet. He was famously clumsy. All his classmates teased him mercilessly. Butterfingers, Thumbs, Trippy McFallstein—they were always dreaming up new names to mock him with. Yes, Brendan knew he was a danger to others and to himself. At home, his father had gently but firmly banished him from the basement art studio after the

---

19 Technically speaking, Murderball is not played the world over. Cultures where Murderball is not played have developed their own equivalents. All of them involve weaker, nerdy children being pelted, whipped, or beaten by bullies with handy objects. In the jungles of Borneo, children play Murdervine. In Afghanistan, it's Murderrock. In Turkey, it's Murderkebab. In France, it's Murdercrepe, and so on.

20 *Sadist*: A person who enjoys inflicting pain. See also: Mathematics Teacher.

21 *Masochist*: A person who enjoys having pain inflicted upon them. Good jobs for masochists include hammer-tester, rodeo clown, and crash-test dummy.

nine-hundredth time he had accidentally crushed some delicate sculpture or piece of art. His mother said he was just growing too fast and he would eventually grow out of his clumsiness, but Brendan had his doubts.

Knowing all this, it was hard to believe that he was the last person in the game, backed into a corner, waiting for Chester to pulverize him. *How?* he asked himself. *Why?* But he knew the reason. The reason was Marina Kaprillian, a ninth-grader of surpassing beauty who was currently leaning coolly against the wall with a tittering group of her friends watching the action. The students who had been eliminated from the game early watched with relish as the humiliation continued, relieved to escape relatively unscathed. The audience grew as more were knocked out and so did the humiliation. The added opportunity for embarrassment was the fact that gym classes, due to the small number of students, were co-ed. Unlike most high schools, gym class and sports were a low priority compared to academic pursuits at Robertson Davies Academy. As a result, physical education suffered from funding shortfalls in favour of Chess Club and the Debating Team. Brendan was desperate to impress Marina or at least make her notice him. Staying in the Murderball game seemed like the way to catch her eye. So, despite all his physical shortcomings, he had made a superhuman effort and here he was on the verge of devastating personal injury.

There's an old saying: be careful what you wish for. Now he was standing in the middle of the gym, wishing she would look anywhere else. Chester was going to cream him and he would look like a total goof.

Brendan looked to the sideline where his friends gathered, faces screwed into varying expressions of horror on his behalf. Harold's chubby hands half-covered his round face as if he couldn't bear to look but at the same time couldn't pass up a chance to witness such exquisite carnage. Dmitri, small and blond, shook his head and motioned for Brendan to just play dead. Beside Dmitri, Kim gave Brendan a thumbs-up. The expression on her face suggested she wished she were in Brendan's place. She was a true tomboy and loved physical contests. Of all his friends, she was the only one who was at home in the gymnasium: her shorts and T-shirt actually fit, and she stood with one hip cocked, looking quite sporty. She kept her hair cut in a trim little bob that framed her oval face neatly. One graceful eyebrow was arched as she slowly shook her head in disbelief. Apart from Kim, Brendan's little gang of nerds lived mainly in their minds and found physical activity difficult at best and distasteful at worst.

"*CHES-TER! CHES-TER! CHES-TER!*" The chanting of the crowd took on a feral edge.[22] They sounded less like high school students and more like a pack of hyenas baying for blood.

Brendan looked away from the little knot of supporters and back to his inspiration. His eyes sought out that

---

22 *Feral* is a word that refers to an animal that once lived in a domesticated state but has returned to the wild. Housecats become feral, recovering their hunting insticts when returned to the wild. Same with dogs. I once had a tame snail who ran away and turned wild. When I found him, I knew he'd gone feral. His behaviour was the same but there was a dangerous glint in his eye.

special face … her face. There she was! She was looking at him! In spite of his pimple, she was looking at him.

"I am so gonna smear you all over this floor, Brendan Clair!" Chester's heavy voice cut through Brendan's daze. Brendan turned to see Chester sneering at him from across the floor.

"No need for taunting, Chester." Mr. Davenport, the gym teacher, his voice nasal and piercing, chided over the noise of the crowd. "That's poor sportsmanship." Mr. Davenport was thin and wiry with a horrible comb-over. He wore a red sweatsuit with "Robertson Davies Academy Magicians" stencilled on the front. Mr. Davenport was a physics teacher but he doubled as a phys. ed. teacher because he had a secret desire to be an athlete, a desire that had no hope of ever being fulfilled. As a result, he took grim pleasure in inflicting physical exercise on his students.

"Whatevs." Chester shrugged and wound up his massive arm. The inflated rubber sphere was clutched in Chester's banana-like fingers, the surface dimpling as he reared back to launch a massive throw at Brendan as he squatted, cornered.

Suddenly, Brendan felt a surge of anger. He was tired of being sneered at. He was tired of having a giant pimple on his forehead. He was tired of being afraid. How dare this big guy humiliate him in front of his friends and, more importantly, in front of the girl of his dreams? He shouted in his mind, *NO!* He gritted his teeth and clenched his fists. Gathering himself like a panther, he let loose with a feral cry.

"Graaaaaaaaaaaaaaaaaa!" Brendan launched himself across the floor at Chester, driven by all the pent-up frustration of being a nerd. Chester's eyes opened wide in surprise. At first, the lunge was quite impressive. The onlookers held their collective breath as Brendan surged forward. Unfortunately, Brendan was unaware that his shoelace was untied. He stepped on the offending lace and tripped himself spectacularly. He face-planted on the hardwood and slid with a skin-erasing squeak on the waxed surface, ending up spread-eagled at Chester's feet.

Brendan rolled over onto his back, blinking up at his adversary. Chester grinned evilly and cocked the ball back for the *coup de grâce*.

"Nice one, dorkmaster!" Chester said with relish. He slam-dunked the rubber orb squarely into Brendan's upturned face.

Fifteen minutes later, Brendan was assuring the nurse, Mrs. Barsoomian, that he was fine. His nose had stopped bleeding and the ringing in his ears had subsided. His face, normally somewhat pale and spotty, was an angry red welt from ear to ear. He looked like the recipient of an intense and localized facial sunburn. His glasses hadn't broken but they had been mashed into his skull, leaving a welt around his eyes. He held up his hand to ward off another cold compress. "I'm fine, really, Mrs. Barsoomian."

"Are you sure? You can lie down and rest a while longer if you wish." The thin dark face of the nurse was full of concern. "I can put some lotion on your face. Or a bag of ice, maybe." Mrs. Barsoomian was a sweet little woman with dark hair and kind brown eyes. Brendan felt embarrassed by the attention.

"No thanks." Brendan smiled and winced at the sudden pain. "Really, I'll be fine."

"I get more patients from Murderball than from any other source." Mrs. Barsoomian shook her head in irritation. "It should be outlawed."[23]

"Yes, ma'am. In a perfect world, I'd never play again but Mr. Davenport wants to make a man out of me."

"Someone should make a man out of Mr. Davenport," Mrs. Barsoomian said darkly.

Brendan pushed himself off the examining table and stood, woozily. "Can I go now?"

Mrs. Barsoomian eyed him critically, then nodded. "All right. Come back if you feel any dizziness."

"Yes, ma'am."

Released from the nurse's office, Brendan walked out into the hall to find Kim, Harold, and Dmitri waiting for him.

"Holy tomato face!" Harold said in awe. "That is, I don't mean to say your face is juicy and a great source of lycopene. I mean that your face is the exact shade of a ripe tomato!" Harold fumbled in his bookbag and fished out a crimson crayon. He held it up to Brendan's face. "See? I was right! Tomato Red!"

"Thanks for your sympathy, Harold," Brendan growled, batting the crayon away from his face. He tried to arrange his glasses so that they didn't irritate his sore face.

"Nice technique." Kim shook her head. "You jumped right into that ball. You got a death wish?"

---

[23] Indeed, Murderball has been outlawed in a number of countries around the world. The United Nations has tried to institute a universal ban on the sport but the Russians have used their veto to block the motion. Many believe the powerful Ball Manufacturers Association of Kamchatka to be behind the veto.

Brendan shrugged and started walking down the hall toward their next class, chemistry with Mr. Bowley. "I dunno. Just got tired of waiting for him to cream me, so …"

"You decided to attack him with your face?" Kim scoffed. She hitched her green kilt up even higher on her hips, accentuating the long coltishness of her legs. She tended to roll her waistband over to inch the kilt into miniskirt territory, technically against school policy. Not even the teachers had the courage to call her on it. Kim didn't take kindly to rule-quoting. "Super-dumb."

Brendan had given up wondering why Kim hung around his little group of losers. She was sporty, confident, and cool. He'd overheard lots of boys who'd called her cute but only when they were sure she couldn't hear them. Her fierce brown eyes would burn holes in anyone who tried to chat her up. Kim tolerated Brendan, Harold, and Dmitri for some unknown reason. Maybe they were just so hapless that she didn't have to worry about them asking her out or behaving like normal high school boys. She could be quite abrasive even if she did count you among her circle of friends. "What possessed you?"

"I don't know," Brendan said, "I just felt tired of being scared of guys like Chester. I just …" He trailed off. Marina Kaprillian stepped out of the cafeteria doorway flanked by two of her girlfriends. Brendan stopped short with his mouth slightly open. "I uh … uh …"

Kim followed his gaze and stopped at his side. "Oh brother." Kim frowned and tugged at his sleeve. "Come on, Brendan. Marina Kaprillian is not for you."

Marina and her friends saw Brendan standing in the middle of the hall as students passed on either side and they immediately erupted in fits of giggles and went off down the hallway still giggling about something one of them had said with a glance in his direction. Brendan felt himself blush, but he doubted it would be visible over the redness of his face.

"Can you hear me, Brendan?" Kim said, rapping him on the head with her knuckles. "Anybody in there?"

"Ow," Brendan yelped. "That hurt."

"I'm telling you," Kim insisted, jerking her thumb toward the retreating gaggle of girls. "You and that girl … not gonna happen."

Brendan was suddenly angry. He turned on Kim. "Why not? Am I such a loser that she could never like me? Huh? Is that it?"

Kim was taken by surprise by the outburst. She opened her mouth to say something but caught herself.

"What? What were you going to say?" Brendan saw that she was sorry, but he didn't feel like stopping. He had to vent at someone. "You think I'm not good enough for her?" Brendan demanded. "She's out of my league. Is that it? I'm a pimply, goggle-eyed, tinsel-toothed loser. Is that it?"

"No. I wasn't going to say that." Kim looked at him. For an instant, Brendan saw something other than disdain in her eyes: a glimmer of … what? Sympathy? Then it was gone. "Forget it!" She snorted in disgust and set off down the hall toward the chemistry class. The knapsack on her back swung back and forth to match her strides, her field hockey stick poking up out of the top like the arm of a metronome.[24]

---

[24] A *metronome* is a device used to help musicians keep a proper tempo while playing music. It is not a very stylish garden dwarf.

"What's with her?" Dmitri asked.

"I should apologize," Brendan said, starting after her. He stopped. "But I'm not going to. She was kind of mean, too."

"I'll talk to her," Harold offered. He was her lab partner and they shared a desk in the next class. "I'll soften her up." Harold shook his head and lumbered after her.

Brendan and Dmitri started walking. "Why was she so down on me liking Marina? I mean, sure, I haven't got a chance but a guy can dream, can't he?"

Dmitri shrugged. "I don't know. Maybe Kim has a crash on you. Have you ever thought of that?"

"The word is crush, not crash." Brendan often had to correct Dmitri's English. Brendan frowned. "And no, I don't think that's it. It's something else …" He felt a hand on his shoulder. He turned to see Dmitri looking up at him. Dmitri had a gentleness about him that came from always being too small to rely on brute force. His family had immigrated from Poland and they were not very well off. He was an outsider in more ways than one. Brendan had gravitated to the smaller boy for that reason. Dmitri'd had to learn English on his arrival and so had had a hard time making friends. He and Brendan had hit it off almost immediately when they had been assigned seats beside each other in homeroom. Nerd magnetism, Brendan called it. Dmitri was a whiz at math and science, which was a good thing since Brendan was practically useless at both. Brendan helped him with the language, concentrating on the slang words that the other kids used in the halls.

Dmitri smiled, more of a lopsided smirk. "There are worse things to be brave about than a pretty girl."

Brendan grinned. "Thanks, D. I don't know why I bother. She thinks I'm a joke. If she thinks about me at all."

The bell rang to announce the start of class.

"Uh-oh," Brendan gasped.

The two boys took off at a dead run. Mr. Bowley was a tyrannical old man. They called him Bowelly Bowley but never to his face. Mr. Bowley was a stickler when it came to punctuality. He would stand with his pocket watch in his hand and if you arrived even a second late, he would close the door in your face and point you toward the office to get a late slip.

When they arrived at the door, miraculously it was still open. Not believing their luck, the two boys hurried into the room, taking the assigned workbench that they shared at the back of the room. Brendan checked to see if Kim was still angry. She sat at the front of the room beside Harold. She had her back turned to him. She was looking at the front of the class and though he couldn't see her face, he could sense by her rigid posture that she was angry.

Brendan followed her gaze and was surprised to see that Mr. Bowley was not there in his customary place at the front of the class glaring at the students. The chemistry teacher, in his pristine white lab coat and polished spectacles, never missed a day of school. He was never sick, never late, and never absent. The students were all certain he was an android programmed by the Board of Education to torture young minds.[25]

---

[25] Though it sounds far-fetched, recently an android teacher factory was discovered in the former Soviet Union. They were manufacturing android science teachers completely devoid of human feelings. Studies revealed that they were completely indistinguishable from human science teachers.

Today, however, Mr. Bowley was nowhere to be seen. Instead, another man leaned casually against the desk. Dressed in a well-tailored sleek grey suit with a pale green silk vest, the man was tall and thin. His face was ... there was no other word but perfect—high cheekbones, a long powerful nose, and expressive grey eyes. He smiled at the class.

"I'm sure you are all wondering where our dear Mr. Bowley has got to. I am happy to say he is perfectly healthy, safe, and sound. Better than sound, truth be told. Mr. Bowley has won the lottery. Understandably, he has decided to take a little time off to absorb his good fortune."

A buzz of whispering erupted from the students. Everybody was busy consulting with their neighbours. Everybody but Kim. She crossed her arms and glared at the man as he raised his hands for quiet. The man seemed to sense her disapproval and, as he turned his head slightly to meet her gaze, he winked. Brendan found the gesture so odd, almost as if they knew each other. He would have to ask her after class ... if she was talking to him. At last the buzz subsided. The man spoke again in his beautifully modulated voice.

"Until he returns, I am your substitute teacher. My name is Mr. Greenleaf. I think we shall get along very well indeed."

THE SUBSTITUTE

The class was mildly stunned by the fact that the grim and cheerless Mr. Bowley had won the lottery. It was hard to imagine such a serious and practical person ever wasting money on a ticket in the first place. Still, the girls in the class were delighted by the change in scenery. Mr. Greenleaf was a definite improvement on Mr. Bowley in the looks department. Already, he was the subject of a number of whispered, giggly conversations.

The sight of Mr. Greenleaf standing at the front of the classroom had sent a weird shock through Brendan's brain. He was overcome by an odd tingling sensation as though a chill breeze had washed over him from an open window. He turned his head and looked out at the late November sun blazing down on the parking lot, igniting the chrome fixtures of the cars and turning each door handle and side-view mirror into a shining star. The world seemed so intensely clear, deeper in detail and richer in colour. *What is going on? That ball must have knocked something loose.*

Brendan shivered and rubbed his eyes, trying to focus. Ow! He clutched at his chest. He felt an intense, itchy, burning sensation over his heart. *Am I having a heart attack? Am I going to be a story in the newspaper? SEEMINGLY HEALTHY BOY KEELS OVER DEAD.* Then he realized the sensation was on the surface of his skin and not deep in his chest. He pulled down the collar of his T-shirt and saw that the pale scar was red and inflamed. The spiral had been on his chest over his heart ever since … well always. His parents said it was a leftover from the time when, as an infant, he had pulled on the tablecloth and spilled some hot tea on himself. A fluke accident that had left the curious scar. It had never given him any trouble before.

He felt something jab into his ribs.

"You okay?" Dmitri whispered. The smaller boy was looking at Brendan with concern. "You look a little … funny."

Brendan faked a smile and shrugged. "Yeah. Just after-effects from a ball in the face, I guess." He let his collar cover the mark and tried to concentrate. He looked up and saw Kim looking at him. He smiled weakly and waved but she didn't look happy. He'd seen her angry before but this was something else. She seemed downright hostile. She was staring daggers at the substitute teacher, but he didn't seem to notice. Either that or he was just ignoring her.

"Chemistry!" Mr. Greenleaf's clear, musical voice savoured the word. "What exactly is it?"

Belinda Tindal's hand shot up. She was a sallow-faced girl with pigtails and enormous braces who could always be counted on to nerd out at the slightest opportunity. Brendan could sympathize. His braces were a pain but hers were of the variety that drew comparisons to antique car bumpers or the cowcatchers on the front of old steam trains. Belinda had also been cursed with every blight that an adolescent girl could suffer: crooked teeth, a spray of pimples across her cheeks, and poor eyesight, just like Brendan, but he had to admit that they all seemed so much worse on her. Still, her disadvantages didn't seem to deter her from calling attention to herself by being intelligent. Any self-respecting teen would have clammed up and laid low. Brendan had learned that lesson early and well after a painful wedgie from Chester and his pals.

"Belinda!" Mr. Greenleaf smiled and indicated with a graceful flick of his hand that Belinda should speak.

"You know my name?" Belinda said, confused. In the three months she had been coming to chemistry, Mr. Bowley had never remembered her name. He'd called her Betty, Betina, Barbara but never Belinda.

"Of course." Mr. Greenleaf smiled gently. "I make it a point to learn every one of my students' names. Chemistry is …?"

Belinda flushed in the face of the concentrated power of the substitute's smile. She rose from her seat and fiddled with her heavy black-rimmed glasses for a second then announced, "Chemistry is the science that deals with the composition and properties of substances and various elementary forms of matter." Belinda said this with the utmost gravity. Eyes were rolled throughout the classroom.

Mr. Greenleaf nodded gravely in response. "Yes. Absolutely. That is a very good textbook definition of what chemistry is. Thank you, Belinda." Belinda sat down, blushing furiously. "A little bit dry, though, don't you think? What does chemistry mean to us?"

Chester could always be counted on to make a smartass comment. "It means total boredom!" This aroused a few snorts of laughter from Chester's cronies. Chester always had someone to confirm his brilliance in the form of a gang of oafish boys who'd grown large seemingly overnight. Chester grinned and cracked his knuckles loudly, eliciting another round of laughter.

"Chester." Mr. Greenleaf's voice cut through the laughter like a knife. His grey eyes latched onto the large boy's and held them. "There are no boring subjects, only boring people."[26] He grinned and showed perfect white teeth. Though he was smiling, Mr. Greenleaf did not seem particularly amused. Something terrible and predatory in the smile made Brendan hope the substitute teacher never smiled that way at him. Indeed, even the thick-skinned Chester managed to realize he was in dangerous waters. Brendan's nemesis visibly shrank back into his seat. Brendan couldn't help feeling slightly gleeful. He turned to see if he could catch Kim's eye but she was still focused on the teacher. The expression on her face was fierce. *If she was a cat, she'd be hissing right now!*

After what seemed like an age, Mr. Greenleaf barked a sharp laugh. "Ha. Boring indeed." The threat in his face was gone, replaced with an amused smirk. "Chemistry may seem boring on the surface, but that is only because you are looking at the surface." He picked up a piece of white chalk and tossed it in the air. He caught the chalk, closing his hand over it completely. "Chemistry allows us to change the nature of things and make them"—he opened his hand to reveal that the chalk had changed colour from white to pink—"different." The class gawped in silence.

He closed his hand again, opened it, and the chalk was blue. Again, Mr. Greenleaf closed his long fingers over the

---

[26] While a nice sentiment, this statement is not true. There are many boring subjects. I would list them but then you would be bored.

chalk. "We can unlock the secrets of matter and transform it into something altogether new and wonderful." He opened his hand to reveal a hummingbird, sitting calmly in his palm. The hummingbird rose from Mr. Greenleaf's hand and hovered for a few seconds, the hum of its tiny wings thrumming in the sudden hush of the room. Then it flitted once in a circle around the teacher's head as if in salute and flashed out the open window into the sunshine. The class gasped and broke out into spontaneous applause, cheering and hooting.

Brendan sat with his mouth open. He was at the back of the class and therefore farthest from Mr. Greenleaf when he executed the amazing transformation. Brendan looked at Dmitri and saw that the smaller boy was smiling involuntarily and clapping his hands along with the rest.

"That was completely awesome!" Dmitri said brightly.

"Totally awesome," Brendan corrected in a whisper. "No one says completely awesome."

"Totally awesome, then," Dmitri corrected himself with a sigh.

Brendan wasn't so sure. He thought what he'd seen was kind of spooky and disturbing. He looked over at Kim and saw that she also was not impressed.

He turned back to the front of the class to find that Mr. Greenleaf was staring right at him. The teacher raised a dark, elegant eyebrow and smiled in a lopsided, knowing way as if he sensed Brendan's discomfort. Brendan's stomach turned over. His hand rose involuntarily to his chest. The itch over his heart seemed to intensify. Brendan felt a wave of dizziness sweep over him.

Mercifully, the door to the classroom burst open to reveal Ms. Abernathy, the vice-principal of RD Academy.

Her green flannel trouser-suit was practically bristling with indignation. Her perma-frown[27] was on full blast.

"What is going on in here?" Ms. Abernathy demanded. All noise ceased immediately, sucked into the black hole[28] of Ms. Abernathy's disapproval. The children stopped clapping and lay their hands on their desks. Some sat on their hands just to make sure they wouldn't be incriminated. Others looked as though they would like to make their hands disappear altogether—anything to avoid detention under the baleful[29] glare of Ms. Abernathy.

It never paid to incur the wrath of Ms. Abernathy. She was the second in command to Principal Singh who was a very jolly, easygoing sort of person. Ms. Abernathy handled all discipline. If a student crossed the line, that student ended up in her office and could suffer anything from writing lines, to extra assignments, to weeks of detention, or could even be expelled.

---

[27] A *perma-frown* is a facial feature that displays permanent disappointment and disdain that many persons develop in conjunction with their jobs. Usually it is manifested as a deep furrow between the eyebrows and perpetual turndown at the corners of the mouth. There are rumours of a special plastic surgery facility that specializes in providing management officials with the perma-frown but these rumours are unsubstantiated.

[28] A *black hole* is not really a hole at all. It is a super-dense sphere of matter that is the result of a star imploding. Gravity is so strong on the surface of the sphere that even light can be sucked into it. More tests will be required before it is known if disapproval would suffer the same fate.

[29] *Baleful* is a word meaning evil or full of suffering. Not to be confused with baleful in the sense that "the barn is baleful," that is to say full of hay bales. I doubt you would confuse the two as someone's eyes could hardly shoot out bales of hay, but still … it doesn't pay to overestimate the intelligence of one's audience.

Her line of sight now rested squarely on the students of grade nine chemistry.

"I said ... *what is going on in here!*"

"Uh ..." Belinda started.

"UH is not a *word*, Miss Tindal! Write that out *one thousand* times! Have it on my desk tomorrow morning."

Belinda gulped and fell silent. The rest of the class stared at their desktops and tried to find a way to exist without breathing.

"My dear Ms. Abernathy." The warm tone of Mr. Greenleaf could not be more different from the harshness of the vice-principal's voice. "I'm so glad you could come and look in on us." He glided gracefully between the desks and placed his hand on Ms. Abernathy's elbow. The VP's face took on a blank, puzzled expression. "I'm so delighted to meet you!" Mr. Greenleaf added pleasantly. Ms. Abernathy looked down at the elegant hand of Mr. Greenleaf, pale on the green flannel of her suit jacket and then she looked up into those grey eyes. That look was her undoing.

She locked eyes with Mr. Greenleaf and he smiled a warm, lovely smile. Something happened then that no one in the class had ever seen before. Ms. Abernathy's perma-frown seemed to waver and then melt away altogether. The corners of her mouth, so conditioned to dip downward, quivered, convulsed, and then, bit by torturous bit, turned upward. Ms. Abernathy, to the shock of the entire class, was smiling.

"Oh. I uh ... oh." Ms. Abernathy blushed and practically giggled.

"I'm sorry if the children were being noisy, but I must take responsibility for the hubbub."

"You?" Ms. Abernathy said, bewildered.

"I'm afraid so. They were so excited by the ideas we were discussing that …" Mr. Greenleaf's eyes swept the room and he continued, "they just couldn't contain themselves."

Ms. Abernathy seemed completely stymied by this idea, but another smile from Mr. Greenleaf seemed to stun her into acceptance. "Oh, I see. Well. I guess some enthusiasm for learning is a good thing."

"Indeed, my dear Ms. Abernathy, indeed. Well put!" Mr. Greenleaf guided her to the door. "Well, this visit has been a treat. I'm sure you have many things to do."

"Yes. Yes, of course, Mr. Greenleaf. Many things to do."

"Don't let us keep you," he said and let her drift out the door. "One last thing. Miss Tindal needn't do those lines at all, need she?"

Ms. Abernathy turned in the doorway and a hint of her old rancour flared in her eyes, but before it could take root, Mr. Greenleaf fixed her with another of his glacier-melting smiles and she stammered, grinning, "Of—of course not!"

"Fine! See you in the staff room for lunch then? Maybe we could have a cup of tea together?"

"Yes, that would be—" Her response was cut off when Mr. Greenleaf shut the door firmly. For a second or two she stood framed in the window of the door looking mildly confused. At last, she turned and wandered away with a look of pure mystification on her face.

Mr. Greenleaf turned to find the entire class staring at him with undisguised awe. He grinned and sketched a comical bow then glided smoothly back to the front of the class. "Chemistry is a wonderful discipline. Chemistry is in everything. It allows us to manipulate the very essence of the universe. Everything is connected, and the study of these connections is what human beings call science. Shall we get down to business?" Mr. Greenleaf picked up the chemistry textbook from his desk and began leafing through it.

Brendan was as shocked as everyone else, but he felt something stirring inside him. He had never seen Mr. Greenleaf before, but he couldn't help feeling that he recognized him from somewhere. What the teacher said resonated within him. He couldn't help himself. He raised his hand. Mr. Greenleaf pointed at him and Brendan blurted, "How did you do that? With the chalk and the bird. How did you do it?"

Mr. Greenleaf looked up from the book. He fixed Brendan with his gaze and his mouth quirked into a sly, not unfriendly grin. "The world is full of surprises, Brendan. Things are not always what they seem. People are not always what they seem. The trick is to be open to seeing what is really there." He winked.

Brendan sat with his mouth hanging open, unable to respond.

Mr. Greenleaf snapped the book shut and tossed it onto the desktop with a thud. "Valences! Who can tell me what they are?"

Belinda's hand shot up immediately. The class commenced but Brendan hardly noticed. He was feeling strangely dizzy. The substitute teacher had made him feel disoriented and he couldn't concentrate.

"Wake up!"

"Huh!?" Brendan blinked.

"Class is over," Dmitri said. "Time to go. Didn't you hear the bell?"

Brendan sighed with relief. He was more than happy to get out of that classroom.

OPINIONS

Brendan stood up and followed the flow of students out the door and into the crowded hall. He cast a glance back at Mr. Greenleaf, expecting the man to be watching him, but the substitute was leaning on his desk chatting with a gaggle of girls. Even Belinda, usually terminally shy outside of academic situations, was standing with the others, albeit at the back of the group. The gawky girl was obviously quite smitten with the new teacher just like every other female.

Well, not exactly every other female. Kim slammed her chemistry book into her knapsack and stomped out of the room without a backward glance. "Let's get outta here," she grumbled as she walked past Brendan. Dmitri and Brendan shared a bewildered look, waited for Harold to catch up, and then followed Kim out the front door.

They caught up to her at the bike racks where she was tying her bag to her scooter with a bungee cord.

"What's your problem?" Brendan demanded.

"I haven't got a problem," Kim snapped. Seeing the look on Brendan's face, she sighed. "Don't like that guy, that's all. He bugs me. Don't know why."

Brendan got the feeling she wasn't telling the whole story, but he didn't press her. "Who wants to go to Papa Ceo's for a slice?"

The suggestion was met with immediate approval from Dmitri and Kim, but Harold's face fell. "I'm not supposed to eat things outside of mealtimes."

Brendan sympathized. His own mum would flip if she found out he'd been eating pizza before dinner. She railed at him about eating greasy food making his acne worse. *How could it be any worse?*

"You don't have to eat anything," Brendan insisted. "You can just have a diet pop … or a salad or something."

Harold thought about it for a moment then nodded. Brendan was relieved. He didn't care about the pizza, really. He just wanted to hear what the others had thought about the new teacher and his incredible chalk trick.

They set off across Queen's Park Crescent by the Royal Ontario Museum. The giant weird crystal perched on top of the limestone building looked like an alien spaceship.[30] Many people didn't like the new crystal but Brendan thought it was kind of cool. He'd been inside the structure on the night of the opening and had wandered all over inside. His father was playing in a jazz quartet for one of the parties, so while his dad played, he explored. The odd angles of the ceilings and walls had been really neat.

---

[30] The Michael Lee-Chin Crystal was opened to the public on June 3, 2007. The abstract crystal structure perches on the front of the original stone building and was met with mixed reactions by the public. There were many other suggestions for a structure to embellish the front of the museum: a giant pyramid, an enormous leather hat, and a massive blob of real mashed potatoes. Fortunately, the crystal was chosen over the mashed potatoes because of the ongoing cost of adding fresh butter to the structure every morning.

They turned away from the ROM and headed south to Hoskin Avenue. Brendan was about to broach the subject but Harold beat him to it.

"What do you think of this Greenleaf guy?" Harold asked. As he walked along, he was sketching in his book with a pencil. He was always drawing and he was quite talented. In a few strokes, a hummingbird appeared on the blank page. Brendan marvelled anew at Harold's gift. He wished he had some comparable talent. If he did, he certainly hadn't discovered it yet.

Kim grunted but didn't say a word.

"He certainly made chemistry more interesting," Dmitri said. "He has a very interesting teaching style."

"Those tricks he pulled were amazing," Brendan opined. "The chalk changing colour and the humming-bird? Cool."

"I'm sure he must have had the chalk up his sleeve," Dmitri said, "Or in a false pocket in his vesk."

"Vest," Brendan corrected. "Not vesk."

"Vest!" Dmitri repeated. "Right."

"And he totally shut down Chester, that's for sure," Harold said with a grin. He had flipped the page in the sketch pad and was feverishly carving a portrait of Mr. Greenleaf with a lump of charcoal on a fresh sheet of white. "I bet he's a magician!" Harold offered, "and maybe he had an accident during a show. Like he accidentally sawed a woman in half for real. On stage. That would be wicked, right?"

"I think that's highly unlikely," Dmitri commented.

"Still, it'd be wicked, right? Am I right?"

"Blah, blah, blah," Kim suddenly cut in. "Who cares. He made a bird appear! Big deal. You guys act like he's some kind of genius. Anybody can learn a magic trick. He buys a book at a joke shop and you guys think he's Gandalf."

Brendan frowned. "Oh, yeah? Like you could do a magic trick." It was a lame thing to say but he was just annoyed.

She sneered and reached over her shoulder to grip the handle of her ever-present field hockey stick, jutting out of her knapsack. "Why don't I put you to sleep with my magic wand."

"Ha-ha!" Brendan sneered back. "Do you want me to push that for a while?" He pointed at her scooter which she was currently guiding along, holding the handlebars. Her silver helmet dangled by its strap from the field hockey stick.

Kim smiled. "Naw. Thanks. I can manage."

Brendan loved that scooter. It was a lustrous, lovingly restored Vespa in metallic candy-apple red with a black leather seat. He had begged Kim on a number of occasions to give him a ride, but she always said no. The insurance wouldn't allow it. He envied her having such an amazing ride. Kim leaned her scooter against a telephone pole outside Papa Ceo's Pizza and they joined the line for slices.

Brendan marvelled that Kim never bothered to lock her scooter. "Aren't you worried that someone's gonna steal it?"

Kim grinned wolfishly. "Who'd dare to steal from me?" Looking at that smile, Brendan decided he wouldn't want to cross her.

They got their slices and sat on the bench outside the window. Brendan bit into the hot, melting cheese and savoured the garlicky tomato sauce beneath. No one did a better slice than Papa Ceo. Harold looked on with a woeful expression until Brendan inevitably said, "I can't eat all mine. You want half, Harold?"

Harold gladly accepted the half slice. It had become a ritual between them. Kim shook her head at Brendan.

"You aren't helping," Kim scolded.

"Aw, it's only a half slice," Brendan said, shrugging. "No harm done."

Dmitri was holding a veggie slice that was easily bigger than his whole head. Brendan had bought it for him. Dmitri's family didn't have a lot of money so Brendan spotted him a slice or a pop from time to time. He thought that the tutoring Dmitri gave him in science and mathematics was easily more valuable than a slice or two.

"I don't like him," Kim said suddenly. "If I were you guys, I'd keep away from him." She said this to all of them but she looked at Brendan when she spoke. To accentuate her warning, she popped a giant jalapeño in her mouth and chewed. No matter how much junk food Kim ate, she always stayed lean.

Harold shook his head, gazing enviously at her pizza. He had already inhaled his. "And it was pretty cool how he knew everybody's names, like right away. That just proves he's a magician. How else do you explain the bird?" Harold demanded.

"Sleight of hand," Dmitri mumbled, with his mouth full. "I've seen magic shows on TV. It's all illusion."

"Looked pretty real to me," Harold said. "Hey, Brendan? You all right?"

Brendan had been sitting looking at a poster in the nearby bus shelter, his pizza drooping in his hand. "Hmm?"

Harold waved a hand in front of Brendan's face. "Earth calling Brendan!"

Brendan raised his head and looked at his friends. "What?" he said dumbly.

"Have you established a psychic link with the alien spaceship yet?" Harold asked sarcastically.

"Very funny," Brendan said. "I was just looking at that poster. You ever heard of her?"

They all looked at the poster. In ornate Celtic script the title read "Deirdre D'Anaan: One Night Only at Convocation Hall."

"My mum's going to that," Harold said, wiping his mouth with a napkin. "She's a folk singer or something."

"Pretty," Dmitri said.

Brendan stared at the picture of the woman. The entire poster was her face. She was beautiful but in a very intimidating way with piercing grey eyes and a haughty expression. Her hair spread out in a red, tangled mass about her head. The artist had manipulated the image so that her hair melded with a border of green vines and wildflowers. The eyes seemed to peer right into Brendan's heart they were so alive.

"That's a cool picture," he said and turned to look at Kim. She was sitting stock-still, her pizza forgotten. She stared at the poster with a fevered intensity bordering on fury.

"Kim? Are you all right?"

Kim blinked. She realized they were all staring at her. "Huh? Yeah. I'm fine. Fine."

Dmitri tossed his napkin into the garbage bin and picked up his books. "I have to go. My mother gets worried if I don't head straight home. Are you taking the subway, Harold?"

Harold nodded.

Brendan watched Kim as she stuffed the last piece of her pizza into her mouth. She was acting so weird today. He decided to push his luck. "That Mr. Greenleaf *is* pretty strange," Brendan said. "I don't know what to think of him. He's kind of … spooky. Do you know him from somewhere, Kim?"

Kim stopped in the act of putting on her silver helmet. "What do ya mean?"

"It just looked like you knew him in class," Brendan said.

"Huh," she jammed the helmet onto her head and did up the strap. "At my old school. He subbed there once. That's all." She fell silent, making it obvious she wasn't going to elaborate.

"I don't know," Harold said, gathering up his drawing materials and stuffing them into his knapsack. "Anything's better than old Bowel-ly."

"Millionaire Bowel-ly," Dmitri corrected. "He's won the lottery now."

"That's so amazing," Brendan said. "Do you think it's true?"

Kim straddled her scooter. "I wouldn't trust anything that guy said. You shouldn't either." She kicked the pedal and the engine roared to life. Without another word she sped off west along Harbord.

They watched her go.

"What's up her butt?" Harold asked.

"No idea," Brendan said. "I think it's something to do with the new substitute teacher."

"Greenleaf?" Dmitri said. "You think so?"

"Yeah. I think he's kind of odd, too. Don't you?"

"No weirder than any other teacher." Harold shrugged. "Let's go, D. See ya, Brendan." He headed off north toward the subway station, pulling his sketchbook out as he went.

Brendan frowned. "There's something about him that's … I don't know. Familiar."

"You've met him before?" Dmitri asked.

"That's just the thing. I'm sure I haven't but as soon as I saw him, I felt something. It's like some part of me *should* know him or recognizes who he is. Does that make any sense to you?"

Dmitri looked at Brendan and said finally, "Uh-uh."

Brendan's shoulders sagged. "Me neither. Ow." His hand gripped his chest.

"What's wrong?" Dmitri asked.

"Nothing," Brendan tugged the collar of his T-shirt down to expose the left side of his chest. "I've had this scar since I was a baby and it's been bugging me today." The scar was red and inflamed. Brendan raked his fingernails across it.

Dmitri pulled Brendan's hand away. "You'll only make it worse. 'Scratch today and cry tomorrow,' as my babka would say." The smaller boy was always quoting his ancient Polish grandmother. "That's worrying. You should get it looked at. It could be skin cancer. Moles can turn into—"

Brendan pulled his shirt back over the mark. "Never mind. Let's just forget it. See you tomorrow."

"Later on," called Dmitri, jogging to catch up with Harold.

"Just 'later,' Dmitri!" Brendan called at his friend's back. "Later!"

He watched them go, then turned to look at the ad again. Those eyes. He scanned the poster and saw that the concert was tomorrow night. He studied Deirdre D'Anaan's face. Like his weird feeling about Greenleaf, he felt he recognized this woman from somewhere. Maybe he'd seen her on TV or something. The memory was just on the tip of his brain. Annoying, he thought. *Maybe my dad has one of her albums or something.*

He decided to let it go for now. He popped the last piece of crust into his mouth and tossed his napkin in the litter bin. He started walking toward home.

HOME

He walked along the sweeping turn that was Spadina Circle, where Spadina Avenue split in two to accommodate an old brick building and joined up again for the plunge into Chinatown. He was trying to enjoy the last semi-warm day of autumn. On his right was Lord Lansdowne Public School, an unlovely box with a concrete playground.

Why do they pave playgrounds? he wondered for the thousandth time. What's fun about falling and scraping the skin off your palms? Brendan had done that too many times to count.

The one thing that redeemed the building was the huge black stone that sat in front of the school by the sidewalk. He always reached out over the fence and brushed his hand across its rough surface for luck.

He picked up his pace and turned the corner as a streetcar rattled and shrieked along the track heading south. He found himself in front of the Scott Mission. This close to dinnertime there was a lineup of people who lived hard on the street. They were all waiting for the hot meal the mission offered every day. He always felt bad for these people. His father always gave them money if they asked for it, which annoyed his mother.

"You shouldn't give them money," she would say. "They'll just spend it on drink."

"Or food," his father would answer.

"I'm not just trying to be mean," she would counter. "I think you should give to a charity that can help them get off the street."

They would argue back and forth. Brendan couldn't tell which was the right way to be. Walking down the line of dirty, haggard faces, he always felt slightly guilty that he had a nice home and could buy some pizza while these people had nowhere and nothing to look forward to.

He passed the mission and found himself in front of the Silver Dollar, a seedy little bar that often pumped out loud music.

Brendan smiled and waved when he saw the old guy sitting on an overturned milk carton.

"Hey there, Finbar," Brendan said with a wave. "Didn't see you for a couple of days. I was worried."

"Hallo, Prince Breandan," said the man, who was wearing a heavy woollen overcoat in spite of the mild weather. He waved back with one large, gnarled hand. He was usually here near the Silver Dollar drinking a cup of tea from a thermos. "I was a little under the weather. Right as rain today, though! Lovely day though, in't it?"

"Yeah!" Brendan waved back.

Brendan stopped and reached into the pocket of his jacket. He pulled out a packet of shortbread cookies he'd stuck there that morning when leaving the house. "Biscuits?"

The old man grinned, showing a surprising set of even white teeth. "Sure and you're a little star."

Brendan watched as Finbar tore the cellophane packet open and took out a cookie, pinched daintily between rough, calloused fingers. He dunked the cookie in the tea and raised it to his mouth. "Glorious."

Brendan smiled. He didn't know where Finbar slept or why the old man hung around on this street corner, but he had struck up a sort of friendship with him, sharing pleasantries and biscuits on his way to and from school these last two months. Finbar didn't ever go into the mission. He didn't talk to any of the street people. He seemed to have a home but Brendan didn't know where it was.

"Off home, lad?"

"Yeah."

"Mind if I stroll along with ye a ways?"

"No problem." Brendan waited for the old man to gather up his thermos and tuck it into his shopping bag.

He'd met Finbar on his way home from RDA the first day. The old man had been sitting on a milk crate at the mission and Brendan had felt compelled to say hello. They'd struck up a conversation. As the weeks went by, he'd learned the man's name but little else about him.

"Let's be off then," Finbar said, hefting his canvas shopping bag. They set off into Kensington Market.

As they walked through the narrow, busy streets, Finbar rattled on about whatever caught his eye. He was very entertaining. Brendan's mother would have probably had a fit if she knew that her son was hanging around with a strange old man. Brendan didn't mention Finbar to his parents. He liked the old guy.

"Good day at school then, My Prince?"

"Yeah. It was okay."

"Ye look like ye've got yerself the beginnings of a black eye there."

Brendan reached up and touched his eye. Wincing, he shrugged. "Yeah. Gym class."

"Ah, yes. A necessary evil in the growth of any young man." The old man laughed and Brendan grinned.

Brendan didn't know why he called him that: My Prince. Just something to say, he supposed. Brendan liked the gravel in the man's voice and his accent. Finbar said he was from Ireland, but he wouldn't reveal anything else about his past. Brendan respected the man's privacy. Brendan had never known his grandfather on either side and he liked to think of Finbar as a kind of surrogate grandpa.

"Well, I should be off now," Finbar said as they reached the heart of the market. "I'd best be home before dark."

The man's clear blue eyes crinkled in a wreath of wrinkles as he smiled and waved Brendan on.

"See ya, Finbar," Brendan said, watching as the old man headed south, whistling and swinging his shopping bag as he went. Brendan watched until he lost sight of Finbar in the crowd of pedestrians.

A few minutes later, he stopped outside a small café. Car seats had been strewn haphazardly around the weedy patio in front of the plate glass window. Gold letters painted on the glass read "I Deal Coffee." He looked through the window and saw his father finishing a sale, handing a customer a bag of ground coffee beans.

People liked Charlie Clair. He made them feel like they were the most interesting person in the world while he was talking to them, not that it helped: Brendan's dad wasn't exactly super-successful in any of his many careers. He played music, painted, sculpted, did some freelance graphic design, but working at I Deal was his main source of income. If Brendan's mum hadn't been able to pull down a decent living as a designer of window displays for the posh shops on Bloor Street, they would have been struggling. As it was, they had a comfortable home. Brendan and his sister each had their own room.

Maybe Brendan's dad wasn't a superstar compared to some dads, but he was Brendan's favourite person. He was kind. He always had time to talk when Brendan needed him. He had tried to teach Brendan to play the piano and the guitar, but Brendan had been hopeless, as clumsy at that as he was in anything that required some dexterity. Even so, his dad was patient and wasn't disappointed with Brendan for not being able to master any of the skills he loved.

Brendan's dad waved at the customer headed out the doors and saw Brendan standing outside. He waved, obviously happy to see his son. He frowned comically and pointed to his wrist where a watch would be, if he ever wore one. This was a joke between them. Brendan's mum was always exasperated when anyone was late for dinner. Brendan grinned back.

"See you at home," his father mouthed silently, winked and turned to the next customer in line. Brendan gave the thumbs-up sign and turned away.

He walked briskly down the street and turned at Crawford, walking the last few metres to his house. He turned up the walk just as his sister was arriving on her bike.

"Hey, Nerdio. How was nerd school today?"

Brendan shrugged. "Nerdy. How was jerk school? Jerky?"

With that bit of wit deployed, he launched himself up the steps to the front door.

FAMILY

Brendan's house was the third in a row of identical Victorian townhouses, the nineteenth-century equivalent of condos for the working folk of the young city of Toronto. Each had a minuscule rectangle of front yard and black wrought iron fence to ward off intruders as long as the intruders were too small to leap the three-foot height of the fence and had no hands to lift the latch on the front gate. A pensioner in an electric scooter could probably ram the fence and knock it down, if so inclined. Brendan took the creaky wooden steps to the green front door two at a time closely followed by his sister, Delia.

He was just about to clear the top step when he felt Delia swat his ankle, causing his feet to tangle up. He fell with a crash, his books spilling everywhere. His glasses spun across the wooden porch.

"Enjoy your trip?" Delia sneered as she stepped over him. She flung the door open and went into the house.

Brendan painfully picked himself up off the floor. Delia was an expert at using his clumsiness against him. He was easily taller and stronger than she was, but she'd always managed to win every fight they'd ever had. She was sneaky and she cheated. Jamming his glasses back on his face, he gathered his books and followed her into the hall.

Dumping his books on the side table, he set off for the kitchen.

"*Shoes!*" his mother's voice admonished from the kitchen doorway ahead. Brendan grumbled and turned back, kicking off his running shoes and reaching for his house slippers. His sister was already pulling on one of hers but had foolishly left the other on the mat. Brendan took the opportunity to throw Delia's remaining slipper out onto the lawn.

"You are such a child," she snorted, heading out to retrieve the slipper.

"I know," Brendan said with a smile. As soon as she was out the door, he closed it and locked it from the inside. Satisfied with his petty revenge, he set off for the kitchen.

"What's for dinner, Mum?" he called as he headed straight for the fridge.

His mother straightened up and ran a forearm across her sweaty face. She had been peering into the oven. Her pale, freckled face was flushed with the heat. She was still wearing her grey suit, the one she called her prison uniform, but over it she wore a red apron with the words YES, IT'S SUPPOSED TO BE BURNT LIKE THAT! emblazoned across the front.

"Mac and cheese. And don't eat anything. It'll be ready in half an hour."

Brendan opened the fridge and pulled out a can of pop. "Okay. I'm just gonna drink this."

Delia crashed through the back door and pointed at Brendan with her slipper. Her hair was full of dry leaves. "Mum! He locked me out! I had to run all the way around and climb the fence to get in."

"You could have knocked on the door," Brendan suggested sweetly.

"I wouldn't give you the satisfaction."

"Brendan!" His mother shook her head. "Can't you two just stay out of each other's way for one hour? Honestly, it's ridiculous."

"What's ridiculous?" Brendan's father came in the front door, catching the last few words of the conversation. "And who locked the front door?"

"Dad," Delia whined. "He's the biggest jerk. He threw my slipper into the yard."

"After she tripped me on the steps."

Brendan's father grabbed them both in a hug that was part affectionate and part wrestling hold. As they struggled in his grasp, he sighed. "Ahhh! There is no joy like a harmonious homestead. It's familial bliss as brother and sister share a magical moment. Isn't it wonderful, Ellie?"

Brendan's mother laughed and joined the clinch, taking the opportunity to kiss both her children while they were relatively helpless. "It warms the heart, Charles, dear husband. It warms the heart!"

Delia squirmed free and wiped her cheek. She was fifteen and totally disgusted with the mere *idea* of living with other humans who called themselves her family let alone being *kissed* by them. "*Mum*. That is *gross!*" She fled into the hall and up the stairs, wiping her face and making retching sounds.

"Dinner in half an hour," Mum shouted just as Delia's bedroom door slammed shut. "You too, Brendan."

"I'll be down in the workshop," Dad said, kissing his wife on the cheek. He headed for the cellar door.

"Can I come watch, Dad?"

"Sure, Brendan. Just don't touch anything unless I tell you it's all right."

"Okay, Dad," Brendan said, inwardly cringing at his father's delicate reminder of his native clumsiness. "I won't break anything, I promise."

"Remember to wash up," Mum said, turning her attention to the salad.

Brendan followed his dad down the creaky wooden steps that led to the basement of the house. The smell of damp and sawdust was pungent in his nostrils.

The basement was his father's domain. The space was long and narrow so he'd made dividers out of wood and plasterboard to section off different areas for different purposes. At the bottom of the stairs there was the gas furnace and the water heater. When he was younger, Brendan used to like to pretend the white cylinder of the water heater was a killer robot in an evil space army. He had battled the water heater on many occasions and it still bore the scars from the wooden sword his father had made him years ago. With chagrin, he remembered the time he'd gotten his head stuck under the furnace while chasing a super-bouncy ball. His parents had been forced to call the fire department. Delia had a field day with that one.

The next part of the basement was the workshop, a tiny cubicle with a workbench along one wall. Tools dangled overhead like metal fruit. Here, his father did mundane repairs, fixed furniture, and did woodworking. They headed into the next area: his father's art workshop. Brendan's father reached up and pulled a chain, turning on a bank of halogen lights overhead.

This is where Brendan's father did his artistic work, "his real work," as he called it. Easels held half-finished canvasses. On a low bench sat a block of wood surrounded with shavings. A winged gargoyle was half-carved, captured as though it were in the midst of crawling out of the wood block. In one corner, a glass booth, sound-proofed as best as possible, formed a miniature recording studio where Brendan's dad rehearsed his music and recorded songs. An elderly iMac slept on a table near the sound booth ready to record any tunes Brendan's father might come up with, its screen dark.

Some might call Brendan's father a jack of all trades, dabbling in many fields. He managed to sell enough of his paintings and carvings to bring in a steady if modest income. The workshop was Brendan's favourite place in the house, next to his own room, and he thought his father was just about the coolest person in the world.

Brendan watched as his father picked up his chisel and mallet and started to tap ribbons of shavings from the block of wood. In moments, the leg of the gargoyle was roughed out. Brendan was quietly in awe of what his father could do with his hands. The concentration and precision were beyond him. His father had tried to teach him woodworking, too, but with typically poor results.

"Dad? You ever think you got the wrong kid?"

His father stopped hammering and looked at Brendan. "Why would you say something like that?"

His father's tone was so sharp, Brendan felt he'd said something wrong. "No reason. Well, I mean, I can't do anything as well as you can. You'd think I'd have some kind of genetically transmitted talent." He tried to laugh and lighten the mood. "I mean, maybe they switched the kids at the hospital by mistake and somewhere there's a kid who builds and plays his own guitars, huh?"

His father didn't answer him right away. His face was flat and expressionless. Then the moment passed. His father grinned at him. "I can guarantee you we got the right kid, okay?" He went back to tapping at the chisel and muttered, "Your sister? Now, there are some doubts …" He turned his head slightly and winked at Brendan.

"Dad!"

"Just kidding. So. How was school today?"

"All right." Brendan shrugged. "We got a new substitute teacher. He's kinda weird."

"Aren't they all?" He turned back to his project. "I have to get this done for the One and Only Craft Show. You like it?" He poked the gargoyle with the head of the mallet.

"Uh … creepy?" Brendan said and he meant it. The gnarled, snarling face of the carving made him a little uneasy.

"Creepy's good. People buy creepy." Brendan's father grinned, placing the chisel on an untouched portion of wood and tapping with the mallet, sending a delicate shaving curling to the ground.

"Dad," Brendan said, "can I ask you something?"

"Of course."

"You know the scar I have on my chest …"

The tapping faltered for an instant, then continued. "Yep."

"How did it happen again?"

"We've told you the story, haven't we?"

"Yeah," Brendan said. "Mum spilled tea and I got this burn."

"Exactly so." Brendan's father blew shavings from the wood and began tapping again.

"It's a weird shape though, huh."

"Sure is." His father stopped tapping and looked at him. "Why do you mention it?"

"Oh, no reason really. It's just that … well, it's been bugging me a bit."

"Bugging you." Brendan's father frowned. "Bugging you how?"

"It's been itchy and stuff. You know."

"Hmmm." Brendan's dad furrowed his brow. "Let's see."

Brendan stood, his head banging into a low beam. "Ow." He winced and rubbed his scalp with one hand as he unbuttoned his white school shirt with the other. He held the shirt open so his father could look.

"It does look a little red," he said. "Maybe your mum should look at it."

"Naw, it's okay." Brendan didn't want his mum to lose her mind as she always did when anyone showed any sign of ill health. He could do without the cloying attention.

"Okay. Well, let's see if it gets better over the next day or two. But do me a favour"—his father winked conspiratorially as he said this—"if it does turn into something serious, don't tell her I knew about it. Then we'll both end up in a hospital. Okay?"

"'Kay." Brendan laughed. His dad could always make him feel better, which was one of his many gifts. "I'm gonna go wash up for dinner."

Brendan headed for the stairs.

"Hey, B! I almost forgot!"

Brendan turned back to see his dad digging in his pants pocket. He held up two thin strips of paper. "A friend of mine gave me tickets to a show tomorrow night. He played guitar on her last album so she shot him some freebies. Wanna go with me?"

Brendan stepped closer and took one of the tickets. "Deirdre D'Anaan," he whispered.

"You've heard of her?" His father was mildly surprised.

"Not really," Brendan said quickly. "Just saw a poster today."

"She's playing Convocation Hall. It's an early show: 7 p.m. Your mum shouldn't mind too much. I thought we could come home for spaghetti night and then go to the show."

Brendan couldn't stop staring at the ticket. A coincidence? He shivered.

"Are you all right, B?" his father asked.

Brendan shook off his chill. "Yeah. Yeah. Fine. Sure, I'd like to go."

"Good." His dad smiled. "Now go wash up. And tell your mother I'll be there in a minute."

SECRETS

The next day, Brendan awoke feeling better. He had slept well, but he knew that his sleep had been filled with vivid dreams. He could barely remember them on waking. He was left with the impression that someone had been searching for him, calling him in a dark and trackless forest, but he had chosen not to make his presence known. He hadn't been frightened, just not willing to be found.

He met Dmitri and Harold at the corner of Harbord and Spadina and they got to school in time for homeroom. Brendan had hoped to talk to Kim, but she came in just at the opening bell and plunked into her seat without giving him a chance to say a word.

The rest of the morning, he bided his time. In English, French, calculus, and biology, he tried to get Kim's attention, but she was more focused than he'd thought possible on the teachers and the lessons. He decided he would have to wait for lunch, hoping he might get her alone. He didn't know why it was so important. He just had a feeling that she knew more about Greenleaf than she was saying.

In gym class, Mr. Davenport was feeling sadistic as usual. He put them through a gruelling session of calisthenics. Brendan didn't mind the stretching and push-ups. At least there was no chance of him tripping over himself.

And when you were doing a push-up, you weren't a long way from the ground.

Chester Dallaire was at his best, or worst, depending on your point of view. He had no problem with all the push-ups and sit-ups. Brendan had long ago learned to stay far away from him if possible. To begin with, Chester was the first of their class to really develop B.O. and perfect it. To be exposed up close could lead to watering eyes, hallucinations, paralysis, and, in extreme cases, death. The other reason he kept his distance was the prospect of being the victim of one of Chester's hilarious "pranks." Pranks in Chester's repertoire included supergluing shoes to the floor or holding down a victim and farting into his face. Sometimes, like today, he merely settled for a jolly "pantsing." Chester waited to strike until Mr. Davenport was busy in the equipment room hunting down a medicine ball. The victim was a skinny kid named Miles Horsten, who stood with his head down and his shorts around his ankles as the class roared with laughter.

Brendan stood with Harold and Dmitri, but they didn't join in. They had all been victims in their time and found nothing to laugh at in another kid's humiliation.

"I'd like to get that guy," Harold grumbled.

"He is a jerker, that's for sure."

"Jerk, Dmitri," Brendan corrected. "Not jerker."

"What?" asked Dmitri.

"I said it's not jerker, it's *jerk*."

In the uncanny way the world has of wanting to get you destroyed, the laughter chose this very moment to fade out and the whole class heard Brendan pronouncing, very clearly, the word "jerk." There was an audible gasp.

Chester Dallaire stiffened. He turned his large face and skewered Brendan in a glare of hatred. Brendan felt like an escaping convict caught flat-footed in the beam of a searchlight.

"What did you call me, Tinsel Teeth?" he growled.

Brendan flushed. He hated being reminded of his braces. He felt like he was going to be sick. Brendan opened his mouth to make a quick denial, but before he could say a word, he saw the blushing face of Miles, tears running down his cheeks as he pulled his gym shorts up. Instead, he just stared back at Chester with what he hoped was a defiant expression on his face. His heart was playing a drum roll against his ribs. He prayed he wouldn't wet himself. He felt Harold and Dmitri shuffle closer to him. He wasn't sure if they were showing support or trying to put his body between them and Chester's fists. Probably the latter.

Chester frowned. He barked a laugh, "Ha. Brendan Clair doesn't think this is funny. Is there anybody else who doesn't think this is funny?"

There was a predictable silence. Chester was about to make further comment when Kim's voice cut him off.

"I don't think it's funny," she said, pushing away from the wall where she'd been leaning. "And I doubt anybody else does either. If they weren't all afraid to talk, they would agree. Brendan obviously doesn't care for your sense of humour. Harold and Dmitri also think you suck." Brendan could hear Dmitri and Harold gulp. She sauntered easily over to Brendan and stood beside him. "I think you like picking on people smaller than you because you're a loser and a coward. But I'm not afraid of you." She cracked her knuckles and looked straight into

Chester's face. Her expression showed no anger or bravado. It wasn't a challenge. It was a simple statement. The conviction in her eyes made Chester hesitate.

"Who said to stop stretching?" Mr. Davenport's peevish voice broke the tension. He stood in the doorway holding an enormous leather ball. "On the floor, people! On the floor."

Chester stared at Kim a second more before turning to Brendan and drawing a thumb across his own neck in an obvious "you're dead" gesture. Chester turned to walk away when the strangest thing happened. One of the floorboards beneath his feet gave way with a loud shriek. He squawked and tried to shift his weight, but the floorboard under his other foot gave way too. His legs drove downward and he was stopped only by his groin slamming into the floor.

Brendan gawked with the others. Everyone erupted in laughter as Chester clutched himself while trying to lever his lower half out of the floor. Brendan couldn't believe his eyes. He happened to look over at Kim to find she wasn't laughing. She stood with her hands on her hips, smirking slightly.

"Now *that's* funny," she said. Then she pointed at Brendan. "You're lucky I feel so sorry for you." The bell rang to mark the end of class. Kim spun on her heel and headed for the girls' change room without looking back.

Brendan turned to watch as Chester's pals hauled him out of the floor by the arms. They helped him limp toward the boys' change room.

Brendan went to examine the floorboards where Chester had fallen through. The floor had just given out. It was an accident, right? A pretty convenient one. He turned in time to see Kim's back disappear through the change room door.

"All right, everybody," Mr. Davenport called. "We'll have to end class there. Go to lunch."

Brendan joined Harold and Dmitri as they headed off to change, buzzing with excitement over Chester's humiliation. As he listened to them re-enact the event, he glanced over to where Marina Kaprillian stood with her little entourage of friends. As soon as he saw them they fell silent for an instant then burst into girlish giggling. Then something amazing happened: Marina Kaprillian, the object of his adolescent desires, looked at him and smiled. The confrontation with Chester hadn't threatened his equilibrium, but one look from her caused him to trip over his feet and fall headlong into the doorframe.

They sat and ate in silence, Dmitri his stinky sandwich and Brendan his cold soup. Luckily, the doorframe hadn't split his skin, but he had a large goose egg on his scalp. Mercifully, it was above his hairline so he could effectively hide it. Mrs. Barsoomian had shaken her head when she saw Dmitri and Harold helping him up the hall to the nurse's office. She had examined him, held her fingers up, and asked him to count them and made him count backwards from one hundred. At last, she was satisfied that he hadn't suffered a concussion and sent him on his way with a bag of ice and a gentle scolding.

Brendan was feeling gloomy. His clumsiness had ruined his moment of triumph, made him look like a fool after looking the hero. He wanted to talk about it but Dmitri wasn't in the mood. He was in study mode, his face buried in his textbook. Restless, Brendan got up to take a walk.

He headed up the main corridor past the doors to the auditorium. The walls of the hall were hung with old photographs of the school's history, black and white images of young men frozen in time, their haircuts stiff and their bodies pale as ghosts. Robertson Davies Academy had once been a boys' school. It had become co-ed only two decades ago. He paused to examine an old photo of the 1936 Senior Varsity Lacrosse Team, young faces earnestly staring out at the camera from long ago.

At first, he didn't realize he was hearing voices. He looked up and down the hall. There was no one nearby. He listened harder.

"Your presence here will attract attention," a female voice hissed.

"Nevertheless, I feel Brendan needs watching ..."

The voices were coming from the auditorium. He recognized the smooth tones of Mr. Greenleaf.

Greenleaf seemed a little annoyed. But with whom? Feeling sneaky, Brendan crept closer to the closed doors of the auditorium. They were solid wood with two small windows at head height. He could just peek into the window and see who the sub was talking to. *That wouldn't be spying, would it? No!*

It was dim inside the auditorium. The only light was from the windows high up the walls by the stage. The seats ranged away in dim rows a few feet from the doors. Mr. Greenleaf was leaning against a seat in the back row, his arms crossed. He was talking to someone Brendan couldn't see.

"... have no control over where I go and what I do. I was just a bit worried. My sister is coming into town and I knew I'd have to keep an eye on him. She has her own ideas, you know."

Brendan almost gasped out loud when he saw Kim step into view. She pointed at Mr. Greenleaf and hissed, "I got the assignment. We've only just managed to locate him and I'm supposed to be watching him. You have no business being here. He doesn't know anything and I want it to stay that way for as long as possible."

"As do I, dear."

"Don't *dear* me. Just your presence here complicates things. It could trigger the …"

"What are you doing?"

Brendan whirled to find Dmitri staring at him. His rapid movement caused him to lose his balance. He tripped and fell against the door, which rattled loudly in its frame.

"Nothing," Brendan whispered. He grabbed Dmitri by the strap of his knapsack. "Let's go get some fries. I'm hungry all of a sudden."

"What? Fries? I don't …"

Brendan pushed him along the hall and through the closest door to the cafeteria just as the auditorium door swung open. Brendan breathed a sigh of relief. *I don't think they saw me.*

Dmitri was staring at him as if he were insane.

"What?" Brendan demanded, trying to lighten the mood. "I really wanted some fries."

THE REST OF THE DAY crawled by for Brendan. He went from class to class in a daze. He couldn't seem to concentrate on anything his teachers were saying. More than once, he was reprimanded for not paying attention. His goal became to simply make it through the day and go home as quickly as possible.

He was determined to ask Kim about Mr. Greenleaf. She obviously knew the guy better than she said she did. Why had they been talking about him in the auditorium? If Dmitri hadn't come along he might have heard something important.

He planned to wait for Kim after school and have it out with her. So he was quite disappointed when the close-of-day bell rang that she managed to slip out of physics without saying anything to him. He got caught in a clot of students, trying to swim against the current. In his typical clumsy way, he managed to drop his bag and spill the contents out everywhere underfoot. By the time he chased down all his pencils and pens, hurried down the main stairs, and burst out the front doors of the school, Kim was long gone.

He stood there, at a loss. He realized that he didn't even know where she lived. He didn't even know which direction she took. She drove a scooter and wore a silver helmet, he knew that but nothing else. The more he thought about it, the more he realized that he knew very little about her. She had attached herself to their little group on the first day of school two months ago and had defended them from the worst of the first-year hazing.

He headed down the steps for the walk home. The sky was still bright but darkness came early at this time of year. The air was crisp and fresh. He took a deep breath and finally started to feel like himself when he felt a sudden burning on his chest that took his breath away. Before he could react to the sensation, a hand fell on his shoulder.

"Going my way, Brendan?" The smooth musical voice sent a shiver down his spine.

He looked up into the face of the substitute, Mr. Greenleaf.

A LONG WALK HOME

The instant Brendan felt Mr. Greenleaf's hand on his shoulder, the itch in his chest suddenly flared. He gasped involuntarily and clutched his chest.

Mr. Greenleaf's face showed obvious concern. "Are you all right?"

"Fine," Brendan mumbled. He forced himself to ignore the burning itch and lower his hand. He smiled weakly. "Must be allergies or something."

Mr. Greenleaf dropped his hand from Brendan's shoulder and the boy felt an instant lessening of the discomfort. "Where are you off to now, Brendan?"

Brendan shrugged. "Home." Brendan instantly regretted admitting his plans. "It's quite a long walk; through the park and across the U. of T. campus, then down into the market." He tried to make it sound far to discourage Greenleaf from walking with him.

"Ah, the same way I happen to be going. Shall we stroll together for a while? I don't want to cramp your style. I'm just across the park, okay?"

Brendan shrugged again. "I guess." He didn't know what else to say. He didn't want to let it slip that he'd heard anything in the auditorium. Add to that the display in chemistry and the strange way he'd been feeling, he would rather not have had any company on the walk home, let alone this weird guy, but he couldn't think of any way to get out of walking with him. He started out across the street and the substitute matched his stride.

He glanced sidelong at Greenleaf as they waited at the crosswalk for the green light. *What's the deal with this guy?* To Brendan and all of the kids he knew, there were some things that just weren't done. One of them was being seen walking around with your teacher after school. Teachers and students were supposed to move in different circles, and those circles were never meant to overlap. That was a law of nature and every high school kid respected it. *But here I am breaking the Universal High School Code.*

"Coming?"

The light had turned green while Brendan was musing. Mr. Greenleaf was looking back at Brendan from a few steps out into the crosswalk. His grey eyes twinkled with amusement.

After crossing busy Queen's Park Circle, they ambled down the path that led under the trees of Queen's Park.

"Parks …" Mr. Greenleaf broke in on his thoughts. The tone of his voice was bitter. "They always make me a little sad."

"Sad?" Brendan looked around but didn't see what was so sad about the green grass and stately old trees. Squirrels clustered around people sitting on blankets. The grey furry creatures begged for scraps, scrambling for crusts of bread and potato chips.

"Sad." Mr. Greenleaf nodded. "Parks are a pale, tame version of the way the world used to be. Before the buildings and the cars and the roads, the world was green and lush, untamed and unpredictable. There were wild creatures. You never knew what might happen. It was darker and more alive. The trees and the rocks were more than objects, they had voices of their own."

Oh my god. Brendan's heart sank. *He's a nutcase. I'm stuck with a nutcase in the park.* He quickly scanned the area to make sure that if this weirdo were to do something to him, there would be plenty of witnesses. He was relieved to see that quite a few people were taking advantage of the last warm days of the fall. People were walking dogs, couples were strolling the paths hand in hand and there were joggers and a woman with some twins in a double stroller. Brendan relaxed.

"You think I'm crazy." Greenleaf chuckled. "I don't mean they spoke out loud. Well, not all of them anyway. Still, they had their ways of reaching us." He stared off into the distance for a moment as they walked along the path toward the other side of the park. Suddenly, derisively, the man growled, "Now even the poor squirrels forget their natural distrust of man. Their nature has been subverted. Now they beg for handouts instead of running and hiding from man."

"Free bread is hard to resist," Brendan said. They were passing a park bench where an elderly man in a baseball cap was holding crusts of bread out to the grey squirrels. The squirrels would actually scrabble up the legs of the man's jeans and sit on his knee while they ate the bread. Most people thought it was cute, but Brendan had to admit there was something kind of pitiful about the way they begged for the food. The squirrels were fat and almost tame.[31]

---

[31] The grey squirrels of Queen's Park are notoriously fat and friendly. There are more wild and fearsome squirrels in other

There was ferocity in Mr. Greenleaf's tone that belied his cultured, elegant manner. Brendan turned his gaze on the park surrounding him and tried to imagine it as a wilderness filled with danger but couldn't quite manage it. Granted, the squirrels could be quite vicious if you didn't fork over a crust of bread in short order, but that hardly counted as dangerous.

"Brendan?" the teacher said suddenly. "You spell it wrong."

"Huh?" Brendan grunted. "What do you mean, wrong?"

"In the old Irish language it is spelled B-r-e-a-n-d-a-n."

Brendan said, "Yeah. That's how my parents used to spell it, but when I got to school everyone kept spelling it wrong so I just changed it. Easier that way."

"Ha," Greenleaf snorted. "People always like things the easy way. Shortcuts. Simplification. Something is always lost when you take the easy way. When you take the shortcut, there was something you missed seeing the long way around."

"Yeah, I guess," Brendan mumbled. *Why am I trapped walking with this crazy guy? Why didn't I say I lived the other way and just go hide? You're such a dumb-wad, Brendan.* "Whoa!"

As the thought occurred to him, it was as though the gods of Dumbwadness reached down and knocked him off balance for a laugh. The toe of Brendan's running shoe

---

parts of the city, most feared of all being the albino white squirrels of Queen West who haunt the grounds of the mental health
facility. Or at least, I am told they are frightening by the people
who live at the mental health facility.

managed to find a dip in the path. He tipped forward, his hands going out to block his fall, the books under his arm scattering like birds. *Here I go again*. He resigned himself to falling on his face.

He never hit the ground. Mr. Greenleaf snared his elbow in a grip of steel, pivoted on his heel and flung Brendan around until he stood upright again facing the other way. Brendan blinked in surprise.

"How did you …?"

Mr. Greenleaf smiled smugly and offered Brendan his books, balanced in a neat stack in the man's hand. Brendan looked around at the ground. Not a single book had fallen. Dumbly, he took his books.

"How did you do that?" he asked again. Mr. Greenleaf gave another of his little bows and laughed. "I've always been fast on my feet. I wasn't always a stodgy teacher in a dusty classroom." Greenleaf fastidiously wiped his hands on a pale green handkerchief he produced from his pocket. "People aren't always what they seem. Sometimes they are much, much more. Sometimes, it takes a little while for them to realize their true nature. Some people aren't even people in the traditional sense."

Brendan stared blankly as Mr. Greenleaf tilted his head back and laughed again. "I've confused you, haven't I? Never mind. Let's just say all people are people! Some are less than they think. Some are more than they know. And some can't even imagine what they truly are." The teacher's eyes caught Brendan's and held them. He felt like a deer halfway across a highway as a truck bore down. "I have a feeling you're one of the latter, *Breandan*." Greenleaf said the last word with a strange, foreign inflection that seemed somehow to insinuate that missing "a" in a deep and affecting way. Brendan felt a wave of dizziness wash through him. All he wanted to do was break loose from the substitute's stare.

"Yeah, right. O-okay," he managed to stutter. "Thanks. Anyway, I gotta get going." *This guy is seriously weirding me out!* "My mum is waiting for me." *Nice. Run to your mummy. What a nerd!* "Have a nice day!" Brendan groaned inwardly at his awkwardness. Before he could open his mouth and utter any more inane things, he turned away from the substitute teacher and started off down the path. He could almost feel Mr. Greenleaf's eyes on his back as he hurried away. The man was probably laughing at his lame escape.

Brendan walked for a few strides until he felt he had put a good distance between him and the substitute teacher. Satisfied he'd left it long enough, he took a sneaky glance over his shoulder to find that Mr. Greenleaf was gone. He was nowhere to be seen. Brendan stopped and scanned the park, right to left, but there was no sign of Mr. Greenleaf anywhere. *How could he have left the park so fast? That's just weird. But he's weird, so what was I expecting?* Suddenly, a tiny bird zipped down from the trees in a streak of colour aimed directly at his face. Brendan held up an arm to shield himself, but there was no impact. He carefully lowered his arm to see a hummingbird hovering a metre away, the same hummingbird Mr. Greenleaf had conjured from a piece of chalk in chemistry class the day before. The minute creature hung in space for a few seconds, its wings humming, then darted up into the branches of a tree and disappeared. Feeling totally freaked out, Brendan set off across the park.

"I SEE IT IN YOU NOW!"

Brendan hurried across Spadina and followed it as it curved around the island of university buildings stranded in the centre like stone ships.

Leaving the university behind, he passed the elementary school with its paved playground. His thoughts returned to Mr. Greenleaf, who had saved him from a fall moments before. He stopped. *How had he managed that?* Not that Brendan was big and heavy, but still, Mr. Greenleaf was no giant. He'd flung Brendan around like a bag of feathers.

He found himself stopped beside the huge rock that stood in front of the school. Why did he like to pass it every day, run his hand over it? He could have easily taken a different route home. He wasn't really sure. The rock had always held a certain fascination for him. Its bumpy black surface was out of place on this busy street. When he was younger, he'd liked to pretend that it was magical and had transported itself to its present spot for a dark purpose.

Brendan snorted. "Yeah, right. That's one dangerous rock!" he murmured to himself. "You're just having a freaky day and you're all freaked out."

Nevertheless he felt an urgent need to lay his hand on the surface of the stone. He looked right and left. There was no one in the yard or on the sidewalk. The cars rushed by, oblivious. He shifted his books to his left hand and reached out his right hand, leaned over the low metal fence that surrounded the rock, and laid his fingers on the cool, bumpy surface.

Nothing. Just a stone. *Idiot. Of course it's just a stone. What else would it be?* Fortunately, the sidewalk was still empty.

"You're losing it," he mumbled to himself. "It's been a weird day, and now you're mumbling to yourself. Snap out of it."

His scar itched fiercely. He fought the urge to dig under his hoodie to scratch the spot and set off again on his normal route past the mission and the Silver Dollar. The line of street people was forming, and there, again, was Finbar, sitting on his milk crate. He felt reassured by the old man's presence.

"Hey, Finbar," Brendan called with a wave. Finbar just looked at him, head cocked to one side. Brendan slowed down and stopped. "What?"

"I can see it," Finbar said. "I can see it in ye now, no mistake. You're becoming your true self."

Brendan's heart sank. Was everybody going crazy? He had never seen the old man behave so strangely before. Maybe he'd had a stroke. He didn't look right. His blue eyes were fever bright.

"Are you okay, Finbar?" he asked.

Without warning, Finbar reached out with a rough hand and clamped down on his wrist. Though he was old, he was not feeble. The grip was vise-like, the skin calloused and rough. It was not painful but it felt firm. He pulled Brendan close. Brendan's nose wrinkled at the intense smell of the old man's body. "You'll be wanting to find it. I know where it is, My Prince. I know. Only I can show ye."

"I don't know what you're talking about," Brendan said, trying to pull away, but Finbar wouldn't let him go. "Cool it, okay, Finbar? You're freaking me out."

"Remember. If you want to find it, ye have to find me!"

"Hey!" a harsh voice barked. "Let go of that kid."

A uniformed police constable suddenly appeared, grabbed Finbar, and pulled him away from Brendan. The old man didn't struggle. He just stared at Brendan with the same fevered intensity. "Remember!" he said once more and then tore free of the policeman's grasp. The policeman tried to grab him again, but the old man was surprisingly spry and evaded the cop, hopping out of range of his clawing hand. That's when things went from bad to worse.

Finbar stumbled and staggered out into the road. Although the traffic was stopped for the light, a bicycle courier was weaving through the stopped cars. He crashed into the old man, sending them both to the pavement. Finbar struck his head against the curb with an audible crack.

A crowd of pedestrians immediately gathered. The policeman hauled out his radio and called for assistance and an ambulance. "Give him some air," the cop was shouting. The cyclist was cursing at the state of his bent wheel.

"Crazy old man! What was he doing? He's totally wrecked my bike!"

Brendan stood in shock, looking down at the slack face of the old man he'd been saying hello to every day for the last few months. Finbar's cap was off, lost under the crowd's feet. Brendan could see he was still breathing. An off-duty nurse was lending a hand, cradling his head in her lap and pressing on a cut that oozed blood between her fingers.

Brendan felt sick. He couldn't help feeling responsible. He had no idea what Finbar had been raving about and the old man had kind of scared him, but he didn't like to see him hurt.

The ambulance arrived, and the emergency workers brought out a stretcher. They placed a backboard on the ground and carefully lifted the unconscious man onto the board and then onto the stretcher, strapping him safely into place. Someone found Finbar's cap and placed it on his chest.

The policeman lowered his radio. "Where ya takin' the old guy?"

"Western General," one of the ambulance workers replied. In all the confusion, the policeman had forgotten about Brendan and got into a police cruiser to lead the ambulance to the hospital. Brendan was left to wander home on his own.

He arrived at his house to find that dinner was almost ready.

When he came into the kitchen, his mother didn't see him at first. She was bent over the stove, her face inches from the steaming saucepot, sniffing and critical. She nodded once and straightened up, obviously satisfied. Seeing Brendan, she pointed a warning finger at him. "You better not have piled your books on the hall table."

When Brendan didn't answer, his mother looked at him more carefully. The expression on his face immediately put her on the alert. "What's happened? Are you all right?"

Brendan shook his head. "I was walking home, and I saw this old man get knocked down by a cyclist." He was reluctant to tell her everything, how he knew Finbar and what the man had said.

"Is he all right?"

"I don't know. They took him to the hospital."

"Oh, dear." She wrapped her arms around him and hugged him. "I know this must be hard for you. You're such a sensitive little boy."

"Mu-um! I'm fourteen. I'm not a little boy!" But she was kind of right. He had never liked seeing anybody hurt. When he was really little, she'd found him crying while watching an episode of *The Three Stooges*.

"I'm sorry. I just worry about you. Can I get you anything?"

"A diaper maybe?" Delia's voice piped up as she entered the kitchen.

"Delia!" his mother snapped. "Your brother just witnessed an accident! He needs a little sympathy right now."

"It's okay, Mum." Brendan gently extricated himself from her arms. It had been a long time since she'd held him that way. It felt good, but it was strange when he now stood almost a foot taller than she. "What are we having?"

"Spaghetti with puttanesca sauce! Your favourite! That should cheer you up. I must have had a premonition that you'd need a lift."

"Cool!" Brendan smiled for his mum, but inside he was still shaken up from the accident.

"And you didn't leave your books on the hall table?"

"No way, Mum," Brendan lied. He'd have to grab the books off the hall table as soon as dinner was over. He plunked down in his chair and reached for a piece of bread from the basket in the centre of the table. Hopefully, his mum would let the incident drop.

"No bread. Not until your father gets here! He called to say he's on his way." She picked up the wooden spoon and stirred the sauce again. "How was school?"

Brendan frowned. *Well, not the greatest. I've had a couple of massive head traumas over the last two days. My scar is turning into melanoma. The girl I adore laughs at me compulsively.* Aloud he said, "I'm fine, really."

Delia sat down opposite him. She snapped open a can of diet pop. "Mum, I'm going to the rec centre tonight with my friends Katie and Jenn." All her friends hung out at the rec centre where they could giggle and watch boys playing basketball. Girls!

"Is that so?" Mum opened the cupboard over the sink and took out plates. "Homework first."

"Mu-UM …" Delia began to whine in the annoying way she had.

"Yes. Homework!" Mum turned away to fill the plates with pasta from the strainer in the sink. Delia sneered at Brendan and reached for a piece of bread, digging into the butter with her knife.

"We're waiting for Dad!" Brendan said loudly.

"Yes!" Mum whirled around and pointed the pasta lifter at Delia. "He'll be one more minute!"

Delia dropped the bread and glared at Brendan, who grinned back. Sadly, when Mum's back was turned again, Delia flicked her knife and sent a gob of butter sailing across the table to splat on the front of Brendan's shirt.

"Hey!" he began to protest, but at that moment, Dad came in through the door, his pant leg held tightly in a bicycle clip and a shiny silver bike helmet on his head. His hands were covered in black grease, and he headed straight for the sink to wash them.

"Darn bicycle chain. It falls off every ten feet!" He rinsed his hands and dried them. Satisfied, he turned with a flourish and a bow. "Clairs! I am arrived! Let the rejoicing commence!" He took his wife in his arms and spun her around once, eliciting a shriek from her as she tried to avoid spilling the contents of the plate she was holding. He set her back on her feet and gave her a kiss on the cheek.

"Gross," Delia protested. "We're going to be eating here in a minute!"

Her father made a pouty face. "What's the matter, Delia? Oh, I know! You want some kisses, too!" He reached for his daughter. She reared back in horror, brandishing her butter knife. Her face conveyed a disgust reserved for plague carriers and affectionate fathers.

"Do *not* touch me!"

"Oh no, Brendan. She has a knife! Watch out!" Dad laughed and sat down in his customary chair as Mum set a steaming plate of spaghetti drenched in the fragrant sauce in front of him. He picked up a fork and began winding noodles around it. "So, children, how was school?"

Brendan opened his mouth to tell his father about Finbar, but Delia interjected. "Dad, can I go to the rec centre? Everyone's going to be there."

"I'm not going to be there," Dad said, stuffing a forkful of noodles into his mouth. "How can you say that everyone is going to be there when I'm not going to be there?"

"Da-ad."

"What did your mother say?"

"She said I could."

"No, I definitely did not. I said you have homework to do."

"But if I get it done? Then can I?"

Mom and Dad exchanged a glance, psychically connecting as mothers and fathers have since the beginning of time. "Fine. But the homework has to be done!"

Delia practically danced in her seat. She picked up her fork and dug in.

Brendan toyed with his food, adding grated cheese and pushing the noodles around. His father frowned. "Brendan? Everything all right?"

"Huh? Oh, yeah."

"He saw an accident today," Mum offered.

"Really? What happened?"

Brendan reluctantly repeated the censored account he had given his mother earlier. When he was done, his father shook his head. "Poor old fella. Hope he'll be okay. People used to have someplace to go when they were losing their marbles. Now they just end up on the street."

"Was there a lot of blood?" Delia asked. "Any brains or things like that?" She was really into slasher horror movies, the gorier the better.

"Just leave it," Brendan snapped. "I don't want to talk about it."

An uncomfortable silence hovered in the room until his father eventually broke it by repeating his question: "Apart from the mayhem, school good today?"

"Um … yeah, I guess. The substitute teacher, Mr. Greenleaf, was weird again."

His father laughed. "Then everything was as it should be, eh?"

"Yeah." For an instant, Brendan was tempted to tell his

father about Mr. Greenleaf, the walk in the park, the weird feelings he had been having, but he decided against it. They wouldn't get it. Delia would rip him mercilessly. His parents would think he was just having some teenage freak-out or something, and make him sit through a prolonged analysis. Ugh. He shovelled some pasta into his mouth. It tasted good. He felt a little better. He started to relax. After all, everything was right with the world: his sister was being a total brat, his dad was cracking horrible jokes as his mum shook her head and rolled her eyes. This was his family. This was normal.

Still, as he looked around the table at the people he'd known all his life, he couldn't suppress a feeling that things were going to change, that his life would never be the same. Something was coming that would alter the life he had known.

Brendan, would you chill? What is wrong with you? One smack with a ball and a kooky teacher and you totally lose it. Come on. He made a conscious effort to throw off his gloomy state of mind, concentrating on his father's accounts of the strange customers he'd served that day. Usually, his father's hilarious stories cheered him up, but the dark feelings lingered all through dinner.

The dinner ended with Brendan washing the dishes and Delia drying. He was just putting the last dish in the cupboard when his mother said, "Wow. Have you been using something new on your skin?"

"No," Brendan replied, confused. "Why?"

His mother frowned and reached out to touch his cheek. "It just looks clearer today than usual."

"Yeah," Delia interjected. "Most days your face makes me want to barf, but today, I just gagged a little."

Brendan whipped the wet dishtowel at her, but his sister ducked easily out of reach. "Too slow, Dorko!"

"Why are these people my children!" Mum sighed.

Delia laughed and ran out of the kitchen, in a hurry to get her homework done and get to her rendezvous at the rec centre.

"You need any help with anything else, Mum?" Brendan asked.

"No, you go do your homework. And your skin does look a lot better."

Brendan felt his cheeks redden with embarrassment. He wasn't used to compliments from girls, even if the girl in question was his mother. He went back down the hall to retrieve his books. As he passed the mirror on the wall by the coat rack, he decided to take a look to see what his mother was talking about. He leaned in close to the mirror and studied his face.

"She's right," Brendan whispered. The usual cluster of zits that plagued the corners of his mouth was fading. The giant angry, potential-Siamese-twin[32] pimple between his brows was half the size it had been that morning. "Wow." Well, one thing had gone right today, even if he had absolutely no control over it. Brendan grabbed his books off the hall table before his mum saw them and went up to his room.

Brendan's room was at the very top of the house, a converted attic that he reached via a steep set of narrow

---

[32] Brendan is exaggerating, of course, but there is one documented instance of a man growing a twin out of his forehead in Eastern Turkey. That is to say, the man was in Eastern Turkey, not his forehead. Well, to be accurate, both the man and his forehead were in Eastern Turkey. And the twin as well.

stairs that were more like a ladder than a real stairway. Brendan had begged for the room even though his mother and father had been dubious. The steep steps and his natural clumsiness were a dangerous mix. In the end, he'd prevailed. Delia was fine with him taking the attic room. She had a room with a tiny balcony to herself looking out over the street.

Brendan hoisted himself up into the room and tossed his books onto the small single bed. He stood up and immediately cracked his skull on the roof.

"Ow," he grunted aloud, rubbing his scalp. He'd lived in this room for years and he still banged his head every day like clockwork. Shaking his head in self-disgust, he went to his desk and sat down at the computer, being careful to duck beneath the slanted wooden beams that sloped overhead. He'd cracked his skull even more lately as he had shot up a foot in the last couple of years.

The room was small and cramped. As a result, Brendan had to keep the place meticulously tidy. His sister's room was liberally carpeted with dirty clothes and half-eaten food. Brendan had always been a neat freak. His cleaning habits gave Delia further fuel for her nerd insults, but Brendan didn't care.

The slanted roof was plastered with movie posters, mostly sci-fi films. A small bookshelf held comic books and paperbacks. His bed was small and narrow, tucked under the eaves next to a tiny bedside table. On the table sat a combination iPod dock and clock radio. He reached over and switched on the iPod; after a few clicks, music filled the small room.

Brendan had a wide range of musical interests. At school, everyone fell into categories: punk, goth, metalheads, emo kids, euro house music fans. Everyone seemed to feel the need to lock themselves into a certain genre. For comfort, he supposed. Belonging to a group made things easier in high school.

Brendan found it funny that a school like the Robertson Davies Academy, even though it was a melting pot of nerds and misfits gathered from the four corners of the city, was still full of cliques and clans. Some were thought to be nerds by other nerds.[33] You'd think a nerd was safe to be a nerd at nerd school but no such luck. Brendan had so far managed to remain outside any group. He had banded together with Harold, Dmitri, and Kim. Together they formed their own group. He and his friends were like the ubernerds, ultranerds, and nerd untouchables.

Which made it even weirder that Kim had latched onto them. He couldn't figure it out. Maybe she was a nerd on the inside. Kim always seemed a little exasperated with him and his friends, but she hadn't dumped them so far. *The year is young*, he reminded himself.

HE JUMPED when his father knocked on the ladder—he didn't have a door for his room. Sitting up, he managed

---

33 *Nerd* is a term that first appears in the Dr. Seuss opus *If I Ran the Zoo*. It has come to refer to a person who passionately pursues intellectual activities, esoteric knowledge, or other obscure interests that are age inappropriate rather than engaging in more social or popular activities. To be judged a nerd by other nerds is a sad situation to find oneself in. There have been some pretty wonderful nerds throughout history: Socrates, Copernicus, Einstein, Leonardo da Vinci. I don't care if Galileo could carve on his snowboard: he observed that the Earth revolved around the sun, which is way cooler, if you ask me.

not to knock his head again. His father's head and shoulders popped up through the hole in the floor.

"You ready to go?"

"Go? Go where?"

"The concert tonight. Remember? I got the free tickets."

Brendan had forgotten. He groaned inwardly at the thought of going to see Deirdre D'Anaan at Convocation Hall. Going to see a show was the last thing he felt like doing. He'd rather just lie down and take it easy tonight after all he'd been through today. He opened his mouth to try to beg off but stopped. The picture on the poster loomed in his mind. He recalled how he had felt when he'd seen it in the bus shelter by the pizza shop: like destiny was calling.

"Let me change out of my school stuff."

"Cool. Ten minutes in the lobby, Mr. Clair."

THE CONCERT

They walked through the chill of the autumn evening. Brendan was basking in the afterglow of his streetmeat,[34] a special treat that he and his father had picked up on the way. Soon they were standing in front of the polished wooden doors of the concert hall.

Convocation was one of Brendan's favourite buildings on the whole university campus. As a little kid, Brendan had come here to see Christmas concerts and hear chamber music with his mother, and he always looked forward to being inside the place. The seats, already full of buzzing concert-goers, were dark and polished oak, arranged in a circular pattern around the central stage.

Brendan's dad presented the tickets to the usher, who guided them to their seats, a bench about halfway to the stage.

---

34 *Streetmeat* in Toronto parlance is a sausage from a street vendor. A local ordinance prohibits the sale of any hot food on the streets of Toronto save for the hot dog or sausage. The limitation on the choice of cuisine has led to fierce competition between vendors to provide peripheral enticements to attract customers. These include offering a wide array of types of sausage, from the Polish garlic to the spicy Italian, presenting a bewildering array of condiments, and even one instance when a vendor offered a free kitten with each sausage sold. The vendor in question had his licence revoked in short order.

As they sat, Brendan's dad pointed at the stage. "She doesn't have any drum kit," he observed. "All acoustic. This should be interesting."

Looking at the stage, Brendan took stock of the instruments. The stage was arranged in sections, each devoted to a type of instrument. One area had a number of stringed instruments: fiddles of various sizes, a mandolin, and a guitar. Next to that was a rack of small drums and percussion instruments: tabla,[35] bongos, bells, and blocks. A rack full of different woodwinds glittered under the house lights: whistles, flutes, and fifes. Finally, in the centre of the stage was a simple, low stool. There were no microphones at all.

"There're no amplifiers," Brendan said. "How will they fill the hall?"

"I don't know." Brendan's dad frowned. "The hall's pretty good acoustically, but that's the thing with this performer, she insists on playing halls with no amplification. She's a bit eccentric. She's a recluse, and she doesn't perform live very often, but she has a dedicated, almost cult following."

At that point, the lights began to dim and a ripple of excitement coursed through the audience. This was the part of every show that Brendan loved the most, the moment before any note had been struck, before

---

[35] The *tabla* is an instrument originating in Northern India. It is a small drum played with the hands, as opposed to a drum that is played with the feet called the footbla. This latter is played by a very few people who have acute control over their feet. The footbla is not as popular because it is both difficult to master and incredibly stinky.

judgments were made, when all the audience perched on the edge of their seats, eager to be delighted. After an endless instant, the thrum of a harp was heard. The stage blazed into being as if conjured into existence by some magical power. The wail of a violin and the pounding of an Irish drum throbbed in counterpoint to the lilting, dancing tones of the harp. The musicians had taken their places in the darkness and now they sat or stood on the stage, playing feverishly.

Effortlessly, Deirdre D'Anaan commanded the focus, her red hair hanging about her gorgeous face as her fingers danced across the strings of her harp, resting between her knees. She wore a long gown of forest-green velvet embroidered with twining vines of golden thread that chased each other along her arms and around her neck. Her eyes were closed in concentration, and her lips curved ever so slightly in a faint smile. She looked like a dreaming angel.

Brendan wasn't aware of anything but the music. The sound was like nothing he'd ever heard before. He had seen Celtic musicians before, heard reels and jigs and Irish ballads, but the music Deirdre played was something altogether different.

He had no idea how long the song went on, but it ended with a final flourish of the drum. The hall echoed with the last note for a long moment before the crowd erupted into applause and roars of approval. Brendan fell back against the bench. He was breathing hard, and his clothing was soaked with sweat. The scar was aching anew, burning and prickling as though the wound were fresh.

Brendan's father sat down, still applauding. He turned to Brendan and said, "Wow! That was incredible.

Thirty-five minutes non-stop! I …" He hesitated, his brow furrowing. "Brendan? Are you okay?"

"Huh," Brendan mumbled. "Yeah. Fine … just a little … I don't know … tired?" Brendan pushed his fingers under the frame of his glasses and rubbed the bridge of his nose.

His father frowned. "You don't look fine." He laid a hand on Brendan's forehead. "Whoah. You're really warm. Are you sick?"

"Nah. I don't think so."

"Maybe we should go …"

"No!" Brendan sat up. He was suddenly aware that he had spoken quite loudly and immediately felt very self-conscious. In a more quiet tone he added, "No. I'll be okay. Let's stay."

His father frowned. "You sure?" Brendan could tell that his father wanted to hear more but would leave if Brendan asked him to. But Brendan didn't want to go. Despite the weird way he was feeling, he wanted to hear more, had to hear more. There was something in the music that he needed.

"Welcome." Deirdre D'Anaan's voice filled the hall. She didn't shout or raise her voice, but it was as though she were speaking directly into his ear. Her voice was rich and vibrant with a lilt of accent that Brendan couldn't place. "Old friends and new, we're glad you've come. What a grand hall and glorious night. On such a night we may bring the seen and unseen together. Can you feel it?" She raised her arms. "The spirits gather. They are drawn to the sound."

"Oh brother," Brendan's father snorted. Others nearby looked at him sharply. Brendan felt the urge to join them in disapproval. It sounded hokey but there was something happening here. He could sense it. He believed she was telling the truth. He believed that she was talking to him.

"This is a special night for those who choose to see. Open your eyes and your heart. I'd like to sing a special song tonight. It's called 'The Misplaced Prince.'"

Some members of the audience sighed aloud at her words. Brendan felt tempted to sigh as well.

Having spoken the words, she lowered her hands to the harp and struck a chord. Brendan shivered at the sound. The woman raised her clear voice in song. The words she sang were in a language he didn't understand, soft and sibilant, full of yearning. But as she sang, the words became clearer. He began to understand.

Who is he that left his home
Cast out in the world alone?
To live his life in strangers' care?
The Prince of Neither Here Nor There.

His glory hidden, dark and deep
His spirit leaden, forced to sleep
Who will wake him? Who would dare?
The Prince of Neither Here Nor There.

Come back, my prince, and join us soon
Your people wait beneath the moon
To welcome you back in the fold
With gifts of amber, jade, and gold.

Come home.

Come home.

The words and the music were so haunting that Brendan couldn't resist joining in the song. He looked about him and saw there were others singing as well. His father looked at him wide-eyed.

"Since when do you speak Gaelic?"[36]

Brendan didn't understand at first. Had he been singing? In a language he didn't understand? It didn't seem to matter to him. "I don't … I must have heard this song before, or something," he answered. Something above caught his eye, and when he looked up into the vault of the domed ceiling, he gasped.

The air was alive with lights like tiny flitting fireflies chasing one another about. As he watched, the lights became more defined. He saw that they were tiny winged figures fluttering about in the upper reaches of the hall. The variety of little creatures was astonishing. Dark-eyed snouted creatures with the leathery wings of bats flapped among them. Here and there, tiny human figures covered head to toe in colourful feathers soared on invisible air currents with exquisite bird wings. They moved in time to the music.

He pointed upward. "Do you see them? It's beautiful."

Brendan's father followed his gaze with a worried expression. "See who? See what?"

All the while, the music continued. The chorus repeated, "Come home! Come home!" The harp and the fiddle kept up a counterpoint with the drum, throbbing in

---

[36] *Gaelic* is the native and ancient language of Ireland. Few people speak it as a native tongue any more but Irish children are taught it in schools. Despite the efforts of the Irish government, the language is slowly dying out.

Brendan's chest, infusing his whole body with the rhythm. He began to sway, holding his arms out to the sides.

"Come home! Come home!" he sang. He felt a powerful surge of joy. He wanted to move! He wanted to leap and run and shout. He pushed past his father into the aisle.

"Brendan," his father said sternly, grabbing his son's arm. Brendan twisted free and stepped down the aisle toward the stage, where Deirdre D'Anaan sang the next verse, her voice like a magnet to the young boy. Her eyes were blazing grey stars. Her fingers flew over the harp strings, and as Brendan watched, he saw that a tiny creature wove in and out of her fingers as she played. It was like the others inhabiting the upper air of the vault, but when it stopped to stare, perching on the top of the sound post of the harp, its tiny eyes were fierce and it grinned in an unpleasant way that chilled Brendan's heart.

See him come and take his place
At last to join the noble race
Sound the trumpet! Split the air!
The Prince of Neither Here Nor There!

The Dark and Light shall be as one
The children of the Moon and Sun
Shall be redeemed, the world to share
The Prince of Neither Here Nor There.

Brendan looked about him, his father forgotten. In the crowd, some people stood out. They were more vibrant, more powerful presences. They were as different from the others around them as wildflowers are from blades of grass.

He turned his attention back to the stage and found himself staring directly into the bottomless eyes of Deirdre D'Anaan. The tiny creature perched on her shoulder, and it was pointing directly at him. She sang and it was like a fist clenching around his chest, constricting his breathing.

It's time to rise and take your place
To feel the sun upon your face
To face the truth if you may dare
Oh Prince of Neither Here Nor There!

Suddenly, the scar on his chest flared, obliterating his senses. He fell backward into someone's arms. He looked up and expected to see his father but he was shocked to see it was Kim.

"Did you see them? Did you see them?" he gasped.

Kim just shook her head. "Can't you ever stay out of trouble?"

THE DREAM

Kim and his father helped him out of the hall. He was a little dizzy, but the farther he got from the sound of the music, the more stable he felt and the more he was sure he'd experienced some kind of hallucination. *I mean, little creatures? Flying things? Give me a break, right?*

The concert had continued despite his episode. Deirdre D'Anaan hadn't missed a beat. To his relief, he wasn't the only one to be transported by the music. Though some had taken to the aisles to dance spontaneously, none had been affected as deeply as Brendan had. Between Kim and his dad, they had managed to steer Brendan to the exit.

Standing out in the fresh, cool air, Brendan felt a little better. If he was honest with himself, he hadn't felt bad in the hall—quite the opposite. He had felt completely alive. *That was amazing. I was totally going to make a fool of myself! I was going to go up on the stage and dance around like a lunatic but ... I didn't care!* Part of him regretted that Kim and his father had pulled him away.

"Are you okay?" his father asked for the umpteenth[37] time.

---

[37] *Umpteen* no longer exists as a proper number. In ancient times, it was used by uneducated people who couldn't count past nineteen and so they would refer to anything over nineteen as "umpteen." The word still lingers on as an idiom that describes a number that is basically uncountable.

"I'm fine," Brendan assured him. "I just … needed some air."

"You really gave me a scare there, bud." His father was clearly trying to sound unconcerned but his laugh rang a bit false. "I thought you were gonna do some stage-diving."

Kim stood back, arms crossed, and said not a word.

"What's your problem?" Brendan asked.

"No problem," she said evenly.

"You look pissed."

"Well, I'm not. Not at you anyway."

"Well, who are you pissed at, then?" Brendan was feeling belligerent and a little tired of her odd behaviour. "And what are you doing here anyway?"

"Hey, Brendan. Just hold on," his father interjected. "Your friend Kim was a big help."

"I'll bet," Brendan muttered.

"As I said," his father repeated, "Kim was a big help. I don't think you should be so disrespectful."

Brendan wanted to say, *Dad, butt out! She's been sneaking around and talking about me behind my back. I'm sick of it.* Instead he muttered, "I guess so."

"You're welcome," Kim snorted. "I'd better be going. See ya, Mr. Clair." She plunked her helmet on her head and tightened the strap.

"Thanks, Kim," his father said. "See you soon."

Brendan watched her disappear around the side of the building and he heard her scooter cough to life and roar away.

"You've never mentioned her before," his dad observed.

"She goes to my school."

"Really?" His father arched an eyebrow. "Hmmm. Like

I said: I'm surprised you've never mentioned her before. She's cute."

"Dad!"

"Come on! I'm just thinking she's cute, is all."

"She's just a friend of mine, Dad."

His dad winked knowingly. "I see. Say no more …"

"Dad," Brendan groaned. "It's not like that."

"Like what? Who said anything about anything being like anything?"

"Well, it isn't like that."

"Gotcha."

"Oh, brother."

"You okay to walk?" His father's face was suddenly full of concern. "We could take a cab …"

"Dad, relax." Brendan rolled his eyes. "I'm fine. We could go back in if you want. I promise, I'm okay."

His father looked at him critically then said, "Naw. Let's go home. I have an early day tomorrow anyway."

"I'm sorry, Dad. I ruined your night out."

"Not at all. I'm not really into that Celtic stuff, y'know. I like the rock and roll." He punched Brendan in the arm. "I say we get some barbecue pork and head home, huh?"

"Okay."

An hour later, after a delicious stop at the Golden Stone Barbecue Restaurant, Brendan climbed into his loft feeling totally exhausted. He was still reeling from the concert experience.

Leaving his father and mother talking in the kitchen, he went upstairs to his room. They'd both been looking at him a little too closely as he kissed them good night like they were expecting him to freak out or something. He knew his father would be telling his mum about his episode at the concert. He groaned at the prospect of their concern.

Picking the iPod up off the dock, he flung himself down on the bed. He didn't feel in the mood for the Ramones. *Too harsh*. He clicked over to the RECENTLY ADDED playlist and scrolled down to find the new Wintersleep he'd downloaded before going to school. There it was, down at the bottom. He sat up suddenly, bumping his head again on the sloping roof.

"Ow." He rubbed his scalp and peered at the screen of his music player. There was a new entry. He froze in mid-rub.

"What is this?" he asked the empty room. He read the name. "Deirdre D'Anaan?" He racked his brain. Had he downloaded this by accident? He couldn't remember downloading any of her music. Maybe his father had done it. What was the alternative? Had someone stolen his iPod from his knapsack, put some new music on his deck, then put the iPod back?

"Just another weird thing on the weirdest day ever," he mumbled.

He clicked on the entry and the album cover came up on the screen.

The picture arrested his attention. She was just as beautiful as he remembered from the hall that night. The picture was so vivid. She seemed to stare out at him from the tiny screen. The title of the CD was traced in the wooden carved vines: THE FAERIE BANQUET.

Brendan frowned. *You should just wipe it. Get rid of it. You know what the music did to you. Mum and Dad are downstairs right now discussing the possibility that you might need a lobotomy. Erase it, fool.*

"Well, I might as well give it a listen." He slotted the iPod into the dock and pushed play. He lay back on the bed and waited.

A harp rippled softly in the dark. The lilting harmonics of the strings were joined by Deirdre's voice. Clear and strong but completely controlled, the notes soared, sending shivers across Brendan's skin. He closed his eyes to let the sound wash over him.

Throbbing with emotion, the harp was lush and vibrant. And when Deirdre D'Anaan sang, her voice was so personal, as if she were singing for him alone. The woman's face filled his mind's eye. She looked so familiar.

Then it hit him. Those eyes. They were just like Greenleaf's! The more he looked, the more he felt that this woman and Greenleaf could almost be related—cousins or even brother and sister.

The music was soothing. As he changed into his pyjamas, he looked over at the single gable window that filled the end of the room. Moonlight angled in low across the floor. Trees, their leaves backlit by the moon, swept like dark shadows back and forth with the wind. Their movement was restful, hypnotic. He was safe here in his little world. He could relax. So he did. In a few minutes, his breathing deepened and he fell asleep.

Something in the music tugged him out of his slumber. Brendan opened his eyes and saw that the ceiling above him was no longer made of plaster and wooden beams. The poster of a space marine firing a laser cannon at swarming aliens was obscured by a mass of dense vines. Brendan sat up, his head brushing the trailing leaves. The whole room had changed. The centre of the roof was gone. Overhead the stars shone down, cold and densely packed.

"Hello, this is weird," Brendan said out loud. His breath came out in a frosty cloud. He realized he was cold. "Is this a dream?" He looked at his hands. They glowed softly white in the pale light of the moon. He looked down to see he was still wearing his pyjamas—a pair of flannel plaid trousers and a T-shirt.

He stood up and stepped to the centre of the room. He found himself on a stone parapet. The wooden floorboards were gone and in their place were heavy stones crusted with moss. A low wall surrounded him. The trapdoor remained in the same place, the top of the ladder poking up. The music seemed to be coming from below. Shivering, he descended the ladder.

The music was louder here. The hall had undergone a similar transformation, plaster walls replaced by stone, and framed pictures replaced with woven tapestries. Brendan passed his sister's room. The door was open. Looking in, he was shocked to see the green vines woven throughout the room, twined through the mass of clothing on the floor, tangled around his sister's bed. A half-eaten sandwich was oddly cradled in a nest of leaves. Delia lay beneath a blanket of dense vines, her face pale and peaceful in the moonlight. If left to their own devices, the vines would soon cover her face and smother her. Brendan felt alarm but the music beckoned him, urging him toward the living room.

The familiar room was utterly altered. He recognized the richly carved hall from the artwork on his iPod. His parents' comfortable, overstuffed furniture was barely visible under a carpet of vines. Where the TV usually occupied the corner, a large wooden chair loomed. In the chair, so real, more real than she could possibly be, sat Deirdre D'Anaan.

In the picture, she had been beautiful. Onstage, she had been incandescent. In person, she was breathtaking, terrifyingly radiant. In the eerie light, her pale skin glowed with a cold fire. Her long, nimble fingers, each decorated with golden rings, caressed achingly beautiful music drawn from the harp she held on her lap. The harp was exquisitely carved, inlaid with woods of many different hues, its surface polished and smooth. On her shoulder perched the tiny creature from the CD cover and the show that night. The little wings, veined and transparent like an insect's wings, fluttered once, twice. The little eyes glittered in the pale glow of the moon streaming through the broad front window. It glared warily at Brendan as he came to stand in front of the woman's chair.

"Is this a dream?" Brendan asked. His voice sounded so loud, a jarring contrast to the rich sound of the harp.

She didn't stop playing. She raised her eyes to his, and he felt a shiver of delight that she should waste a gaze upon him. "A dream? No. I have wrought a Sending. Such are my gifts: I am a Weaver. I pass the thread through the loom and make tapestries for the mind's eye. But I have no time to waste. What I do is exhausting."

"What do you mean?" Brendan frowned. He felt like a child, an infant in front of her. Looking directly into her shining eyes was like looking into the sun. He wanted to hide his face but he made himself hold her gaze.

"You left the hall tonight before I could accomplish my goal. I rarely perform for the People of Metal.[38] I had to

---

[38] The People of Metal is the Faerie name for Humans. Humans have a love for iron, steel, tools, and machines that pound the world into shapes of their choosing. Faeries prefer to use less

see you for myself." The woman raised a hand and pointed a long, elegant finger at his chest. His scar flared in agony. "I have come to dispel the glamour that has hidden you for so long. The Ward is failing. Soon, you will come to understand who and what you are. Enemies search for you. Soon, they will be able to see you."

"Enemies," Brendan gasped, clawing at his chest. The pain was deepening. "I don't understand."

"No. You were hidden among Humans until you were old enough to defend yourself, choose for yourself. You cannot possibly understand. You must learn your true heritage and find your true strength before you are destroyed or turned to darkness."

"Turned to darkness? I'm a high school student! What darkness?" Brendan shook his head. "I must be dreaming. This is some kind of post-concussion thing. I'm going to wake up and everything will be back to normal."

"Foolish boy!" The woman frowned, and for the first time, Brendan sensed something dark and dangerous behind her beautiful eyes. The mark on his chest ignited with fresh, crippling pain. As he fell to his knees, gasping, she said, "You have no idea of the danger you are in. I am trying to save you!"

"You have a funny way of showing it!"

"Breandan! You have a destiny. There is no use trying to escape it." Her voice was impossible to deny. The tone was fell[39] and it throbbed with power.

---

invasive methods, choosing to manipulate the inner energies of nature to achieve their goals.

[39] *Fell* in this instance is not the past tense of fall but an adjective meaning dark and dangerous. It wouldn't make much sense if she suddenly fell down in the middle of a menacing sentence, would it. That would be silly.

Brendan staggered to his feet. He had to get away from the music, from the power of her voice. The strange way she said his name, like Mr. Greenleaf. The thought that they were related came back, stronger than ever. "Who are you, exactly? Why should I trust you?"

"There is no time," Deirdre said. "This Sending is exhausting to maintain." Indeed, lines of strain creased her brow. "Listen to me."

"No!" Brendan cried. He staggered across the floor and through the door that led to the hall.

The walls, the carpet crawled with vines that coiled around his ankles and wrists, making him stumble. Something buzzed past his ear. The little creature had left Deirdre's shoulder and zipped about his head, shrieking. The whir of its tiny insect-like wings was maddening. Brendan batted at the creature but it ducked away easily. Suddenly, the thing dove at his chest, scuttling under his T-shirt. The feel of its tiny hands scrabbling across his skin filled him with revulsion.

"Get away!" Brendan shouted, slapping at the thing with both hands. "Get off me!" He was starting to panic. He banged into the wall and fell on his hands and knees. Instantly, the vines clutched at his hands. A sharp pain in his chest made him cry out. The little creature had bitten or clawed him!

Then the creature, having slithered out from the shirt, flew up and hovered in front of him, holding something in its hands. Brendan's eyes went wide. It held a glowing spiral shape in its tiny fingers. While Brendan looked on in fascination, it opened its jaws to reveal rows of minute, needle-sharp teeth and began to devour the glowing shape, shredding it like a pastry and popping the pieces in its mouth with relish.[40]

The shape was somehow familiar. "My scar," Brendan whispered in horror. "It's eating my scar!" He looked down at his bare chest, exposed by the rent in the cotton shirt. In place of the scar there was merely an empty patch of reddened skin. "That is so gross!" He swatted at the creature, but it darted out of reach and continued its feast.

"*The Ward is broken*," the woman's voice intoned. "Now you will know your true nature! You will live among the People of Metal no more. You shall come to the Fair Folk!"

Brendan spun around to find Deirdre standing in the hallway behind him. She was tall and dire, filling the doorway. Her face radiated an aura of strength and authority. She spoke, and her voice was as irresistible as a hurricane, as inevitable as an earthquake. "The People await you. Your true family awaits you. You will return to us! You must be prepared before it is too late. There are those who wish to harm you. They will try to turn you to a dark purpose." She reached for him.

"I don't know what you're talking about!" Brendan shouted. "I'm with my family! Who wants to harm me? You're the one with the crazy vines and the creepy little, scar-eating thing! Why should I listen to you?"

"You must listen," Deirdre demanded. "I don't wish to frighten you. I wish you to understand!"

"No," Brendan whimpered. "Leave me alone." He backed away, tripping over a snarl of vines. He had to escape. "*Mum! Dad! Help me! Don't let her take me!*"

---

[40] And by relish, I mean enjoyment, not the condiment.

Scrabbling against the clutching vines, Brendan hauled himself hand over hand into the kitchen. He pulled free of the clinging tendrils with a final heave. He grabbed the edge of the kitchen table and pulled himself to his feet. He gasped in horror.

His mother and father sat at the table with a pot of tea and a plate of biscuits between them. The vines had completely engulfed his parents. His father's head lay on the table, his mouth open. Leafy fingers clawed down his throat. His mother sat with her head thrown back, a mass of crawling leaves engulfing her. The only part of her that was recognizable was her left hand, where her wedding ring glinted in the silvery light.

"No!" Brendan screamed. "*No! Let them go! Let them go!*"

A thick root twined around his foot and jerked him off balance. He crashed to the tile floor of the kitchen as vines swarmed hungrily over him, enveloping him, pinning his limbs uselessly to his sides. The vines wormed their way up over his shoulders....

"Let me go! What do you want from me?" he shrieked, writhing desperately.

"You are one of us," Deirdre whispered. "You must join with us or be overwhelmed. The darkness is coming for you. You must join us. It's your only hope of survival!"

At last he could stand it no longer. "*Nooooooo!*" he screamed. His open mouth filled with vine, choking him, strangling him.

"Brendan!" He was being shaken. "Brendan! Wake *up!*"

His father's voice was calling.

Brendan opened his eyes and looked up into the faces of his parents. Their eyes were filled with concern. He sat up and saw he was in the kitchen. His pyjamas were soaked with sweat, lying cold and damp against his skin. He shivered.

"Brendan, are you okay?"

"Huh? The woman …" Brendan croaked. His throat felt raw. "She's going to hurt you. She's trying to get me."

His parents exchanged a worried look. Brendan blinked away the sting of sweat and looked around him. The vines were gone. Tea dripped from the tabletop where two cups lay overturned. Mum's favourite china teapot was shattered on the floor beside him. Brendan looked up at his parents again.

"You're all right," he said softly. "You're okay."

"We're fine." Brendan's mum bent down and pulled his head to her chest. "We're just fine."

"It was a dream, son." His father ruffled his hair, reassuring him. "Everyone's okay."

A REVELATION

Brendan looked around the kitchen, blinking stupidly. "But … how did I get here?"

"You were sleepwalking, Dorklord," Delia's acid voice sneered. "And screaming like a little girl."

She was leaning against the kitchen doorframe, her dressing gown wrapped around her. Her hair stood out like a tatty halo.

Brendan shook his head. It had all seemed so real … more than real. He still felt the grip of the terror and the sound of the otherworldly music.

His mother released him and stood up. "I'll get this mess swept up, then we'll put on some hot milk."

"Give it to him in a baby bottle, too," Delia said, rolling her eyes. She left the doorway and went back up the stairs.

Brendan let his father help him to his feet. He still felt shaky.

"I should probably just get to bed, Dad."

"Sit."

Brendan looked at his father's face and saw there was no escape. He pulled out his chair at the table and sat down as he watched his father fetch the milk from the fridge and his mother clean up the mess he'd made.

It seemed so real, Brendan thought. *But it couldn't have been. It was a dream.* He winced as the fabric of the T-shirt brushed against his chest. When his parents weren't looking, he surreptitiously[41] pulled the collar of his T-shirt down and looked at the space over his heart. Where his scar had been for all the years of his life, there was now a patch of reddened, irritated skin. The odd spiral scar was gone. He quickly covered up the mark again before anyone saw.

His father took a seat opposite him as his mother heated the milk in a pan. "We're worried about you, Brendan," his father began seriously.

"Dad, I'm fine! It was just a bad dream like you said," Brendan insisted.

"I don't know," his dad said. There was worry plain on his face. "We've had a couple of calls from the school nurse. You had some kind of confrontation with a bully at school and you hit your head ..."

"It's nothing," Brendan groaned, secretly cursing the kindly Mrs. Barsoomian. "I got tagged in the face in Murderball. And I banged my head on a door. Really. I'm just clumsy. You know that."

His mother sat down, putting a cup of hot milk in front of him. Ever since he was a child, his mother had made him hot milk when he was sick or upset. He picked up the cup and blew gently on the surface of the milk, watching a skin form on the top. When he looked up, both his parents were looking at him with sober expressions on their faces.

---

41 *Surreptitiously*. How do you like that for a word? It means discreetly or sneakily. I could have just said sneakily or discreetly, but I didn't, did I? Deal with it.

"Oh." Brendan suddenly understood. "Oh, no way! I'm not on drugs or anything. It's not like that. Besides ... how could I afford drugs on my allowance? Huh? Ha!" They didn't find his joke funny either.

"What are we supposed to think?" his mother asked. "You've been behaving so strangely. And your father said you had some kind of episode at the concert tonight."

"Episode? No! It wasn't an episode," he said hurriedly. "I was just ... tired and ... I don't know." He thought back to the concert and how he must have looked. If he'd been watching himself, he would have thought the same thing as his parents. "I was just getting into the music. Really. It's nothing to worry about. I'm a teenager. I'm supposed to do weird stuff."

"But we do worry," Brendan's father said. "It's a dangerous world and we want you kids to be safe. You have to be careful."

"I am, Dad."

"Well, we still worry," his mum repeated. "And we think it's time you knew something. We wanted to tell you before but it never seemed like the right time." She looked to his dad before continuing. "We're concerned that some of these episodes might be subconsciously linked to this ... situation."

His mother fell silent. Brendan groaned inwardly. His mother had studied psychology and she liked to use it on him whenever the opportunity arose. Brendan steeled himself for her amateur psychoanalysis. His father reached out and took his mother's hand, squeezed it. His mother took a deep breath and looked at Brendan.

"I want to say, first, that we love you. I've loved you

from the moment I saw you, Brendan. You have made your father and me so happy in so many ways."

Brendan was puzzled. "I love you too, Mum. And you, Dad." Normally, not even Chester's tortures would be enough to draw this admission from Brendan, but he sensed this was not like any discussion he'd had with his parents before. He knew this was a time to set aside his usual embarrassments.

"We have tried to give you a good home and a good family. We've done everything we can for you...." His mum faltered. "I don't know how to tell you. But we want you to know the truth." Her voice cracked.

His father took over. "Brendan, you aren't our natural child. That is to say, you are our son. You are my son and I love you, but you weren't born to us."

Brendan stared in disbelief. "What are you saying?"

"We adopted you when you were a baby." His mum blurted it out suddenly, her eyes full of tears. "You were so beautiful. Just a perfect little baby boy and we loved you immediately and we've never stopped."

Brendan felt a chill run through his heart. "I'm adopted?"

"Yes," his father said. "It makes no difference to us, and it shouldn't to you. You are loved here and no child has ever been more wanted."

Brendan didn't know what to say. He sat in silence for a full minute as he tried to find his words. Finally, he said, "Why are you telling me this now?"

His mother took his hand. "We were worried. You are our son in everything but biology. We were worried that you might be having problems that are due to your genetic inheritance...."

"Or even psychologically," his father added. "Perhaps, on some level, you are aware that we aren't your biological parents and you're having … problems because of those suppressed feelings."

Brendan didn't know what to think. He looked away from his parents' faces to the cupboards and the stove and the pots hanging above the sink. This was his home. He had never even dreamed that he didn't belong here.

Suddenly, his mind was filled with the voice of Deirdre D'Anaan: *Now you will know your true nature!* He couldn't get his head around it.

"Does Delia know?" he said at last.

"No," his father said. "She was very young when we got you. We have never told her. We decided you should know first."

Brendan suddenly felt angry. "Now? Now I should know? You've kept it a secret this long and you think telling me will help me in some way?" He pushed his chair back and stood, jostling the table and spilling his milk across the tabletop.

"Brendan!" His father stood. "Do not speak to your mother in that tone."

"I won't," Brendan sneered. "If I ever meet her." He instantly regretted what he'd said. His mother covered her face with her hands and began to sob. His father was at her side in an instant, encircling her shoulders with his arms.

Brendan felt so ashamed of himself. Why had he said something so cruel? She was his mother. She had always been there for him and now he had repaid her with cruelty.

"I …" he stammered. "I'm sorry, Mum. I didn't mean it. I—"

His father raised a hand and smiled sadly. "I know. She knows too. It's all right. Just head on up the wooden hill now. We'll talk more in the morning."

Brendan wanted to go and hold his mum and make her understand that he was sorry. Instead, he made his way to the loft and flung himself down on the bed.

"Who am I, really?" he murmured to the space marine in the poster on the ceiling. *Talk about the worst week ever. Maybe if I'd never made it to the end of the Murderball game, all of this wouldn't have happened.* He thought it would take forever to get to sleep, but the concert, the bizarre dream, and the revelation had sapped him completely. He flung an arm over his eyes and fell almost instantly asleep, a sleep that was thankfully devoid of dreams.

PART 2

Freaking Out
and Running

Another Note
from the Narrator

Certainly, not an elegant name for the next section but it accurately describes the action. Accuracy is important in narration. What if I'd called the next section

BRENDAN PETS A LITTLE DOG
AND EATS A COB OF CORN

Ridiculous, I think you'd agree! There is no petting of dogs (little or large) and no corn is present in the narrative. You would have been confused, angry, and upset. You might have come to my home with torches and pitchforks and taken your vengeance upon me. I wouldn't enjoy that, to say the least. Especially since I just had some landscaping done on the front yard, and it would break my heart to have an angry mob trample my geraniums. (Or gerania? I'm not certain of the plural form of geranium. Still, it's beside the point.) I don't want you to wreak your revenge upon me for the inaccuracy of my section titles. (Of course, I doubt that you would be able to find my house, even should you raise a vengeful mob. I live in a subdivision of Helsinki and the streets are very windy. I'm sure you'd get lost and there's nothing that takes the wind out of an angry mob's sails like endlessly wandering around, searching for the object of their fury.)

Let's move on. Brendan is on the verge of some big changes. He's discovered some shocking facts about himself. These shocking facts are just the tip of the iceberg, I'm afraid. It's time to start freaking out and running.

SEEING THINGS

Breakfast was strained. Brendan's parents tried to be hearty and upbeat, but he could tell they were worried. His sister was her usual sensitive self. Whenever his parents weren't looking, she flipped him the loser sign on her forehead. His parents kept sneaking looks at him, as if they were expecting him to lose it at any moment.

His father was off early to the coffee shop. His sister also left for a volleyball practice before school. Brendan was relieved to have a chance to talk to his mother alone. He waited until she came downstairs in her work suit. She was gathering up her notes and stuffing them into her briefcase when he finally worked up the nerve to approach her.

"Mum?"

She stopped what she was doing but she didn't look at him.

"I'm sorry, Mum. I was mean last night," he said softly.

She looked up at him then, her eyes bright with tears. "I know. It's a lot to accept. Maybe, we shouldn't have told you ... but we were worried about you."

"Mum, I know," Brendan said. "I'm sorry I've been weird lately. I guess it's just hormones or something. I want you to know that you are my mum. No one else. That will never change."

She started to cry, wrapping her arms around him and squeezing him tight. "I'm so glad you said that. I always want to be your mother. I don't regret anything." She pulled away and looked up into his face. "I know what you're thinking—why tell you now? Well, there is another reason."

Brendan felt a lump form in his stomach.

"While you were out last night, a woman came here asking for you," his mother told him. "She said she was a relative of your father's ..." She paused and frowned slightly. "Your biological father. She wanted to see you."

"What did you say?"

"I told her the truth," his mother said. "You were out with your dad. She said she would wait. I told her that wasn't acceptable. We would have to talk to you first before you had any contact with your biological relatives."

"What did she say to that?"

"It was weird," his mother said. "She didn't say anything for a long time. She just stared at me. It was kind of scary. It felt like she was barely restraining herself from physically attacking me."

"Did you call the police?" Brendan asked. "She sounds a little crazy."

"Not yet," his mother said. "Your father is going to talk to our lawyer today, to see what the legal implications might be. That's why we felt we had to tell you. We didn't want you to find out from anybody else."

Brendan's mouth hung open in shock. Strange people claiming to be his relatives? His dream? Greenleaf and Kim conspiring? There were so many strange things happening to him. He'd forgotten to ask his father about the music on his iPod. He'd have to do that tonight when he got home.

"What did this woman look like, in case she tries to talk to me?"

His mother frowned. "That's another weird thing, I can't really remember. I only have a vague impression that she was tall and her hair was blond. I've been racking my brain but I can't come up with anything else. Maybe she scared me worse than I realized."

"Did she give you a name?"

His mother shook her head. "No. When I asked for it she said, 'Your *people* will know it soon enough.'" She shivered. "The way she said it was so, I don't know, vicious. I was pretty frightened. I was glad when you guys came home."

"If she comes back, you should call the police."

"I will. You be careful, too," she said and kissed his cheek. "And about everything else … your past history. We love you. I know there will be difficult things for you to deal with but as long as you remember that, we're going to be fine, understand? We just have to keep talking about it, okay?"

"Yeah," he said, a lump forming in his throat. "I'll remember." He kissed her cheek and set off out the front door.

Dmitri was waiting at the corner of College and Crawford. Brendan was glad to see him today. He was glad to see anyone normal.

"Did you get the calculus homework done?" Dmitri asked.

"No." Brendan groaned inwardly. "I just fell asleep last night. I didn't get to it. I'll try and do it during my free period. Is it hard?"

Dmitri pursed his lips. "You can copy mine if you want to."

They walked in silence for a couple of blocks. Brendan was wrapped up in his thoughts of last night's dream. It had seemed so real. Deirdre D'Anaan sitting in his living room with the vines choking his family. Then there was his parents' revelation, and the weird visitor. Had the woman at the door been Deirdre D'Anaan? No. Not likely. She was onstage at the time. So now there were two strange women to deal with. It was all too much. He needed help.

"D," he said finally, "what do you think about dreams?"

"Dreams? Like while you're asleep?"

"Yeah. What are they? Do you think they're important?"

"Important?" The smaller boy shrugged. "I don't know. Some people think that your dreams are your subconscious mind processing what your waking mind takes in. Your brain is like a computer, and when you go to sleep it continues to process data in a random fashion."

"Huh," Brendan grunted. "I guess that makes sense."

"Then there's my babka's point of view," Dmitri said.

"She believes in all sorts of crazy things. She says dreams are a way for spirits to speak with us directly. It's a kind of teleconferencing for the spirit world." Dmitri tossed his head. "She also believes her cat gives her stock tips."[42]

"Is she crazy or what?"

"Well, she has a fairly healthy stock portfolio ... but I can't say I share her point of view. The human brain is a pretty amazing thing. We understand very little about how

---

[42] Do not take your cat's advice in business dealings. I speak from experience. My cat was my investment manager for three years. I now own over seventy thousand squeaky mice and an acre of swamp in Siberia.

it actually works. Who can tell what dreams actually mean?" Dmitri looked sideways at Brendan. "Why this interest in dreams? Had any interesting ones lately?"

"Naw. Just curious. Some reading I was doing." He changed the subject. "Are you going to the field hockey game after school? We should support Kim." *And maybe I can finally corner her and make her talk.*

"I wouldn't miss it. All those girls in short skirts beating each other with sticks? Is there any finer entertainment?" Dmitri grinned.

"You are truly creepy," Brendan said, laughing.

"I won't argue with you."

They were walking past the elementary school and the huge rock when Brendan heard snoring. Heavy and ponderous, it sounded like the wheezing of an elephant. He stopped and looked around. It sounded as if someone was sleeping nearby but there was no one around.

"Who's snoring?" Brendan asked Dmitri.

"What?" Dmitri asked in return.

"There's somebody snoring right here. Can't you hear it?"

Dmitri looked at Brendan like he was a little nutty. That was happening a lot lately. "I can't hear anything."

"Well, I can." He looked around once again and saw that there was no one around, just him, Dmitri, and the huge black rock.

Brendan stepped over in front of the large stone. The snoring seemed to be coming from behind it.

"Come out of there," he demanded. "You can't sleep there."

"Brendan?" Dmitri came and stood beside him. "Are you okay?" Dmitri laid a hand on his arm.

"I hear snoring. I think somebody's sleeping behind the stone." Brendan shook off his friend's hand and stepped over the short white fence that surrounded the stone. "Come out of there, right now." He had to prove to Dmitri that he wasn't crazy. He walked around the stone and looked down. There was nobody there.

Now he felt foolish. He had been sure he would find someone. He scratched his head and leaned on the stone. Suddenly the snoring was very loud. With a snort like someone stirring in his sleep, the rock under his hand shifted almost imperceptibly.

Suddenly, a loud deep voice rumbled in his ear. "Get yer greasy hands off, punk."

Brendan jumped away from the stone, jerking his hand back as if he'd been stung. He staggered backward and fell over the fence at Dmitri's feet.

"Brendan! What happened?" Dmitri helped him to his feet.

"D-didn't you hear that?" Brendan stammered. "It was the rock." He pointed at the stone, inert and stone-like as ever. "It yelled at me!"

"Brendan, I didn't hear anything." Brendan looked into his friend's face and saw only worry there, the same worry that had been on his parents' faces last night and at break-fast this morning. He decided to change the subject.

"Never mind." Brendan waved Dmitri away. "I'm fine. Just a little tired, I guess." Dmitri didn't look convinced.

"C'mon," Brendan said. "We're gonna be late." He took a final look at the now-silent rock and strode up the street.

Dmitri had to hurry to catch up with Brendan. The scowl on Brendan's face pre-empted any attempt at conversation. Dmitri was worried. He'd never seen his friend behave this way before.

Brendan was scowling to cover up his bewilderment. He was sure he'd heard someone speaking to him and was terrified he was losing his mind. What made it worse was the fact that the world just seemed so noisy all of a sudden. The birds seemed louder. Every car driving past sounded like a freight train. The leaves in the trees rattled in the wind and the sound was so acute that he felt they were speaking. If only he could listen to them more closely, he might catch a word or two of their conversation. He clenched his teeth, resisting the urge to clap his hands over his ears.

They reached the park and started along the path that would carry them diagonally across the green to the school. The wind was gusting strongly, plucking at his jacket and keening in his ears.

"*Winter is coming.*" The wind's whistling resolved into a haunting voice. Brendan stopped so suddenly that Dmitri ran into him. The wind spoke again. "*Smell the snow. The devouring winter comes.*"

Brendan whirled and grabbed Dmitri. "What did you say?"

Dmitri stared into Brendan's eyes, inches from his own. "I ... I ... didn't say anything."

"Are you trying to freak me out?" Brendan's eyes were wide and wild, white showing all around the pupil. "I heard someone speaking. I heard a voice. How are you doing this?"

Dmitri didn't know what to say. He stepped back in confusion. Brendan saw how frightened his friend was, and with a great effort, he reined in his own terror. "I'm sorry, D. I didn't mean to scare you ... I ... I don't know what's going on. I'm just feeling really weird. I can't explain it."

"It's okay. I understand." Dmitri smiled to reassure Brendan, but his eyes said that he clearly wasn't comfortable.

"Why don't you go on ahead," Brendan suggested. "I need a minute to myself. To clear my head."

"Are you sure? You don't seem well."

"Yeah, yeah. I just need a minute. I'm tired, that's all."

Dmitri didn't need much convincing. "All right. I'll see you in homeroom." He quickly set off across the park but not without a worried backward glance.

Brendan sank down onto a park bench. He'd lied when he said he'd felt tired. Quite the opposite, he felt completely wired. His nerves were jangling, he felt more acutely aware of everything around him. He could sense each blade of grass reaching for the weak rays of the sun. He felt their yearning, their despair as they seemed to know that autumn was ending and they were doomed to die.

What is happening to me? Am I losing my mind? He felt close to tears.

"Food? Food? Food?" sang a chorus of tiny voices. They were high and silly sounding like when he swallowed helium out of a balloon or when his dad sped up recordings of his voice to make him laugh.

Brendan looked around in confusion. There was no one nearby. "Hello?"

"Food? Food? Food?" the voices repeated, more insistent this time.

Brendan looked down and gasped.

A gang of chubby grey squirrels had gathered around the bench. Not unusual, for they congregated whenever a person stood still, hoping for scraps of bread or potato chips. Their beady black eyes fixed Brendan with fevered intensity.

Suddenly, their tiny mouths opened in unison. "Food? Food? Food?"

Brendan practically choked, rubbing his eyes in disbelief. "You ... you're talking!"

The squirrels scampered closer, forming a ring around Brendan's trainers. "*Food? Food? Food?*" The little voices were annoyed now. Tiny paws stretched out in entreaty. It was such a human gesture that Brendan answered, "I don't have anything."

One of the squirrels suddenly reached up a paw and seemed to pull its head off. Brendan gasped. It wasn't a head. It was a hat. Standing amid the squirrels was a small man with big black eyes and a twitching nose. He was dressed in a suit of grey fur, roughly stitched together. In his hand was a minute[43] silver object, a forked stick made out of metal with a cord strung between the tips of the two tines. It was a tiny slingshot! The little man sneered at Brendan.

"What's the deal, buddy? You gonna give us some bread or what?" The voice was high and squeaky.

---

[43] By *minute* (pronounced my-nyoot), I don't mean a minute (pronounced mi-nit) made up of sixty seconds. I mean minute (pronounced my-nyoot), which is another word for very small. I suppose a minute (pronounced mi-nit) is a small part of an hour, one might say. A Minute (pronounced mi-nit) Man was a nickname for American soldiers in the Revolutionary War. But they were not minute (pronounced my-nyoot) but capable of being ready in a minute (pronounced mi-nit). A very important difference. Tiny soldiers would certainly have been defeated in short (pardon the pun) order.

Brendan swallowed, gasping for air. "I … I …"

"C'mon, you selfish jerk. I can smell that tuna sandwich in your knapsack. Fork it over."

Brendan lurched to his feet. "This can't be happening," he choked.

An old woman who was walking along the path stopped short at Brendan's outburst. "Are you all right?" she asked.

Brendan stared at her, then back at the little man, still standing amid the pack of rodents. Wild-eyed, he looked back at the old woman. "Don't you see him?"

"See who?" She looked down at the little coven of squirrels. "The squirrels?"

Brendan whipped his head around to glare at the little man, who smiled sardonically up at him.

"The little man! Right there! He's *right there!*" Brendan's voice rose toward hysteria. The old woman suddenly decided that she had better places to be. She backed up a few steps and then turned to hurry back the way she had come.

"Are you gonna give us something or what?" the tiny voice demanded.

Brendan shook his head, moving away from the pack of squirrels. "You can't be real. You can't be *real!*" He tripped over the corner of the bench and fell backward, dropping his knapsack.

"C'mon, lads!" the tiny man cried. The squirrels swarmed forward, their little paws scrabbling at the flaps of the pack, worming their way inside.

"Hey, that's mine!"

The tiny man leapt easily onto the bench. He moved like the squirrels, in quick darting leaps. "Back off, biggun! It's ours now!"

Brendan made a grab for his bag but a sudden pain stung his ear. "Ow!"

The tiny man was reloading his slingshot, grinning. His mouth was filled with sharp rows of teeth. "Go ahead, punk! Try that again! Lord Chitter will sting you again!"

That was the final straw. Brendan screamed and turned tail. He ran as fast as his legs could carry him. He ran as if the hounds of hell were on his heels. He ran …

Straight into a tree.

He saw stars … with angry squirrels dancing among them … then blackness.

A STORM IS COMING

When he woke, someone was standing over him. His eyes watered and his head ached. Blinking to clear his vision, he first saw Kim's scooter, then her frowning face, her head tilted to the side. She looked to be torn between wry amusement and concern.

"Rise and shine!"

"Huh?" Brendan sat up and immediately regretted it. His head pounded. He probed his scalp and found a large goose egg on the side of his skull. He hadn't broken the skin but it certainly hurt. *Okay. That's three in three days. I have a streak going.* "I was being chased. I ran into a tree."

"Chased by who?" Her eyes narrowed. "Chester and his pals?" She whipped her head around, searching for a threat.

Brendan opened his mouth to answer and promptly snapped it shut again. What was he going to tell her? He was attacked by squirrels? That he'd seen a little man in a fur coat with a slingshot? That the wind was talking to him? He shook his head, wincing again at the pain.

He'd been desperate to question her about Greenleaf but now he felt a little too ridiculous to begin an interrogation. He brushed the dry leaves from his clothes instead and mumbled "Never mind." Then, with alarm, he gasped, "My bag ..." He suddenly realized he'd left it at the bench.

Kim held it out to him. "I found it on the path. It looks like an animal got into it."

He took it from her and examined it. The straps were gnawed through and his sandwich was missing, but otherwise, everything was accounted for. He opened his mouth to thank her but he almost choked before he could say a word. Something fell out of his mouth. Looking down on the grass, he saw his braces glinting in the weak sunlight.

"Oh no," Brendan groaned. "My parents are gonna kill me." He stuck a finger in his mouth and ran it over his teeth, checking to see if they were all accounted for. They felt strange: smooth and even. He had always been self-conscious about his crooked teeth but they didn't feel crooked any more. He wished he had a mirror. He grabbed the braces and stuffed them into his pocket.

"That's a shame," Kim said, offering a hand to help him to his feet. He accepted it and rose to his feet.

"Thanks," Brendan mumbled.

"Don't mention it." Kim raised an eyebrow. "Hmmm." She studied Brendan, casting her gaze from his head to his feet and back again.

"What hmmm?" Brendan demanded. "Hmmm what?"

"Nothing," she said softly. "Just thinking. You look … different. Has anything weird happened today?"

He wanted to shout, *Yes, I'm totally losing my mind! I was mugged by rodents! And a tiny guy was dressed like a squirrel!* Instead he said, "No. Nothing really. I'm fine."

She eyed him a little longer and then snapped her fingers. "I know what it is! Your glasses! You aren't wearing them."

Brendan's hand automatically went up to his face. She was right. They were gone. He must have lost them while being chased through the park. "Oh, crap. That's all I need." He looked around and saw nothing but leaves and grass. "I must have dropped them somewhere ..." He stopped short. *How can I see the leaves and the grass? I can see everything perfectly without my glasses!* As he continued to look around, he marvelled at the clarity of his vision. He'd always worn glasses. He couldn't get contacts because he had astigmatism.[44] The glasses were practically a part of his body. Now he was seeing with remarkable clarity, better than he'd ever had even wearing glasses. He looked across the park and read the lettering on the side of a van moving along the street. DAN'S PLUMBING: LET ME TAKE A LOOK UP YOUR PIPES! He laughed aloud.

"You seem pretty happy for a guy who's lost his glasses and run into a tree," Kim said, arms crossed.

Brendan realized he had a goofy expression on his face. He tried to settle down. "I dunno. Maybe I'm delirious."

She looked at him critically. She changed the subject. "You were acting really strange last night."

Brendan shrugged. *Wait a minute*, he thought. *Isn't this convenient? She just happens to be here every time something weird goes down.* Aloud he said, "Yeah, I'm fine. Lucky you just happened to be there, huh. And you just happened to find me here. I guess I'm just lucky, huh?"

"Yeah, you're lucky. You're lucky I hang around you at all, dude." She softened the words with a laugh. "Hop on." Kim jerked a thumb over her shoulder. "We better motor

---

[44] *Astigmatism* is a visual defect caused by the unequal curving of the refractive surfaces of the eye—usually the cornea, or lens of the eye. Astigmatism therefore makes wearing contact lenses impossible. Astigmatism is also difficult to spell. I like saying astigmatism. Astigmatism. Astigmatism. Astigmatism. Okay, I'm done ... astigmatism.

if we want to be on time. Let's find your goggles and get outta here."

"Never mind," Brendan said. When he saw her puzzled expression, he quickly said, "I've got a spare set at home and we're late already." He moved to the scooter before she could protest and swung his leg over it. He wrapped his arms around Kim's waist. She throttled the scooter up and they sped away.

Brendan clung on for dear life as Kim swerved through the trees, the grip of the tires precarious on the dew-slicked grass. He tried to concentrate on the newfound acuity of his sight rather than her breakneck driving. He thrilled at the detail in the trees and leaves, the intricate patterns in the clouds. When they came to the road, Kim didn't slow down, timing their arrival at the intersection perfectly with the changing of the lights. She shot through a crosswalk, weaving deftly among pedestrians and cyclists and skidding to a stop at the front steps of the school.

Brendan dismounted, his knees wobbling. "Thanks for not doing any wheelies."

"No problem," Kim said with a wink. "Next time!"

"Ooooo! Look at Brendan and his girlfriend." The mocking voice of Chester Dallaire assaulted Brendan's ears. "Or is it boyfriend? I can't tell! She's more like a guy than a girl!"

Chester sat on the steps with a pair of his cronies, Dean Spitz and Abdul Khun. They all shared an appreciation for the finer things in life: bullying, vandalism, and body odour.

"Like you'd know a real girl if she bit you on the butt, Chester." Kim dismounted and rolled the scooter to the bike rack.

"Nice helmet, chrome dome." Another round of guffaws. This was truly choice bully comedy.

"It takes so little to delight a tiny mind. C'mon, Brendan." She walked straight up the steps past Brendan.

"Hey." He pointed at the scooter. "Aren't you gonna lock it?"

"I say it again: who would dare steal from me?" She glared pointedly at the three boys in front of her. They reluctantly slid out of her way and she climbed the steps. Brendan went after her. He reached the top step when he felt his foot catch on something. He sprawled on his hands and knees in front of the open doors of the school.

The laughter of Chester and his buddies swelled. Brendan angrily pushed himself to his feet and picked up his bag. He smouldered with anger. Chester did things like this to him every day. Today, he wasn't in the mood. He'd really had enough of falling down and tripping and running into things. He turned around to glare at Chester. When Chester looked into Brendan's face, the laughter died on his lips. Brendan felt as if Chester could see a darkness in his eyes, as if he didn't look helpless or scared. He was furious and Chester was uneasy.

"Brendan," Kim said, pulling at her friend's arm. "Don't bother with them."

Brendan jerked free of her grasp. He stared Chester down. "That's the last time I let you get away with anything, Chester." He pointed at the bigger boy and spoke in a voice that he scarcely recognized himself. "Get lost!"

The instant the words were out of Brendan's mouth, it was as though a cloud had passed before the sun. Chester's face went slack and his eyes became blank. His voice was totally flat as he said, "Right away." He then turned and set off at a dead run. Abdul and Dean stared after him as he sped across the parking lot, turned up Avenue Road, and disappeared behind the Museum of Ceramic Arts. Abdul and Dean looked at Brendan, their faces filled with confusion and dread. Robbed of their leader, they shuffled up the stairs, keeping well away from Brendan as they hurried into the school.

Brendan was oblivious to their reaction. He shivered. He felt as though he'd just run a marathon. He reached out to grab Kim's shoulder, slumping against her. "Wha …? What just happened?" Brendan felt a wave of exhaustion wash over him. He gripped Kim's arm to stop himself from falling. "Whoa."

"Just take a deep breath, Brendan. You'll be okay."

In a moment, Brendan was feeling better. He looked up to find Kim staring at him. "I can't believe it," she breathed.

"What can't you believe?" Brendan asked.

"Do you know what you just did?" she hissed. "Do you have any idea?"

"I didn't do anything," Brendan said, confused. "All I did was tell him to get lost."

"You really don't understand." Kim shook her head. "This is all happening too fast."

Brendan was tired of the cryptic comments. He pointed an accusing finger at her. "That's it. I've had it. I don't get you. The more I think about you, the more I think you have some weird agenda."

Kim didn't say a word. She scanned the front of the school to see if anyone was watching.

"We're going to have this out right now," Brendan continued. "Either you tell me what's going on or—"

"Or what?" She smirked at him.

Brendan couldn't think of a good threat. He changed his tack. "I heard you talking to Greenleaf."

Kim stiffened. "What are you talking about?"

"In the auditorium yesterday! I heard you talking about me."

"Eavesdropping isn't very polite," Kim said quietly.

"Tell me what you were talking about," Brendan demanded.

"I can't do that," Kim said.

The bell rang. Classes were starting. Neither of them moved. Class was forgotten.

"Well, maybe I should go and talk to Mr. Greenleaf." Brendan started up the steps.

Kim stepped in front of him, blocking his way. "Oh, no you don't!"

"Why not?" Brendan was secretly delighted that he'd hit a nerve. "What's he going to tell me?"

Kim was about to respond when she was cut off by the harsh voice of Ms. Abernathy.

"What's going on out here?" She stood in the open door of the school, glaring at the two truants. "The bell has rung. You are both late."

Brendan froze. He had never been on the receiving end of a tongue-lashing by Ms. Abernathy. He had only watched others be dressed down by her. He tried to speak but all that came out was a strangled squeak.

"I asked you a question!" Ms. Abernathy barked. "What is going on out here?"

Brendan tried to clear his throat and make an excuse but Kim cut him off. "We're having a private conversation."

Brendan had never seen such an expression of complete

shock on a human face before. Ms. Abernathy stared in disbelief. "No one speaks to me in that manner."

"Well, I just did," Kim said evenly. "Deal with it!"

Brendan thought the vice-principal was going to have a heart attack. Her face turned an interesting shade of puce. Her eyes bulged with outrage. "You … You … You …" the woman stammered.

"We'd like to finish our discussion so why don't you run along," Kim said. "Now!"

Ms. Abernathy quivered with rage. She reached out and grabbed Kim by the arm. "You are coming with me, young lady."

Kim looked slowly down at the offending hand and then back into Ms. Abernathy's eyes. "First of all, I am not young. Secondly, I am not a lady. Thirdly, take your hand off me if you ever plan on using it again."

Ms. Abernathy's mouth dropped open. She was about to speak but something in Kim's eyes made her snap her mouth shut with a click. She let go of Kim.

"Better," Kim said simply. A peal of thunder rolled across the sky. The three people on the steps looked up. The sky was clear. There was no imminent threat of rain, just a few white clouds drifting. The thunder rolled again.

"That's odd," Ms. Abernathy said softly.

"Uh-oh." Kim's voice was filled with dread. "This is gonna be bad."

Brendan didn't understand. He looked up into the sky again. Without any warning, a finger of lightning lashed downward from the empty sky, blasting into the middle of the sidewalk with a deafening bang. He was thrown from his feet, skidding along the steps and smacking into the metal railing. He tried to blink away purple spots from his eyes, the after-effect of the lightning strike. When he could see again, he found himself staring at the most beautiful and terrifying woman he had ever seen.

She was tall and graceful, her long legs sheathed in black, tight-fitting leather trousers. She wore a bodice,[45] brocaded with intricate lightning patterns. Her long, pale blond hair flowed over her shoulders in a wintry cascade. Her face ... oh her face!

"So beautiful ..." he breathed.

"Ah, nephew!" She smiled. Brendan's heart shuddered. The sensation was like being smiled at by a hurricane. "At last we meet. They tried to hide you but I've found you at last."

Kim had fallen on the steps beside Ms. Abernathy. She staggered to her feet. "He's not for you, Orcadia."

"Ki-Mata," the woman said, chuckling. "You're the best they could come up with? How sad."

Brendan, still dazed, was trying to figure out what was happening. "Who are you?"

The woman smiled her ferocious smile. "I am your aunt Orcadia, my dear child. I've come to take you away from these weaklings. Together we have work to do. Together we are destined to do great things." She took a step closer, and Brendan smelt ozone burning in the air around her. "Together we shall destroy the Humans and take our world back."

Brendan cringed away from her outstretched hand. She pouted prettily. "Don't be afraid. I don't bite."

---

45 A *bodice* is a close-fitting, often laced-up top worn over a blouse. Very few people wear bodices any more: vampires, people who want to look like vampires, and the odd evil Faerie.

"See here." Ms. Abernathy stepped into Orcadia's path. "You have no business being on the grounds of Robertson Davies Academy! You must leave at once."

Brendan couldn't believe his eyes. Ms. Abernathy was crotchety, mean, and annoying but he had to admit, she had guts. He felt he should warn the vice-principal that she was out of her depth but he was having enough trouble trying to stand up.

Orcadia looked at the vice-principal with a disdainful smile on her perfect face. "I'm not going to leave the grounds. But I'm afraid you are." She lazily pointed a finger at Ms. Abernathy, and a jagged string of blue energy lanced out from her pale fingertip to engulf the hapless VP. Then, with a negligent flick of the wrist, Orcadia sent Ms. Abernathy cart-wheeling through the air to disappear over the edge of the roof.

Satisfied, Orcadia turned her attention to Brendan and Kim on the steps. "That was fun but I'm losing my patience. Brendan, come along."

PURSUIT

Brendan looked into Orcadia's face. Her eyes were icy blue. In fact, her skin had a tinge of azure underlying its pale chalk surface.

"I'm waiting," Orcadia snapped.

"Orcadia, give it up," Kim said. "*You* have no place here. Your actions threaten us all."

"Shut up, you little fool," Orcadia hissed. "You have no place here. He's my nephew, son of my brother Briach Morn. Do not presume to tell me what to do, dung beetle!"

"Hey!" Brendan had suddenly found his tongue. "You tossed the vice-principal onto the roof!"

"Yes, I did." Orcadia smiled. "Wasn't it hilarious?"

"Hilarious?" Brendan was incredulous. "She might be dead!"

"Why should I care? Humans are like cockroaches, Breandan, they breed and breed. When you step on one, a hundred spring up to take its place," Orcadia said. "Now, come with me. You needn't live in this filthy world of Humans any more. There is a whole new world for you to explore." She smiled again and held out an elegant hand to him.

In spite of his horror, Brendan found himself compelled to take that hand. There was something mesmerizing about her voice, something intoxicating about her beauty.

Still, something in his mind was repulsed by her.

"Cockroaches?" he said. "We aren't cockroaches. Who do you think you are?" he managed to croak. "I don't want to come with you. Why don't you leave us alone?" He stepped away from her, taking his place beside Kim.

The woman laughed, a sound like the peal of bells in a dark cathedral. The sound pounded against Brendan's skull, threatening to upset his precarious balance. He steeled himself not to act on the urge to fall to his knees. "It's not polite to laugh at people," he said, annoyed.

"Oh my." The woman grinned, a fierce expression that held no mirth. Her teeth were a deep, startling blue. "That is so sweet! He thinks he has the right to comment on my manners. I, who was old with power at the quickening of the world, who was old when the People of Metal first cringed in their caves at the sound of the thunder. How dare you question my manners, whelp?"[46]

"Whelp?" Brendan said angrily. "I don't even know what a whelp is but it doesn't sound good to me. If you're going to insult me, use words I can understand."

The woman narrowed her eyes. "Ignorant little child! You dare to question me?" she thundered. She gnashed her teeth and bright blue sparks flared between them. She seemed to expand, to tower above Brendan. Her pale face twisted with rage. Even as his heart shrivelled in fear, Brendan felt a yearning. She was cold and beautiful like the glaciers he'd seen in Alaska on a cruise with his

---

[46] A *whelp* is a newborn puppy. The insinuation of the insult is that it's somehow bad to be a newborn puppy. I don't know about you but I like newborn puppies. Except for when they pee on the carpet, but even then, they're kind of cute.

parents. She was poised above him, ready to crush him, grind him underfoot. He raised his eyes to the chips of flaring ice that were hers and waited to be destroyed.

"Enough, Orcadia." Kim's voice shattered the moment. "He doesn't want to join you."

The woman's head snapped up, releasing Brendan from the spell of surrender. He shivered and stepped back, tripping on the bottom step and falling hard on his bum.

Kim stepped out in front of Brendan and faced the woman. "Orcadia, the truce stands. He is not for you to take or destroy."

"Fool," Orcadia spat. "Step aside or perish."

Kim looked so small in the face of the dark woman's fury. In her RDA school uniform, short school kilt, grey cardigan, and knee socks, she was hardly a match for the force of nature seething on the pavement of the parking lot. On her back, Kim carried her green nylon knapsack with her trusty field hockey stick poking out of the top.

"You know the Law," Kim said in a chiding tone as if Orcadia were an unruly child. "He cannot be touched."

"Indeed, I know the Law. I don't respect the Law but I know it: he may not be interfered with so long as he bears the Ward. The Ward is gone."

Kim stiffened. "What?"

"It is gone. Removed by a Weaver.[47] See for yourself."

---

[47] There are several different types of Faerie Disciplines, what we might call Magic. The Disciplines allow Faeries to manipulate the Energy of the Earth to affect matter, mind, and even time. Weaving is one of these disciplines. A Weaver is a Faerie who has the power to manipulate magical energy. They can do this in any number of ways, depending on the craft they prefer. Some use music. Some use visual arts such as painting or carving. Some

Kim whirled and stared at Brendan. "Is it true?"

Brendan gaped. "Is what true? I don't know what anybody's talking about!"

Kim's hand lashed out and tore open the front of Brendan's school shirt. Buttons flew everywhere. She was impossibly strong for such a slender girl.

"Hey," Brendan protested. "That was a new shirt!"

"Shut up, idiot!" Kim snapped.

"Don't you call me an idiot! Idiot! Whelp! What's with you people?" Brendan began but he stopped when he saw the stricken expression on Kim's face. She stared at the spot where Brendan's scar had been until just the night before. Now there was only a reddened patch of skin. The irritation was already fading.

"Where's the Mark?" Kim demanded.

"I had a dream last night," Brendan explained. "Deirdre D'Anaan came and her little … flying thingy ripped my scar away!"

"That interfering …"

Orcadia laughed. "He is ready to be initiated. I will do the honours."

"I'm not going anywhere with you, nutcase!" Brendan shouted.

"Why didn't you tell me?" Kim snarled at Brendan.

"Tell you what?" Brendan snapped back. "That my scar's gone? Why would I tell you about it? I have athlete's foot! Should I alert the media?"

---

quite simply weave, but that's a little bit obvious. They are vital to the continued existence of the Faerie People, as they allow the Fair Folk to live in hiding alongside human beings.

Kim rolled her eyes in disgust and whipped around to face Orcadia, taking a defensive stance. Brendan couldn't believe it. She was actually going to fight this woman? "Are you nuts? Let's run!"

"I am your protector. Get behind me," Kim said, shoving him back.

"Protector? You can't take on that woman!" Brendan couldn't believe what he was seeing. This kind of stuff happened in the movies or in comic books. Orcadia looked like a total badass and Kim, grade nine student at Robertson Davies Academy, was acting like she was going to throw down with this total nightmare. "I'll say it again. Let's run!"

"His instincts are good, Ki-Mata," Orcadia sneered. "You can't hope to resist me."

"Ki-Mata? Kim, what is she talking about?"

"Zip it, Brendan," Kim snapped impatiently at him. Then she snarled at the smirking stranger. "You will not take him. He is under my protection. And we are in the open, where the People of Metal will see."

The cold laughter froze the air again. "What care I for the Humans? Vermin! The bird doesn't ask the worm's permission before devouring it! When we take back the world, they will know of us soon enough. They will have no choice! Ki-Mata? You honestly think you can stop me from taking him? Oh, that is rich." Orcadia raised her arms slowly from her sides until they were spread like wings. As she did so, her body levitated off the pavement until she hovered a metre off the ground on a cloud of crackling energy. "Your house will keen[48] for you, Ki-Mata

---

48 *Keen* means weep or mourn. It is an old Irish word. Not that the

Na Graål. Alas, they will have no body over which to perform the rites." Lightning crackled in icy blue filaments surrounding Orcadia's form, outlining her in a nimbus of shuddering violet. She looked like a crane,[49] black as midnight, ready to spear a fish with its sharp beak.

"Don't, Orcadia," Kim demanded. "Not here. The Law forbids it." As she spoke, Kim reached over her shoulder and pulled her field hockey stick out of her pack. It was nicked and scratched, the tape fraying on the handle, and Brendan doubted it would be very effective against the woman levitating in front of them.

"A field hockey stick? Are you kidding?" Brendan cried. "Do you have something a little nastier in there? I'm thinking a machine gun …" He stole another look at Orcadia. "Or maybe a rocket launcher?"

Kim sneered at him, "Just stay out of my way!" She pushed him behind her.

This isn't happening! It can't be! I'm gonna wake up and realize all of this was a dream. Any time now! Like right now! Or maybe now?

"Laws are made for weaklings," Orcadia hissed. "I am my own Law!"

"No," Kim said, flexing her shoulders. "The Laws are there for our protection as well as the Humans'. We can't survive without them."

"Laws were made to be broken, so …" Orcadia shrugged. With a final peal of exultant laughter from her, the air itself ignited.

---

word is used by old Irish people. It's a word from olden times. That were Irish. You know what I mean.

[49] The bird, not the construction vehicle.

Or so it appeared to Brendan. A wave of blue fire flared out from her. She was like a star going supernova. In the instant before Brendan buried his face in his hands, he saw Kim whack her field hockey stick against the concrete paving stones. He waited for the end.

It didn't come. He crouched, his arms over his head, waiting to be incinerated, but nothing happened. Instead, his nostrils were filled with the sharp smell of burning wood, like the fires his father made when they went camping. Because his father always managed to find the dampest wood available, his fires were more smoke than flame. Now there was heat, uncomfortable heat, but he wasn't being burned alive.

He tentatively lowered his arms and stole a look. His mouth dropped open in amazement. Kim stood in the path of the blue flame, her field hockey stick firmly planted on the concrete. She was humming softly, a haunting, lilting sound that seemed to fill the air around them. Brendan couldn't believe his eyes. Radiating from the hockey stick, a thick, thorny hedge sprouted in a protective shield. The branches of the hedge were large and black, glistening with sap. Wherever the white fire touched the foliage of the hedge, the sap bubbled and spat, turning to gas and dissipating the heat. Brendan followed the thorny brambles and discovered that the hedge sprouted from a single tiny crack in the pavement where a shoot of green vegetation had managed to force its way out into the light. Kim seemed to be coaxing the wall of thorns from this single small sprout.[50]

---

[50] This action is a good example of Faerie "Magic." Faerie Magic is sympathetic: it can only manipulate an already existing situation. What I mean is this: Kim couldn't make a barrier of thorns grow

The heat from the fire was intense. Brendan could feel his hair curling and crisping. The hedge wrapped around them in a cocoon of branches. If he hadn't been in danger of being incinerated, Brendan would have felt more awe than terror.[51]

"What is going on?" he cried. "How are you doing that?" He grabbed Kim's arm.

The contact startled Kim, her singing faltered, and the hedge contracted. The heat washed closer and their clothing smoked.

"Don't touch me! I have to concentrate," Kim shouted at him. Brendan dropped his hand. She picked up the tune again and the melody steadied. The hedge inched outward again and the heat lessened. Sweat beaded on Kim's brow.

Brendan peered through the branches and saw Orcadia. Her face was twisted with rage. She raised her arms higher. The heat intensified. Kim groaned and the hedge contracted. Brendan studied Kim as she struggled to keep her composure. She clutched the field hockey stick closer, her knuckles whitening on the wood. Her shoulders trembled. Sweat ran down her face and plastered her hair to her forehead. Obviously, the strain on her was tremendous. Brendan had no idea what she was doing or how she was doing it, but he doubted she would be able to do it for much longer.

He had to help her. But how? Who were these people? How could they do these amazing things? They seemed to know him. He'd believed Kim was just an ordinary

---

on the moon because no plants would be available for her to manipulate. And she would suffocate because there is no air on the moon, but that's beside the point.

[51] Sadly, his life was in danger of being snuffed out so he was practically wetting his pants.

teenage girl, a high school kid like him, and now she was making trees grow out of nowhere and fighting weird women who could float in the air and shoot lightning from their bodies. What could he hope to do? And why was nobody calling the police?

Beside him, Kim gasped and the hedge contracted.

You've gotta do something, Brendan. He looked around him. The parking lot was behind the school, hidden from the busy street. No one was in sight. Kim gasped again. He felt desperation grip him. *There has to be something I can do!*

In an answer to his mental cry, a switch flipped in his mind. His vision sharpened as if someone had placed a set of goggles over his eyes that allowed him to really focus clearly. He saw each blade of grass, each leaf. He saw the texture of the flame coursing from Orcadia and realized that she was channelling the stray electrical energy from the atmosphere around her, her body like a conduit for the free electrons that might normally form bolts of lightning during a storm. He cast his vision further. He saw how fiercely Orcadia was concentrating to maintain her assault.

That's it, Brendan realized. *Break her concentration. Then we might escape. But how?*

In a large oak tree just across the parking lot, he saw a flock of sparrows, crouching in the boughs, taking shelter from the storm they sensed was coming. Their tiny minds appeared to Brendan like glowing motes. It was almost as if he could sense their thoughts.

Fear. Fear. Hide. Shelter, they tittered.

Their tiny minds were so simple. Brendan recalled the squirrels he'd encountered earlier in the day. They were motivated by their quest for food. *Maybe I could make a suggestion to these birds, something along the same lines.*

Beside him, Kim staggered, falling to one knee. He didn't have much time. Orcadia's joy was palpable as she felt the end was near. He had to concentrate. He focused on the birds and sent them a single thought. *Food! Food! Food!*

He sensed their interest. *Food?*

He also sensed their fear. *Storm?*

Food! He concentrated harder. He tried to send them reassurance. The heat was growing and it added urgency to his message. *Food! Lots of food!*

Yes! Their tiny minds were excited now! *Where food?*

There! There! He sent them a powerful image of Orcadia's billowing, ash-blond hair. The birds exploded from the tree, rising from the branches en masse. With a single purpose, they made a beeline for Orcadia's head.

For her part, Orcadia was concentrating too hard to notice the birds until they struck.

"Aaaargh!" she cried. The white fire faltered and went out. She tried to bat the birds away as they pecked at her scalp, but the thought of food drove the sparrows to greater efforts.

Delighted, Brendan turned to Kim. Calling the birds had made him light-headed with fatigue but he saw that Kim was in worse shape. Her face was pale and haggard. She leaned on the field hockey stick. The hedge withered, its many branches turning to fine grey dust as Brendan watched in stupefied wonder. The wind swirled the dust away, leaving only the tiny shoot of green sprouting in the pavement, unscathed.

"Holy! That was totally sick. How did you do that?" When Brendan turned to Kim with this question, she was staring at him in a similar state of amazement.

"How did *you* do *that*?" she demanded.

"Uh, I don't know," Brendan answered, suddenly self-conscious. "I just kinda talked them into it."[52]

"You talked to the birds?" Kim was incredulous. "But you've had no training, no initiation."

"He is gifted, indeed." Mr. Greenleaf's voice interrupted Kim. He strode down the school steps, neat as a pin in a green suit and yellow vest. The hummingbird perched on his shoulder, its tiny eyes full of impossible intelligence. As Brendan watched, the bird shimmered and changed into a small woman with swiftly beating wings. Her clothing was woven of iridescent feathers of green and blue. She caught Brendan's eye and winked.

Brendan just stared. "There's a little person on your shoulder!"

Greenleaf laughed. "This is my companion, Titiana. You may call her Titi." The tiny creature waved. Brendan was struck dumb with amazement.

"Can we concentrate, here," Kim demanded. "This is a disaster. We have to get out of here."

"We always knew he'd be special." Greenleaf smiled at Brendan. "But, indeed, there's no time for discussion now. You have to get him to safety. She's occupied for now but those birds won't distract her for long."

"Nice of you to show up after the fight." Kim stabbed an accusatory finger at the teacher. "This is your fault.

---

[52] Speaking with animals is a Discipline unto itself. And I don't mean just talking to animals. I do that all the time. I have a guinea pig named Mr. Pants who listens while I read the newspaper to him every morning. Faeries are capable of speaking to animals and listening to their responses. There's a big difference. The Faerie Gift is amazing while what I do is merely a bit pathetic and lonely.

First you show up here and stick your nose in and then your sister breaks the Ward."

"Deirdre overstepped her bounds. I just wanted to find him but she is overeager. It doesn't matter now. What's done is done." Greenleaf shrugged.

"Easy for you to say," Kim snapped.

"What are you talking about?" Brendan demanded, shaking off his stupor. "Wards and Laws and all that. Somehow, you people know more about me than I do."

"I'll kill you all," Orcadia shrieked, cutting in on their conversation. She tore at her hair, trying to drive away the birds.

"You must go! Take him to the Swan. He'll be safe there." Greenleaf's eyes narrowed. "I'll attempt to distract her for a time. Hopefully, I can delay her long enough for you to get away." Mr. Greenleaf raised his hands and closed his eyes. Instantly, the wind began to quicken into a stiff breeze. In seconds the breeze became a stiff wind then a gale, whirling around Greenleaf as he stood in the centre of a funnel of dust and leaves and stray bits of paper. "*Go!*" he shouted over the roar of the wind.

Kim didn't wait another instant. "C'mon." She grabbed Brendan by the shirt and pulled him to her scooter. She jammed her field hockey stick into a saddlebag and jumped on. She drove her foot down, gunning the motor. "Get on," she demanded.

"Why should I do anything you say?" Brendan shouted. "I don't know what's going on. Who are you people?"

"Certainly, who we are is important," Kim said urgently. "But what's more important is who you are. You are a Faerie. You're one of us."

"Fairy?" Brendan was confused. "What do you mean, I'm a fairy?"

"A Faerie! One of the Fair Folk," Kim said, exasperated.

"But …" Brendan began.

Orcadia chose that moment to ignite. Brendan felt the birds' minds wink out as they were incinerated. They dropped to the ground, lifeless and smoking in a ring around Orcadia's feet. Brendan felt a sharp stab of shame. They were just innocent birds. He'd lied to them and now their deaths were his fault.

"Now, you will all die!" Orcadia shouted.

Greenleaf suddenly threw his arms toward Orcadia. The funnel cloud carved across the pavement and enveloped her. She shrieked, but her voice was muffled by the wind. The cloud lit up from within with flashes of lightning as she struggled to escape. The funnel cloud lifted off the ground and rocketed skyward.

"No time to explain. If you don't want to be a dead Faerie, you'd better move your ass right now," Kim threatened.

Brendan had no choice. He jumped onto the scooter behind Kim and wrapped his arms around her waist as she sped away.

OVER AND UNDER

Despite his tight grip around Kim's waist, Brendan almost fell backward over the end of the scooter as it shot forward. He stifled a shout as Kim wove through the parked cars at a speed certain to break both their necks. Without slowing, she swerved around the end of the building, vaulting onto the lawn, and zoomed straight for Queen's Park Crescent with its steady hum of cars. Brendan watched in horror as she gunned the motor and headed for the thickest traffic.

"Are you out of your mind? Slow down!" Brendan shouted in her ear. "You're gonna kill us."

"Holy Mother of the Moon!" Kim spat. "Would you just relax and try not to get your skirt caught in the wheel, Granny?"

Brendan was about to shout a retort but terror stole the words away. They shot into traffic without slowing in the slightest, Kim sailing into a gap between a limousine and a gigantic SUV. Car horns honked. Tires squealed. Brendan buried his face in Kim's shoulder waiting for the inevitable collision. He clenched his entire body around Kim as if she were a rock in a tossing ocean.

"Loosen up, will ya," Kim grunted. "You're gonna break me in two." Brendan didn't let go of his grip. He waited for the screech of tires that would announce their painful demise, but it didn't come.

Seconds passed. He was still alive. He mustered his courage and peeked over Kim's shoulder.

They were heading south in the long turn around the provincial Parliament, accelerating smoothly. Brendan couldn't believe how fast they were going. He noticed something else. Usually, Kim's scooter had the high-pitched whine shared by all vehicles with small engines, but as they zipped along, Brendan realized he wasn't hearing that sound. Instead, emanating from the engine was a low, harmonic hum that shifted through a spectrum of sound depending on their speed. It almost sounded like a choir of tiny voices. He looked down and saw that where he had assumed the scooter was built of metal and plastic, it was actually an amalgam of different woods, skilfully carved with strange symbols up and down its chassis. The saddle was beautifully tooled leather, the pattern a series of swirling lines chasing each other across the surface. The scooter's lines were sleek and perfectly harmonious. It was more like an animal than a machine.

"I thought this was a gas scooter," Brendan shouted over the wind. "What does it run on?"

"Trapped zephyrs,"[53] Kim called back.

***

[53] A *zephyr* is a lesser spirit of the air. There are many types of spirits, all with different powers and properties based on their home elements. Water Spirits, Fire Spirits, Wood Spirits, and more are embedded in objects by Artificers to create magical tools. What's an Artificer? If you don't mind, I'm getting tired of this footnote. I'll get back to you later when you absolutely need to know.

"Trapped what? *Yaaaaaaah!*" Brendan screamed as they approached an intersection, weaving through the cars stopped at the red light.

Kim ignored Brendan's cries of panic. She gunned the motor as she timed their approach to the intersection of College and University perfectly, the light winking green as she sailed through. They flashed down the wide boulevard, weaving through the cars.

Brendan opened his eyes, surprised that he wasn't dead. The wind ruffled his hair. He relaxed his grip ever so slightly. "Where are we going?" Brendan asked. He was not entirely over his initial fear but was starting to enjoy the ride. A little. The speed of their passage and the beautiful hum of the engine's song were exhilarating.

"Someplace safe," Kim said dismissively.

"Why don't we go to my house." His father might be at home. Maybe they could get him to help, call the police.

"No way."

"Why not?"

"Orcadia knows where you live. She's already been sniffing around there. If you go back there, you'll put your family in danger."

Brendan hadn't thought of that. Orcadia had been the mysterious relative his mother had talked to last night. He shivered at the thought. His mother had no idea what danger she'd been in. He decided, whatever happened, he'd try to keep these weirdos as far away from his family as possible. "Then where *are* we going? To the police?"

"The police? Ha! They can't help us." Kim shook her head. "No, we're going to a place I know. It's a safe place, neutral ground, a meeting place called the Swan of Liir."

"Never heard of it."

"You wouldn't have. It's for Fair Folk only."

"What if we get separated? How will I find it?"

"If we get separated, you'll never find it. No one can find it on their own. You have to be shown the way."

"But if something happens to you …"

"Nothing's going to happen to me."

"But what if it does?" Brendan insisted.

"Will you quit whining? If anything happened to me, well then, you'll probably die," Kim snarled. Brendan's mouth snapped shut. "But nothing is going to happen to me, so shut up and let me drive. I have to concentrate, and I can't do that with you whining in my ear."

The sudden wail of a siren cut off their conversation. Brendan looked back over his shoulder and saw a police cruiser pull out from a side street. The red and blue lights on the roof of the car were flashing and the siren screamed. There were two officers in the car, one female constable driving and the other, a man, speaking into his radio. They didn't look happy.

"We should pull over," Brendan suggested. He had never been in trouble with the police and he didn't want to start now.

Kim laughed. "Not today." She glanced up at the swath of sky visible between the tall buildings. Brendan looked up and saw purple clouds spreading south, almost as if they were following the scooter's progress. "Uh-oh. Looks like Greenleaf couldn't hold her. We have to get to safe ground. She's coming for us."

"Why does she want me? Is she really my aunt? Where's my father? My mother?"

"Do you ever stop asking questions? Just shut up.

Everything will be explained to you when we get to the Swan," she barked. "Try to relax!"

"Relax? I'm attacked by some crazy woman. I can talk to squirrels and birds! People are trying to kill me! You've basically kidnapped me and I'm supposed to *relax!*" Brendan's voice cracked. He was about to lose it.

"Like I said," Kim repeated, "everything will be explained when we get to the Swan. If we don't get to the Swan, it won't matter."

"Is it far?"

Kim looked up at the darkening sky. "Far enough. Just zip it and hold on! I've gotta shake the fuzz."

Kim continued her swerving route down University Avenue. The scooter slalomed from lane to lane, barely missing vehicles on either side. The police were hampered by the traffic but the siren was clearing the way as motorists pulled over to allow the cruiser through. The police were slowly gaining ground.

"Pull over to the curb immediately!" A policeman's voice was amplified through the public address speaker on top of the cruiser.

"Maybe we should stop now!" Brendan said hopefully.

"Do you always do whatever you're told?" Kim laughed.

"When it's the police telling me, yes!"

Brendan felt sure that Kim would slow now. Up ahead, the light at Queen Street turned red. Cars streamed across their path in a thick flow. They would certainly be killed if they tried to cut across. The scooter did slow slightly as Kim scanned for a way through.

In front of them, a fist of lightning slammed into a Mercedes convertible that was just few metres ahead. The car sizzled as the rainwater turned to steam and its paint crackled. The stricken vehicle swerved, smashing sideways into a van. The crunch of metal and the smell of scorched rubber stung Brendan's nostrils.

"She's here!" Kim shouted. "Time for an alternative route."

She angled the scooter to the right, aiming it at the sidewalk. They bumped over the curb, Brendan almost being jarred loose, and fishtailed through a group of pedestrians, narrowly avoiding a collision with a sausage vendor's cart. People shouted in anger and shook their fists.

"Sorry!" Brendan called.

The police cruiser screeched to a halt at the curb. A female officer leapt out and began to run after them while the other went to investigate the accident caused by the lightning strike.

"Halt!" the female cop shouted.

Kim ignored the command. Swerving across the sidewalk, she jumped the curb again, shooting across the intersection diagonally.

"Oh sweet Christmas!" Brendan shrieked.

"Yee-haw!" Kim crowed.

They had almost made it to the other side of the intersection when a transport truck turned in front of them. The broad side of the van loomed, a mass of wheels with a flatbed laden with coiled wire for some construction site.

"Hang on!" Kim cried as if there was an alternative.

The scooter tilted. She turned side on to the truck, and they slid along the pavement, the dark, greasy underside of the truck bed passing above them. At that instant, lightning struck the coiled wire on the bed of the truck. The impact was followed by a shower of sparks that curtained over them as they slid out the other side of the truck. The shock wave that followed deafened Brendan for a moment, but amazingly the two of them were still on the scooter.

Kim thrust her leg against the pavement and threw them upright again. She gunned the motor, and the scooter zoomed along the curb down Queen Street. They had left behind them a wake of swerving cars. The traffic was snarled in the intersection.

"We've gotta get out of the open," Kim shouted. "We're too exposed."

Brendan was completely incapable of speaking. His throat was frozen and his eyes wide with shock. He'd always thought that chases in the movies were so cool and that he'd like to be in one. Now he was in one, and he wanted it to stop. To add to his horror, Kim pulled an object from her blazer pocket and stabbed at it with her thumb.

"You're going to make a phone call?" Brendan squealed. "Now?"

"Keep your panties on," Kim said.

"May I point out we're involved in a police chase on an unstable, two-wheeled vehicle ..." He trailed off when he caught sight of the cellphone.

Instead of being made of plastic like the cells he was familiar with, it was a small featureless palm-sized block of wood. When Kim pressed the centre of the wood with her thumb, the wood began to glow with patterns of light that settled into the shape of a keyboard. A crack appeared along the edge of the block, and it flipped open to reveal a tiny glowing screen.

"A wooden cellphone?"

"Cool, huh," Kim said. "It's a Faerie thing. We like organic stuff. Metal and plastic don't mix well with us. The Artificers finally figured out how to copy the Human technology."

"Artificers?" Brendan asked.

"Shhh!" She pressed the phone against her ear and guided the scooter up onto the sidewalk. Pedestrians dove for their lives.

"Yeah." Kim was speaking into the phone. "We're on our way. We've got some cops on our tail. I think we've lost them but we'll need some damage control.[54] I'm going underground so I'll be out of touch …"

She tapped the block of wood with her thumb and it returned to its original state: a wooden block. She tucked it into her pocket and leaned over the handlebars of the scooter. Rain continued to fall in hard, cold droplets, stinging Brendan's exposed face and numbing his hands.

"Hold on," Kim shouted. She twisted the throttle grip with her right hand and they sped up. In the distance, sirens wailed. The cops at University Avenue had obviously called in about their little jaunt.

---

[54] Usually, Faeries are able to hide their existence very effectively from the Human populations they are hiding in. Of course, sometimes situations occur in which they have to cover up obvious breaches in secrecy (like riding a scooter through town while being pelted by balls of lightning). When these problems arise, Faeries rely on Fair Folk moles who are embedded in the media and in government positions to spread misinformation and doctor evidence to cover up Faerie involvement. The Faeries' greatest defence is that Human beings would rather believe anything besides the idea that magical beings share the Earth with them.

A scream of terror rose behind them and then another. Brendan craned his neck to look back and saw that something was cutting a swath through the crowd of pedestrians on the sidewalk. A canine howl rose from many throats, chilling his blood. It seemed very close.

"What *is* that?"

"Orcadia's hired some help!"

Kim cut right and zoomed through an open door into the perfume section of a department store. A security guard shouted something incoherent. Kim shot along an aisle lined with glittering bottles, scattering white-coated sales clerks in a flurry of paper scent samples.

Brendan looked back and saw two canine shapes burst in the door after them. He didn't get a good look at them because Kim chose that moment to reach out an arm and sweep hundreds of bottles of perfume off a shelf. The bottles fell and shattered on the floor. Brendan was about to protest the wanton destruction of property when the scooter skidded in a sharp right turn and shot down the escalator to the lower level.

"Did you have to smash that stuff?" Brendan shouted, his teeth chattering with the impact of each step.

"Throws the hounds off the scent," Kim explained. "Buys us some time."

"Where are you taking us?"

"Underground," Kim said.

That much seemed obvious to Brendan as they hit the bottom of the escalator and swerved through kitchenware.

They sped down the wide aisle and past a coffee shop. The subway entrance loomed, but heavy glass doors barred their way. A homeless man, begging with a cup as he opened the door for shoppers, saw them coming and grinned.

"Ride it, Ki-Mata!" he shouted as he swung the door open.

"Thanks, Tik!" Kim guided the scooter through.

"You know that guy?" Brendan asked.

"One of us," Kim explained. "We're everywhere!"

"How many of you … us are there?"

Kim was about to answer but a security guard reached out to grab them as they sailed past.

"Halt!" he shouted.

"I guess he's not one of us," Brendan said sarcastically.

Kim ignored Brendan. She also ignored the security guard. She gunned the scooter and guided it straight for the entrance to the Queen Street subway station, a set of tiled stairs heading farther underground.

"Oh, no!" Brendan cried.

"What's the matter? The subway is an excellent alternative mode of transport. Very green!" Kim seemed very merry, given the circumstances.

"Aaaaaaaaaaaaaaaah!" Brendan screamed.

"Hahahahahahahahaa!" Kim laughed like a maniac.

They shot off the top step and plunged down the stairs. Both of them ducked instinctively, fortunately, or the lower ceiling of the entrance would have decapitated them. They landed hard on each step. Kim struggled to keep a grip on the handlebars as the tires thudded down the steps. Two businessmen in sensible suits and ties, on their way to the food courts, pressed against the walls on either side to avoid being mowed down.

Kim guided the scooter to the edge of the platform and launched it onto the tracks. Brendan screamed and buried his face in Kim's shoulder. Surely now they would die.

When he looked up again, they were speeding down a subway tunnel. He concentrated on holding tight to Kim. The last thing he wanted was to fall off in the dark and crack his head open or, worse, land on the third rail and be fried to a crisp.

Light bloomed ahead as they sped toward the next station.

"King Street subway, next stop!" Kim intoned in the flat tone of a Toronto Transit Commission driver. "Change here for King streetcar!" She laughed at her own imitation. Brendan tried not to be sick.

King Street, Brendan thought. *I never thought I'd see it from down here.* Men and women in business suits holding newspapers and briefcases looked down at them, slack-jawed, as they motored through the station. Something in Brendan relaxed. If he weren't going to be in so much trouble, he now thought, the ride would actually have been quite fun! A line of elementary school children, probably on a field trip, stood ranged along the platform at the far end. They waved and hooted at Kim and Brendan as they rocketed past like it was the coolest thing to see two kids riding a scooter through the subway. Brendan had never felt cool before. He had never been the centre of attention in a way that wasn't him making a total fool of himself. He let go of Kim with one arm and waved to the kids, who cheered.

Of course, he immediately fell off the scooter.

He bounced and rolled along for a few metres and ended up on his hands and knees in darkness. He groaned. Sitting back on his haunches, he took stock. His palms hurt. They were probably skinned and bleeding. He felt his legs and discovered he'd torn his grey trousers and his knee was bleeding freely. Apart from that, there was no serious damage. Nothing broken.

Farther up the tunnel, he heard Kim screech to a halt. The headlight of her scooter swung wildly in the darkness. He heard her shout in alarm.

Light filled the tunnel. The glaring illumination seared the darkness.

Brendan whirled to stare as the blunt silver wall of a subway train swelled to fill the tunnel. He froze in terror, his expression a mirror of the driver's in his tiny control cabin.

Faced with the oncoming train, Brendan looked to either side but there were only sheer blank walls of concrete.

"*Help!*" he screamed, not expecting any. In despair, he threw his arms over his face, waiting for the impact.

THAT'S THE WAY I TROLL

He was yanked off his feet. He wasn't expecting that. He was expecting to be smashed into bits from the front. The roar of the train filled his ears, but now it was below him.

He dared to open his eyes and immediately wished he hadn't. He was dangling above the train, his feet centimetres away from the silvery roof of the cars as they flashed past. He felt slightly ill.

Worse was yet to come. Hanging by the scruff of his neck, the fabric of his grey RDA blazer cutting into his armpits, he looked up and saw his rescuer.

In the strobe light of the train cars passing below, he caught a stuttering glimpse of a large face as square as a concrete block with a lantern jaw and cavernous yellow eyes. A grotesque parody of a human face, it was in every way harsher and more savage-looking. One large tooth jutted from its lower jaw, poking almost into his captor's slitted right nostril. Its skin was blue and rough like the hide of an elephant. As Brendan took in all the details of the thing's face, the thing stared at him, wide-eyed.

The yellow eyes narrowed to slits and the huge nostrils sniffed wetly. "Hmmmmmmm." The voice was deep and rumbling like rocks dropping into an empty oil drum. "Hello. Are you lost or what?"

Brendan was at the end of his endurance. He'd been attacked, chased, and nearly run over by a train. He'd heard squirrels talk and narrowly avoided being struck by lightning. Now a huge blue man was holding him helpless above the subway tracks. His mind decided that if this huge monster were going to eat him, it would be better if he weren't awake for it. Brendan passed out.

When he came to, he was immediately aware of two things. One: he hadn't been eaten, a positive development. He wanted to check his hands and feet to see if they were all present and accounted for but it was too dark to see. Two: he was moving. Well, he wasn't moving himself, he was being carried. Something large and thick was clamped around him. It smelled powerfully. Not a bad smell but weird, like a very stinky armpit full of cinnamon. As his eyes began to adjust to the light, he was able to pick out more detail. He was being held in place by a large arm, thick as a young tree and just as solid. The arm was attached to a body of suitably large proportions. The body was draped in a thick woollen fabric, scratchy in the extreme. At the moment, they were shambling along a rough stone corridor.

As they swayed along, the giant thing hummed softly to itself. "*Bum ba bum ba bum! bum ba bum ba bum! bum ba bum ba bum bum!*" Brendan recognized the tune: it was the old *Hockey Night in Canada* theme.

Brendan felt panic begin to well up. He started struggling against the iron grip of the creature holding him. "Let go of me!"

"Na! Don't whiggle. No whiggling, please." The low rumbling voice echoed off the stone. "Borje don't appreciate the whiggling."

Brendan stopped wiggling. "Where are you taking me … Borje?"

"Patience, little master. 'S not so far."

Even as the creature spoke, the light was growing stronger. Brendan craned his head to look ahead and saw a bluish glow outlining what looked like a door.

Borje walked straight up to the door, a thick, heavy portal, and took out a steel key. Spray-painted slogans in a language Brendan couldn't read covered the door, and a few crudely drawn rude pictures adorned it as well. The huge blue man named Borje tapped the key against the door, which glowed with a faint silver light for an instant before swinging open with the squeal of rusty hinges.

"Home, shweet home," the creature Borje called as he carried Brendan over the threshold.

They were in a rough cavern cut out of the native stone. In one corner sat an overly large table with two oversized wooden chairs beside it. On the table were stacks of hockey pucks in tottering piles that covered most of the tabletop. In the far wall, a fireplace held pride of place, a merry fire crackling in the hearth. A huge overstuffed armchair sat directly in front of the flames. A smaller end table sat nearby and a large remote control lay atop it. On the wall over the mantelpiece was the largest flat-screen TV Brendan had ever seen. The place seemed quite cozy in a stone-caverny kind of way.

The door clanged shut. Borje placed Brendan on his feet. Brendan turned to look at the door, an impenetrable slab. He was trapped with the thing called Borje.

In his precarious and exhausted state of mind, he thought that the objects hanging on the wall were skulls. He blinked, rubbed his eyes, and looked again.

"Hockey helmets?"

The wall was covered in ice hockey helmets, row upon row, lovingly arranged and polished. Each had a tiny plaque that told which professional player had once worn the headgear. There were also shelves full of gloves from the ultra-modern to the ancient and decaying leather gauntlets that players had worn a century or more ago. Brendan looked around the room and saw that it was a hockey shrine, a museum to the sport. Rows of hockey sticks ranging from gnarled wooden clubs to plywood laminate to aluminum to one-piece composite leaned in cleverly designed wall racks. The rafters and roof beams were hung with hundreds of hockey jerseys. Most of them were from the Toronto Maple Leafs[55] but there were other teams as well.

Looking up into the curved recesses of the ceiling, Brendan could see more odds and ends of hockey history dangling from the rafters: shoulder pads, elbow pads, hockey pants, more sticks and helmets from every era of the sport. He gasped when he looked into one stone alcove and saw a squat silver cup lit from above by a single spotlight. The cup was so shiny it was clear it had been lovingly polished. Brendan looked more closely, and his eyes bugged out as he read some of the inscriptions on the base.

"Is that what I think it is?" he breathed.

---

[55] The Toronto Maple Leafs are the Toronto professional hockey franchise. They are one of the most famous and most enduring hockey teams in the world. Their fans are fanatical despite the fact that, as of this publication, they hadn't won a championship in over forty years. Their fans are both fanatical and masochistic.

"Yo. The original Stanley's Cup." Borje beamed. Then his huge face became slightly sheepish. "The one they have is a replica. I couldn't resist! They never announced that the original whent missing." He winked and grinned. "But she ain't missing, nah? She's right here!"[56]

Brendan traced his fingers over the engraved lines on the trophy. "This is unbelievable," Brendan said in awe. If his father had seen this collection he would have wet himself, wept for joy, and then died. His father was a huge hockey fan and played on a team called the Jokers, made up of comedians and artists who played charity games in Toronto. Brendan sometimes joined them. The awe in seeing such a collection pushed aside his terror for a moment. "Where did you get all this amazing stuff?"

"You like my hockey memorabiliums?" The heavy voice took on a childlike quality. "Many years, I've been collecting."

Brendan moved closer to peer at a white helmet with a scrawled signature and the number 21 on the side. "Borje Salming?"[57]

---

[56] Lord Stanley, Governor General of Canada, donated the Silver Cup in 1892 to be presented to the best amateur hockey team in Canada. It later became the ultimate professional hockey prize, going to the winner of the National Hockey League playoffs. The cup has been accidentally left on buses, streetcars, trains; dropped in swimming pools; been lost, found, lost, and found again a number of times. Borje's claim to have purloined the original cup is not so hard to credit, considering how many times it has gone missing in the past.

[57] Borje Salming was one of the first European hockey players to play professionally in North America. A stalwart defenceman, he was a fan favourite for many years. In retirement, he followed many important pursuits, including designing and selling his own line of underwear.

"Yo! My favouritest of players. A good Swhede, like me. I am Borje, too. Same name!" He giggled like a child. "I, Borje, left Swheden many years ago. Centuries in the fact. I come aboard a ship whith Lucky Leif himself."

"Leif Eriksson?" Brendan whispered. "The Viking?"[58]

"That's the one! I were in the crew." Borje thumped his chest with one massive fist. "They leave Borje behind. Hey, think I, bad luck! Not me, *Leif* bad luck. I stay. Whander here and there. End up here. Toronto built up around me."

Brendan turned to look at Borje and was amazed that he wasn't afraid of the hulking creature. Borje stood close to eight feet tall, with massive shoulders and arms that hung at his sides like thick tree branches. His head was as big as a large pumpkin and sprouted with greasy blond hair. He was wearing a blue and white woollen hockey jersey (one he'd made himself by the look of it) with a lopsided white maple leaf on the front.

"Uh … this is really cool and everything, but I really need to find Kim. You know Kim?" With some difficulty, Brendan decided he had to return to his current situation.

"Of course." Borje smiled and slapped his chest. "Ki-Mata good friend of Borje!"

---

[58] Leif Eriksson, or Lucky Leif, is believed to have discovered North America in the tenth century. Accompanied by a group of adventurous Vikings from Greenland (of which Borje claims to have been one), Eriksson made landfall somewhere on the island of Newfoundland. They built some huts, collected some wood and wild grapes, then returned to the Greenland settlement. Borje appears to have been left behind in the New World and is therefore assumed to be the first permanent European settler in the New World.

"Yeah, nice," Brendan said. "Well, she said I have to get to the Swan so maybe I should be going."

"You can't go." Borje frowned, his brows beetling together over his bulbous nose. "There are Dwharfs about in these tunnels."

"Dwarfs?"

Borje shook his shaggy head. "Bad persons. Scavengers and whaylayers of folk. When they move in, there go the neighbourhood. They travel in gangs in the under tunnels and prey on the wheak. I stops them when I can."

"Which leads to my next question," Brendan said, trying to be delicate. "What exactly … are you?"

Borje laughed like a boulder falling down a well. "Oh. I am Borje and I am a Troll."[59]

"A Troll? A Troll. Of course you're a Troll. Why not?" Brendan felt he was about to lose his mind. "Okay. Last question: where are we?"

"This is my home. I live here. Under the Air Canada Centre, home of beloved Maple Leafs!" He placed a vast blue hand over his heart and cast his eyes upward in adoration. "So handy! I have easy access to new souvenirs for collection. Borje loves the beautiful frozen game!"

Brendan's stomach suddenly rumbled, and Borje's smile vanished. "But Borje is bad host. Enough talking for now. You must be hungry."

---

[59] *Trolls* are a race of mythical beings that originated in the frigid mountains of Scandinavia. They are easily recognized by their characteristic skin: a thick, rough hide with a deep blue colour. Their natural habitat is mountainous terrain where they tend to live in remote caves, though some, like Borje, enjoy living underground. They are incredibly strong and resistant to most magic. And they tend to smell quite powerfully.

Borje reached over and scooped Brendan up in one shovel-like hand. In three strides, Borje crossed the stone floor and deposited Brendan in one of the large wooden chairs at the table. With one arm he swept the pucks onto the floor. As he did so, Brendan managed to catch a glimpse of the signatures on the pucks of many famous players. The Troll picked the remote off the small table and pointed it at the TV. A hockey game suddenly filled the vast screen.

"Borje PVR'd it last night. She's gonna be a good one." He pulled aside a tapestry to reveal a tidy kitchen with a stove and fridge. "Borje make you some food!" The Troll snapped his huge fingers. The sound was like a gunshot. "Borje make nachos! Ha!" With a clap of his massive hands—it sounded like a gunshot—he disappeared into the kitchen and let the tapestry fall to cover the door.

Brendan sat in the giant chair. It was the first time he hadn't been running, screaming, and being chased in what seemed like a very long time. He looked at his watch. It wasn't working. He couldn't tell what time it was.

"Crap! I've got to call home. Mum'll be freaking out." He hauled his knapsack off his back. Although one of the straps had broken, he hadn't managed to lose it along the way. He fished around in the bag and found his cellphone. He flipped open the screen and his heart fell. He looked at the small screen and saw something he'd never seen before. Usually, if the phone was getting no reception, the normal home screen would show but there would be no bars in the corner. Now, however, his phone didn't even show the home screen, just a miniature blizzard of electronic snow.

As he held the phone, it began to burn his hand with a prickling heat that grew in intensity. In seconds, he was forced to drop the handset. He clutched his hand in pain, red welts standing out where the phone had touched his fingers and palm. Then he remembered what Kim had said.

"Metal and plastic don't mix well with us."

Brendan refused to accept it. He reached for the phone on the floor and grabbed it. He instantly cried out and dropped the phone again. As he watched, stunned, sparks fountained from the cell and the entire handset melted into a puddle of plastic slag. He looked at the blob that had been his cellphone.

Part of his mind was asking, "Is that covered under my insurance plan?" while another was asking, "Where can I find another phone?"

He scanned the room but didn't see anything resembling a phone. He wasn't surprised. "Why would a Troll need to phone anyway?" He hopped down from the chair and went to the door. He was almost afraid to touch it after the phone incident, but he had to get out of there. Borje didn't seem threatening but … he was a Troll! That couldn't be good! Trolls hid under bridges and ate people. He didn't want to push his luck. Brendan couldn't even remember the route he'd come by. He'd read in a book once that if you kept turning left, you would eventually escape a labyrinth. This was the closest to a labyrinth he'd ever encountered so hopefully that logic would work.

He tentatively pushed on the door. There was no handle. He'd thought the door was made of metal but he realized now that it wasn't. It was warm to the touch and had a glassy texture like nothing he'd ever felt before. The door didn't yield to a gentle shove. He pushed harder. Nothing.

He almost jumped out of his skin when the Troll called from the kitchen, "Do you like anchovies?"

Anchovies? On nachos? "Yeah. Love them!" He pushed with all his might on the door but it wouldn't budge. He backed up and prepared to throw himself against the door when he was interrupted by a loud banging on it.

"Open up!" Kim's voice was muffled but still recognizable. "Come on, Borje! Open up!"

Borje came bustling out of the kitchen holding a vast platter of nachos and wearing an apron that read HAIL TO THE CHEF with a version of the U.S. presidential seal that pictured the American eagle holding a spatula and a wooden spoon. "Coming!" He slammed the platter down on the table, sending a few stray tortilla chips scattering on the tabletop. Wiping his vast hands on the apron, he hurried to the door. Brendan stood back as he pulled the steel key from his pocket and tapped it on the door. Again, the door glowed faintly with a silver light and swung open to reveal Kim, her school uniform slightly torn and smudged with soot. Her face was similarly smeared. In her right hand she was carrying her field hockey stick. In her left, she held a set of wooden scooter handlebars.

"So there you are," she said. "I thought I'd be scraping you off the front of a southbound train, but thanks to Borje here, you're all in one piece."

She tossed the handlebars onto the floor with a clatter. "Too bad I can't say the same for my scooter. Og and the Artificers are going to kill me."

Borje beamed. "I've made some nachos. Are you hungry, Ki-Mata?"

"Starved," Kim announced. Without a second glance at Brendan, she marched to the table and vaulted into one of the high chairs. She wrinkled her nose when she saw the mound of chips loaded with cheese and toppings. "Anchovies?"

"He said he whanted them!" Borje pointed a knobby finger at Brendan, who simply stared.

Kim sneered at Brendan. "Figures." She began to pick the salty fish fillets off the chips with her fingers.

"So I like anchovies," Brendan said defensively. "Sue me. I've had it. Tell me what's going on!"

Kim shook her head, licking her fingers. "It's not for me to say. I was told to Ward you and that's what I've done. Now I have to deliver you to the Swan. So why don't you just have some nachos and try to get some rest. We're safe for the moment."

Brendan wasn't satisfied. "Why should I go anywhere with you? You aren't the person I thought you were. And you say things like 'your human family'! Like I'm not human."

Kim just stared at him thoughtfully, chewing a mouthful of chips.

"If I'm not human, what am I?" Brendan shouted. "*What am I?*"

Kim shrugged and said simply, "I told you. You're a Faerie."

"You said that before," Brendan said, annoyed, "but what does it mean?"

"A Faerie. A Faerie with a capital F-a-e-r-i-e! An old-school Faerie. One of the Fair Folk, an ancient race of magical beings."

Brendan stared at her in disbelief, then burst out laughing.

NACHOS, MARSHMALLOWS,
ANCHOVIES

Kim watched him laugh, wipe his eyes, and wheeze as she calmly devoured more of the nachos. She made a face.

"Do I taste ... marshmallow?" she asked in disgust.

"I like marshmallows," Borje mumbled.

"Hold it," Brendan gasped after he managed to get control of himself. "Hold it just a second. You're telling me I'm a fairy? Me? A fairy? Like Tinkerbell?"

"No." Kim rolled her eyes, picking a stray anchovy off her corn chip. "No. *Not* like Tinkerbell. Tinkerbell is a total misrepresentation of what Faeries are. We aren't tiny little things that flit around and wave wands.... Well, for the most part we aren't. There are lots of different kinds but none of them are as silly as that."

Brendan had finally managed to stop laughing. He stared at Kim in disbelief. "You honestly believe what you're saying, don't you. You actually think you're a fairy."

"I don't think," Kim stated. "I know. I am a Faerie. And so are you."

Brendan tried to take this in. "And him?" He pointed at Borje.

"No," Kim said calmly, as if talking to a child. "Obviously, Borje is a Troll."

"I already told him this," Borje complained.

"Is there a difference?" Brendan asked.

"A big difference," Kim answered. "There are a number of different races that inhabit the world beyond Human awareness: Faeries, Trolls, Dwarfs. Look, I don't have time for a history lesson. We're safe in here for a little while but the Wards on that door won't hold in the face of a concerted effort by Orcadia and her helpers. Borje is a Troll and so he is basically neutral. His home is protected under the provisions of the Truce but Orcadia doesn't appear to respect it any more. She wants you and she'll stop at nothing, not even the Sacred Truce."

Brendan held up his hands. "Hold it! Hold it! *None of this makes any sense!* What Truce? Who is that crazy woman? Why does she want to kill me? I haven't done anything to her."

"She doesn't want to kill you, necessarily. She wants to turn you ... never mind! It doesn't matter. It's what you represent. You could shift the balance. There are some Fair Folk who don't like the status quo. They want to go to war with the Humans. We have to get you to the Swan. We have to get you initiated. Once you're initiated, you will be in a better position to defend yourself."

"Initiated?" Brendan couldn't absorb anything she was saying. "Initiated into what?"

"I've already said too much." Kim wiped her mouth with her sleeve. "Listen, I didn't ask for this job. I was assigned to protect you. Now that fool Deirdre D'Anaan has ruined everything by breaking the *glamour* that allowed you to hide in the Human world. The only way to ensure you survive and don't go over to the Darkness is to get you to the Swan and get you initiated. I intend to do that."

"Why should I trust you? I didn't even know your real

name until this afternoon. Ki-Mata? *Is* that even your real name?" Brendan said sullenly.

"Yes, it's my real name," Kim said. "At least, it's the one I share with others. I have another name, a secret name as well, but that is only shared with those I trust. Breandan is your true name. You'll get your secret name when you are initiated." She stood up. "I have to get you to the Swan so that can take place."[60]

"So you never were my friend," Brendan said. "You were lying to me all along."

Kim didn't answer. She thoughtfully licked salsa off her fingers. "If it makes you happy to believe that, fine."

"I want to go home," Brendan said.

"Whether you believe it or not, that's where I'm taking you," Kim said softly, without looking at him. "You'll go to the Swan and be among your own people again."

"I'm talking about my mum and dad ... and even Delia. I want to go home to my house."

"Impossible." Kim shook her head. "They'll be tracking their way back there now. They'll be watching for you. You won't be safe. *They* won't be safe."

He stomped to the door and slammed his fist into it. He immediately regretted it. His knuckles stung but he swallowed the pain. "Open this door right now. I demand that you let me go! This is kidnapping!"

Kim glared at him. "Kidnapping?" She hopped down from the chair and casually pulled the field hockey stick out of her knapsack as she crossed the floor to stand in

---

[60] In the Faerie culture, one's secret name is very important. Those who know it have power over an individual.

front of Brendan. He unconsciously pressed his back against the door, shrinking away from her. "I'm tempted to add assault and battery to my list of crimes. But I assure you of one thing, and this you must believe if you believe nothing else. If you do not come with me and do exactly as I say, you will die. Or worse."

"What could be worse than dying?"

"Do you really want to find out?"

Brendan didn't know what to say. He looked into her eyes and he saw that she was absolutely serious. Kim put her stick back in her knapsack. "Rest's over. We have to go."

"Wait." Brendan's voice stopped her. "How can I take you seriously? I mean, put yourself in my shoes. I'm just supposed to believe you and follow you anywhere you say? You have to give me some proof."

Kim cocked her head and looked at him, considering. "Fine. You had a spiral mark on your chest over your heart. I've never seen it but I know it was there." Brendan's hand went to the spot of its own accord. She continued, "It's what we call a Ward, a magical safeguard. A Ward is a kind of magic seal, in your case, a mark on your flesh. A glamour was embedded within just after you were born."

"Whoa, whoa, whoa!" Brendan interrupted. "What's a glamour?"

Kim crossed her arms, the very picture of exaggerated patience. "A glamour is a magical illusion, a manipulation of earth energy that warps perception. There are many kinds but basically, it makes people see things differently from the way they actually are. In your case, the glamour allowed you to live hidden among Humans without their knowing you were Faerie. It also hid you from Faerie eyes. And now that magic is gone."

"Yeah, it's gone," Brendan whispered. "That woman's little creature ate it in my dream last night."

Kim nodded. "All the more reason to hurry. The glamour is wearing off. Look."

She pointed to a mirror, more a slab of polished metal that leaned against the wall by the door. Brendan stepped in front of it and gasped.

He was looking at his own reflection but it was slightly altered. His skin was paler even than normal but it shone with health. The giant pimple he'd been nursing all week was completely gone. All evidence of blemishes, zits, or blackheads (the bane of every teen's existence) was gone. His hair, normally a bland sandy brown, was shot through with streaks of amber and gold. He held up his hands before his face. The fingers seemed longer, more perfectly formed. He sighed in wonder. He grinned and was shocked to see that his teeth, crooked the day before, were now straight and even, white as snow.

"You're taking on Faerie form. Soon the glamour will dissipate completely. Humans will see you for what you really are. That would be bad for us all."

"Why bad?"

"Because we have a touchy relationship with Humans. They like to think we magical races, like Faeries, Trolls, and Dwarfs, don't exist, and as long as we don't do anything too outrageous or flamboyant, the Truce is maintained."

That was a little disturbing so he focused on Kim. He looked Kim up and down. She was still wearing her school uniform: green kilt, green blazer, and white shirt. She looked like a normal schoolgirl. "And you're like me?"

She gave a nod, smirked, and flicked her wrist. Kim shimmered as though she were going out of focus, then her image sharpened again. Her clothes had not changed but her face was different. Not that it had been altered in any major way. Her features were somehow more defined, more elegant.

Her hair, normally a dull brown, was a lustrous and shining chestnut shot through with strands of silver. She held out her hands and from her palms sprouted tattoos in the shape of vines. As he watched, dumbstruck, the vines, glittering and golden, twined up her forearms and out of sight under her shirt sleeves. She smiled, revealing teeth that shimmered with a tinge of gold as well.

The corner of her mouth quirked up and the smirk widened. "So? Believe me now?"

Brendan gulped. "I don't know what I believe any more." He suddenly looked at Borje. "Is that what you really look like?"

Borje rumbled with laughter and pulled at his cheek with his fingers, making his grotesque face slightly more ugly. "Yo! This is all Borje. Good and ugly."

"Okay," Kim snapped. "Show and tell is over. We have to get going."

"Hold it!" Brendan said. "One more question."

Kim sighed. "Make it quick."

"You said the Ward was placed on me at birth, right?"

"Yeah," she said impatiently.

"By who? Who wanted me hidden?"

Kim frowned. "I should let Ariel tell you. He's the Eldest among us."

"Come on," Brendan pleaded. "I really want to know."

Kim sighed again. "It was your father. Your true father."

Brendan was silent then, trying to absorb this bit of news. Then he said, "Where is he? Will I meet him?"

"That's a bit complicated," Kim said. "I'll have to let Ariel explain." She tapped the door with her stick. "Right now, we have to get to the Swan. Okay?"

Brendan shrugged. "What choice do I have?"

"Now that's the first smart thing you've said today." Kim grinned. Turning to the Troll, she said, "Borje? The door!"

Borje raised his hands in protest. "Nay! Not the front door. They whill be expecting that." He raised the tapestry that led to the kitchen and gestured one giant hand for them to enter.

They followed Borje across the kitchen. He seemed to love shiny things. The stone countertop was crammed full of the latest appliances: a blender, a shining toaster, a microwave, a food processor, and many other chrome-encrusted gadgets. Borje stopped in front of the fridge, a monolithic slab of stainless steel glimmering in the overhead light.

Borje patted the polished metal surface lovingly, caressing its smooth surface as if the appliance were a favourite pet. "Amana has a secret, don't you, girl?" The huge Troll chuckled to himself. He bent over and lifted the entire fridge in his massive hands. Grunting with the effort, he turned and put the fridge on the floor.

Where the fridge had been was a gaping rectangular hole in the natural rock of the wall. A cool breeze drifted up from the hole. Brendan stepped closer and peered down into the hole. Steps, roughly carved from the stone, led down into darkness. The walls ran with water. Brendan felt his stomach sink.

"This is handy, Borje," Kim commented, inspecting the entrance.

"Ya! When I moved down from the old hockey arena Maple Leaf Gardens a few years ago, I had to use subway tunnels. Risky! But when I got here, there whas so much construction, nobody noticed when I borrow few tools and do a little digging of my own." The vast bulk of his chest jiggled with childish laughter. "I dig right under their noses. Now, I can go and whatch the baseball game if I whant or go to the train station or even down to the Harbourfront whithout going upside. Very convenient!"

"It'll do," Kim decided, all business now. "C'mon, Brendan. Let's move."

"No way," Brendan said firmly. "I'm not going down there."

Kim glared at him. "There's no other way."

"I've had enough of tunnels. It's dark and I can't go down there. And another thing …"

"You're scared?" Kim offered, eyebrow cocked in derision.

Brendan flushed angrily. "Shouldn't I be? You've said yourself that people want to kill me or capture me. Why, I have no idea! And now we're going to blunder around in the dark? That's your plan?"

Their argument was interrupted by a blood-curdling, shrieking howl. The cry echoed through the stone and into Brendan's head like the scratch of fingernails on a chalkboard. His skin crawled as the wailing howl sounded again, closer this time. He felt panic climbing up his throat.

"Kobolds!"[61] Kim's head whipped around and her pale skin became paler still. "They've got the scent," she cried. "They're coming fast. We have to go."

"They whon't dare come through here," Borje growled. "They can't break my Whards."

"Given time, Orcadia could do anything," Kim said. She turned and glared at Brendan. "She'll risk anything to get hold of Brendan. We have to go now."

Brendan decided he'd rather brave the tunnels than face whatever was making that howling. He looked up into Borje's yellow eyes and tried to smile. The Troll smiled back, a slightly terrifying proposition, considering the state of his teeth. Brendan reached up and grasped one giant finger and shook it. "Thanks, Borje. I don't really understand everything yet, but I think you're a friend."

"That's enough for me," Borje rumbled. "It's a pleasure and an honour to have helped, Your Highness." The Troll dipped his head in an awkward bow.

Kim glared at Borje, who snapped his mouth shut.

"Highness? You called me prince back at the school. What is that all about?" Brendan demanded. A gut-wrenching howl cut off any reply. Kim grabbed Brendan by the arm and hauled him down the steps.

"Go, Leafs, go!" Borje cried as they plunged into darkness, and with that incongruous exhortation ringing in his ears, Brendan entered Toronto's Undertown.

---

61 *Kobolds* are another magical race of Germanic origin. They are shape-shifters and expert trackers. Kobolds are akin to Dwarfs but smaller in stature, preferring dark subterranean tunnels to the open air. They are incredibly mischievous and devious, with a loathing for most Humans.

THE TUNNELS

The steps were uneven. More than once Brendan had to thrust out a hand to brace himself against the stone wall. His hands were soon frigid and slimy with whatever microbes clustered in such miserable underground places.

Brendan had lost count after sixty-seven steps. He was becoming disoriented as he stumbled after taking another step downward where there was no step to be had. He almost turned his ankle when his questing foot encountered the floor.

"Which way?" Kim said in the darkness. Her voice was surprisingly loud, echoing off the stone walls.

"I have no idea," Brendan said. "I can't see a thing."

"It's funny," Kim said, her voice now closer. "You are able to do some things naturally but others, like your Faerie Sight, they haven't kicked in yet."

"Faerie Sight?" Brendan asked.

"It's impossible to describe. Let's just say, to keep it simple, Faeries can see really well in the dark. Obviously, you haven't got the knack yet, so …"

A soft yellow glow flared to life in the darkness. Kim held her field hockey stick aloft. The curved head of the stick was wreathed in a golden nimbus of flame. When his eyes finished smarting at the sudden glare, Brendan marvelled to see that the wood of the stick was not burning. "How are you doing that?"

Kim snorted with laughter. "You're so new, it's hilarious." Looking at Brendan's face, she sensed he didn't see the humour. "Seriously, you've got a lot to learn. But we've got to get moving. We'll talk as we go. First, we have to decide which way."

She raised the club and their surroundings came into focus.

Brendan saw they were in a rough-hewn, circular chamber where three passages joined. Scrawled on the walls was the ubiquitous graffiti. "Dwarfs!" Kim shook her head in disgust. "There are three possible routes and they aren't marked in any way. Ridiculous Troll! I'll have to go back up and ask him." Kim started back toward the stairs.

A howl from above and an angry Troll shout dissuaded her against that course of action. "They've arrived at Borje's. We'll just have to pick one and go."

At the sound of the piercing howling, Brendan's heart raced anew. He looked around at their options. Three darker patches of blackness stood in front of them, three different possible directions.

"Go left," Brendan said.

"Why?"

"In a labyrinth, always choose the left passage and you'll come out eventually."

"Did you read that in a kid's book?" Kim snorted. "This ain't no labyrinth. I've been in the real deal. Kitsune Kai in Kyoto tried to trap me in one a while back.[62] *That* was a

---

62 *Kitsune Kai* is a Fox Spirit renowned in the Faerie World. Japanese Fair Folk tend to be shape-shifters, capable of taking

labyrinth. This is just a few tunnels." She thought for a moment and shrugged. "But I suppose left is as good as any other choice. They all smell rank. Mould and Dwarf farts, a pungent combo. All right. Let's go."

She started forward with Brendan close on her heels. He didn't want to lose her down here.

At first, their choice seemed a good one. The passage headed straight on with a gentle downward tendency. Brendan could actually see quite far ahead down the tunnel. On the walls, here and there, were spray-painted inscriptions in angular letters in a language he couldn't read.

"What do they say?" he asked Kim.

"You don't want to know," Kim said, shaking her head. "Dwarfs love graffiti. And they love swearing. They're not so keen on spelling."

As they made progress, Brendan started to relax a bit. They were moving at a steady clip, and he had to concentrate on breathing regularly to keep up the pace. Kim didn't seem to tire at all.

The terrifying cries of their pursuers became less frequent and more distant. Brendan began to feel that the danger was less immediate. Kim slowed their pace slightly, allowing Brendan to better study the tunnels.

He could see details in the rock walls, striations, and cut marks. Borje had employed the tools only when necessary to widen the path or connect existing caverns and natural tunnels. Brendan had never even imagined that such places existed. The oppressive weight of the city poised above

---

animal form whenever they choose. Kai is one of the most powerful of all Japanese Fair Folk.

him made him feel as though he was going to suffocate. To take his mind off his fear, he decided to talk.

"This is amazing," Brendan marvelled. "How could this exist below the city without anyone knowing?"

"Humans see what they want to see. They don't venture down here much," Kim said. "They don't need to. We're way farther down than the deepest subway tunnel or basement. But this is nothing compared to, say, New York, Tokyo, Cairo, or London. They are so honeycombed with catacombs it's ridiculous. Toronto is a young city. Give it a few hundred years and it will be Swiss cheese down here."

"There are people … Faeries like you in other cities?" Brendan asked, incredulous.

"Like you, too," Kim said pointedly. "Oh, yeah. Everywhere in the world. We live right under the noses of the People of Metal, in their cities, sometimes right in the open and the Humans don't even know it."

"People of Metal?"

"That's what we call the Humans."

Brendan tripped over a pile of plastic objects and almost fell. Looking down, he saw a litter of empty cans, discarded CD cases, and refuse.

"Dwarfs again," Kim explained. "They steal anything shiny and toss what they don't like. The original litter-bugs."

Brendan caught up to Kim and asked, "How is it that nobody finds out?"

"About the Dwarfs?"

"About them and you and all of this!"

"We're experts at deception. We disguise ourselves with charms and glamours. We keep out of sight and don't draw attention to ourselves. Many Faeries live right alongside

Humans, work in their businesses and live in their neighbourhoods but we keep it quiet. Otherwise, Humans would totally freak out. Ever heard of the witch hunts? In the Middle Ages?"

Brendan seemed to recall something about people being condemned as witches and burned at the stake in olden times. "They were Faeries?"

"Yeah. Faeries who weren't careful enough to keep themselves secret," Kim said. Her expression darkened. "Or assumed wrongly that they could use their gifts to help their neighbours and not pay the price. The only protection is in secrecy for us. And there's the Sacred Truce."

"The Truce?"

"That's it," Kim said curtly. "That's all I'm going to say."

Brendan was frustrated. "I need to know more. You expect me to follow you and not ask questions?"

"That would be ideal, yes."

"Well, tough beans! Why do you call Humans People of Metal?"

"It's like this. Our people, your people, Fair Folk, we like to go with the flow. We bend nature rather than break it. We manipulate the natural forces that exist within the Earth. Does that make sense?"

Brendan thought about it. "I think so."

"Humans, the People of Metal, they break things. They force things. They cut things up to make them fit their plan."

"You make the Humans sound … I don't know … cruel."

"It's their nature. They can't change it. It's programmed into them," Kim said.

"Still, why 'People of Metal'?"

"Ah, okay! The thing is, things went along just fine for thousands and thousands of years," Kim explained as they hiked along. "Humans and Fair Folk co-existed. They had respect for our ways and we could stay out of theirs. It was a big world. Sadly, things changed when the Humans found a way of taking the bones of the Earth and turning them to their will. They learned to dig the metal from the Earth. They made more and more effective tools to carve her flesh and each other's. Their mastery of metal made them masters of the Earth, and they drove us into hiding. Iron and steel are hurtful to us. When they realized this, there could be no more cooperation between our people. They became the People of Metal, and we faded into legend."

Brendan felt a powerful stab of sadness. Her description of Humans made him ashamed. "Hey, not all of them are bad. My mum and dad recycle. They go to the Earth Day celebrations. They really worry about the environment."

"Maybe they do and maybe they don't." Kim looked somewhat skeptical. "I'm not saying that some Humans aren't good. There are good and bad in the world of the Fair Folk, too: hence Orcadia. And we've learned to adapt. We live alongside Humans and slip through the cracks. Though they can be destructive, Humans are fascinating, vibrant, and imaginative. And now, some seem to understand that they can't continue to destroy the Earth and expect Her to provide for them. We just hope it's not too late. There are those who think that one day we may be able to reach a compromise and share the world like we used to do. Some think that you might be a big part of that." She stopped talking for a moment and sniffed the air. Satisfied, she said, "Anyway, we have more important things to take care of right now."

"Like what?"

"Like I think we went the wrong way."

They turned a corner and found themselves facing a blank wall.

"Oh no." Brendan could suddenly feel the ominous weight of the city, the tons of rock suspended precariously above them. His chest constricted and his breath came in gasps. "I don't want to die here. I can't breathe!"

Kim slapped him on the back. "Come on, Brendan. You have to pull it together. We just have to retrace our steps. We passed a few tunnels on either side. We'll try each one."

"Go back? Toward those Kobold things? Are you nuts?"

"Well, we can't sit here while you bawl like a little girl. We have to keep moving."

"I'm not bawling like a little girl," Brendan snapped. "If we keep moving we're just going to get more lost." He stood up and tried to control his breathing. He *couldn't* panic. He had to keep calm or he was lost. "I wish someone would show us the way," he said aloud.

"Careful!" Kim grabbed his arm. As if in answer to his call, a fluttering filled the small chamber where they stood. Kim groaned. "Too late."

Out of the tunnel they'd come from, a small splotch of blackness stuttered into their midst. Brendan's eyes went wide in horror.

"Oh great," he moaned. "It's a bat! I hate bats. Cover your hair."

"Well, that's a fine how-do-you-do!" said a tiny voice. "I'm not a bat and I have no interest in your hair."

Brendan stared at Kim. "Did you say that?"

The creature swooped at Brendan's head and lashed out with a tiny foot, catching him on the tip of the nose. "No, you giant fool. I said it. And I meant it. I'm liking you less and less by the minute."

Brendan uncovered his eyes and stared at the tiny winged creature hovering in front of his face. It was the size of a bat, no bigger than his hand. It had the wings of a bat, leathery and translucent. It had ears like a bat, long and wide, thin as parchment, and they swivelled in the thatch of black hair covering its head. It had the body and face of a man. Its big black eyes bulged out, their gaze focused on Brendan. The long, pointy nose sniffed the air. "Listen, Skreet didn't come here to be insulted, you know. Skreet was summoned. Who summoned Skreet?" He sneered and brushed his hands against his little leather jacket. He wore small motorcycle boots complete with rows of silver buckles.

"Summoned? I didn't summon anyone," Brendan said, trying to keep a safe distance between himself and the creature.

"He doesn't know … he isn't initiated yet. He's been living outside among the Humans," Kim said.

Skreet's face became devious. "He doesn't know the rules? He's a total green? Oh, this is excellent. Delightful!"

Kim groaned. "Be careful, Brendan. You have to be very careful when you make this bargain. Skreet will hold you to the exact letter."

Brendan's nose stung from the blow he'd received a moment earlier. "What bargain? What are you talking about?"

Skreet flitted close to Brendan's ear, rubbing his tiny hands together. "*You* summoned me. You said, 'I wish someone would show us the way.' When a Fair Folk speaks such words with sincere intent, a Summoning occurs.

So"—he flitted once around Brendan's head and stopped, hovering before the confused boy's face, hands spread in invitation—"you summoned me! Now we bargain."

Brendan looked to Kim for guidance. She sighed. "You can summon a Lesser Faerie …"[63]

"Lesser Faerie? *Lesser* Faerie! How insulting!" Skreet squeaked indignantly.

"What would you prefer? Midget Sprite?" Kim said caustically.

"We prefer to call ourselves Diminutives, for your information," Skreet said with a tiny sniff of disdain.

Kim rolled her eyes and continued, "Lesser Faeries can be summoned to perform tasks, but you must strike a bargain with them."

"What kind of bargain?" Brendan asked, warily eyeing the tiny flapping person.

"You have to give something in exchange for their service," Kim explained. "But you have to be careful! If you leave any loophole, they will try to trick you."

Skreet's face took on a wounded cast. "Don't malign me, you giant spoilsport!" He puffed out his chest. "I'm honest as the day is long. I've never once cheated on a deal. Never once." He flitted over and lighted on Brendan's shoulder. "So, my fine young lad, what is your desire? Tell me! Tell me! I am eager to serve."

---

[63] *Lesser Faeries* are tiny relatives of the Fair Folk. They vary in shape and appearance but they often resemble tiny animals or birds or even fish. They survive by pretending to be members of these mundane species. Lesser Faeries are far more numerous than Fair Folk. No one knows exactly how many of them there are in the world because they refuse to sit still long enough to be counted.

"Show us the way out of here," Brendan blurted. Kim frowned so he added, "To the lake! The way out to the lake!"

Kim shook her head ruefully. Skreet was delighted, however. "Fine! Perfect! Excellent! Grand! A noble task easily executed for a person of my vast capacity." He grinned slyly. "I know the Undertown like the back of my wing. Hee-hee. Now, what is the payment?"

Brendan grimaced. He dug his hands into the pockets of his soiled blazer. In his right pocket, his hand closed around something metallic. He pulled his hand out and opened his palm to reveal his braces.

Skreet flitted in and sniffed the metal bands. "Bah! No thanks. Silver they are not."

Brendan dug in his left pocket and felt a thin flat packet that crinkled in his hand. He pulled the packet out of his pocket and held it up. Gum. Sugarless spearmint gum. "I have this?"

Skreet's eyes bugged out even farther. "Is that what I think it is?" He licked his lips.

"If you think it's gum, then yes."

Skreet's face lit up. He spun and corkscrewed through the air in a circuit around Brendan's head like a tiny comet. "Oh! Bliss! Joy and bliss again. Gum! Sweet gum! Lovely, chewy gum! This suits Skreet to the tips of his wings! The bargain is struck!"

Brendan heaved a sigh of relief. "Great," he said. His grin vanished when he saw Kim's sour face. "What? He's going to lead us out of here."

"We'll see," Kim said. "All right, you little pipsqueak. Get us out of here."

A howl ululated down the corridor followed closely by a shrieking, mirthless laugh. It sounded much closer than before. Brendan's blood froze. Skreet raised an eyebrow. "Hmmm. The plot thickens. Hounds upon thy tail. Speed is of the essence, I assume?"

"Now!" Kim demanded.

Skreet sneered at her and then waved to Brendan with a little bow in mid-air that turned into a somersault. "This way, Boon Companion.[64] This way."

He set off up the corridor down which they had come. Brendan jogged after him with Kim bringing up the rear.

Brendan tried to keep Skreet in sight but the little Faerie was very quick. Brendan began to panic when his guide turned the corner and disappeared from view. Rushing around the bend, he breathed a sigh of relief to find Skreet holding station in front of a side corridor.

"Come along, Boon Companion. Don't dilly-dally." Skreet darted into the opening. Another howl raised the hair on Brendan's arms. The sound was very close and seemed to be coming from the corridor directly ahead, the one they'd come down in the first place.

"Move." Kim shoved him from behind into the side corridor. She hauled out her field hockey stick and followed him.

Skreet led them on a winding path through the darkness. He would speed ahead, leaving them in fear that he had run off but when they rounded the next bend, he was always there, waiting impatiently. They traversed natural caverns with oozing walls furred with mould. At one point, they entered a brick-lined tunnel, ancient and

---

[64] Any person who strikes a bargain with a Lesser Faerie becomes their Boon Companion for as long as the bargain lasts.

crumbling, with foul-smelling water sluicing down its centre. Always the howls came behind them. Every so often, the sound would fade as though the pack had lost the scent but soon they would find the trail again, drawing closer once more.

Brendan couldn't tell how long they'd been moving. Time disappeared in the darkness of the Undertown. He was exhausted, cold, and shivering. His shoes squelched with water and his trousers were thoroughly soaked. He had begun to doubt whether Skreet actually had any idea where they were going. The only thing that kept him going forward was the thought of the Kobolds catching up to him. The sound of their howling was terrifying enough without having to see them in the flesh.

At last, he saw a light up ahead. The light was steady and strong and could only come from good old electric light bulbs. His heart lifted. Maybe they were going to escape after all. He rushed forward and burst into an open space.

They were in a chamber that looked like a recent construction. The walls were of poured concrete painted a utilitarian grey. Conduits holding wires and pipes ran along the walls. The light came from banks of fluorescent lights high in a ceiling forested with pipes and ducting. Two huge steel pipes ran diagonally from the upper right wall down through the lower left wall. The sound of surging water and the labouring of pumps was deafening. Affixed to the pipes in the middle of the room was a platform accessible via a short flight of metal steps. The platform was taken up by a square metal box about the size of a portable toilet with a man-sized metal hatch. The hatch had a wheel lock in the centre.

"Skreet has brought you to the way out!" Skreet shouted proudly, landing on the metal wheel. "A way out, by water. As you instructed."

"This is the way out?" Brendan said skeptically. "How are we supposed to get out of here? What is this place?"

"It is a construction of the People of Metal!" Skreet hopped up and pointed at the wheel. "Spin this! Open the door. Close door. Let the metal box fill with water. Open the inner hatch and jump in the pipe. Zip along like a salmon in a stream! Boon Companion pops out into the lake like a cork from a bottle, like an arrow from a bow. Like an egg from a chicken! Pop. Gaaaah!"

Kim swung the field hockey stick, barely missing the little Faerie. "You little sneak. Sure we'll be shot out into the middle of Lake Ontario! Two hundred metres under the surface!"

"Skreet was never asked to make sure you'd be alive!" Skreet wailed. "Boon Companion! Don't let her kill me! I did as you asked." Skreet flitted up in the air out of reach of Kim's stick.

Brendan's heart froze as he suddenly realized where they were. In the last couple of years, the city had initiated a deep-water cooling system for office buildings in downtown Toronto. These pipes were part of that system. One went up from the lake, the other back. Now he understood why Kim was so furious and why she'd been so paranoid about bargaining with the little Faerie in the first place. Brendan had not been specific enough. Kim raised the field hockey stick for another swipe.

"Kim!" Brendan shouted. "Stop!"

Kim paused and looked at Brendan. "Why should I?"

Brendan looked up at terrified little Skreet, clinging to

a pipe above them. He knew what it was like to be small and helpless. In his mind's eye, he saw Chester Dallaire poised to smack him with the Murderball, the bully's eyes filled with triumph. He shook his head.

"It isn't his fault. He just did what I asked. It's my fault. You warned me to be specific and I wasn't."

"I admire your empathy." Kim looked at him thoughtfully for a moment then she frowned and lowered the club. "I still think he deserves a kicking."

Skreet cautiously flitted within range, his eyes suspicious. When he saw that no one was going to hit him, he cocked his head and looked at Brendan in open curiosity. "That's not the way it's supposed to be. You're supposed to get angry. Curse me to the Seven Pits and the four Fiery Infernos and the Endless Voids."

"I'm too tired," Brendan said.

Skreet darted over and tugged at Brendan's soiled lapel. "Thank you, good sir, kind Friend, Noble Bargainer. You are truly a good-hearted soul."

"And you are not," Brendan said fiercely. "You've led us to a dead end. You've led us to our deaths. Thanks for nothing. Here's your payment." He held out a single white morsel of gum.

"*Whhhhaaaaat!* You said the whole pack!"

"No," Brendan said smugly. "I said gum. Never how much gum, only gum. Be happy I don't give you half a piece."

Skreet frowned but he nodded. "Fair is fair." He snatched the piece of gum from Brendan's fingers. "Oooo, you are shrewd. Shrewd, I say, and no mistake. Still! You are kind. Skreet will not forget, Brendan, Boon Companion." With a final circuit of Brendan's head,

Skreet sped away between the narrow bars of a ventilation grating.

Brendan wished he could escape the same way when the howl sounded in his ears. It was loud even over the sound of the machinery. Alas, the vent shaft was far too small to admit him or Kim. The howling increased in volume and ferocity.

"They're almost here! What are we going to do?" Brendan shouted. Kim held her field hockey stick out in front of her in both hands, ready to defend the entrance. Brendan searched through the chamber for another way out. He spotted a set of metal doors. He ran across the room, ducking under the massive pipes, and threw himself against the doors. They didn't budge. He grabbed the metal handle and tried to turn it. It was locked tight.

"Come on, Kim! Help me!" The howling was danger-ously close now. He grabbed the door handle and heaved with all his might. The handle came off and he fell hard on his butt. He scrambled to his feet. "Use your magic hockey stick, why don't you?"

"I can't."

"Why not? Grow one of those thorny hedges. Slow them down."

Kim shook her head. "Doesn't work that way. I can only manipulate green things that already exist. I can't create them out of thin air."

Brendan thought back to the encounter in the parking lot. All of the briars had grown out of that one slip of a plant in the pavement crack.

"So what now?"

She dropped her knapsack to the floor, straightened her kilt, and spat in her hands.

"What are we going to do?" Brendan cried to Kim as he rejoined her in front of the dark mouth of the corridor.

"I'm going to face them here," Kim said grimly. "I'm away from my element. The good news is, so is Orcadia. She's a member of the Skyclan. They thrive in the open where they can draw on the open air. It'll be the Kobolds that give me the most trouble. I'll try to hold them off as long as I can. Just stay behind me."

Brendan wanted to say that it wasn't much of a plan but there didn't seem to be any point. It was his fault they were stuck in this dead end. Now they were going to be torn apart by some crazy devil things and he couldn't do a thing to save himself. He looked up at the hatch on the side of the pipe.

"Why not?" he said gloomily. "It can't be any worse than being eaten by dogs." He ran up the metal stairs to the hatchway and started to spin the wheel.

"What are you doing?" Kim demanded.

"I'm opening the pipe," Brendan said. "Maybe there's some way we can ride this flow out into the lake. Then we'll at least have a small chance of surviving."

The wheel turned easily because the machinery was new and well maintained. When the wheel stopped moving, he hauled the door open. A small amount of water poured out over his shoes. He had expected a torrent but there was only a trickle. Looking inside, he saw that there was another chamber big enough for a man to stand upright and a wheeled hatch on the far wall. *For maintenance. Like an airlock on a submarine. They would get into this chamber wearing scuba gear, flood the chamber, and go into the pipe to fix it.* He turned to shout his discovery to Kim. "Hey, Kim. Maybe we could—"

"Never mind me. Just go, Brendan!"

A long, triumphant howl froze his blood. He spun and looked down at Kim. She was backing toward the metal steps.

He looked to the doorway they'd entered from. At first, he could see nothing in the dark mouth of the corridor. Then he heard a wet snuffling, huffing sound. Shadows separated themselves from the greater darkness, and poking snouts sniffed tentatively into the room. Satisfied, the creatures edged into the light. The Kobolds had found them.

DOWN THE TUBES

Four of the creatures faced them. Brendan had been expecting fantastical beasts but they were more like the hyenas he'd seen at the zoo: large dogs with the colouring of pit bulls, dark brown with lighter brindle stripes. Saliva dripped from their gaping jaws as they stood panting on the concrete floor. They raised their muzzles and their nostrils flared. Brendan had never seen dogs with eyes like these, yellow as topaz and glinting with intelligence. They bared their sharp teeth, saliva drooling in thick ropes from their underslung jaws, and growled deep in their chests as they sighted Kim and Brendan.

"Far enough," Kim's voice rang out. She raised the stick above her head. "Just stay right there."

As one, they howled, a deafening sound that echoed off the concrete walls of the room, drowning out the sound of the pumps. The howl decayed into a series of sharp yaps that sounded like laughter.

"I'm warning you," Kim snarled. "One more step and you'll regret it."

Brendan gasped as the coats of the dogs began to ripple and flow. As one, the dogs reared up on their hind legs. Before Brendan's astonished eyes, the dogs transformed into bipedal humanoids. They were all dressed in furs, roughly sewn together into garments. Tall triangular ears flicked back and forth at the top of their flat skulls. All of them had long noses with wide, flat nostrils. Feral yellow eyes glared at Kim, warily watching the stick as it circled above her head.

They suddenly began laughing, a harsh barking sound that set Brendan's teeth on edge.

"Ooooo! She's got a stick!" one cackled.

"Oh, how terrifying!" another howled.

The Kobolds began to yip uncontrollably, rolling on the floor and nipping at each other.

"Laugh your heads off, if you like," Kim said evenly. "But if you come any closer, you'll regret it."

One of the Kobolds shook himself and got to his feet. "Oh, we ain't going to come any closer," he snarled. "We was just told to find you, corner you. The mistress will be here right quick to take you in hand, my darling. But you do look very tasty …" He licked his lips with a long pink tongue.

"Out of our way!" Kim demanded. "*Now!*"

The Kobolds cringed at the sound of her commanding voice. They were part dog, after all. Brendan began to think they might have a chance, but then he heard Orcadia's icy voice.

"I don't think so, Ki-Mata." Orcadia sauntered into the room, looking cold and beautiful in her midnight leathers. The Kobolds scampered to her side. She absently scratched each of them behind the ears as though they were harmless puppies rather than intelligent beings.

"Dear girl, you've led us a merry chase but it's over now. Greenleaf was a nuisance but I sent him off with his tail between his legs. Now I have you. You can't escape. Let me have him and you may go back to your clan. We don't want conflict."

"Are you joking? Conflict is all you've ever wanted," Kim spat. "He is my responsibility until I get him to sanctuary. I intend to accomplish my task."

"Foolish girl. You'll never make it to the Swan." Orcadia's tone darkened. "You are literally out of your element. Forest magic has no place here. Your tricks won't work here. Look around you." Orcadia waved a hand at the sterile room, concrete and metal lit by harsh fluorescence. Wires ran along the walls. "Not a single growing thing for you to manipulate. Your discipline is not suited to this place. That stick in your hand is exactly that—a stick. Now hand over the boy before I become impatient." She laughed again.

"You're as out of your element as I am, Orcadia. There's no sky above you, or hadn't you noticed?"

Orcadia smirked. "The Humans have been so kind as to bring the sky to me." She raised an elegant finger and a crackling bolt of blue fire arced from an electrical wire passing along the ceiling above to dance upon her fingertip. "Handy, isn't it? The game is up." She sniffed. "Or are you expecting the boy to help you?" Her icy eyes focused on Brendan, and his heart quailed. "He may have gifts but he has no idea how to use them. He's as helpless as a baby."

Kim stood poised in readiness. Brendan sensed his friend's uncertainty. He had no idea what the two Faeries were talking about, but he got the feeling that what Orcadia said was true. Kim needed help.

Maybe he had lost some basic survival instinct. Perhaps he'd finally lost his mind. Whatever the reason, he felt the same kind of anger and frustration that he'd felt when Chester held the Murderball over his head. He was tired of helplessness. He was tired of running. He was tired of being spoken about as if he weren't there. The anger overcame his fear, and he stepped out of the hatchway.

"Listen, you weird, crazy … crazy woman!" He couldn't think of anything more articulate. "I don't know who you think you are," Brendan said, growing louder and more confident as he spoke. "I don't know who you think I am. I don't care. This is over right now. I have had it with running! I'm done! So you just take your stinking, drooling … *dogs* and get out of here!"

The Kobolds howled with laughter and began their yapping mockery anew. Brendan expected Orcadia to laugh in his face. The effect on the woman was completely unexpected.

"Ugnh," Orcadia grunted, as if she'd been struck. "Ugnnnooo! How? How can he …?" Orcadia took a jerky step backward. Then another. "He's Compelled me? He has the Voice of Command? How?" She took another step back. Her arms went out and gripped the concrete doorframe as though she was made of metal and a giant magnet was pulling her back into the corridor. The Kobolds stopped their racket and stared at their mistress in whimpering confusion. Their eyes flicked back and forth between Orcadia and Brendan. They didn't know what to do.

Brendan stood with his mouth open in shock. A wave of dizziness swept over him. He felt leaden and fatigued. "What's her problem? Why is she …?" The look on Kim's face stopped him. Kim was looking at him with undisguised amazement. "What did I do?"

"You gave her a Command," Kim said, mounting the steel steps. "But she's trying to resist it."

"What's a Command? I don't understand."

Kim looked at Brendan with what might have been a grudging respect. "You're a bag of surprises. You have no training but it would appear you have some raw talent. You did the same thing with Chester on the school steps today. Remember?"

Brendan recalled the stricken look on Chester's face and the way the bully had run off without a backward glance. "Are you kidding me? *I* did *that?*" He looked at Orcadia, who was straining against some invisible force. "Me?"

"Yes, pal. You. And now we have to get out of here before she overcomes the Command." Kim pushed past him and looked into the hatch. "This will have to do."

Brendan was still focused on Orcadia as she strained to control the urge to leave. "That's insane. I did that?"

"Congratulations—now can *we* get out of here?" Kim said, her voice heavy with sarcasm. She grabbed Brendan by the arm and swung him around until he was in the hatch. "Open that up." She pointed at the inside hatch. "That's our way out."

"Are you nuts? It goes right down into the middle of the lake. We'll drown!"

Kim grabbed the front of his shirt and shouted in his face. "We don't have any choice. At least we can get in and close the door. We'll be safe for a while until I can call for help." Kim shoved him backward into the chamber. His heels caught on the frame of the hatch, and he fell with a splash in the cold water on the floor of the chamber. Kim threw her knapsack in after him, whacking Brendan in the back of the head.

He pulled himself to his feet using the wheel of the inner hatch. "There's no need to—" He didn't get to finish: the world detonated.

He was thrown against the inner hatch, his head banging painfully on the hard surface. Blue light washed over him. He shook his head to clear it, looking out into the room.

Orcadia hovered in the air. All around her the floor was scorched. The Kobolds whined and cringed away from their master, terrified by the release of energy. Kim's hair danced in the storm of static electricity but she still stood, barring the way.

"That's better," Orcadia purred as she floated toward them. "I don't know how you managed that, nephew. Very impressive! You obviously have great natural gifts. I was careless. I left myself open. It won't happen again. You have great power waiting to be unleashed. I can help you. Come to me and learn your true potential. Come along before I lose my *patience*." The last word came out in a seething hiss.

She raised her hand and gestured toward the power cable running along the wall. A blue sparking ribbon of energy leapt from the cable into her open palm as if she were leaching electricity from the grid into her body. The lights overhead flickered.

"This is your last warning, Ki-Mata," Orcadia announced. "Stand aside."

"Sorry, Sparky." Kim shook her head, bracing herself. "You're gonna have to go through me."

Orcadia shrugged. "If you insist." She cocked her arm back and hurled a ball of energy directly at Kim. Kim swung her field hockey stick and struck the ball squarely. There was a blinding flash and Kim was flung backward, sailing through space and slamming into the frame of the hatch. Her hair and clothing steamed. She lay slumped on her side, not moving.

Brendan was horrified. He looked at Kim, inert on the floor. She was still breathing but was completely unconscious. He crouched down and took hold of her shoulders.

"Kim," he shouted. "*Kim!*" She moaned but didn't awaken.

"Now it's just you and me," Orcadia said, as if reading his thoughts. The woman's eyes glowed with triumph. "Poor little boy! So confused. Don't worry. Auntie Orcadia is here to make everything right. You don't even know why this is happening, do you? Don't worry. Everything is going to be fine. Join us and be a part of the change that is coming. You could be a True Prince in the world we will create. Does that interest you?"

Brendan was silent.

"You've tasted a little of what you might become, Breandan. I will guide you, instruct you. You will be my apprentice."

Brendan looked at her face, so pale and beautiful. Part of him wanted to say yes. Maybe it wouldn't be so bad to follow her out of this dark place and do as she wished. He was tempted.

Brendan looked down at Kim, resting against him. Her face was pale and her breathing ragged. Her school uniform was scorched, charred around the edges. What would happen to her? She was annoying. She had pretended to be his friend for months while hiding her true intentions. *True. But she was trying to help me. I have to choose someone to trust. Everything has turned upside down in the last couple of days. My parents aren't really my parents. People want to capture or kill me. I'm not even Human.*

Orcadia's voice broke into his thoughts. "You look like

your father." Her voice was thoughtful. "Your mother certainly, yes. But the eyes: that's your father for sure."

Brendan looked up at her. "You know my father?"

"I should say so," she chuckled. "He was my brother." She saw Brendan's shocked expression. "I don't call myself your auntie for nothing, you know." Orcadia cracked her knuckles elaborately, like a safecracker preparing to open a safe.

"Come now, get out of the way. I'll kill her and we'll go," Orcadia said impatiently.

"No," Brendan said firmly. "I won't let you."

"I'm losing my patience." She raised her hands. They crackled with blue fire.

Brendan made his choice.

He grabbed fistfuls of Kim's blouse and hauled her into the maintenance chamber. As an afterthought, he grabbed her field hockey stick, now charred and blackened, lying on the floor.

"Where are you going, Breandan? You can't hide from your auntie Orcadia!" Orcadia drifted closer.

He ignored her. He grabbed the open hatch and pulled. The Kobolds leapt forward, transforming into hounds as they came. One of them jammed its slavering snout in the doorway as Brendan tried to push it shut. He punched it hard on its wet nose. With a yelp, the dog retreated. Brendan slammed the hatch shut with a clang.

"You can't esca—!" Orcadia's voice was cut off as the hatch closed. All sound was muffled, but Brendan thought he heard a scream of frustration, which was satisfying, but when he thought about how miserably trapped he and Kim were in the tiny metal chamber, he felt foolish. Their reprieve was short-lived: either they would be forced to come out of the hatch eventually to face Orcadia and her drooling canines or they would have to try the pipe, which was certain death by drowning. Brendan's grim musings were interrupted by a sudden clanging thud against the outer hatch.

The metal had seemed reassuringly thick when he'd slammed it shut on the canine horrors and their mad mistress. Now a massive dent appeared in the hatch.

"Are you serious?" Brendan shouted at the hatch.

He was answered by another clanging thud. The hatch bowed farther in.

"Oh, come on. I mean, I was totally ready to accept my death in here, and you won't even grant me that dignity you … stupid … *dog things!*" He kicked the hatch in frustration and immediately regretted it. His foot throbbed. "Ow. Ow. Ow. Ow."

He sat with his back against the inside hatch and rubbed his foot in his hands. He didn't think he'd broken anything but it sure hurt.

The darkness wasn't complete. A small red indicator light on the wall by the inner hatch was the only illumination. Brendan pulled Kim up so that they were sitting side by side. Thuds rang against the hatch like a bell. The hatch was holding but for how long? He put his arm around Kim and waited.

The scrape of claws raking across the outer hatch interrupted his moment's reverie. Could they cut through steel? *I guess I'll find out soon enough.* And the noise! Deafening. So deafening, in fact, that at first he didn't notice the knocking on the inner hatch.

During a lull in the Hounds' assault, he realized that he'd been hearing the tapping for quite some time, but he hadn't clued in that it was coming from the inner hatch, not the outer.

"Hello?" Brendan said softly. Then louder, "*Hello?*" Easing Kim back against the wall, he banged on the hatch and was answered by a series of ringing taps. "Is there someone out there?" The taps came rapidly.

Now what? He had no idea who was rapping on the outside of the hatch. If he opened it, would there be some horror even worse than the Kobold pack and Orcadia? Renewed clawing and thudding on the outer hatch made him decide. *It can't be any worse.*

He wrapped his hands around the wheel on the inner hatch. Grasping it in both hands, he spun it as hard as he could. The hatch opened suddenly with a rush of water. The water was making the return journey from the office towers above, so it had absorbed some heat, but it was beginning to fill the chamber up quickly. Brendan felt the field hockey stick bump against him. He grabbed it in his left hand and wrapped his right arm around Kim's chest, pulling her upright to keep her above water.

Suddenly, two Human-shaped figures burst out of the water, a man and a woman, smiling in the red light. Their skin was dark and slick, water beading on its surface.

"Hey, buddy," the man said. His soft brown eyes were smiling. "What's up?"

Brendan didn't know what to say.

"You look like you could use a hand," the woman said, raising a long-fingered hand to Kim's cheek. In the dim light, Brendan could see that both of them, male and female, sported long, bristling whiskers that stuck out a great distance below their noses.

"You're ..." Brendan stammered. "You're Faeries, too?"

The woman laughed, a gentle coughing bark. "Not exactly. We're Silkies.[65] Water Folk." She turned to study Kim's face, lolling at Brendan's shoulder. "Is she hurt?"

"I … I … I don't know. She was attacked by—"

As if mentioning her was enough to renew Orcadia's fury, the chamber was rocked by a violent impact. The water sloshed back and forth. Another blow finally knocked the outer hatch out of true. Light flared around the edge of the hatch frame.

"I have you now," Orcadia hissed. "Like fish in a barrel."

The water began to drain out of the chamber into the room beyond.

"We must go," the newcomer said urgently. She fished something out of a small pouch at her hip and stuffed it in Brendan's mouth before he could protest. "Chew this."

"Huh, gug!" Brendan reflexively bit down and his mouth was filled with a salty, musky flavour, not unpleasant but extremely odd. *Like some kind of seaweed jerky*, he thought. The man grabbed Brendan by the arm, and the woman took hold of Kim, forcing a small wad of the green paste into Kim's mouth as well.

The strangers hauled Brendan and Kim out into the tube. The current slammed into them like a freight train. The force of the water drove the air from Brendan's lungs. Terrified and disoriented, he plunged down into cold wet darkness.

---

[65] *Silkies*, or *Water Folk* as they often call themselves, are akin to Faeries. They inhabit lakes, rivers, and seas around the world. Excellent swimmers, they can breathe underwater and swim to great depths. They tend to travel in groups, as they enjoy the company of others of their kind. In ancient times, they gave rise to the legends of the mermaids, helping distressed sailors to safety. In recent years, their habitat is increasingly threatened by pollution and industrial waste. They can leave the water for short periods of time, but they prefer the depths of their watery homes, staying away from Humans or "Drylanders," as they call us.

THE WATER FOLK

Brendan thrashed and heaved in a panic. He was drowning! His lungs were filling with water! He was ... He was ...

Not drowning even though he was sucking water in and out of his lungs! Somehow, he was breathing the water! After the initial weirdness of the sensation, he found he could settle down and breathe more evenly. He laughed, sending a silvery string of bubbles out into the water.

"Relax," the man said into his ear. "Enjoy the ride."

"How am I able to do this?"

The man explained, "It's water weed. We grow it for visitors. My sister and I don't need it. Silkies can breathe water naturally."

Brendan stared.

The woman grinned, showing even, pearl-white teeth. "I am Oona, and my brother is called Miv. We heard the commotion and we came to investigate."

"Lucky for you we did," Miv said, winking a big brown eye. He twitched his whiskers in amusement. Brendan was reminded of seals he'd seen at the Metro Zoo.

"I'm a little out of my element, here," Brendan said, marvelling that he could speak underwater. His voice sounded dull and muffled in his ears. "Kim got hit with something back there and she's unconscious. She said we needed to get to a place called the Swan?"

The siblings looked at each other and nodded. "We can take you close," Oona said. "Now hold tight. We're coming to the gate."

Brendan craned his neck to look forward. A faint glow was approaching from below. Occasionally, he bumped against the sides of the pipe, but for the most part, Miv guided him unerringly, spiralling down the pipe.

The glow grew stronger, and soon Brendan could make out a chrome filter grate at the bottom of the pipe. Miv and Oona gently turned against the current and lowered themselves feet first, kicking against the flow of water, slowing their own and their charges' descent.

Oona handed Kim to Brendan. He struggled to hold her upright against the current while he waited for the Silkies to open the grate. The pause gave him a chance to examine his rescuers.

At first Brendan thought they were wearing wet suits, but when they moved their limbs, the faint light refracted off their slick hide. Their skin was covered in dense hair like a seal's fur. Their arms were long and slender, ending in fingers joined by webbed skin that allowed them to swim easily. They went barefoot, and their toes were long, splayed, and also webbed. As they worked on the hasps that sealed the grating, they anchored themselves by curling their toes around the bars. They gently waved their hands in the water.

Looking at them working, Brendan suddenly realized that they were dressed only in loose-fitting loincloths made of a silvery material that looked like fish skin. The cloths were held in place by a belt of woven weeds. With a shock, he noticed that Oona was bare-chested. He blushed and looked away. Oona saw him do it, and she twitched her whiskers playfully at his discomfort.

The grating swung open soundlessly on well-oiled hinges. The Silkies ushered Brendan into the open water, closing the grating after them. Looking more closely at the lights while the Silkies fastened the hasp, Brendan could see that they weren't lanterns, at least not electric lanterns. The bulbs of light were pods of some kind, a string of bulbous seaweed flowers that emitted a soft, greenish glow.

"Glow-weed," Miv told him, seeing his curiosity. "We grow many different types of weeds as tools and utensils. We shouldn't hang around here too long."

"The computers that monitor the system have motion sensors," Oona explained. "If they sense the grate is open, they send an alert to the controllers and they send a Drylander work crew. We don't want to draw attention to ourselves."

"Drylander?"

"That's what we call the Humans."

"Does anyone just call them Humans?" Brendan asked.

Miv screwed up his face in distaste. "How boring! Calling everything exactly what it is!"

"It's less confusing," Brendan pointed out.

Brendan looked around but there was nothing to see outside the circle of light save for murky dark water. "Where are we exactly?" Brendan asked. "I mean, are we far from the Swan?"

"Not so far," Oona said reassuringly. "But we should be going. Miv will take Ki-Mata."

Brendan looked down at Kim's inert face. Miv laid a

gentle hand on his shoulder. "Have no fear. She is safe with me."

Reluctantly, he let the Silkie man take Kim from him, and Miv tucked her under his strong arm. Driving downward with his splayed feet, he shot forward into the water, disappearing after a few strokes into the murk.

Oona reached up and tugged a glowing bulb free of the wreath of weeds and handed it to Brendan. Taking it in his hand, he was surprised at how warm it was. He smiled gratefully at Oona. She sensed how fearful a ride through the dark lake might be for one of the uninitiated. She extended her hand with a friendly nod. He took it, marvelling at the strength of her elegant fingers and their odd texture. With a kick of her feet, they were off.

He had no idea how fast they were going. Guessing speed was impossible when there were no landmarks or reference points. Brendan had seen the surface of Lake Ontario many times while driving with his parents along the expressway. The lake seemed more like an ocean sometimes with huge slate-grey waves capped in white driving against the jetties. He looked in the direction he assumed was up and saw nothing but darkness outside the perimeter of the glow-weed's reach. Strange. Something didn't seem right. He thought about it for a moment before he realized what was bothering him.

"Where are all the fish?"

Oona looked back at him with a puzzled expression. "There are no fish. They are all gone."

Brendan couldn't believe it. "There have to be some fish."

"Oh, there are some eels." Oona stopped, hanging in the dark water, her face sad and serious. "There are some that scrape the muck for food in the deepest part of the lake. But no true fish remain, nor otters nor beavers nor any creature that swims. The lake is dead. Even we do not live here. We come to see if any life has taken hold. We patrol the waters to make sure nothing goes amiss. We try to punish the worst polluters by fouling their machinery and sabotaging their factories."

"How is that possible?" Brendan asked, but even as he spoke the words, he knew. Pollution and overfishing, oil spills and chemicals dumped in the lake had sterilized the waters. How many times had he seen news reports saying that the waters were too full of disease to swim?

Oona's eyes flashed with anger. "Drylanders have destroyed the lake, annihilated every living thing, and snuffed out the very soul of the waters." Brendan could feel her anger burning in her voice. "Drylanders! We must obey the Truce but it is bitter for us."

"What is this Truce? People keep mentioning it but no one explains it." Brendan called out to her.

"An agreement, forced on our kind by the Drylanders long ago," Oona answered.

With a flick of her powerful hands and feet, Oona increased her speed through the cold murk. Their conversation was at an end. Brendan kept his mouth closed, partly because the water they ploughed through made his lips flap if he opened his mouth and partly because bits of weed and dirt would get into it. The sensation was odd, as though he were flying through the water. He held on to Oona as tightly as he could. He didn't want to be left behind in the dark watery wasteland of the lake. He thought about what Oona had said: the whole lake dead. What had the lake been like before people had come and poisoned it? He couldn't even imagine it. The lake had always been a thing of beauty to him. Now he realized he was only seeing the surface. Beneath the waves, Humans had made a desert.

Time passed with the rush of water in his ears. At last, he marvelled as the floor of the lake came up to meet them. His heart fell again as he saw the rubbish strewn on the lake floor. Tires, shopping carts, rubbish bins, plastic bags, cans, bottles, and a million other discarded objects were half-buried in the sterile muck. They skimmed along a few metres above the lakebed and a metre or two below the surface. He could make out the lights of the shoreline and the wake of a boat, one of the ferries heading out to Centre Island.[66] Daytrippers travelled out to the amusement park there and to ride bicycles on the island paths on the weekends.

Oona took them in among the frothing waves churned up by the ferry's wake, corkscrewing in the turbulent water. Her mood appeared to have lightened somewhat. Brendan got a glimpse of what she might be like when she was in a happier time. She flashed a smile at him, a glimmer of white teeth in the darkness at his side.

They swam to a stop as they approached a series of regular, dark columns furred with green algae fronds.

---

[66] The Toronto Islands were originally a peninsula connected to the mainland by a long spit of land. In 1858 a storm blew a hole in the peninsula, in effect cutting the islands off from the mainland. Humans believe the storm was natural, but it was actually part of the Ward conjured by Ariel to create The Ward's Island. But I'm getting ahead of myself ... and I wouldn't want to run into myself should the part of myself that's ahead of myself suddenly decide to stop for some reason.

Oona guided them along through the massive pillars of the ferry dock, coming into shore. The water was finally shallow enough for Brendan to stand upright. He queasily placed his feet among the garbage and stood up.

His head came up out of the water beside Oona's. He took a deep breath and immediately started to cough.

Oona slapped his back. "You have to get used to breathing air again," she said, laughing at his spluttering. "Give it a moment."

Brendan coughed heartily for a few seconds, spitting and choking until he had control of himself. Water flowed freely from his mouth and nostrils as he emptied his lungs. The bow wave from the ferry washed over him, filling his mouth with dank, oily water. He choked anew.

He was in the middle of the second coughing fit when Miv's head, hair slicked back with water, broke the surface. He raised Kim's head above the water. She was stirring but still not fully awake. "Here you go," Miv said. He pushed Kim into Brendan's arms. "We have brought you to the Island of the Ward as you have asked us to do. The Swan is here. We can do no more." Miv and Oona turned away.

"Wait!" Brendan grabbed Oona's shoulder. "Where are you going? I need you."

Oona smiled ruefully and shook her head. "No. We go this far and no farther."

"Why?" Brendan shifted Kim so he could get a better grip on her. He was starting to feel cold. "Can't you live on land?"

The Silkies laughed. "No, no! Nothing like that. We can survive on the land for a time," Miv told him. His dark eyes turned to watch the ferry easing into the concrete pier. "We choose not to. We will leave you here.

Goodbye, Breandan. Don't worry. I'm sure we'll meet again."

Miv disappeared under the waves with barely a splash to mark his passing. Oona gripped Brendan's forearm and squeezed. "Remember what you've seen." She raised a dripping arm and pointed ashore. "Follow the path. There are signs for eyes that can see. The Swan awaits you. Good luck." She winked and disappeared after her brother.

Brendan was left standing in the cold stinking water. Kim floated in his arms.

Now what? What am I supposed to do?

As he watched, he noticed a smudge of cloud roiling over the lake. Lightning flashed within the disturbance. The cloud was moving out over the lake from the centre of town. He had lost Orcadia in his trip under the lake but only for a while.

She was coming.

He jumped when the voice shouted from above him.

"I see you down there!"

THE WARD'S ISLAND

"Are you deaf, kid? I'm talkin' ta you!" the voice demanded angrily.

Brendan looked up and saw a man in a waterproof coat and hat staring down at him over the edge of the pier. "What the hell do you think you're doing?"

"U-uh," Brendan stammered. "I was just … uh … swimming!"

"Ya can't swim there! Are ya stupid or what? The water's filthy! You could get cut to pieces by the props. Get outta there."

"Okay," Brendan mumbled. He hefted Kim under the arms and dragged her up onto the bank. The mud made the footing slippery and she was a dead weight. He fell a number of times before he managed to get them up onto the grass, where he collapsed beside her to catch his breath.

The man was still looking at him, taking in Kim with a critical eye. "What's wrong with her?"

"Uh …" Brendan thought quickly. "She fell in and … she fainted from the cold. She's fine. I'll take care of her."

"Just stay right there." The man pointed at Brendan, indicating he was not to move. As he turned away, Brendan saw him take a radio from his belt. The man spoke quietly into it, and Brendan was sure he was calling the police. For a moment, Brendan toyed with the idea of just sitting, waiting for the police to come, but a look at the storm cloud boiling across the lake changed his mind. He knew that the police wouldn't be any help against the likes of Orcadia. He had to find this place, the Swan. He had to get some answers.

He became aware that he was hearing music. A band was playing at one of the halls on the island. Brendan had been here for picnics in summers past. He knew there was an amusement park on one of the islands with little kiddie rides and a couple of restaurants and bars. He'd never heard of one called the Swan. He watched as a small airplane rose up over the trees as it took off from the Island Airport. He wished he could just fly away like that plane but here he was, shivering in the grass. What was he supposed to do now?

He reviewed his situation. He knew he was on one of the Toronto Islands, the small scattering of islets that sat offshore from the city. But which one? *The Island of the Ward*, Miv called it. He slapped his forehead. Of course. Ward's Island. He'd read somewhere that it was named after a man named Ward, but now that he knew about Faeries, he wasn't sure that was really where the name came from.[67] His father had played a gig there last summer at the Ward's Island Community Centre. Again, he couldn't recall a place called the Swan, but he didn't know the island well.

---

[67] Weirdly, Ward's Island isn't even an island but a part of the larger Centre Island. Why anyone might call part of an island an island boggles the mind. People who live on islands are always a bit eccentric, and by eccentric, I mean weird.

One thing was for certain, he couldn't just sit here. Orcadia was coming, and the ferry operator was calling someone on his radio. Time was of the essence. "It's up to me, then," he said through chattering teeth.

He got to his feet and pulled Kim up with him. Carrying an unconscious girl around with him seemed like a sure way to attract attention, but he had no choice. He imagined that it looked very bad. *Hi! I found this girl and I'm taking her home! Not good*, he thought ruefully. The man in the white uniform watched him lift Kim and shuffle away. Brendan was certain the man was suspicious. He could feel the glare following them as he hauled Kim away. Brendan half-dragged, half-walked her to the convergence of paved paths that led away from the ferry pier. He had to find the Swan before the man could call someone to stop him or Orcadia caught up with them.

A street lamp cast a bright white light down over the signpost that listed possible destinations with pointed arrows.

"Centre Park. The Dock. Cycle Paths. The Marina. Ward's Island Community Centre." No sign indicating a place called the Swan. "Now what?" He was about to turn away from the sign when something weird happened.[68] The central pole of the signpost began to grow!

A further foot of green post sprouted out the top and a sign unfolded. Written in an elegantly quaint hand, the sign read THE SWAN OF LIIR THIS WAY! Brendan rubbed his eyes and stared, but it wasn't a hallucination. The sign pointed in the direction of the Community Centre,

---

[68] As if weird things weren't happening all the time.

straight up the path toward the interior of the island in the direction of the music he'd been hearing. He hefted Kim and started off down the path.

The music swelled louder the closer he got to the Community Centre. Kim groaned, her head lolling forward as he struggled with her along the paved path. People passing gave him funny looks. He soon came to the edge of an open space. Reggae music was thumping, and the voices of people having fun, shouting, and whooping drifted from the open doors of the Community Centre. Light spilled from the broad windows and the wide double doors.

A cluster of people stood smoking outside the door. Soaked in sweat and steaming in the cool air after the heat of the Community Centre, they were laughing and chatting happily, but they stopped when Brendan shuffled past with his cargo.

"She's not feeling well," he explained lamely.

"Do you need a hand?" A young man stepped toward him.

"No! No thanks," Brendan said quickly. "We're fine. Her parents are inside. No problem!" The man frowned suspiciously. Brendan hurried past and came to the entrance, where an older woman with grey hair braided at the back and wearing a tie-dyed dress that spread out around her like a tent was sitting at a small table.

"Hi there," she said, cheerily. "Five dollars each, please." Then the woman noticed Kim. "What's the matter with her?"

"She's fine. Just a little sick. Flu maybe? She's flu-ey, y'know. Flu." *Flu-ey? Nice one, dummy.*

The woman's face went from cheerful to suspicious in short order. "What's going on here?"

"Nothing, really," Brendan said. "I'm looking for a place called the Swan. The Swan of Liir? I was told it was near here?"

The wind was picking up, lashing the trees. A few drops of rain struck his face. The small hairs on the back of his neck began to rise. Orcadia was getting close, and he still didn't know where the Swan was. He didn't want to be caught out in the open when he was so close to the sanctuary Kim had insisted they find.

The smokers decided it was too cold to stay outside and shuffled into the hall. "Weird weather," one of them said as they pushed past Brendan and Kim. He didn't know how far away Orcadia was, but he felt instinctively that he didn't have time to sit around.

"There's no place named the Swan on the island." The woman stood up. "You stay right here. I'm going to call security …" She picked up her cellphone and flipped it open.

Brendan turned away from the desk and looked in the direction of the city. The cloud bank had stopped. It appeared to him that the clouds had halted in a roughly semicircular line about two hundred metres from the building. He could see rain falling and lightning igniting the interior of the clouds, but they seemed to have stopped in their advance as if they'd run up against an invisible wall.

"No need to call security, Pearl," a deep voice rumbled. "I know these two."

Brendan turned and looked up into a dark smiling face wreathed in knotted dreadlocks. The man was easily the biggest man Brendan had ever seen. No, that wasn't true. He wasn't as massive as Borje, but Borje was a Troll and

Brendan assumed that Trolls ran to the large side. This man wore a tight T-shirt with a portrait of Bob Marley stretched almost beyond recognition by his massive chest. His bare arms squirmed with muscle and were adorned with raised markings, scars in the shape of lions' heads. His shaggy, dreadlocked hair was like a ropey mane draped over his broad shoulders. Twined in the strands of hair were beads and bands of metal, gold wire, and lumps of coloured crystal that glimmered in the lights overhead. His skin was like dark chocolate. In contrast, his eyes shone as blue as sapphires. He raised his massive hands and smiled, displaying an impressive array of gold teeth.

"Where you been, man? We been waitin' for you." He clapped Brendan on the back and laughed a deep rolling laugh so merry that Brendan almost sagged with relief. Anyone with a laugh like that couldn't be bad. He stopped laughing when he took in the state of Kim. "What be the problem with the little miss?" the man said. "The flu, is it? Hey! I got just da ting!" He reached down and plucked Kim up as easily as a child and lifted her in his arms. Kim moaned softly and snuggled into the broad chest. "We get you set straight in no time!"

"You know them, Leonard?" the doorwoman asked.

"That I do, beautiful, sweet Pearl! You don't worry your pretty head no more about it!"

The woman blushed and smiled. "Oh, well. All right. Yes." She sat down and giggled like a little girl.

"Follow me, mon." Leonard turned and walked along the side of the wooden hall. Brendan followed, giddy with relief.

Leonard led him to an open space beside the Community Centre. The grass was close-cropped and lush, twinkling with dew. The lights from the building spilled about halfway across the open square of lawn. Brendan remembered from the last time he'd been here that this was a lawn-bowling club in the summer.

"Thanks for rescuing me there," Brendan said. "I was kind of at the end of my rope."

"No problem, mon," Leonard said. "I been told to watch for you. There be folks who want to meet you. Now let's get in out of the cold, eh?" Leonard looked up at the sky.

"Orcadia is right on my heels," Brendan said, pointing at the stationary clouds to the south.

"She can't come any closer, mon. Don't fret! You be safe now. The Ward protects you."

Brendan was about to ask for an explanation of when this would happen.

"You!" The voice surprised Brendan. "Stop right there."

Brendan turned and saw a man in a dark security uniform. He held a walkie-talkie in his hand and pointed at Brendan. "What's going on here?"

"Going on?" Brendan repeated, trying to think fast. "Uh … she …" He jerked his head at Kim. "She's really tired. And sick! She's tired and sick. Yeah. So I was helping her. Yeah."

Before the guard could lay a hand on Brendan, Leonard stepped between them. "Simon," Leonard said in a friendly tone. "You can let me handle this. I know the boy, and what he says is true."

Simon the security guard stopped in mid-reach. Leonard was very intimidating, a mountain of muscle. The security guard looked up into Leonard's face. He was easily a foot shorter than the black man, but he was one of those short people who wear their small stature as a badge of defiance.[69] "These kids are coming with me."

"I don't tink so, Simon," Leonard said. The tone of his voice was velvet but there was steel hidden within it.

"You can't intimidate me," Simon said, wavering.

"I'm not trying to intimidate you … yet," Leonard said. He grinned, and his golden smile was ferocious. A soft rumble sounded in his deep chest, an animal growl like a hunting cat. His eyes flashed in the lightning. In the flicker of light from the sky, Brendan thought for an instant that he saw another face interposed over Leonard's benign features. The face of a snarling lion leered hungrily down at Simon the security guard.

The smaller man took an involuntary step back. "Uh … good. Right," he stammered. "So, you know them?"

"Absolutely," Leonard assured him. Any hint of danger in the big man's face had vanished. Leonard patted Simon's shoulder and grinned hugely. "You should get back to your office. It gonna rain!"

"Good idea," Simon agreed after the slightest hesitation. He pointed his flashlight at Brendan and said, "No more swimming! It's dangerous around the docks. Remember that!"

Brendan nodded. "You got it! No swimming. Thank you!"

With a nod, Simon turned and walked away back toward the ferry dock.

---

[69] There have been many short overachievers: Alexander the Great, Napoleon Bonaparte, and Billy Joel are just three examples.

Brendan watched him go, mouth open in surprise. He turned to Leonard. "How did you do that? Is it magic?"

"Do what, mon?" Leonard asked innocently.

"I don't know," Brendan said, suddenly unsure of what he'd seen. "For a second I thought you were … never mind. Never mind. I'm just glad you worked your magic on that guy."

Leonard laughed, flashing his golden teeth. "No magic unless it be the magic of my personality." He rolled his blue eyes and laughed again.

"I'm just glad you were here." Brendan suddenly felt an urgent need to be under cover. The wind had picked up, and he felt a few more prickles of cold rain. "I have to get to a place called the Swan. I saw a sign and it said it was this way."

The blue eyes held his face. "You saw the sign, did you?"

"Yeah," Brendan went on urgently. "I don't have time to explain, but I was told I'd be safe there. Kim needs help, and there's this crazy woman after us with Kobolds and stuff."

"Kobolds, is it? That sounds bad, mon. We should waste no time. You don't need to worry. We be safe here on this part of de island. This is the Ward's Island, after all." Leonard chuckled deep in his chest. Leonard cradled Kim in his massive arms. "Follow me."

As he strode around the side of the building, the rain began to pelt down. Brendan trotted at his heels, glancing back warily at the dark clouds.

"Is it far?" Brendan asked.

"It's impossibly far if you don't know where to look. You'd never get there in a million years, though you search and search." The big man laughed, then suddenly stopped. "Or it could be no farther away than your fingertips."

They made their way around the back of the building where Leonard stopped, facing a blank wall of white boards that were peeling and chipped. "We're here!"

Brendan looked around in confusion. "What? Where? Where are we?"

"The Swan of Liir," Leonard explained. "De finest Faerie establishment in the West."

"Is there a trap door or something? A tunnel?" Brendan asked. He reached out and tapped his foot on the wall. Flakes of paint were dislodged from the planks but otherwise it seemed like a solid wall.

"As I say before," Leonard said, his voice full of mirth, "never in a million years will you find it though you search and you search. There is a trick and a pattern." He turned and faced the wall. In a clear voice he cried, "I could use a drink!" Then he took one step sideways to his left, turned counter-clockwise once, twice, three times. Then he reached out one giant dark hand, extended a finger, and tapped the wall.

For an instant nothing happened. Then a bright musical tone rang out, suffusing Brendan's being with a warm, welcoming, musical note. Leonard reached out and tapped the weathered surface of the wall. Instantly, the planks began to fold into tiny squares, revealing an empty space behind the wall that expanded and expanded like a jigsaw puzzle falling to bits. At last there was a doorway in the wall where none had been before. Light and warmth flooded out of the opening. Brendan heard the sound of voices and music.

Leonard turned to him and winked. "Never in a million years." Leonard chuckled at Brendan's rapt expression. "Shall we?"

Leonard held out his hand, and a shining golden handle sprouted out of the wood under his grasp. He tugged on the handle and the door swung open. Heat, noise, and honey-coloured firelight washed over him. Leonard stood aside and gestured for Brendan to enter.

Brendan took a deep breath and stepped across the threshold.

THE SWAN

The first thing that struck Brendan was the overwhelming noise. A palpable wave of sound assaulted him, a mixture of music, shouted conversation, braying laughter, and the drone of television commentary.

The next thing that registered was the smell: a combination of flowers, heavy spice, and wood smoke. The mixture was unlike anything he'd ever smelled. The closest comparison would have been what his house smelled like on Christmas Eve when the fresh scent of pine mixed with the spicy cinnamon and cloves his mother used when she made mulled wine. Add to that the warm earthy smell of gingerbread, and you were getting close.

His eyes adjusted last. After the darkness outside, the brightness of the pub was blinding. Yes, pub, for indeed, the Swan seemed to be a pub.

The decor was typical of the pubs he had been in on his family trip to Ireland a couple of summers ago. Framed ads for Guinness stout were displayed on the walls. The ceiling maze of rafters were hung with a bewildering array of ornaments, dried flowers, glowing crystals, candelabra, and strange antique tools whose purpose Brendan could only guess at. The room before him was jammed with small round wooden tables ringed with little three-legged stools, and these tables were in turn jammed with people enjoying a variety of beverages. Around the walls, large booths were also crammed with patrons. A massive stone fireplace dominated the wall to his left, a fire burning merrily. Little insects chased each other in and out of the flames, catching the updraft of warm air and tumbling out into the room only to dart in again. Brendan's mouth dropped open when he realized the creatures weren't insects: they were Lesser Faeries! *Diminutives*, he corrected himself. They darted in and out of the flames like moths, chattering and laughing.

Brendan tore his eyes away from the fire. A wooden stairway led up into the smoky rafters on the right. On the far wall, a long mahogany bar glowed under the light of torches jammed into sconces on the wall. The rustic atmosphere was slightly marred by the TVs hanging over the bar and the giant flat screen in the centre of the wall to his left. He looked closer and saw that the frames of the TVs were all ornately carved out of wood. The screens flickered with sporting events, news broadcasts, and infomercials largely ignored by the patrons. He was about to turn away from the screens when a familiar face flashed on the news channel.

Chester Dallaire's face sneered from the screen. The picture was taken from a class photo. A caption underneath the photo read LOCAL BOY MISSING! HAVE YOU SEEN HIM?

Brendan groaned, "Oh, no! What have I done to Chester?" A sudden burst of music distracted him from his misery.

A small band occupied a booth in the corner. Crammed elbow to elbow into the tiny space, they managed to strike up a lilting reel. There was a fiddler, a man playing a harp, and another beating on a flat drum with a two-headed stick he held in the three middle fingers of his left hand. They were in mid-song, banging out a lively reel. The people at the surrounding tables and booths were clapping along, and one person was on top of a table doing a complicated dance that seemed to involve only his feet. The clapping and shouts of encouragement were almost drowned out by a DJ standing in the opposite corner of the room at a table on a raised platform. She was mixing heavy beats and tribal rhythms that wouldn't have been out of place in any of the clubs downtown. Her ears and nose were pierced with studs, and her hair stood up on end as if it were frightened of her scalp. Some people had cleared away a few tables, and they were gyrating to that music. The two musical sources and styles were totally at odds, but as Brendan listened, they seemed to resolve into a complementary counterpoint that was a melding of the old and the new. He wished his father could hear this music. He would love the beautiful chaos.

The most startling thing about the Swan was the clientele. Everyone was a Faerie. Every table was taken up by Faeries of every description, crammed into tables, leaning at the bar, staring up at the TV, where a hockey game was underway. The air was full of tiny Faeries, flitting in swarms through clouds of wood smoke, sitting on the rafters, their wings drawn up against their tiny backs.

Brendan shook his head in wonder. He thought the scene couldn't get any weirder and then … a cellphone rang. A Faerie with hair an unnatural shade of green fumbled in her handbag while everyone pointed at her and jeered.

The bartender shouted, "No cellphones in here! House rule!" And rang a bell. The crowd began chanting and pounding on the tables.

"No cells! No cells! No tweet, twitting, bleeting bells. No cells! No cells! Curse them to the seven hells!"

"One more time, Edie, and you owe us all a round!"

"Turn it off!"

"Sorry!" She pulled out a slim piece of wood that was glowing and pulsing. She keyed the power off. When she was done, she held it up to jeering applause.

Brendan looked around at these faces and realized they weren't so completely removed from his world. He might have a kinship with these people. Then Leonard's deep voice bellowed, cutting off all conversation and bringing the music to a sudden halt.

"People, he is here! The Misplaced Prince has arrived!"

There was a sudden hush. After the initial din, the silence was deafening. All eyes shifted to Brendan as he stood just inside the door of the pub. He didn't know how to react. He shifted from foot to foot, tried to lean Kim's stick against the wall but only managed to drop it with a clatter to the polished hardwood floor. He swallowed hard and finally raised his hand and waved lamely to the throng. "Hey?"

A rich, jovial voice boomed out, "Sure it is himself, the Prince of Neither Here Nor There! In the flesh!"

A great barrel-chested man dressed in a three-piece suit about two sizes too small for him burst through the crowd, his arms spread wide in greeting. His face was florid, cheeks red, and eyes bright blue. "There he is and isn't he just a picture."

Brendan was lifted off his feet and crushed in an embrace that smelled of whisky, pine, and some muskier scent he couldn't identify. When Brendan thought his ribs would finally break, the man released him from the bear hug. The man's grimy, calloused hands clasped Brendan's upper arms as the watery blue eyes looked him up and down.

"And isn't he just a fine figure of a man, I ask you? Could he be any better?"

"Sir ..." Brendan started to speak but the man cut him off.

"Sir! Did you hear it? 'Sir' he calls me? Me being his very own uncle? Sir indeed!" The man laughed and smacked Brendan so hard on the shoulder that he staggered against the wall.

Brendan recovered his balance and looked at the man. "You ... you're my uncle?"

"I surely am! On your mother's side. Say hello to your uncle Og."

Brendan didn't know what to say. He studied the man's face. Could there be any resemblance? The eyes maybe? The shape of the face? "I don't know what to say. This has all been a bit crazy."

Og bent over double laughing at that. "Crazy? Yes indeed, it is crazy! Mad! Mad as a bag of otters! Ah you're one of us, through and through, me old son! Come now! You'll have a drink!" He began hauling Brendan by the arm toward the bar. Brendan didn't resist. He couldn't have if he wanted to. Uncle Og's grip was powerful and his calloused fingers were begrimed with oil. "Whisky fer the lad!"

Finally understanding Og's intention, Brendan dug in his heels and resisted. "Thanks. No! I don't drink. I'm only fourteen!"

Og found this hilarious as well. "He's fourteen! Fourteen, he says." Tears streamed down the man's red cheeks as he laughed again. "Only fourteen and such a terror ye've wrought up and down the city entire. We've been watchin' yer progress on the local news!" Og beamed down at Brendan.

"On the news? They saw the chase on the news?" he breathed.

"Och, they didn't know what was happening, sure enough. They put it down to hooligans and freak weather systems! They always explain us away. Makes 'em feel more comfortable if there's a logical explanation for the shenanigans we get up to, bless 'em. Are ye sure you won't have a drink?"

"I was told that if I came here I'd get some answers." Brendan suddenly stopped and gasped, "Kim! She's been injured!" He turned to look for her but she and Leonard were gone.

"Do not worry. She is being seen to as we speak," Og assured him. "She's tough as nails, our Ki-Mata. She'll join us in short order. Peace!" He laid a hand on Brendan's shoulder again and guided him toward the booth, and he let himself be led. "It's answers ye want, is it! Ho! Ho! A curious lad, just like yer uncle Og! Answers indeed!"

"The boy's right." A mellow voice cut through Og's wheezing mirth. "He has a right to an explanation."

The owner of the voice was a tall and austere man dressed in a simple yet expensive-looking grey suit of a slightly old-fashioned cut. His hands were long and white and his face was as pale as snow. His features were almost feminine, yet he radiated subtle strength, authority, and power. Looking into the pale grey eyes, Brendan felt from him an overwhelming calm but also a great world-weariness, as if this being had seen too much to ever be truly happy.

"Breandan," the newcomer said soothingly, "come and sit. Take your rest. It is time to tell tales. Our folk"—he paused and smiled at Brendan—"your folk love tales. You have much to learn and little time so let us not waste another moment."

"Of course, of course, we should get down to business," Og agreed.

Rain lashed the windows of the pub and brought with it a renewed sense of urgency to Brendan. "Orcadia is on her way. She's trying to kill me. We've got to get out of here."

The man rested a hand on Brendan's shoulder, and immediately Brendan was relaxed and at peace. "Fear not. This is the Ward's Island. The Ward here is strong, woven by the goodwill and combined Art of all who come here." He waved a hand to take in the walls of the place. "According to our Law, no Fair Folk may strike at each other within the precinct of the Ward. Orcadia may not risk hurting you because of the dire consequences. She is powerful, certainly, but even she would not try her luck against the assembled will of all those here. Now come. You must be hungry and tired. You will eat and drink while I tell you what you need to know about your history and your situation. Then you must rest for there is much to do." He extended an elegant hand toward the corner of the room where a booth was hastily being cleared for them.

As he threaded his way through the tables toward the booth, the Faeries he passed reached out to gently pat him on the back or shake his hand. Some simply stared at him like he was a weird, rare animal—a unicorn or a Sasquatch. He found the attention disconcerting. Brendan didn't respond well to public scrutiny. He prayed that he wouldn't trip over his own feet and fall on his face. He managed to cross the room without bumping more than a couple of tables and sloshing a few beverages.

With relief, he slid into the wooden bench, and the man sat down opposite him. Og pushed in beside Brendan. A woman appeared beside the table as if by magic. Brendan had not seen her arrive … she was just suddenly … there. She was wiry and lean with the yellow eyes of a wolf. Fixing Brendan with an intense, appraising stare, she grinned, showing gleaming white teeth. "Food and drink, if you will, Saskia," the man said gently. Saskia nodded once and disappeared. Watching carefully this time, Brendan thought he saw a blur of movement, almost too fast for him to see. Saskia reappeared behind the bar on the far side of the room a second later. Sensing his stare, she cocked her head and winked a yellow eye at him. Brendan gulped and turned away.

"First, I should introduce myself. I am called Ariel. Of all the Fair Folk here, I suppose you would call me the most senior."[70]

"So you're the boss?" Brendan asked. Og giggled at that, which Brendan found a little annoying.

"No. We really have no hierarchy, per se. We operate in a more or less democratic fashion. I am a spokesperson by consent of the group." He waved a hand to indicate the entire room. Brendan was suddenly aware of how quiet the pub had become. The TV screens still swirled with images but no one paid them any attention. All eyes were on him. The whole room seemed to hold its breath.

---

[70] Ariel is an ancient Faerie who has made many appearances throughout history. According to legend, he was the inspiration for the character of the same name in Shakespeare's *The Tempest*.

"Don't let them make you nervous, Breandan. They rarely get to see history in the making. You're a bit of a legend, you see."

"A legend? Are you kidding me?"

Ariel laughed softly. "I promise, I will never kid you. I'm too old for that." A smile flitted across Ariel's face as he leaned back in his seat. "I think the best thing to do is let you ask whatever questions you want to ask. I will try to give you answers as best I can. We can move on from there."

Brendan found himself at a loss. Where to start? There was so much he didn't understand. Although he was curious about his own situation, he decided to start at the beginning. "Where do Faeries come from?"

"Same place Humans come from." Og laughed raucously and punched Brendan's shoulder.

"Og," Ariel said sharply. "He means, what are the origins of the Fair Folk."

"I know. I know." Og subsided with a sheepish grin. "Just havin' a laugh."

Ariel steepled his long fingers and stared up into the rafters. "My! You have to begin with the most difficult question of all. I will do my best." He paused for a moment, his eyes closed as he decided how to begin. The audience seemed to gather in around them, and the musicians, responding to the deepening mood, began to play softly.

At last, Ariel began to speak.

TWO TRIBES

"There is a legend among our people about our origins. Whether it is true or not, no one knows. The story goes that at the beginning of the world, the Mother created the world in all its beauty. The stars were so thick in the heavens that the Mother could run her fingers through them, stirring them in the sky like leaves on the surface of the black lake of the cosmos. She gathered great handfuls of stars and formed Sun and Moon, her first children. Sun and Moon were brother and sister, each beautiful in their own way and well loved by their Mother. They were the joy of her heart. They shared the sky and knew peace.

"Next, she gathered more stars and pressed them into a vast ball and this was the Earth. On its surface she sprinkled soil and seed, rain and snow, and then she breathed upon it and so filled it with the potential for life. The Sun and Moon shared the sky and cast down their light upon the Earth and their Mother as she walked. Where her feet fell upon the ground, seeds sprouted and grew. Forests and fields of flowers sprang to life, reaching for the light with eager leaves. She looked upon what she had made and it pleased her heart.

"She roamed the Earth for an age, taking pleasure in what she had wrought, but at last, she became dissatisfied. She longed for someone to share this world with. So she took two fistfuls of sand from the shore of the ocean and she dipped them in the salt sea. Taking great care, she formed the wet sand into two figures, one with her left hand and one with her right.

"With her right hand she formed the first Human, proud and tall. With her left hand, in a mirror image of the Human, she formed the first of the Fair Folk. They were alike, yet different as siblings are wont to be. Yet they both pleased her greatly.

"The Sun and the Moon looked down on what she had done, and they were jealous of the attention she gave her new children. They didn't like to see their Mother doting over them.

"They were also jealous of each other. They argued over who was most important, who was most powerful, and who held the larger place in their Mother's heart.

"They became bitter toward each other and that bitterness led them to try to win the hearts of their Mother's new creations. Brother Sun whispered in the ear of the Human, filling him with pride and arrogance. He encouraged the Human to mistrust the Fair Folk. He taught him how to dig in the Earth and find metals to make tools to cut the Earth and subdue her. This is why we call Humans the People of Metal.

"Sister Moon likewise led the child of the Mother's left hand away and taught him that he was most favoured. She showed him hidden mysteries: the rhythm and flow of the Earth, the movements of the stars, the secrets of growing things, and the hidden heartbeat of the universe. So the children of the left hand were more in tune with the natural world, and their empathy gave them long spans of years.

"The other wedge driven between the two peoples was the fact that though the Fair Folk were long of life, they rarely produced offspring. The Humans were very fertile and soon they spread across the green face of the Earth, digging, cutting, and shaping the world to fit their wishes.

"The children of the left hand and the right hand began to dislike each other. Brother Sun and Sister Moon poured malice and bile into the ears of the Humans and the Fair Folk. Soon the two peoples took up weapons, and a war was fought with dire losses on each side.

"When the Mother returned from a journey through the stars, she was dismayed at the rift between them, their quarrelling and hostility. Everywhere was devastation and suffering. She was furious with her children, Sun and Moon, for bringing disharmony to her creation. So she separated the night from the day and banished the Sun and the Moon to the far reaches of cold space, imprisoning them in an endless cycle that held them always apart except for rare times when the Sun and the Moon share the sky. Even then, they try to blot each other out whenever the opportunity arises, for they cannot put aside their jealousies, each blaming the other for their imprisonment."

Ariel smiled sadly. "And so, the Mother made the Humans and the Faeries lay down their weapons and make a Truce. They would share the Earth and respect each other. Having established the peace, the Mother then went away again beyond the stars, for she had other worlds to tend. Time passed. The Humans dug and cut and burned and bred generation after generation. The Faeries kept themselves apart and the peace held. After thousands of years, the Humans forgot all about the Truce, and Faeries to them became only stories, passed down from generation to generation until the truth was lost.

"But we Faeries are not so fertile. The generations pass but slowly to us. We live long and our memories do not fade. Now we keep the Truce because our numbers are small. Our only hope for survival is to live quietly between the seams of the Human world. And so we endure."

The tall man smiled at Brendan and asked, "Does that answer your question? I've had to skim through the details, and we Faeries love details, but that is our story ... and your story, too."

Brendan blinked. He looked down at the table and found a platter of cheese, bread, and slices of ham. A bowl of soup steamed at his elbow. Beside the bowl was a clay tankard brimming with foaming liquid. He had been so engrossed in Ariel's story that he hadn't noticed Saskia returning with the food. He started when he looked up to find her smiling her fierce smile at him. "Thanks." She nodded and blurred away again.

He was suddenly ravenous. Needing some time to absorb what Ariel had told him and to formulate his next question, he picked up a slice of ham and draped it over the dark bread. After adding a lump of cheese, he took a bite. The food was simple but perfectly satisfying. He chewed thoughtfully, savouring the flavour and swallowing at last.

"So, Humans don't really know there are Faeries?"

"For the most part, no," Ariel said. "Only those we allow to see us for what we are know of our existence, and those are rare indeed. They must be trusted with our great secret, and so we only reveal ourselves sparingly. Some suspect our existence but cannot confirm it because we live among them and hide ourselves with glamours to keep our existence secret."

"Glamours?" That word again.

"Manipulations of the Earth's energy ... you might call it magic."

Brendan recalled all the strange experiences he'd had over the last couple of days. He thought about his ability to use the birds for his defence and what Kim had said about him Compelling Orcadia. What other explanation was there besides magic? "What are the Arts?"

"Ah," Ariel laughed and shook his head. "Another question that is impossible to answer without an age of time. Some say I am the wisest of my kind, but even so, I would not be able to give you an answer you might understand."

"Why not?"

Og piped up, "Explain the wind! Explain the sea! Explain the stars in the sky. The Humans would try and break them down and tell you 'The sea is a body of water' or 'The stars are balls of gas' or some such. True enough but it doesn't explain the power of the sea, the way the stars affect our souls. Faeries don't label these things. We try to experience them on a deeper level and manipulate the energy they represent."

Ariel nodded in agreement, adding, "A crude explanation but accurate."

"I'm nothing if not crude." Og grinned and raised his glass of amber whisky. "And I am sometimes accurate." He knocked back the whisky in one gulp and wiped his mouth on his sleeve.

"Og is too humble," Ariel said softly. "He is one of the greatest Artificers our people have ever produced. That requires steady hands and a keen mind."

Brendan looked sidelong at his professed uncle. "An Artificer? Kim mentioned them. What is an Artificer?"

"One of the disciplines of the Art. Artificers craft objects. In the past, Faeries like Og would forge magical weapons, rings of power, armour of invulnerability. Nowadays, our needs are different."

"We Faeries don't like the metal, see. It can hurt us," Og said, waving for another whisky. "In strong enough concentrations it can kill us. In alloys, it can make us sick or give us allergic reactions based on the amount of iron in it. So I and people with my Talent, we make items for our folk to use out of proper materials. Lately, the Fair Folk have been fascinated by Human technology like … those televisions. Artificers find a way to make them work without being harmful to us."

"So you made Kim's cellphone?"

"Och, not me. I prefer more exciting items." Og's eyes lit up. "Engines! That's what I love!"

Brendan said, "Like Kim's scooter?"

"Aye! That's one of mine." Og beamed. "She's my pride and joy."

Brendan gulped. He would rather not be around when Kim revealed what had happened to the scooter and Brendan's part in it.

He changed the subject. "But how could *I* be a Faerie? I mean, how could I have been a Faerie all this time and not known it?"

Ariel nodded. "An excellent question. Until recently, you had a scar upon your flesh. Am I right? A curiously shaped scar."

"Yeah," Brendan admitted. "But it's gone now."

"That scar was a Ward, a Glamour of Protection. There

are many kinds of Wards like the one that hides this place from the eyes of the People of Metal." He swept a hand about him, taking in the whole pub. "The Ward allows the Swan to exist right under their noses without them suspecting a thing. Once upon a time, the Ward covered all the Islands, but over time, we've pulled it back to this little corner. It's all we really need.[71] Woven by many powerful people of our kind, it is maintained by the desires of all who wish to remain hidden. All of us who choose to live in the Human world must bear Wards that hide our true nature and make us appear outwardly as Humans. The Ward that hid your nature from those around you and yourself was the work of one very powerful Faerie of the Skyclan. He was your father, Briach Morn."

The name sent a shiver through Brendan. *My father? My real father?* Up until last night, he had believed his father was the man he'd grown up with, eaten dinner with, played Monopoly with on rainy afternoons. Now everything had changed. Had it only been a day since his parents had revealed the truth to him in the kitchen?

"I can take it from here." The voice was cool and feminine, and Brendan recognized it immediately from his dream the night before.

"You!" Brendan gasped.

Deirdre D'Anaan stepped out of the shadows, pulling a silken shawl from her face. She wore a shimmering cloak

---

[71] Indeed, as explained earlier, Ward's Island is not an island at all but only a part of Centre Island. This is not the only weird thing about the Toronto Islands. The Centre Island Amusement Park is not even on Centre Island but on Middle Island. Again, Islanders are odd people.

that was beaded with rain. She shook out her hair and smiled at Brendan as she stepped toward the table. The crowd parted for her.

"Oi, good to see you, my dear sister," Og bellowed, sliding over and scrunching Brendan into the bench. "You look ravishing as ever." Og patted the bench beside him in invitation.

Deirdre ignored Og. She stood by the table, looking down on Brendan. Her eyes were as powerful as he remembered from the concert the night before, burning with cold grey fire as she held his gaze. Her tiny winged servant, Fith, sat on her shoulder. The Faerie licked raindrops from her hair with its small black tongue.

"I see you made it unscathed despite Orcadia's best efforts," Deirdre said with a welcoming smile. "Well done."

"No thanks to you," Brendan said, trying his best to sound angry, but in the shadow of her beauty, he was finding it difficult. "These people tell me you stripped my only protection away. You could have gotten me killed."

Deirdre opened her mouth to retort but she was cut off by Kim's voice.

"Well, look who's here!" Kim snarled, appearing suddenly at the top of the wooden stairs. She descended, her field hockey stick over her shoulder and a steaming mug in her hand. "Deirdre D'Anaan, who can't keep her nose in her own business."

Brendan was so relieved to see Kim, he wanted to jump up and hug her but Og's beery bulk prevented it. Instead he beamed a smile at her. She sneered playfully in return and sat down beside Ariel. She still didn't look completely well but at least she was sneering again.

Deirdre scowled. "It is my business. He's my nephew."

Kim laughed harshly. "What a kind auntie you are, too. It's a wonderful way to show your affection, removing the only protection he has and leaving him at the mercy of that psycho out there." Kim jerked a thumb at the window where rain pelted the glass and lightning flashed. "What a sweet coming-of-age present. What will you give him for his birthday? A rabid wolverine? One of the Metal Folk's hand grenades?"

"What? I'm your nephew?" There was too much information for Brendan's reeling mind to process. "You're my aunt?"

"And she's me sister and Bob's-your-uncle! Hee-hee-hee! I need a drink!" Og pushed himself to his feet. "Anyone need anything?" Everyone ignored him so he staggered off to the bar.

"I can't believe it," Brendan said, his elbows on the table and his head in his hands.

Deirdre ignored Brendan and sneered at Kim. "Better he knows who he is so he can make choices. We need to guide him!"

"Guide him?" Kim sneered back. "Or control him?"

Ariel raised his hands in a conciliatory gesture. "Peace. What is done is done. We must work together now. Put aside what cannot be changed and let us discuss how to move forward."

"He must be initiated immediately," Deirdre said. "It's the only way he will be safe."

"Agreed," Kim grunted. "As soon as possible."

Brendan slammed his hand on the table. "Hey! Quit talking about me like I'm not here! I want to know what's going on! What initiation? Start talking or I'm going to leave and go back to my home, and you people can blow it out your … *ear!*" He would have said something harsher but his mum hated when he cursed.

Ariel, Kim, and Deirdre stared at him. Finally, Ariel indicated that Deirdre should sit. "You are the Weaver, Deirdre. You should tell the tale."

Deirdre nodded and took a seat. Saskia returned at that moment with a cup of steaming dark liquid, which Deirdre accepted. After taking a sip, she swallowed and lowered her head for a moment. Her hair hung like a curtain around her face. When she raised her grey eyes again, they were full of tears.

"I had a sister. Bir-Gidha was her name and she was fair. To look upon her was to see a spring day walking. She was a joy to behold and gentle of heart. She thought the best of all she met and brought such joy to my heart." Brendan found himself being lulled by her words. Deirdre's voice took on the cadence that he had heard at the concert. He had to try hard to hang on to his anger.

"She had many suitors, for she was beautiful and fair. She could have chosen anyone to be her mate, but as fate would have it, she fell in love with an Ancient One whose heart was dark and troubled. She was a Healer, and she was gifted in those arts so perhaps she thought she might heal the darkness in his heart. His name was Briach Morn.

"He was a Prince of the Elder Times, a Lord of the Skyclan who believed that this world had been stolen from us by the People of Metal. He wanted to shatter the Truce and take back this Earth for the Faerie Folk. He was powerful in his Art, and many followed him. Together with his sister, Orcadia, he led the dark faction that would see the war renewed between the Humans and the Fair Folk."

At the mention of Orcadia, Brendan shivered. "Hold it," he interrupted, drawing a dark glare from Deirdre. He tried to ignore her. "You lost me. An Ancient One? Elder Times? Skyclan?"

Ariel spoke. "The Elder Times are what we call the age before the Truce, when we held the upper hand in the world. Briach Morn was old indeed and very powerful. In those days, he was worshipped by the People of Metal as a god of War and Destruction. We were often seen as such by ignorant Humans who didn't know us. They set us up as gods." Ariel smiled sadly. "You might even know one of my names from those times. I was called Apollo."

Brendan had learned about the gods of Greek mythology from his father, who had read him stories of their deeds. Was he actually looking at Apollo, god of the sun? He could hardly believe it. "So this Orcadia is his sister?"

"Yes. And your aunt."

Deirdre continued her tale. "Their love was fated. They were wed despite the wishes of both their clans. All the Oracles foretold doom for them and much unhappiness, but such was the depth and the power of their love that they chose to ignore the future. My sister seemed to soothe his raging spirit. It was her dream that one day Human and Faerie might live together in harmony, as in the time before the rift between our peoples. Briach Morn listened to her, and we had hope that he might abandon his desire to bring war upon the Human world. Then word came that she was with child.

"We rejoiced at the news," Deirdre said, her voice warming with remembered joy. "You see, Breandan, among our kind, children are a rare blessing. We looked upon the news as a sign that the Oracles might be wrong. A child was certainly a sign of great happiness to come. But we were wrong.

"My sister took to her birthing bed and her labour was long. In the end, her heart failed her. She lived only long enough to see your tiny face and she named you. Then she crossed over. A great light went out of the world."

Brendan felt his eyes prickle with tears. There was a lump in his throat. He longed to see her, his mother. He would never know her. He sensed the sadness of all in the room, watching and listening in the smoky darkness. The crackle of the fire was the only sound. At last, he said, "What about my father? Where is he?"

"Ah," Deirdre breathed. "There is the strand that completes the tapestry. Briach Morn was overwhelmed with grief. His heart was utterly broken. Despite efforts to stop him, he took you from your mother's deathbed, and he worked a powerful Ward upon you. Secretly, he left you among the Humans and then he disappeared. Some say he destroyed himself in his grief. Some say he went off in search of deep magic into the Other Lands that border on our world, that would allow him to destroy the Humans once and for all."

"So he might still be alive?" Brendan asked.

"Those who travel in the Other Lands forget themselves. They rarely return. If he is alive in those dire places, he will not be coming back."

Brendan couldn't help feeling sad. Both of his birth parents were gone. He'd never known them but he still felt the loss somehow.

"Whatever the case may be," Deirdre said, oblivious to his mood, "he left you hidden in the care of Humans, disguised as one of them. No one understands why he did what he did. He loathed Humans, so why would he hide you among them? But he was grieving and who knows the state of his mind.

"No one knew where you were or even what you might look like. We searched for long years. Briach's Ward was extremely well wrought but, at last, we found you. Ki-Mata was sent to observe and subtly watch over you ..."

"And you had to stick your big nose in and blow it," Kim said suddenly. "Thanks for that!"

Deirdre's eyes flashed with anger. "I was doing what I thought was right."

"What about what we all *agreed* was right, you arrogant cow?"

Deirdre's hands gripped the table in fury. Kim's fingers curled around the handle of her stick. They glared at each other across the flat surface, and the crowd held its collective breath. Suddenly Og staggered over, jarring the tabletop and upsetting all the drinks. Instantly, the dark atmosphere was expelled as Kim and Deirdre tried to avoid getting ale and mulled wine on their laps.

"Sorry," Og slurred, a wounded and contrite expression on his ruddy face. "There is no greater tragedy than a spilled drink. It breaks the heart." He raised his own tankard, brimming with foamy beer, and said cheerily, "Still, my pint was saved. Be grateful for small mercies." Unseen by the women, Og winked at Brendan and staggered away, leaving Brendan with the impression that the spillage had not been entirely an accident. He decided to take the opportunity to speak.

"Listen," he said. "This is all really interesting and everything, but I really just want to go back to my parents.

I don't want anything to do with any trouble. I just want to be a normal kid, go to school, and hang out with my friends, you know? So thanks for the story but I'm going home. Put the Ward back on me and make it stick this time."

His speech was greeted by uncomfortable silence. He looked at Kim, but she was inordinately concerned with mopping up beer. Deirdre was silent too. She looked at him sadly.

Ariel broke the silence. "I'm afraid that isn't possible, Breandan."

"Why not?"

"Orcadia and others like her know where you are now. They would never leave you in peace. They see you as the rebirth of their hero, Briach Morn. They will either turn you to their purposes or kill you."

"That's crazy!" Brendan cried. "Kill me? Turn me? I didn't even know this guy Morn existed until today!"

"It doesn't matter to them," Kim interjected. "Your family would be in danger from them, too. Your Human family, I mean. A Ward of the type Morn wrought cannot be renewed. We have not the Art. Your Human parents will see that you have changed. You are Faerie now, and it will become more and more obvious that you are not like them. Certainly, you could disguise yourself using glamours but sooner or later, they would learn of your true nature."

Ariel nodded agreement. "The best choice you have is to join your true people. Only we can protect you and keep you safe."

Brendan sat in stunned silence. How was this possible? Only two days ago, everything was fine. He was a nerd in

Nerd School with an annoying sister and his kooky parents and everything was completely normal. He hadn't realized how happy he'd been. He felt an overwhelming sadness numb his soul. He wanted to cry, partly from sadness and partly from frustration. He hadn't asked for any of this. What right did they have to completely destroy his life?

"Never mind them," Deirdre said lightly. "I promise you, you won't miss them once you get to know your true family. You will come and live with me. I'll teach you my Art. We'll have such a good time together."

Her tone was so glib and heartless that it made Brendan furious. He felt a rage swell in his chest. He glared at Deirdre and pointed a finger, quivering with emotion, saying in a harsh voice he hardly recognized, "You. Shut. Up."

Deirdre D'Anaan's face went rigid. She tried to open her mouth, but it was as though her lips were glued shut. Her eyes went wide. Her face flushed with fury. Fith, sitting on her shoulder, mirrored her distress and anger. He opened his mouth and keened loudly.

A QUEST

"Did I do that?" Brendan whispered in astonishment.

The crowd erupted in astonished chatter. Voices shouted out, "He Compelled her! The Great Deirdre D'Anaan."

"How is it possible?"

"He hasn't been initiated. How could he place a Compulsion on her?"

Ariel seemed as amazed as the rest. "It would appear that you have your father's temper as well as his power. You have Compelled her to silence."

Kim crowed with laughter. "Oh, that is just beautiful! I never thought I'd see the day. The Great Deirdre D'Anaan unable to say a word. So sweet!"

Deirdre glared at Kim.

"I did that?"

"Yes, Breandan," Ariel said sternly. "And it is no small thing. You must understand that you have great power. You must be careful."

"I didn't mean to do it," Brendan cried. "I was … I dunno. I was angry."

Kim laughed again. "Honestly? I've wanted her to shut up for about a hundred years or so." Deirdre greeted Kim's comment with a hiss through gritted teeth that was echoed by a hiss from Fith. Kim ignored Deirdre and went on.

"He's been doing this all day. He sent a Human packing at the school this morning, and he almost did the same with Orcadia in the Undertown."

Ariel's eyebrows went up in mild surprise. Brendan got the impression that little ever surprised the thin Faerie. "You are manifesting many abilities. This is fascinating and dangerous. Obviously, your blood is strong."

"He also exhibited control over a flock of sparrows. It was quite amazing," Kim added. "He's full of surprises, is our Breandan."

"Most of us exhibit one Gift, Breandan," Ariel explained. "You are displaying a most amazing variety. Compulsion and Communion with Beasts are two very different disciplines of the Art. There are others. Leonard is a shape-shifter. Saskia is a Warp Warrior.[72] Perhaps you will exhibit more talents?"

Everyone looked at him appraisingly. Even Deirdre ceased her attempts at speech. Blushing, he said, "I just want to go back to my family and my life."

Deirdre and Ariel exchanged a look. Kim just studied the tabletop, tracing the grain of the wood with her fingertip.

Og had been hovering nearby. "I don't think ye've understood what ye've heard, me lad. What's learnt can't

---

[72] Warp Warriors are a bizarre phenomenon. They are formidable with weapons and have the added bonus of being able to teleport minute distances. These tiny spatial shifts make them very difficult to strike. Many Human legends of invincible heroes were based on the exploits of Faerie Warp Warriors: Achilles, Beowulf, and Lancelot are typical examples. Many modern Warp Warriors end up pursuing careers in professional sports.

be unlearnt. There ain't no going back. You are what you are, my son. You aren't Human and you never were." Brendan looked at him in disbelief. Og shrugged. "You can no more go back to being Human than I could turn into a fish and swim away. We are what we are. And you, my son, are a Faerie." He took a slug of his beer and belched profoundly. "Simple as that."

Brendan couldn't believe what he was hearing. "Is he right?"

Ariel smiled sadly. "I'm afraid so. But it isn't such a terrible thing. Being a Faerie is a great gift. You are special even among our kind."

"There's the prophecy!" Og blurted out. "You could be the One! *Ow!*"

Kim had lashed out and kicked Og in the shin with the toe of her boot. Og hopped and grabbed his shin. "That isn't nice, Ki-Mata. Not nice at all."

Brendan hadn't noticed the exchange. He wasn't paying attention to anything around him. *Never go back? Never?* He felt hollowed out. All the running, all the terror and revelations of the past hours crushed down on his shoulders like a heavy weight.

"Breandan." Ariel's voice roused him from his stupor. "I know this is hard for you. None of us wished it to be this way. Know first and foremost, you are welcome among us. You are not alone."

Brendan looked up into the pale face of Ariel and saw sympathy in the ancient eyes. He looked at Kim and saw her familiar half-smile. Deirdre was silent, of course, but her eyes held his. He turned his gaze upon the gathered patrons of the Swan of Liir and felt their anticipation, as though this was a moment they had been waiting for, something they never dreamed would happen. He sighed and swallowed hard around a lump in his throat.

"How do I undo the ... Compulsion-Thingy?" He jerked his head toward Deirdre.

"A Compulsion is a sincere wish given force," Ariel said. "To remove it, an equally sincere wish is required."

Brendan frowned. He looked at Deirdre and thought for a moment. *She is my mother's sister. She is one of the few true flesh and blood family members I have in the world. I wish I could ask her about my mother. I wish ...* "What was my mother like?" he said.

Deirdre shuddered and breathed deeply. She smiled and spoke. "She was half of my heart. She was beautiful. You remind me of her. I'm sorry I removed the Ward but I was just so happy to find you. Don't think ill of me. I acted out of love." Deirdre's eyes were shining with tears. "You have her smile."

Brendan knew she meant what she said. He felt the truth in her voice. "I'm sorry I told you to shut up."

Deirdre laughed, and it was a sound that lifted his heart despite his sadness. "No harm done, darling boy." She reached out and ran the back of her fingers over his cheek, and he felt tears smart once again in his eyes. "Who knows?" Deirdre said, her eyes shining. "Perhaps you have the talents of a Weaver, too, like me. Or maybe you will be a Healer, like your mother."

He thought again of his Human mother at home, probably worried sick about him. He had always felt awkward and clumsy. He had never had any great talent. His father had tried to teach him music. His mother had introduced him to art. He had never been able to give them the satisfaction of being adept at either. Now he knew that he hadn't really belonged there, and the pain of it was deep. Now he had found his people.

But was that really true? Surely, whomever you love is your family. He shouldn't have to choose. These people may have a claim on him, but his mother and father had been there for his whole life. They had loved him and cared for him, held him when he was sick, and taught him to be the person he was. He made a decision then and there: whatever happened, he would never leave them behind.

He squared his shoulders. "Now what? What's next? I can't stay here and hide from Orcadia forever. Tell me what I have to do."

The Faeries at the table seemed to release a collective sigh of relief.

"I think you're making a wise choice." Deirdre smiled gently, grasping Brendan's hand. "And we all know it is a difficult one."

"So what do I have to do?" Brendan asked.

"The first thing is to get your wild talents under control." Ariel stood. "You must be initiated."

"Initiated?" Brendan balked. "Is this gonna hurt or what?"

Ariel laughed and so did many of those watching. "Not at all. Usually, it happens long before a Faerie reaches your age. There is no pain." He extended his hand. "I will need the amulet, however."

Brendan looked at him blankly. "What amulet?"

"When a Faerie child is born, his parents place a portion of their essence into a token of some kind. The token is then kept close until the child comes of age, when it is integrated into the essence of the child. Thus we ensure continuity from generation to generation. The child knows the parents on a deeper level and becomes fully awake to the world. In your case, the Artificers forged an amulet. It carried the spark of both Briach Morn and Bir-Gidha."

"It is all that is left of my sister. Now it will become part of you," Deirdre said softly.

"I don't have an amulet," Brendan said.

"It was wrought of gold, inset with gemstones. Inscribed with your name in the Ancient tongue: Breandan," Ariel said.

"I've never had anything like that."

Ariel sat back down. "This is not ideal."

Deirdre gripped Brendan's arm. "You're sure? Think hard now. Your Human parents never mentioned anything like it?"

Brendan shook his head. "Nope."

"Great!" Kim threw her hands up. "He lost it."

"I didn't lose it! I never had it!"

"He couldn't lose it," Ariel said. "It's linked to him. It could only be stolen and then only by someone of the Blood."

"Hold it." Brendan held up his hands. "I don't get it. Why do I need this thing? Can't I just get initiated or whatever without it?'

"No." Deirdre shook her head. "Not possible."

"You need the token before you can become fully fledged," Ariel said. "Until you find it, you will be vulnerable to anyone who chooses to strike you down. You will never be safe until you have it back."

"Whoo-hoo!" Og shouted, raising his glass. "A Quest!"

The crowd raised their glasses and cheered. Something in their tone made Brendan's heart sink.

"Oh no," he groaned.

Kim smirked. "Oh no is right."

PART 3

The Quest

Yet Another Note
from the Narrator

Ha! You thought that the whole story would wrap up at the Swan, didn't you! Fools! Burned you! There is at least another third of the story to go!

I mean, honestly! You are holding the book in your hands. There is still a wad of pages ahead of you. Did you think they were just blank pages put there to deceive you? That would be a horrible waste of paper, and I am anything if not conscious of environmental issues.

Or did you think I'd merely doodled little pictures on all the remaining pages? Certainly, my doodling is renowned in World Doodling Circles. In fact, I was once torn between pursuing a career in doodling and being a narrator, but in the end, I decided that the world would be a darker place without me to narrate the important stories.

So, no doodles. Just more story. Brendan has already gone through a great deal of struggle, but there is always more struggling to do. Life is worthless without struggle. Struggling is also a good source of cardiovascular exercise. I struggle three times a week and I'm as fit as a horse. Well, not a horse. Perhaps a small shaggy pony. But I'm fit and that's the important thing.

Without further ado, let us get on with the story.

ALLIES

"A Quest!" Og had cried, delighted. Something about his giddy exclamation had filled Brendan with dread. He looked to Ariel for an explanation.

The ancient Faerie seemed uncomfortable for the first time since their conversation had begun. He pursed his lips and sighed. "Oh, dear."

"Oh, dear what?" Brendan demanded. "What, oh dear? What does he mean, 'a quest'?"

"You have lost your token. You must find it or forever be banished from the presence of the Fair Folk," Ariel explained.

"Lost it?" Brendan said, incredulous. "I've never even seen it before. How could I have lost it? How am I supposed to find this thing? I don't even know what it looks like!"

"When you were taken and hidden among the People of Metal, your father would have given you the amulet. No one could have taken it from you unless they were Faerie."

"Again," Brendan said through gritted teeth. "Anyone could have taken it. I was a baby. A Faerie could have easily taken it. How could I stop them?"

"No Faerie could have found you. You were under a Ward," Ariel insisted. "A powerful glamour forged by one of the strongest of our kind shielded you from Faerie eyes.

Now that the Ward is removed, your true nature will be revealed to Humans. Perhaps more dangerous is that you will be visible to Orcadia and those who follow her. You will be vulnerable until you find your token and undergo the initiation."

"Who could expect me to be able to hold onto an amulet?" Brendan was totally exasperated. "I was an infant! Anybody could have taken it from me. Haven't you ever heard the expression 'Easy as taking candy from a baby'? Well, just substitute amulet for candy and you see my point."

"If it were just any amulet, I would agree," Ariel said. "However, this amulet had its own Wards as well, attuned to you. It would be invisible to Human eyes. Only another Faerie could have removed it from you and to do so would bring dire punishment, should the theft be discovered."

"So some other Faerie took it. Maybe they destroyed it."

"If they had," Og interjected, "you would be dead."

Kim nodded soberly. "Og is right. It contained an essential part of you within it. If it were broken or destroyed, you would perish."

Brendan felt a chill pass over his heart. "I hope it's a sturdy, high-quality item," he said in a dry tone that hid his anxiety.

"Of course it is," Og declared. He thumped his chest and burped loudly. "Made it myself, didn't I?"

Brendan didn't find the declaration reassuring. "So what do I do now?"

"Now you must find the amulet," Ariel said simply, leaning back in his chair.

"It sounds like an impossible task," Brendan said. "How can I possibly succeed?"

Ariel's face became deathly still. "You must. If you don't, you will have no protection. Orcadia and her ilk will find you and either destroy you or turn you to their dark purposes. Your Human family will be endangered. You will have nowhere to hide. Without being fully initiated and integrated to your Faerie powers, you will be a danger to all those around you. You will have no control." He shook his head sadly. "It pains me to cast you out once again when we have only just found you, but this is our Law. We must follow the Law or we are doomed."

Brendan looked at his face and saw that there would be no change of heart. He looked to Kim, and she shook her head. "Can't you help me? At least tell me where to start?"

"Ain't done," Og said, staring at the glass held between his scarred hands, unable to meet Brendan's gaze. "No one in this room can help ye, son. Ye have to do it all on yer own. It's the rules!"

"But we have to help him," Deirdre said suddenly. "He has no idea what to do. He's a special case. Not just because of who he is but because of his circumstances. He is ignorant through no fault of his own."

"Deirdre, no," Ariel said firmly.

"You can't send him out there alone," Deirdre insisted.

"*No!*" Ariel thundered. The entire room fell silent, and even Deirdre seemed cowed. For an instant all the lights dimmed, and Brendan saw a shadow in Ariel's eyes, a hint of the power that lurked beneath his gentle exterior. "He must follow his Quest and retrieve his token. Alone! That is the Law!"

No one spoke. Brendan saw how Ariel commanded them all with the force of his personality. He could easily imagine Ariel in ancient Greece striking fear and awe into the hearts of his worshippers.

Brendan looked around at the Faeries gathered there, the people he had never imagined existing before today, and felt despair. He suddenly didn't want to lose them. "This isn't fair! You pulled me out of my Human life, and now you're kicking me back out into the street?" He looked at Kim beseechingly. "You can't do this!"

"I'm sorry, Breandan," she said softly. "I can't help you any more. I'm bound by the Law as much as you are."

Brendan looked at her, this girl he'd never truly known. He saw how much this was hurting her, too. "Okay. I understand."

"I'm sorry …" she said miserably.

"S'okay." Brendan hung his head. He didn't want to whine. His dad had always told him that life wasn't fair. You had to do your best with what life gave you. He would succeed or fail, but he would do his best. "That name they call you …"

"Ki-Mata."

Brendan stood up from the table. "I think I'll call you Kim, if you don't mind. It suits you."

"You and you alone may call me that," she said. "Be careful, Brendan."

He shrugged. "I'll do my best. Thanks for watching out for me at school. You were a good friend. I just wanted you to know that in case I never get back here."

She smiled but said no more. Og's hand fell on his shoulder. Brendan looked up into the beefy, red face. "Here, son. Take this." He held a ham and cheese sandwich in his hand. Mustard dripped over his knuckles.

Brendan looked critically at the offering. "Is it a magical sandwich?"

"Sadly, no," Og admitted, laughing. "Delicious but not magical."

"No gifts," Ariel said.

"It ain't a gift! It's provisions. He's hardly had nothing to eat, Ariel. You won't begrudge him a morsel for the road?"

Ariel pursed his lips. "Hmmm. All right. I will allow it. Now, Brendan, you must be gone. Return with the amulet and the doors of the Swan will be open to you. Good luck."

Brendan took the sandwich. "Thanks, Og."

"*Uncle* Og! And enjoy the sandwich!" He winked a great blue eye and clapped Brendan on the back. "Just be careful where you bite," he said cryptically.

So Brendan walked slowly across the room toward the door. Faeries called out to him as he wove his way through the crowd, patting his back, wishing him luck. He came to the door and found Leonard standing there, massive arms crossed over his huge chest. There was a slight gust of wind and then Saskia appeared by Leonard's side.

"You be careful, mon," Leonard rumbled. "It be a dangerous world out there!" Saskia smiled at him but said nothing.

Brendan smiled weakly. Leonard pushed the door open to reveal the rainy green. "You come back soon. We'll be waitin' for ya."

Brendan nodded. He took one last look back at Kim, Ariel, Og, and Deirdre. They were all watching him, save Deirdre, who was slightly turned away and looking down at something she held in her hand. Brendan recognized that stance: she was trying to send a text on her phone without anyone seeing. Presently, she stuffed her hand back into her pocket and looked up at him. She smiled at him reassuringly. Og raised his whisky glass while sucking mustard off his knuckles. Ariel nodded. Kim merely looked steadily back and mouthed the words "Be careful." Brendan waved and stepped out into the night.

And so he found himself, immediately soaked to the skin and shivering in the downpour, holding the soggy sandwich. He was miserable, depressed, and alone.

He turned around to look at the Swan but it was gone. The doorway was gone. A blank wall stared back at him. There was no hint that it had ever been there at all. He could not go back.

"Where do I start looking for something that I didn't even know existed?" He felt utterly miserable. He held up the sandwich, which was dissolving in the rain before his eyes. "Even my sandwich is ruined." In disgust, he threw the sandwich onto the grass.

"Ow!" the sandwich squeaked.

Brendan almost leapt out of his skin. "Who said that?"

"Uuuughh," the sandwich moaned.

"Will the weirdness ever end?" Brendan said to the rain. "I'm talking to a sandwich."

As he watched, wide-eyed, the top slice of bread flopped over to reveal a tiny person, her clothes smeared with mustard and mayonnaise, lying on a bed of ham. The person in question had small fly wings and pale mauve eyes. "Oh crap." She picked at her tight brocaded coat, trying to wipe mustard off. "That's not coming out."

Brendan reached down and scooped the person into his hand. Sitting on his palm was a perfectly formed little woman dressed in a tight-fitting red velvet suit. Her hair was fire-engine red and her cheeks were flushed. Brendan peered closely at her. "You're a ... Diminutive?"

"Bah," she spat. "I don't stand by that modern malarkey. I'm a Lesser Faerie and proud of it!" She thumped her chest and tried to stand but fell back onto her bottom.

Brendan sniffed. "You're drunk!"

"Never! Not a bit of it! I never touch the demon liquor. Not me! Ha! Drunk, he says! The idea!" Finishing with a huff of disgust, she glared at him, her tiny arms crossed defensively over her chest. A sly look came into her eye. "Something sweet, now! I wouldn't say no to that! Ya have anything sweet in your pockets, your grace?"

Brendan frowned. Digging into his pockets, he found the packet of gum that he'd used to strike a bargain with Skreet in the Undertown. He held it up.

The little fairy spat. "Sugarless? Poison! Poison, I say!"

"Forgive me," Brendan said sarcastically. Digging in the pocket of his trousers, he was pleasantly surprised when his fingers closed on a small hard object. He pulled his hand out and revealed a small after-dinner mint furred liberally with lint. "How about this?"

The Lesser Faerie's eyes lit up. "*Yes!*" She zipped forward and snatched the mint from Brendan's fingers. Without a moment's hesitation, she stuffed the entire sweet, lint and all, into her tiny mouth. Brendan marvelled that she could even encompass the entire morsel. It was like watching a normal-sized person stick a softball in her mouth. With great effort, somehow, she managed to stuff the whole mint in. "SnarfffffffmmmmmmmmmmmmmmMMMMMMMMMMM!"

The effect was immediate. The tiny creature began glowing, brighter and brighter, as if she were a tiny star. The raindrops falling on her fizzed like drops of fat in a frying pan as they struck her. Brendan had to shield his eyes from the intense glare.

"*Yesssssss!*" The Lesser Faerie began zipping around erratically, shooting here and there at random. "*Sugarrrrrrr!*" she shouted. She dive-bombed Brendan's head and then whirled around his ears in tighter and tighter circles.

"Hey! Calm down!" Brendan cried in alarm.

Then, as suddenly as the fit began, it ended. Her light winked out, and she fell with a soft plop face-down in the mud.

"Sugar …" she mumbled. Snores, impossibly loud for such a minute creature, rose to Brendan's ears. He bent down and picked the tiny woman up in the palm of his hand.

"Great," Brendan snorted. "I'm stuck in the rain with homicidal Orcadia after me, and all I have to defend myself with is a miniature sugar junkie."

"That's not all you have," Mr. Greenleaf said, stepping out from under the trees. "You have your wits and your luck."

Brendan almost dropped the Lesser Faerie in surprise. "Do you people enjoy scaring the crap out of me?"

"Sorry to startle you," Greenleaf said with a smile. Titi zipped out of the darkness to land on his shoulder. After a wink at Brendan she began preening her coat of colourful feathers. "I forget that you can't sense us yet. When you become fully fledged, you will be very difficult to surprise. But to the matter at hand…. You must be off. Time is wasting. My sister texted me that you might need some help."

"I thought cellphones weren't allowed in there," Brendan said.

"Rules must be bent when the situation demands it."

"Does that mean you're gonna help me find this amulet?" Brendan's heart lifted.

"No." Greenleaf shook his head decisively. "Even I can't flout the Law to that extent. As it stands, my even talking to you could be misconstrued. If anyone asks me, I will say that I wasn't aware of your status." Greenleaf looked at the lingering cloud bank. "I will try to give you a little breathing room, that's all. I've been keeping an eye on Orcadia. She is waiting for you to leave the island."

"If I leave this place, I won't be protected, will I? This ... shield-thingy ..."

"The Ward of the Island."

"Whatever, it only assures my safety on the Island. As soon as I leave here, I'm toast."

Greenleaf shook his head. "*If* she sees you leave. I can do something about that."

"I thought no one could help me."

"I wouldn't be helping you directly. If asked, I would say that I was just trying to vex Orcadia, which has become something of a hobby of mine, of late."

"Fine. So how are you going to hide me?"

"I won't hide you." Greenleaf's smile showed a hint of mischief. "I will be you."

Greenleaf reached out and touched Brendan's shoulder. There was a tingling sensation where the hand contacted him. Then, as Brendan watched in astonishment, Mr. Greenleaf shimmered. His features smeared. He shrank slightly in stature. In a matter of seconds, his appearance had completely changed. Brendan stood open-mouthed, staring at an exact replica of himself. "What do you think? Neat, huh?" Even Greenleaf's voice and manner of speaking had changed to sound like Brendan's.

"How did you do that?"

Greenleaf laughed. "A glamour. Now I will leave the Island, and Orcadia, thinking I am you, will chase me. I will lead her on a wild goose chase."

Brendan stared in disbelief. "I can't get over how creepy it is looking at another me."

"Get over it, dude. Now!" Greenleaf struck a very "Brendan" pose. Brendan had to admit, Greenleaf was good.

"Okay."

"I will go and lead her away. I don't know how long I can give you, but you must use the time wisely." Titi waggled a hand at Brendan, then crawled into Greenleaf's shirt pocket, out of sight. Greenleaf turned to go.

"Wait," Brendan called. "Where do I even begin?"

"Remember," Greenleaf said, "you have friends."

"Friends? What friends?" Brendan cried but Greenleaf was already moving. He sped off across the grass and disappeared down the path. Brendan watched himself run away and shook his head. "*That* is weird."

Recovering his composure, Brendan set off after him at a slower pace. The first item of business was to get off Ward's Island.

He tucked the Lesser Faerie into the pocket of his school blazer and trotted along the paved path to the ferry terminal. He knew it would be too late for the ferry, but he had to start somewhere.

He arrived at the pier to find the ferry docks in darkness. A chain hung across the entrance to the dock.

"Now what?" he said aloud.

"The Faerie Terminal," a tiny groggy voice said.

"Huh?" He looked down to see the Lesser Faerie had recovered enough to haul herself up and was hanging out of his pocket. She was looking slightly green.

"We go to the Faerie Terminal."

"We're at the ferry terminal. It's closed."

"Not the ferry terminal, you idiot," she snapped. She pointed off down a path that Brendan hadn't seen before. The path was paved with white stones that shone faintly in the moonlight. A sign stood at the top of the path. In elegant painted letters it read TO FAERIE TERMINAL.

"I've never seen that before."

"Your Faerie Sight is not very reliable, is it?" the Lesser Faerie teased. "There's a whole world that you've been missing, friend. Now let's haul some butt, please."

Brendan had no choice but to do what she asked. He jogged down the path in the direction that the sign indicated.

"Do you mind not bouncing me around too much? I may puke."

"I'll do my best. What's your name, anyway?"

"Basra La Tir."

"Huh." Brendan snorted a laugh.

"What's so funny?"

"I found you in a sandwich, and your initials are B.L.T."

"I don't get it," Basra said.

"Bacon, lettuce, and tomato. It's a sandwich."

"Oh. Sounds awful."

They came around a bend, and the lake spread out before them. Down by the shore a light was shining. Brendan saw movement, people shuffling in the pool of illumination. A flash of lightning erupted out of the water to the north. Thunder rolled across the grey waves. "I guess Greenleaf is doing his part."

Brendan came to the light and discovered a small wooden dock. The waiting Faeries gave him a cursory glance and went back to shuffling from foot to foot in the steady downpour.

"Bloody late again," one said.

"Probably the weather," another offered.

"Bah," the first replied. "What do we pay taxes for?"

"We don't pay taxes,"[73] another observed.

A bell rang out on the water. Brendan peered through the rain and saw a boat looming in the darkness. At its prow stood a tall thin man who wore a bright yellow rain suit topped with a drooping yellow hat.

The boat came up to the dock and bumped against it.

"'Bout time, Ferryman!" the grumpy Faerie grumbled.

The Ferryman didn't say a word. He merely bent and looped a painter[74] around the nearest post. That done, he stood up and held out his hand. One by one, the would-be passengers stepped onto the precariously rocking boat, dropping a gleaming coin into the Ferryman's hand.[75]

---

73 The Faerie is obviously joking. Everyone pays taxes. The old adage is true: nothing is sure except death and taxes. Being practically immortal, the Fair Folk can escape the first but not the latter of these two evils.

74 A *painter*, as it is referred to above, is a short rope used on a boat to attach objects to it. If you thought that the Ferryman had thrown a painter like perhaps Picasso or Van Gogh and tied him around the mooring post, you are a little weird.

75 Ferrymen, Keepers of the Crossroads, and Bridge Guardians are a special category of magical beings. They have their own special guild called "The Brotherhood of the Ways" that accepts only their own kind as members. To be honest, no one else would want to be a member anyway: these guys are really creepy.

Brendan didn't know what to do. He stepped up to the Ferryman and said, "I haven't got any money."

A gasp came from the other passengers. Brendan couldn't see the face under the shadow of the rain hat. Up close, Brendan realized how tall the Ferryman actually was. He towered over everyone. Water dripped from the brim of his hat as the Ferryman stood eerily still despite the rocking of the boat beneath his feet.

Brendan fished in his pocket and pulled out his useless braces. He held them up and said hopefully, "Will you accept these?"

The Ferryman bent closer and sniffed. "Nay. These are not noble metal: gold, silver, platinum only."

"Oh," Brendan mumbled, sticking the braces back in his pocket. "I have nothing else."

"A promise." The voice of the Ferryman was like the rattle of dry sails. "A promise in exchange for passage."

BLT flitted up to Brendan's shoulder. Her eyes were wary. "Be careful, my friend. A promise is a solemn Pledge."

"What do you mean?" Brendan demanded.

"Ferrymen accept only noble metal as payment. Or sometimes gemstones. If you don't have noble metal, they take a Pledge. I warn you, if you make a promise or a Pledge to one such as this, it must be paid in full at some point in the future."

Brendan thought back to the Undertown. He had made a bargain with Skreet and he'd managed to escape any drastic consequences. How bad could it be? This was just a guy in a rowboat. "Well, I have no 'noble metal' and I haven't got any other way off the Island. Unless you can fly me, BLT?"

She shook her tiny head.

"Fine then." He turned to the Ferryman and said, "I promise to pay you later. I need to get to the city."

"The promise is made." There was a wheezing chuckle from the Ferryman. The sound was chilling and mirthless. "Board."

Brendan stepped into the boat with BLT on his shoulder. He sat down on the nearest empty bench. The others around him shimmied away as though they didn't want to catch something from him.

"Why do I feel like I've made a horrible mistake?" Brendan moaned.

"Probably because you have," BLT offered helpfully. She groaned. "Boats don't agree with me."

The boat suddenly jerked, and they were forging through the waves toward the distant skyline of Toronto.

The Ferryman stood in the stern, solid as a rock despite the pitch of the waves. His pale hand lay on the tiller. Brendan could see no engine, but despite that fact, the vessel powered forward, cutting a direct path toward the piers at the harbour front. No one spoke. At least the rain didn't seem to touch them while they were aboard the ferry. It parted on either side of the craft, some unseen force shielding the passengers from the weather. Only the Ferryman streamed with rain, and he didn't seem to mind.

He hadn't realized he'd fallen asleep until the boat bumped against the dock. He shook himself awake to find the towering condominiums looming in the rain all around him. He was at the ferry dock. He was so tired. When was the last time he'd slept? The night before last. He looked blearily about. All of the other passengers were gone. There was only the Ferryman looming over him.

"Out," the Ferryman said, jerking a pale thumb at the dock. Brendan forced himself to stand and step over the gunnels. The Ferryman's hand stopped him.

"Remember." The Ferryman's raspy voice was chilling. "You made a Pledge to a Brother of the Ways. The Pledge will be called in."

Brendan looked into the dark face and saw a flash of icy blue eyes beneath the brim of the yellow hat. He nodded once. The hand was lifted from his chest, and he stepped out onto the solid wood of the pier. He watched the boat pull away and disappear into the misty drizzle.

Shivering, he stood on the pier and thought for a moment. *Where can I go? Greenleaf said I have friends, but who are they? I can't go to my parents. It's too dangerous for them. Who then?*

Then it struck him. He did have friends. *Do I want to involve them in this? It's too dangerous. But ... there's no one else.*

He made a decision. He started off down the pier toward the city. BLT flitted ahead of him, hovering in front of his face.

"Where to then?"

Brendan smiled grimly. "I'm going to get some help."

BABKA

Dmitri finally opened his bedroom window. Brendan had been tossing pebbles for ten minutes and was about to resort to larger rocks when the blond head poked out.

"Brendan! What are you doing? Everyone's looking for you! Your parents are worried sick!"

"I know," Brendan whispered in a raspy voice. "I'll explain everything. Just let me in. I need your help."

"You should just go home."

"I want to but I can't! Please! I have nowhere else to go. You've got to let me in."

Dmitri's head disappeared and the window closed. Brendan waited for what seemed like an hour. He was about to leave when the back door to Dmitri's townhouse opened with a low squeak. Dmitri held a flashlight in his hand.

"Hurry," the small boy said, motioning Brendan toward the house.

Brendan gratefully padded across the dead brown grass of the backyard and into the kitchen. Dmitri was careful to close the door so that it didn't make a sound.

The kitchen was small but cozy, redolent of the smell of Dmitri's mother's cooking: garlic, cabbage, and fresh bread. A small table occupied the centre of the room, surrounded by wooden chairs. A lamp burned in the corner of the counter, casting a warm glow. Dmitri indicated that Brendan should have a seat, then went to the counter beside the ancient gas stove and opened a steel bread box. He retrieved a pan of chocolate cake and a dull knife and brought them to the table. He sat down and cut a square piece of cake and lifted it onto a napkin for Brendan.

"Eat this," Dmitri said quietly. "You look completely worn in."

"Out," Brendan said wearily, "worn out, not in."

Dmitri watched in silence as Brendan devoured the cake. When Brendan was licking the icing off his fingers, Dmitri asked at last, "Where have you been?"

"It's a long story," Brendan replied. "And I'm afraid you won't believe a word of it."

"Let me decide what I will believe," Dmitri said, crossing his arms. He was dressed in flannel pants and a threadbare dressing gown. He wore a faded T-shirt that read POLAND IS FOR LOVERS. His small face was pale and serious.

"Okay." Brendan took a deep breath. "This is gonna sound totally weird but ... the thing is ... I'm a Faerie."

"Faerie? I don't know this word." Dmitri frowned. "What is 'Faerie'?"

"A Faerie! As in Faerie tales? Like Tinkerbell, only not like that either. Aagh. It's complicated."

Dmitri shook his head. "I don't know what this 'Tinkerbell' is. You should just tell me where you have been and—yuck! What is that?" Dmitri's face twisted in disgust as he pointed at Brendan's blazer pocket.

Brendan looked down to see BLT's head and shoulders sticking out over the edge of his pocket. The tiny woman was sniffing the air. "Is that chocolate?" she asked excitedly.

"Chocolate cake," Brendan told her. He looked at Dmitri, who was staring in disgust at BLT. "See, this is what I mean. This kind of Faerie!"

"That is the biggest fly I have ever seen. Why are you carrying such a horrible insect in your pocket? And why are you talking to it?"

Brendan was confused. *A fly? Why can't he see her?*

Before Brendan could stop her, BLT flitted out of his pocket and zoomed up onto the table. Dmitri recoiled in horror as she plunged face-first into the chocolate icing on top of the cake.

"Gross!" Dmitri jumped up from his seat and reached for a newspaper. Rolling it up, he prepared to swat BLT. Brendan leapt up and grabbed his hand.

"Don't, D," he begged. "That isn't a fly! Can't you see her?"

Dmitri looked at Brendan as if he were mad. "See who?"

"He can't see me," BLT announced around a mouthful of cake. She rolled over onto her back in the icing and smiled drunkenly up at them. Her whole body began to glow. "He sees a big hairy fly. We protect ourselves with illusions. He sees what I want him to see." Her eyes lit up. "This is good cake. Sweet! *Sweeeeeet!*"

She commenced a frenzied, erratic flight, buzzing here and there around the kitchen, causing Dmitri and Brendan to duck their heads to avoid a collision. She banged into cupboards and knocked over a jar full of wooden spoons by the stove. Brendan managed to reach up and snatch her out of the air. With great effort, he held BLT as she wriggled. It was like holding on to a shooting star. "How can I make him see you as you are? I need him to under-stand. I need him to believe me."

"If you let him see me, he sees all of us. When that happens, he won't be able to go back. What's done is done." She licked some icing off her fingers and wriggled, desperate to spend her energy. Dmitri was watching this exchange. He looked at Brendan as if he was sure now that Brendan had lost his mind. Brendan knew he would have thought the same if he found Dmitri talking to an insect. He was torn. If he could take back everything and just be a normal person, blissfully ignorant of the secret world that had materialized over the last two days, he imagined he would do it in a heartbeat. Should he subject Dmitri to the kind of craziness that his life now contained?

I know I'm being selfish, but I can't do this alone. I need some help and I have no one else I can trust.

"Brendan? Are you okay?" Dmitri asked, his face filled with concern. "You're talking to a fly."

Brendan groaned.

"All right. How do I do it?" he asked the struggling BLT.

"Are you sure you want to?" BLT managed to ask.

"I have no choice," Brendan replied.

"Okay. All you have to do is say it. But you have to say it with sincerity. Will is everything. That's what makes the magic work."

Brendan let her go, and she recommenced her blazing circuit of the kitchen. Brendan turned to Dmitri and grabbed him by the shoulders. He looked into the smaller boy's blue eyes and said earnestly, with all the honesty he could muster, "Dmitri, I need your help. I need you to see what I can see."

Dmitri shivered. As Brendan released him from his grasp, the smaller boy blinked and rubbed his eyes then looked up into Brendan's face. His jaw dropped. "What ...? Brendan ... you look ... you look different."

"Different how?"

"I can't describe it," Dmitri said softly. "Oh. You aren't wearing glasses. And your pimples are gone. And ... you shine!" Dmitri laughed.

BLT, her energy finally spent, fell to the tabletop exhausted.

"It worked," BLT said wearily. "He has the Sight now."

At the sound of her voice, Dmitri whipped his head around to stare at her. His mouth dropped open. He pointed at BLT. "There is a tiny person on the table."

"Dmitri Krosnow, meet Basra La Tir, Lesser Faerie," Brendan made the introduction. "I call her BLT."

BLT hopped lightly down onto the tabletop and bowed with a flourish. "Pleased to make your acquaintance, I'm sure." Dmitri stared for a moment in dumbfounded shock. BLT frowned and cocked an eyebrow. "Got any sweets?"

Brendan swept her up in his hand. "No more sweets."

Brendan waited for Dmitri to run screaming, lose his mind, and freak out. He was ready to clap a hand over the boy's screams for help. Nothing like that happened. Dmitri turned to him with shining eyes and a huge grin on his face. "My mind blows!"

Brendan grinned back. "It blows your mind, you mean. Yeah, I know. I can hardly believe it myself."

Dmitri grabbed his arm and pulled Brendan down into a chair. "Tell me how this is possible. Tell me everything!"

So, for the next hour, in the quiet kitchen, by the light of the small lamp, Brendan told his friend everything that had happened to him over the last few days. He told him of Greenleaf and Deirdre, the concert and the dream. He told him of Kim and her secret self. He told him of their flight through the Undertown, Borje and Orcadia, the Kobolds and the Silkies, and about the Swan of Liir. It felt so good to be able to tell someone everything and to share the burden. Dmitri interrupted with questions and the occasional exclamation of amazement, but mostly he watched and listened, trying to take it all in. Throughout the conversation, BLT flitted about the kitchen sampling bits of food and exploring the shelves. Brendan made sure she didn't get hold of any sugar, which earned him a few curses and angry glares.

At last, Brendan reached the end of his tale. Dmitri sat in silence, processing what he'd heard. Brendan could almost hear the cogs turning in his friend's mind.

"So, you must find this amulet or else you will be vulnerable to those who wish to hurt you?" Dmitri asked.

"From what I understand, that's the deal," Brendan said. "Once I'm initiated or whatever, I'm off limits and I get certain rights. Not that she seems to respect the rules. Once I'm initiated, I get all my powers and I may be able to defend myself. At least I'll have a fighting chance. The problem is, I have no idea where to look for this thing. It could be anywhere."

"They say you had it when you were a baby," Dmitri said thoughtfully. "When your real father …"

"Briach Morn," Brendan offered.

"Him. When he dropped you off in the Human world. And only another Faerie could take it from you."

"That's what I understand," Brendan agreed. He was amazed that Dmitri had just come on board this whole business. He didn't know how he would have reacted in Dmitri's shoes, but he doubted he would have been so calm.

Dmitri's eyes suddenly went wide. "Oh my! I understand now."

"What? You know what to do? Tell me!"

"No, not exactly. But it's something about my babka. Remember the other day when you asked me about dreams and we talked about my babka?"

"Yeah," Brendan confirmed.

Dmitri's face coloured. "I kind of downplayed that a bit. You see, it is a bit embarrassing. She is a sort of … I don't know the exact word. She claims to be able to see things. In Polish we call such a person a *vrooshka*. Do you know what I mean? A psycho …"

"She's a psychic?"

"That's it! That's the word! People, mainly Polish people, friends of ours and other people who have heard about her, come to visit her. They bring her gifts, sometimes money, and she tries to help them by using her special sight." Dmitri grimaced. "My father doesn't like it. He thinks it is hopelessly old-fashioned and makes us look like ignorant peasants, but the truth is we can use the extra money."

"Do you think she can help?"

"It's just that for the last little while she's been acting a bit strangely," Dmitri explained. "Well, she's always been acting strangely, but she's been oddly focused in her weirdness. Last week, she insisted that my mother take her out to the hairdresser. She wanted a perm and her hair dyed."

"That doesn't sound weird to me."

"She lost all of her hair about five years ago."

"Gotcha."

"We got her a wig and she seemed pleased. When I asked her why she needed her hair done so suddenly, she said that she had to look pretty for His Highness." Dmitri paused to let this sink in. "She has been babbling in her sleep, too. She keeps saying things like 'He has been hiding.' And last night she woke up shouting, 'He rides beneath the waves! He rides beneath the waves!' My parents have been talking about getting her some help. They think she's going senile but now I see that, as impossible as it seems, she was describing what was happening to you."

Brendan thought about this for a moment. "Maybe I could ask her about this amulet. Maybe she knows where it is."

Dmitri shrugged. "I suppose it's worth a try."

"I can't wait 'til morning, Dmitri," Brendan said urgently. "Can we wake her?"

A woman's voice called from the next room. The voice was quiet but clear and spoke in Polish. Brendan heard his name, recognizable but heavily accented.

Dmitri looked surprised as he translated. "That's my babka. She's awake. She says she's been waiting for you, Prince Brendan. She wonders why we're wasting time in the kitchen. What's this Prince Brendan stuff?"

"I have no idea. Come on. Let's go."

Dmitri led Brendan through the swinging door into the sitting room. BLT flitted to Brendan's shoulder and sat down.

"You're getting icing all over me," Brendan complained. BLT answered with a prolonged belch. "Nice. Can you keep it down? You'll wake the whole house!"

"Don't worry," Dmitri reassured them. "It's only me and Babka. Both my parents are working nights this week."

The living room was absolutely full of furniture. The chairs were overstuffed and comfortable, covered with woven throw rugs of many different colours. A television sat on a shelf loaded with rows of little ornaments, painted wooden dolls, and crystal animals. A spray of framed photographs of varying sizes and ages were mounted on the wall over the heavy antique couch. Lying on the couch, cocooned in a thick comforter and with a woollen shawl draped over her bald head, was Dmitri's grandmother or babka, as he called her. A small table lamp shed golden light on her round face.

She was obviously very old. Her face was like an advertisement for wrinkles. A thick fur of white bristles whiskered her chin, and she had a mole the size of a golf ball on her thick neck, also home to a healthy colony of thick white hairs. Despite her age, her eyes were a lively blue. When she saw Brendan, she smiled, and Brendan felt instantly at home in her presence though he'd never met her before. She had always been upstairs in bed whenever he'd visited Dmitri.

The blue eyes were riveted on Brendan as he came into the room. She stared so intently at Brendan that he had to look away.

"She asked us to move her down here yesterday," Dmitri said. "She wanted to watch TV."

Dmitri went to her and spoke gently in Polish. She smiled and beckoned Brendan closer with one hand, heavy with rings.

"Prince Brendan," Babka whispered softly.

Dmitri spoke in Polish to his babka and she answered him. Dmitri translated. "She says you're a prince. The Misplaced Prince."

Brendan suddenly remembered Og greeting him in the same way when he'd arrived at the Swan. What was that all about? BLT darted from Brendan's shoulder and did a loop around the old woman's head. She clapped her wrinkled hands and laughed with delight. She spoke excitedly in Polish to Dmitri, who looked in wonder at his grandmother. The old woman held out a hand, and BLT gently lit in her wrinkled palm. She cooed to the tiny Faerie in soothing tones. BLT responded by stretching out and going to sleep.

"My babka says she used to speak with the Little People, the *Chochlikach*, she calls them, when she was a little girl in Poland. They came to visit her often."

Brendan moved closer, and when he was in reach, Babka grabbed his hand in a firm, moist grip. Suddenly, she was speaking fast in Polish, her eyes bright and her face serious.

A little disturbed, Brendan asked Dmitri, "What is she saying?"

"She says that she sees a dark future for you, but it can be changed if you find what you are seeking," Dmitri translated. "Do you think she's talking about the amulet?"

"Ask her if she knows where to find the amulet," Brendan said eagerly. He waited while Dmitri posed the question. The old lady pointed out the window where the sky was greying toward dawn. "Well? What did she say?"

"She says that she can't see it. A man has hidden what you seek. She holds his face in her mind's eye," Dmitri said.

Brendan knelt down beside the old woman and took her hand in his own. "Can she describe this man?" Brendan waited in an agony of impatience while the question was translated. Babka started speaking, her eyes closed as she concentrated.

Dmitri translated. "He is old. With white hair. He was tall once but now he is stooped over. He is down. No, the correct way to say it would be 'laid low.' He's sick? Or hurt, maybe?"

"Can't she be more specific?"

"She says it doesn't work that way. She sees what she sees."

"I wish she could give us a better description. That could describe any old man at all."

"What can I do?" Dmitri shrugged. "It's not easy to translate accurately."

"I wish we had one of those guys who do those drawings for the police, you know?"

"That would be helpful," Dmitri agreed. Suddenly, his face lit up. "But we do know someone who could do that!" He went to the phone and started dialling.

"Wait a minute! Who are you calling?"

"Harold! He could do it!"

Brendan crossed the room in two strides, plunking his finger down on the phone to cut off the call. "No!" he said quickly. "I can't do that! It would mean that I'd have to tell him everything. It's bad enough that I had to tell you."

"Harold is your friend," Dmitri whispered. "You can trust him."

"It's not that I don't trust him," Brendan said. "I don't want to put any more people in danger. Orcadia isn't exactly a fun person to have breathing down your neck, Dmitri."

Dmitri frowned. "The way I see it, if you don't find this amulet soon, you won't survive. I know that Harold wouldn't want anything bad to happen to you. We're your friends. You have to let us help." Dmitri lifted Brendan's finger off the receiver. "Besides, you don't have to tell him what's going on. He just has to draw the picture."

Brendan weighed Dmitri's argument and found that he couldn't fault his friend's logic. He needed to at least know what the old man looked like if he wanted to have a hope of ever finding the amulet. He looked at Dmitri and nodded. "Okay. But we don't say anything about what's happened to me. He just draws the picture, right?"

"Of course," Dmitri said gleefully and dialled Harold's cell.

Twenty minutes later, Harold was sitting on the sofa beside Dmitri's babka, his tablet open and his charcoal in hand. He'd been awake when Dmitri had called, sitting up waiting to draw the sunrise from his back balcony. He'd ridden his bike over right away when he heard that Brendan was okay and he needed help.

The old woman had sat patiently on the sofa under her blankets while they were waiting for Harold. Her eyes glowed with excitement. She chatted quietly with BLT, giggling like a little girl.

"You speak Polish?" Brendan asked the little Faerie.

"Sure," BLT said. "It's a fun language, very expressive. Lots of interesting swear words."

Brendan had insisted that BLT hide in his pocket when Harold arrived. A giant fly would probably be hard to explain.

"Brendan," Harold said when he came into the living room. "Dude, you're okay! I was worried. I mean, after Chester Dallaire disappeared, I thought maybe there was some kidnapping ring operating in town or something."

At the mention of Chester, Brendan felt a cold lump of guilt in his gut. He would have to take care of that if he made it through this in one piece. "No, I'm fine. But I need your help."

Harold listened as they detailed what they needed him to do. When asked if he could draw a composite sketch from Dmitri's instructions, he shrugged and said, "I can try. I've never really done it before although I do a lot of portrait work ... but that's mostly of my mum's friends' pets."

"Great!" Brendan groaned. "This will never work."

"Let's try," Dmitri insisted. "Babka?"

"*Tak?*" Babka asked.

So, for the next forty minutes as the sky turned from black to grey, Dmitri tried to translate his babka's description of the man she saw in her vision. Harold went through a whole pad of sketch paper. The job wasn't made any easier by the fact that Babka's eyesight wasn't the best. Each time Harold held up his work for her to critique, she would squint and shake her head. Harold would then begin again, scratching and smudging with his charcoal, trying to get the right combination of strokes that would satisfy Babka's inner eye. Brendan and Dmitri watched over Harold's shoulder as he worked.

Finally, Babka announced that she was satisfied. The picture was as accurate as she could make it. The old woman was obviously exhausted.

Harold held up the picture for Brendan to see. He studied the picture closely. The drawing depicted a man with craggy features. His eyes were deep set under heavy brows. The mouth was a chiselled line, and the jaw was heavy and straight.

"Does he look familiar?" Dmitri asked urgently. "Think hard."

"There's something," Brendan breathed. The face did look familiar somehow. It was right at the tip of his brain, so close as to be annoying. "There's something …" Suddenly, he had an idea. "Hey, Harold. Could you draw a hat on the guy?"

"What kind of hat?"

"One of those flat ones that old guys wear, like a squashed pancake sort of, with a brim on the front. You know what I mean?"

Harold nodded. "I think so." He sketched a few lines on the drawing, superimposing a flat herringbone cap on the man's head.

Brendan's eyes lit up. He turned to Dmitri. "When we first asked her about the guy, what did she say? He'd fallen?"

"She saw him falling and hitting his head."

He'd seen someone fall and hit his head. Just the day before yesterday, the old man had been hit by the bike courier. "It's Finbar!" he said softly.

The old woman squeezed his hand and beamed. "*Tak! Tak!* Finbar! *To on!*"

"Yes! Yes! Finbar! That's it!" Dmitri said excitely.

"Couldn't she have just told me his name in the first place?" Brendan said, exasperated.

The woman spoke and Dmitri translated. "She says she didn't have it until you spoke it. Now she knows that it's right."

Harold interjected. "You sound like you know the guy. Do you know where he is?"

Brendan nodded, his heart sinking. "The last time I saw him, he was on his way to Western General Hospital."

FINBAR

"Listen, why don't you guys just go home?"

They were approaching the front of the hospital. The sun was higher now, but it gave no heat. Dmitri had thought far enough ahead to tell Harold to bring an extra jacket for Brendan. "I don't want to drag anybody else into this. It's too dangerous."

"You still haven't told me anything," Harold complained. "Why do you need to find this guy? Who's after you? Why don't you just go to the cops or call your mum and dad?"

"I can't call anyone," Brendan said. "It's complicated."

"We're your friends," Dmitri said simply. "Friends are always there when you need the hand."

"*A* hand," Brendan sighed. "Not *the* hand." Brendan looked at the faces of Harold and Dmitri. He had to be honest. He was relieved that he wasn't alone. "Thanks for the coat, Harold."

"No problem," Harold said. "Just don't wreck it."

Brendan almost laughed. Wrecking Harold's coat seemed like the least of his worries right now.

"C'mon, dude," Harold pleaded. "You gotta tell me what's goin' on. Seriously! I won't tell anybody. I promise."

Brendan sighed. "It's a long story and we haven't got the time. I want you to know that this will be dangerous and possibly quite mind-freakingly weird. If you really want to be part of it, there's no going back."

Harold frowned, his round face thoughtful. He looked to Dmitri, who shrugged and smiled. "It's pretty wicker."

"Wick-ed," Brendan said. "Not wicker. And yeah, I guess it is."

Harold licked his lips and asked, "Will there be cool things to draw?"

Brendan laughed. "Yeah, that I can pretty much guarantee."

Harold made his decision. "Okay, I'm in. What do I have to do? Will it hurt?"

Brendan shook his head. "Just look into my eyes …" Brendan focused Harold with an intense stare.

Harold shifted uncomfortably. "This is kinda weird?"

"Just look into my eyes and shut up, will ya?"

"Gee, Brendan, I didn't know you felt that way about me …"

"Shut up, Harold."

"Okay, okay. Geez." Harold looked into Brendan's eyes.

Brendan concentrated as hard as he could. He could feel Harold's discomfort but he didn't let it distract him. When he felt he was ready, he said, "Harold. I want you to see me as I really am."

Harold frowned. He blinked. Then his mouth dropped open. He pointed at Brendan and stammered, "H-H-He *glows!*"

"I know." Dmitri nodded enthusiastically. "Cool, isn't it!"

Harold looked around in wonder and exclaimed, "This is so freakin' awesome! How is this possible?"

"It's because I'm a Faerie," Brendan explained. "And quit yelling, will ya?"

"A Faerie? Like little flying things with wings? In the garden? Like Tinkerbell?"

"Not like Tinkerbell …"

Harold cut him off, pointing. "Holy cats! Look at that!"

He was pointing at a hotdog vendor's cart set up on the hospital steps. A trio of Lesser Faeries was in the process of stealing a sausage, carrying the tube of meat like a rolled-up carpet between them as they flew away from the cart. The vendor tried to swat them with a pair of barbecue tongs but they dodged easily, screeching with laughter.

"Darn seagulls! Get lost!" the vendor shouted. He couldn't see the Faeries for what they really were.

"Are they real?" Harold asked with wonder. "I mean, like, am I losing it?"

Brendan laughed. "No! They are real. There's a whole world that I didn't even know about until a couple of days ago. I'm a part of it, and I've let you see it too. I hope you don't regret it."

Harold was busy hauling his sketchbook out of his knapsack. "Are you kidding me? This is totally sick!" He found a piece of charcoal and started swiftly sketching the trio of sausage thieves as they shared out their stolen meal in the lower branches of a tree. "I mean. Look at them! Tiny people with wings! It's so cool."

"I like this one!" BLT climbed out from under the collar of Brendan's coat where she had been sheltering. "He seems to appreciate a Lesser Faerie when he sees one."

"You! You!" Harold pointed, his eyes wide. "You've got one on your shoulder."

"Yeah, yeah. I know. Say hello to BLT!"

"Cheers," BLT saluted saucily.

"Wicked!" Harold was delighted.

Shaking his head, Brendan said, "Come on." He started toward the front doors of the hospital. "We have to find Finbar."

Reluctantly, Harold trailed after Brendan and Dmitri, scratching out a few last details of his sketch.

One of the little Faeries noticed him sketching and shouted, "Oi! Fatty! Mind your own business!" He and his friends shook their fists and made rude farting noises. Harold was so delighted with the sight that he didn't even take offence at being called Fatty. He kept sketching until Brendan pulled him into the revolving door.

"Where do we start?" Brendan asked as they stood in the bustling foyer of the hospital. There were people everywhere, patients shuffling around in bathrobes and slippers. Visitors sat in chairs or were lined up for coffee.

"We have to find out if he was admitted," Dmitri said. "This is where my babka came last year when she had a fall in the bathtub. I remember there's an information desk down this way."

Dmitri led them through the central hall of the building until they saw a desk where a uniformed nurse wearing glasses connected by a chain around her neck sat talking on the phone. Brendan made sure that BLT was out of sight. He knew that no one could see her for what she really was, but he doubted that anybody would want to see a giant bug on his shoulder in a hospital. She reluctantly climbed into his pocket.

A sign hung over the woman's station that read INFORMATION confirmed they were in the right place. They approached and stood in front of her, waiting for her to get off the phone. She held up a finger to let them know she was aware of their presence.

Brendan could barely stand still. He could feel the seconds ticking past. So far, he hadn't seen any sign of Orcadia, but he knew Greenleaf would not be able to distract her for long. He had to find Finbar fast and then the amulet.

The nurse hung up the phone and smiled at them. "Hello, boys," she said. "How can I help you?"

"We're looking for someone who was brought here a couple of days ago, a friend of mine. He was in an accident," Brendan explained.

"I see," the nurse said. "Well, what was his name?"

"Finbar," Brendan began. "Finbar …" He suddenly realized he had no idea what Finbar's last name might be.

The nurse frowned. "Finbar what?"

"Uh," Brendan said. "Uh …"

"Uh-Uh? That's a funny name," the nurse said. She was smiling, but her eyes narrowed. "Shouldn't you boys be getting to school?"

Brendan's shoulders drooped. He didn't know what to say. Dmitri piped up. "The truth is, we don't know his last name, Madame. He is a street person with no fixed address. We see him on the corner on our way to school each day. The other day he was involved in an altercation with a cyclist, and the ambulance attendants brought him here. We are worried about Finbar as he doesn't have anyone else in the world as far as we know. We thought we'd come by on our way to school and see if he was all right." Dmitri looked up at the nurse with his big, sad, blue eyes.

Dmitri had a gift for charming adults. His odd diction, the result of learning English as a second language, had the effect of winning their affection. He also knew how to play up his sad eyes to great effect. Brendan could see the nurse melting.[76]

"Well, aren't you the sweetest boys," she said. "I wish there were more kids like you." She swung her computer screen around and started tapping on the keyboard. "Technically, I'm not allowed to release that kind of information." She peered at the screen through the thick lenses of her glasses. "But ... I think the gentleman in room 1721 would benefit from a little visit from you boys."

Brendan heaved a sigh of relief. "Thank you, ma'am."

"And his name is Finbar Shaughnessy," she called as they hurried for the bank of elevators.

The seventeenth floor was an extended care unit for patients who required long-term attention. The boys stepped out of the elevator into a hallway lined with doors. A small sign with an arrow pointing left read NURSES' STATION, COMMON ROOM, ROOMS 1720–1740.

"This way," Brendan said, leading them in the direction the arrow indicated. They hurried down the hall.

"Why are we trying to find this homeless guy exactly?" Harold asked.

"Because my babka told us we had to," Dmitri explained. "She's a psycho."

"Psychic!" Brendan corrected. "I have to find him if I

---

76 Politeness is the one true weakness of adults. When politeness is used properly, a child can achieve almost any result. Sad eyes help a great deal. Adults are so susceptible to sad-eyed children that an entire industry involving the production and sale of pictures of children with giant sad eyes has grown up. The Sad-Eyed-Children Picture Industry employs millions worldwide and grosses more than ten billion dollars a year.

want to find my sort of magical amulet thingy. It's a quest, kind of."

Harold shook his head and grinned. "This is so freakin' cool. I mean, I could be in math right now but instead I'm on a quest for an amulet. This totally kicks math's butt."

Brendan said, with just a touch of sarcasm, "I'm glad you think so."

They turned a corner and found themselves in an open square with a nurses' station in the middle. The nurses' station consisted of a square counter that surrounded a couple of desks and filing cabinets. Working at the desks were two nurses. Patients' rooms opened off the central area. The lighting was subdued, and the mysterious sound of electronic monitors and medical devices hummed and pinged softly.

Brendan, Harold, and Dmitri walked along, looking at the numbers on the doors: "1719. 1720. This is it! 1721!" Brendan announced. He reached for the handle.

"Excuse me." A female voice froze them in their tracks. "Where do you think you're going?"

Brendan turned to see a short, plump woman approaching. She wore a white cotton coat over green scrubs. Her gold nameplate read RITA. She looked at the three boys with her blue eyes and waited for a response.

"We're here to visit Finbar Shaughnessy," Brendan said hopefully.

"Are you family?"

"No. Just friends. The lady downstairs said it would be all right."

"The lady downstairs doesn't run this ward," Nurse Rita snapped. "I do. You can't just barge in here and demand to see a patient."

"We are not demanding to see him, Madame," Dmitri said sweetly. "We would really like to see him, maybe cheer him up." The sad eyes were on full blast.

"Don't try to charm me, young man." Nurse Rita waved a finger in Dmitri's face. "There are rules!"

"Please, ma'am," Brendan begged. "We just want to say hello. Tell him Brendan is here to see him."

Nurse Rita was about to protest, but she stopped when she heard Brendan's name. "Humph. Brendan is it? Well." She looked at each of the boys and made a decision. "You wait here. I'll see if he's awake. If he isn't, you'll have to come back later."

She went to the door of 1721 and opened it a crack. "Mr. Shaughnessy? Are you awake?" They heard a grunt from inside the room and she nodded. "I have some folks here to see you." She nodded at the boys and held open the door. Brendan led the others through.

"He's been asking for you ever since he came in here," Nurse Rita said softly to Brendan. "We didn't even know if you really existed. He's had quite a bad knock and he's no spring chicken. I have to say he's recovered very well for a man of his years." She took one last look toward the bed and closed the door.

Finbar was propped up in his hospital bed, the adjustable bed angled forward and a couple of pillows under his back. The room was bare and stark, the walls a sickly shade of pale green. There was a single chair in the corner, a rolling table, and a cheap wardrobe up against the wall. Finbar's weathered boots rested on the floor in front of the wardrobe.

Finbar did not look good. His head was tightly wound with a gauze bandage. He was dressed in a hospital gown with short sleeves, his stringy arms folded on his lap and his hands clutching a cup of water with a lid on it and a bendy straw. An IV bag hung by the bed, its clear fluid dripping into a plastic tube that was attached to the man's arm. A heart monitor beeped softly above the bed.

Dmitri and Harold hung back as Brendan went to stand beside the old man's bed. Finbar's eyes followed him, the pale blue orbs burning with a fevered intensity. The heart monitor sped up slightly.

"I knew ye'd come," the old man said. "I knew sure as the nose on my face."

Brendan found Finbar's stare a little disturbing. "You did? How did you know?"

The old man laughed a raspy, chesty sound that transformed into a coughing fit. "I knew 'cause ye'd have to find yer token, don't ye? Yer wee necklace."

Brendan's eyes narrowed. "How do you know about that?"

"Sure and I was there when you were left on the doorstep as a babe. Them nuns didn't see ya for what ye was but I did, didn't I?"

"Nuns? I don't understand. What nuns?"

Finbar cackled again. "You don't know the first thing, do ye? Kept ya in the dark all these years, poor lad. Poor Prince *Breandan*." He started to laugh again and broke down into a fresh coughing fit. Brendan grabbed the cup of water and raised the straw to the old man's lips.

Brendan was startled to hear his name spoken in the way the Faeries pronounced it. Finbar was Human. He was positive. He would have seen if he was a Faerie surely. "How do you know me? Tell me!"

Finbar coughed once more and then spat a massive glob of phlegm onto the linoleum floor.

"Gross," Harold observed.

Finbar ignored Harold's comment and focused on Brendan. "You were left on the doorstep of St. Bart's Catholic Orphanage fourteen years ago. I was workin' there at the time."

"Is that true?" Dmitri asked.

"It could be," Brendan admitted. "My parents told me the other night that I was adopted. They didn't tell me where they adopted me from."

"I was there, sure enough, and I knew there was somethin' uncanny about ye. I'd had experience of yer kind before."

Brendan was surprised. "What do you mean? You had contact with Faeries before?"

Finbar's face became guarded. "Never you mind what I mean. The point is I know where to find what yer lookin' for. Hid it meself, didn't I?"

"So tell us where to find it," Brendan said. "And we'll leave you in peace. It's very important."

"I'm sure it is. But I won't tell ya where tae find it unless you promise that you'll do me a good turn in exchange."

"A good turn. A favour, you mean?" Brendan demanded. "Tell me, and I'll decide if I can do it."

"No!" Finbar barked. "You have to promise and that's it! Or else ye can go and search for your treasure high and low. I'll not help ye." Finbar leaned back in the bed and sucked contentedly on his drink, eyes on Brendan all the while, waiting for the boy's decision.

"I recognize this one from somewhere," BLT's voice piped up. She came out of Brendan's pocket where she'd been hiding. Her almond-shaped eyes narrowed in concentration. "He has a strange aura."

Unlike Dmitri and Harold, Finbar didn't seem the least bit shocked or surprised by the sudden appearance of BLT. He merely smirked. "Look at that, will ye. It's been a while since I've seen one of yer kind."

"You seem very familiar to me," BLT said again. "Let me think."

Brendan had thinking of his own to do. He had no idea what the old man wanted. What if he couldn't deliver on the promise? Promises seemed to hold a great deal of weight in his new life. He didn't know what to do.

Sometimes our decisions are made for us. At that moment, all the lights in the room went out. Weak sunlight streamed through the window, but the electrical light failed completely. The heart monitor let out a sickly shriek, then shorted out altogether.

"They're coming," BLT whispered.

"Oh, no," Brendan whispered.

"What's the matter?" Dmitri asked.

"This is bad," Brendan said. He felt terror jangling along his nerves.

"It's just a power failure," Harold offered. "They have, like, emergency power and stuff."

"No. It isn't a normal power failure. I can feel it," Brendan said tightly. "She's coming."

"That crazy woman?" Harold asked.

"Orcadia." Brendan nodded. "She's found me." He whipped his head around to Finbar. "Fine! Whatever you ask, I'll do it. Where is the amulet?"

Finbar wagged a finger. "Uh, uh, uh! Not so fast, me lad. I won't tell you. I'll show you where it is."

"No way! You can't even leave your bed!"

In answer, Finbar tugged the IV out of his arm. Fluid squirted from the needle.

"Also gross," Harold gulped.

The old man swung his scrawny legs out of bed and staggered to the wardrobe, on the way revealing his equally scrawny buttocks through the slit in the back of his hospital gown.

"Now I may barf!" Harold said, covering his eyes.

"I'll get dressed and away we go." Finbar hauled open the door of the wardrobe to reveal his clothes on hangers within.

"Hurry," Brendan cried. He rushed to the window and looked out. Traffic was snarled because the traffic lights had failed. People were honking and trying to get around each other. His heart sank. He felt that everyone was being put in danger all because of him. He turned back into the room to find that Finbar had pulled on his pants and boots and now Dmitri was buttoning up the old man's shirt.

"Let's go!" Brendan shouted and ran for the door. Dmitri and Harold pulled the old man by the elbows and they rushed out into the hall.

Brendan stopped short. The nurses' station was dark. Here, on the inside of the building, there were no windows. The only light came from battery-operated emergency lights over the nurses' desks.

"BLT!" Brendan hissed.

BLT popped out of Brendan's pocket. In her tiny hands she held a mini chocolate bar, half of it already eaten. "What's up, your lordship?"

Brendan groaned. "Don't tell me you're on a sugar high!"

"All right," BLT giggled. She began to spark and glow. "I won't tell you."

"Where did you get that?"

She pointed an unsteady finger at Dmitri and laughed. "His lovely babka gave it to me. What a lovely woman, she is! Thoughtful, you know what I mean?"

"Can you tell me if Orcadia is close?"

"She'll be comin' up the elevator when she comes." BLT giggled, looking unconcerned. She started to sing. "*She'll be comin' up the elevator when she comes! She'll be comin' up the elevator, she'll be comin' up the elevator …*" She collapsed into helpless giggling and tried to fly out of Brendan's grasp. He quickly caught her and, none too gently, rammed her into the pocket of his jacket and zipped it shut.

"And that little Faerie is useful how, exactly?" Harold asked.

Brendan's pocket began to heave and glow from within. "BLT! Gimme a break, will ya?"

Nurse Rita came around the corner. She held a flashlight. "We seem to have had a power failure. Are you boys all right?" Then she saw Finbar. "What are you doing out of bed, Mr. Shaughnessy?" Then she saw he was dressed in his street clothes. "What's going on here?"

Brendan opened his mouth to answer, when there was a crash from down the hall where the elevators were. A rending of metal shrieked through the ward.

"What in the world …?" Nurse Rita began.

Brendan didn't want to wait to confirm what he already knew. "To the stairs!" he shouted and ran for a red exit sign down the opposite hall.

He crashed into the door and flung it open, revealing a

set of grey concrete stairs with a steel pipe railing painted dull grey. With Dmitri and Harold dragging Finbar close behind, they rushed as fast as they could down the stairs by the light of the red emergency bulbs.

As the door was swinging shut behind him, Brendan clearly heard Nurse Rita saying angrily, "And who are you? There are no pets allowed in the hospital. It's against the rules."

There was a low canine growl. Brendan recognized it all too well as the sound of the Kobolds. Orcadia's voice was as cold as ice. "The rules just changed."

The door slammed shut on the yapping laughter of the Kobold pack.

ESCAPE

Brendan was about to run down the stairs with his friends and make his escape when he stopped short. He was stung by guilt. Poor Nurse Rita couldn't be left to face her fate alone. It wasn't right.

Brendan shouted at the others, "Hurry! Get downstairs! I'll be right behind you."

Harold needed no coaxing. With Finbar leaning heavily on him and the railing, the chubby boy started down the stairs as fast as he could. The old man's slouch cap was poised comically on top of his bandaged head. The two of them turned the first corner and disappeared from sight. Dmitri stopped and looked hard at Brendan. "Where are you going?"

Brendan looked back at the door. "I can't leave that nurse to deal with Orcadia and those hounds."

"What could you possibly do? All you should be worrying about is getting away."

"Just go!" Brendan yelled. "I'll be fine. Wait for me outside."

With that, Brendan flung the door open and stepped back onto the seventeenth floor. Flickering lights could be seen from down the hall in the nurses' station. The sniff and snort of the hounds and the murmur of Orcadia's voice reached him. Brendan mustered his courage and headed back toward the nurses' station.

Brendan came around the corner to see Orcadia with her hand around the throat of Nurse Rita. She had pressed the woman up against the wall, and she was speaking straight into the terrified nurse's face.

"I'm going to ask one more time," Orcadia said sweetly. "You will tell me the truth or else I'll let them deal with you."

The Kobolds squatted in dog form, their pale eyes glaring hungrily at Nurse Rita. Brendan saw them for what they were: Kobolds. His Faerie Sight was becoming more acute, able to see through the hound form they projected for Human eyes. Though they were not in hound form, they still maintained some dog characteristics: their stance, sitting on their haunches with their mouths hanging open, was reminiscent of their canine alter egos. Their red-rimmed eyes rolled in their wedge-shaped skulls as they tittered maniacally.

Brendan couldn't imagine what Nurse Rita was thinking right then, her Human eyes telling her she was menaced by slavering dogs. He'd been scared out of his mind while running from the beasts through the Undertown. Nurse Rita hadn't had the benefit of even a day to get used to the bizarre creatures she was facing but somehow she found the courage to defy Orcadia.

"I'm not permitted to release patient information," she managed to rasp. "Leave here at once. The police have been notified."

Orcadia crowed with laughter. "The *police* have been notified? Oh, my! I'm sooooo terrified." She laughed again. "You have no idea how little I care about the police!" She ceased laughing and raised her fist over her head. Her fingers flickered with sparkling flame and she hissed, "I'll ask you one last time: I know a boy came here. Who did he come to see and where is he now?"

"Right here!" Brendan announced, stepping out of the hallway. "It's me you want. Let her go."

Orcadia's head snapped around at the sound of Brendan's voice. She smiled. "Ah. Here he is at last."

"Let her go, Orcadia," Brendan said evenly, though inside he was a jelly of fear. He had trouble keeping his knees from knocking together.

"Of course." Orcadia smiled. She stabbed her finger into Nurse Rita's neck. There was a crackle of discharged energy. Nurse Rita went rigid for an instant then limp as a rag doll in Orcadia's grip. Orcadia tossed the nurse aside, and the unconscious woman slid across the floor, through the door into Finbar's vacated room. Brendan took a quick look and was relieved to see the rise and fall of the nurse's chest. She was alive, at least.

Orcadia turned to fix Brendan with her seething frigid blue eyes. She smiled as she said, "So, you've decided to surrender at last. It's for the best." She walked toward Brendan, her arms wide in a parody of loving invitation. "Come give your auntie a hug, Breandan. I won't bite."

Brendan stood still, watching her approach. The Kobolds trotted tamely at her heels. They grinned at him, revealing rows of vicious teeth.

Brendan's mind was racing. He looked frantically around for any way out. The door to Finbar's room gaped open, but there was no way out save the window. He couldn't fly. *Well, at least I don't think I can*, he thought miserably. *How would I know?*

Orcadia stopped in front of him and wrapped her arms around him. The sensation was like being wrapped in a live power line. Brendan could feel the hum of energy coursing through her, and the smell of her hair was the metallic tang of rain on pavement.

"Dear boy," she whispered in his ear. "You needn't be so afraid of me. I am here to show you your true potential." She pulled away and looked into his eyes. "My brother would want me to take care of you, to bring you into your powers. He can't be here." She smiled, and Brendan suddenly felt that he could believe her, almost. He felt some power working on his resistance. Some part of him knew it was a trick but he was unable to resist her.

Maybe she does just want what's best for me. Maybe all those others are wrong. "But Mr. Greenleaf and Ariel and Kim … Ki-Mata. They say you want to hurt the Humans. My parents are Human. I don't want them to suffer."

"Oh, aren't you a dear." She ruffled his hair. Static crackled from her fingertips. "The Humans took everything from us. They have to pay. But here, if you really like these *parents* of yours"—her distaste for the word was obvious—"we'll spare them. You can keep them as pets. Won't that be nice?" She smiled sweetly.

Brendan felt anger welling inside him. Who was this creature to refer to his mother and father as pets? There was no way he would ever submit to her. "I'm afraid I'm going to have to refuse," he said through gritted teeth.

Orcadia's eyes narrowed to slits. She drew her lips back to reveal her even white teeth in a grimace of rage. The Kobolds whimpered and cowered away.

"All right. I'm through trying to convince you. You had your chance," Orcadia hissed. "Now, you will die!"

And that was when Dmitri smacked her with the fire extinguisher.

Orcadia staggered and fell over. Brendan gave his head a shake and surged to his feet. That's when he saw Dmitri.

"A fire extinguisher?" Brendan asked.

"It's all I could find!" Dmitri explained.

"I told you to get out of here!" Brendan shouted angrily.

"You're welcome!" Dmitri snapped back. "I just saved your ham."

"Bacon," Brendan laughed, on the verge of hysteria. "Saved my bacon!"

"Whatever." Dmitri shrugged. "I knew it was a pork product." Then his eyes went wide and he raised the nozzle of the fire extinguisher. Brendan dropped out of the way as the Kobolds leapt at Dmitri. The small boy triggered the extinguisher, and frigid, pressurized foam gushed into the beasts' faces. Their hungry snarls became canine yelps of pain as they fell to the ground, rubbing their stinging muzzles on the floor to scrape away the chemical coating.

"Nice one," Brendan said, looking at Dmitri's handiwork. His joy was cut short when he felt Orcadia's hand clamp around his ankle like a vise. He looked down at her face, twisted with rage, snarling up at him.

Dmitri fired off another blast of foam directly into her face.

"Arrrrrrrrgh!" she shrieked. "It burns!" She let go of Brendan, and he danced free, pulling Dmitri out of reach with him. Orcadia, blinded, raised her hands and shouted, "I'll kill you!" Her hands ignited in showers of crackling blue sparks as she fired bolts of electricity randomly into the air. The bolts struck the ceiling tiles, igniting them.

She spun around, flailing bolts of power at the walls and the floor, trying blindly to strike at Brendan and Dmitri.

Brendan wanted to dash down the hall to join Harold and Finbar on the stairs, but Orcadia was standing squarely in the way. The elevators were blocked off, too. A bolt sizzled an inch above their heads.

Brendan grabbed Dmitri by the sleeve. "We've got to get out of range." He pulled his friend through the door of Finbar's room. Orcadia swung toward the sound of his voice and fired a blast of energy at the exact spot he had been a split second before. Brendan slammed the door shut.

Dmitri fumbled at the doorknob. "There isn't any lock!"

"Quick! Help me move this!" Brendan ran to the bed and heaved against it. Luckily, it was on rollers so it moved easily. Dmitri helped guide it across the floor until it rested against the door. "The brakes," Brendan shouted. They went from corner to corner kicking at the wheels until all the brakes were down.

"That should hold them for a second or two," Brendan said. He looked down and saw Nurse Rita lying on the floor. "Help me."

He and Dmitri hauled the nurse between them and propped her inside the wardrobe, closing the door. "Maybe they won't notice her when they come for us," Brendan explained. A snarl and crash that rattled the door in its frame made them both jump.

"I wouldn't count on it," Dmitri squeaked. "Now what?"

Brendan didn't know what to say. They were seventeen floors off the ground. He ran to the window and pushed it open. He looked straight down to the concrete forecourt of the hospital. There was no convenient balcony to land on only a floor below as there would have been if this were a story in a book or a Hollywood movie. The door rattled again. Then it began to rain indoors. A heavy downpour began to fall from the ceiling. Brendan couldn't believe it. "Can she make it rain as well as control lightning?" he cried.

The truth was much more mundane. Orcadia's indiscriminate blasts had set off the sprinkler system. The water poured down onto her and the hounds. The Kobolds snarled and yelped in the downpour. They didn't enjoy being wet.

This served to enrage Orcadia further. She fired two crackling blasts of electricity into the floor.[77] The consequences for Orcadia were negligible. She was naturally immune to the effects of her own powers. The Kobolds, however, were not.

Standing in the water pooling on the linoleum tiles of the ward, the Kobolds did a bizarre dance as many thousands of volts coursed through them. Though they were magical beings of more than an earthly nature, they were not able to survive electrocution. After one final yelping whine, they fell in a steaming heap on the floor, stunned, their furry coats smouldering in the artificial rain.

Brendan and Dmitri, listening on the other side of the door, didn't know what was happening out in the hallway.

"That sounded painful," Dmitri said in the sudden silence.

---

[77] Now, anyone who works around electricity is probably aware that water and electricity do not mix well. Water is an excellent conductor.

"Do you smell burning dog hair?" Brendan asked.

They waited in the eerie silence, wondering what would happen next.

"You want to look?" Dmitri asked at last.

"Are you nuts?"

"I'm here so I must be."

Brendan was about to agree with Dmitri when a profound, concussive boom split the air. The door came flying in, sending the bed spinning out of the way and narrowly missing the two boys. The door continued its trajectory and smashed through the window, plunging out of sight. Smoke poured in from the nurses' station as Orcadia strode into the room and stopped, glaring at them. She was quivering with rage. In a voice that was eerily calm, she said, "You, dear nephew, are a difficult little boy. I have offered you everything and you've spat in my face. I will give you one last chance!" Her voice ramped up to an angry shout as she raised her hands. Blue fire bridged between her hands like the electrodes of a mad scientist's machine in an old horror movie. "Join me … or *die!*"

Brendan looked out the window and saw seagulls swooping past the window: not Lesser Faeries this time but the real thing. He had an idea. It was crazy, but they were running out of options. Before Orcadia could fry them where they stood, he wrapped his arms around Dmitri and, with a mighty heave, flung himself and his best friend out the window.

Dmitri began to scream in terror. Brendan ignored him and sent out a call with his mind. He remembered the way he had called the sparrows the day before. Now, he prayed he could do something similar. It was the longest of long shots but he had nothing to lose.

Help! Help! HEEEEEELP! he cried in his mind. He pictured all the seagulls that gathered in the air around Toronto. They swarmed around the garbage Dumpsters and the restaurants. They gathered on the beaches and in the parks. He pictured their broad powerful wings as they soared on the air currents, scanning the land below for anything they might eat. *COME HELP ME! THERE WILL BE SNACKS!*

All this ripped through his mind in a fraction of a second. He felt the air rushing past him as they fell from the window, cold air rippling their clothes. He closed his eyes and sent one final plea. *SNACKS!!!*

The sensation was similar to falling backward onto a trampoline or one of those inflatable bouncy castles that he had loved so much as a child. He opened his eyes to find that they were absolutely surrounded by a cloud of fluttering, flapping feathers. Raucous bird cries filled the air.

Dmitri stopped struggling. "I don't believe it." He started to laugh.

They were wafting gently down toward the pavement. They passed the windows, going more and more slowly. The seagulls had gathered into a sort of raft, interweaving their wings into a single feathery platform. With gentle grace, they coasted to the ground. Dmitri and Brendan rolled off their raft of birds, and it gracefully dissolved into a carpet of screeching seagulls, heads bobbing and twisting as they looked up at Brendan with beady eyes. The caws slowly distinguished themselves into a single word. "*Food? Food? Food?*"

Dmitri and Brendan exchanged a look and then burst into laughter, the kind of laughter tinged with hysteria that only comes from being saved from death by the impossible intervention of a flock of seagulls.[78] Brendan felt incredibly exhausted, drained by the effort of calling for the gulls. Shaking his head to clear it, he looked around and saw that many people were stopped, staring at them as if they had landed in a spaceship or something. Brendan didn't blame them.

Brendan's eye alit on the hotdog vendor's cart. He waved toward the cart and said, "There! Food."

The hotdog vendor was immediately the recipient of the unwanted attention of a thousand seagulls.

Dmitri pointed to the front doors of the hospital. Finbar and Harold were emerging from the revolving door. The sound of sirens approaching swelled in the air. Brendan looked up to see the window they'd fallen from gaping above, and black smoke pouring out of it. For an instant, he saw the shock of Orcadia's pale hair as she looked down at him. Then she was gone.

"We've got to get out of here!" Brendan ran to meet Harold and Finbar, Dmitri at his heels. Together, as the fire engines arrived and the firefighters poured out to battle the flames in their emergency gear, the four pushed their way through the gathering crowd and headed south down University Avenue.

---

[78] That is a very particular and rare form of hysterical laughter indeed!

TO PARKDALE

"The birds caught us!" Dmitri said, dumbfounded. "They caught us!"

Brendan had seen and experienced so many weird things over the past two days that he took the bird rescue in stride. "Where are we going, Finbar?"

Finbar was wheezing hard. The seventeen floors of steps had been difficult for him. Brendan was surprised that he was still on his feet. "Home. Must get home," the old man wheezed.

Brendan had always assumed that Finbar lived rough on the street. He'd only ever seen the old man outside the Scott Mission on his way home from school. "Where do you live?"

"Where I've always lived, o' course." Finbar grinned despite his discomfort. "Where I've lived these eighty years and more."

Brendan couldn't believe his ears. "Eighty years! How old are you anyway?"

The old man wheezed out a laugh. "Old."

Brendan threw up his hands. He'd had enough of Finbar's cryptic answers. His patience was wearing thin. "Tell me where the amulet is!"

Finbar's eyes narrowed. He leaned hard against a lamp pole, catching his breath. "I know how you folk work! I know better than anyone! Promise everything and give nothing. If I tell ye anything, ye'll cheat me."

"Listen," Brendan said earnestly. "I don't know why you don't trust me or … my 'folk.' I'm sorry if you've been cheated in the past. That wasn't by me. I swear I will grant you whatever you wish as long as it's in my power." He pointed back up at the hospital where more fire engines were converging. "I can guarantee that you will get a better deal from me than you will from her. Just tell us where we're going."

Finbar stood chewing on his lower lip. He looked into Brendan's eyes and nodded once, grinning to show his sparse teeth. "All right, lad. I'll trust ye. We need to go to Parkdale. In Liberty Village."

Brendan frowned. "That's west. Down by the Dufferin Gate." Brendan had gone down there a couple of times with his father to the Canadian National Exhibition and to see a Toronto FC soccer game.

"Does anybody have money for a cab?"

Harold and Dmitri shook their heads. "I have about five bucks in quarters," Harold offered.

"That won't even get us all on the Red Rocket!"[79] Brendan said in disgust. "I guess we're hoofing it."

There was no sign of Orcadia as they headed south, but Brendan didn't want to take any chances. They wove a

---

[79] The streetcars in Toronto are nicknamed "Red Rockets." They cruise up and down the streets on fixed tracks, drawing power from electrical lines overhead. Motorists find them a little annoying because they're a little slow and no one likes getting caught behind them. One day, all cars will fly and the speed of the streetcars will no longer be an issue. Unless there are flying streetcars, which will cause the same problem, only in the air.

circuitous route through back laneways and side streets, but always heading southwest. Brendan kept a wary eye out for any sign of pursuit—he felt horribly exposed out in broad daylight but it couldn't be helped.

At first, he was worried about how Finbar would manage. The man had suffered a serious head injury and been in the hospital, but as they moved closer to his home, he seemed to actually improve. His step became steadier and he seemed almost cheerful. Brendan wondered if Finbar could possibly have told the truth about how long he'd lived at his present home. *He's old, sure. But is he older than ninety? A hundred?* He put the thought out of his mind and concentrated on the route.

Half an hour later, following a nervous march across the heart of Toronto, they arrived at their destination. "There she is." The old man pointed at a rough, red-brick building. "Home, sweet home!"

Brendan stood staring at the dilapidated building. "You live *there?*"

"I do."

"What a dump," Harold breathed.

The three boys took a moment to absorb what they were seeing. The building stood on its own surrounded by a chain-link fence. The windows were mostly boarded up or broken, and the only door they could see had two-by-fours nailed into it to keep people out. To drive the point home, a big sign hanging on the fence read

DANGER: DO NOT ENTER.

The building was an odd shape, too. One side of the roof was higher than the other, as though the remaining structure had once been part of a longer one that no longer stood. A free-standing wall jutted out from the side of the building as though the decrepit building were reaching out to balance itself.

Condo towers rose all around the building, all perfectly proportioned, sleek boxes of glass and steel that made the red-brick building look like a misshapen, stunted dwarf standing among giants. The lawns and walkways outside the fence had all been painstakingly manicured and landscaped, while the little building sat in a muddy field, a few tools piled against the wall. A miniature bulldozer sinking into the mire made it look even more forlorn.

"You live *there?*" Brendan asked again. "In a condemned building?"

"It ain't condemned," Finbar said, annoyed. "They ain't goin' to tear it down. It's to become a community centre or some such."

"Looks like a fun place to hang out," Harold puffed. He was bent over, sucking wind. He was fumbling for his writing pad and charcoal. "I'd love to meet other youths here for good clean fun."

"The amulet is in there?" Brendan asked Finbar.

The old man grinned his gap-toothed grin. "Aye, she is, hidden from prying eyes."

"How do we get in?"

"This way." Finbar walked up to the fence and pushed on a section of the chain-link. He looked back at the boys and smiled. "Comin'?"

"You guys are free to go," Brendan said to Dmitri and Harold. "This isn't your problem. You've been great, but I don't want to put you in any more danger."

Dmitri and Harold exchanged a glance. Dmitri folded his arms. "I think we'll stay."

"Yeah," Harold said. "I've almost crapped my pants about ten times but it's been pretty cool." He started to carve the blank sheet of his sketch pad with his habitual lump of charcoal. "Besides, nerds gotta stick together."

Brendan looked at his friends, and he felt a fierce surge of pride. They were great friends: the best! They had helped him out, putting themselves in danger. He couldn't ask them to do any more even if he didn't want to face the next part alone. He knew he had to let them go for their own safety.

He concentrated on what he wanted. He closed his eyes, and when he opened them a moment later, he made a sincere request. "Harold and Dmitri: go home and forget this day."

The two boys blinked. Without a word, they turned and walked away. Brendan watched them until they disappeared around a corner before turning to Finbar.

The old man watched him with his pale blue eyes.

"That must have been a hard choice."

"I wanted them to be safe."

Finbar smiled and ruffled his hair. "Yer a good lad." He went to the fence and pulled a section of the chain-link aside, holding it for Brendan. "After you, Yer Highness."

"What?"

"It's your name, son." Finbar smiled. "In the old tongue Breandan means 'Prince.'"

"Huh," Brendan said. "I didn't know that."

"There's a lot of things ye didn't know, lad. Now let's hop before that mad banshee rears her head."

Brendan took a deep breath and stepped through the hole in the fence.

THE AMULET

Brendan's foot sank ankle deep in mud.

"Gah!" Brendan tried to pull his foot out but he only succeeded in losing a shoe.

"Watch yerself." Finbar chuckled. "It's a mite muddy."

"Thanks for the warning." Brendan glowered.

The old man nimbly climbed through the fence and stepped onto a rock, avoiding the mire. He hopped from stone to stone until he stood on a grassy patch of sod by the wall of the building. "C'mon, lad. Look sharp."

Grumbling, Brendan fished his cold, wet, mud-caked shoe out of the muck and gingerly slipped it back onto his foot. He hopped from stone to stone as Finbar had done until they stood beside a heavy wooden door. The door was secured with a steel padlock.

"Do you have a key?" Brendan asked.

"No need." Finbar kicked the door, and the hasp pulled away from the wooden surface. The door swung open, and Finbar stepped through into the darkness. After a quick look over his shoulder, Brendan followed.

He found himself in almost total darkness. The wooden floor creaked underfoot, making him wonder about the structural soundness of the entire building. He could dimly make out a staircase going up on one side and a corridor that stretched out in front of him.

"Welcome to St. Bart's." Finbar's voice rasped from the darkness. "Formerly the chapel of Toronto Central Prison. It's all that's left of that fine institute of moral correction. I spent some time there as a resident, paroled in 1915 when they shut the old place down."

"You …" Brendan stared at Finbar in disbelief. "That's impossible. That would make you …"

"Old." Finbar smiled sadly. "Older than you can imagine." He looked up around the room and waved an arm at the gloom. "The Sisters of St. Bartholomew got this building for a song. I came and worked as the caretaker. For over ninety years now, it's been my home."

A match flared, casting shuddering shadows on the peeling wallpaper of the walls. Finbar's face was eerily lit from below as he used the match to light an old-fashioned oil lantern. The lamp caught, and the warm yellow light grew stronger as Finbar fiddled with a knob on the side of it. Satisfied, the old man lifted the lantern by a wire handle and held it high.

He pointed. "Up those stairs, the children slept. The nuns as well. The Mother Superior had her office there too. I worked for a few. The kindest was Sister Cecilia, the last of the Mothers Superior: a good Irish lass and a kind-hearted lady, God rest her soul. 'Twas her that took you in that night so long ago."

Brendan looked up the stairs into the darkness. *I've been here before?* He couldn't remember this place but, of course, he'd only been an infant.

"You charmed them one and all, ya did." Finbar chuckled. "Such a sweet little nipper. Had them eatin' out of yer hand." Finbar's tone darkened. "But I knew what ye were the moment I saw ye. I knew, 'cause …"

"Ha!" BLT's shout startled Brendan. The tiny Faerie leapt out of his pocket and buzzed over to Finbar, hovering in front of his face. "You were the one who almost saw us that night!"

"What are you going on about?" Brendan demanded.

"I was one of the Lesser Faeries who left you on the doorstep all those years ago." She was laughing. "And this big fella was the one who picked you up that night. He almost saw us. Ooo. Your father would not have liked that. Not one bit."

"You knew all this time where we were going?" Brendan was incredulous. "Why didn't you say something?"

BLT cocked her head in frank puzzlement. "You didn't ask! And besides, I didn't know the old fart had stolen the amulet. I was just the delivery girl."

Brendan clenched his fists and gritted his teeth. "Faeries!" he snarled. Getting his annoyance under control, he said, "We're here now. Finbar, where is the amulet?"

Finbar smiled. "Down in the cellar."

The old man turned and walked down the corridor. Brendan followed, expecting the floor to give way beneath his feet at any second. BLT fluttered down and rested on his shoulder. "I sure could use a little something sweet right now. To take the edge off, you know."

"Too bad," Brendan said without sincerity.

The corridor led to a kitchen. Brendan was expecting decrepitude but the kitchen was surprisingly neat and tidy. Apparently, Finbar had continued to use it as a living space. On top of the old gas stove he had placed a propane camp stove. Bottles of water stood by the sink and a few cups and plates lay beside them. Some dried noodle soups and cans of beans were stacked on the counter.

Finbar grinned and pointed at the sink. "They gave ye a bath in that there sink. You were naught but a tiny wee thing." He chuckled. He went to a door and pulled it open. Stairs led down into darkness. "Watch yer step, now. The stairs are a little tricky." The old man started down, holding the lantern high.

Brendan tried to imagine himself, a baby, sitting in the little sink. He couldn't. Why hadn't his parents told him about this place? He imagined them coming to find him here and taking him home. He felt a sob welling up inside him, but he forced it down. He went to the stairs and started down after Finbar.

The stairs were indeed tricky. Some of the treads were missing altogether. Bracing himself against the crumbling plaster wall, Brendan made a careful descent. At last, he reached the bottom to find Finbar waiting patiently and holding the lantern to guide his steps.

Junk was piled everywhere in haphazard piles. There were old pieces of broken furniture, tools, building materials, bicycles, boxes of old clothes, and books all stacked in precariously balanced piles. One false move and the whole jumbled mess looked like it would come down.

"This way," Finbar called and began to weave his way deftly through the stacks. Brendan followed at a slower pace, trying to avoid toppling anything.

"You were there when I was left on the doorstep?" he asked BLT.

"Sure." BLT nodded. "I didn't realize it was you. You were just a bairn."[80]

---

[80] *Bairn* is an old Scottish word for child. The origin of the term is unknown. Some say that in the distant past, Scottish people

"So you knew my father?"

"He was my master." BLT nodded. "He had me and Fith drop you off. He was afraid he wouldn't be able to let you go if he did it himself."

"Fith? You mean Deirdre's creepy little creature?" Brendan couldn't believe it. "Why didn't Fith say something about that?"

"We were Compelled to silence by Briach Morn." BLT grimaced. "He was powerful. When he tells you to keep your mouth shut, you really ain't got a choice." She suddenly noticed a stray globule of chocolate icing on her waistcoat and gleefully scooped it into her mouth. Instantly, she smiled and began to flare. Without warning she shot like a rocket into the air, forcing Brendan to snatch her as she zipped for freedom. Brendan managed to hold on to her but bumped into a stack of books, sending them crashing down.

"Mind yerself!" Finbar called.

"Sorry." Brendan cringed. He frowned at BLT but she was oblivious. When he was sure she hadn't had too much sugar to provoke a major freak-out, he relaxed his grip on her. "I have one more question."

"Hmmm?" BLT said dreamily.

"Why did he do it?"

"Do what?" BLT asked.

---

mistakenly believed that children were actually little bears. This seems far-fetched. Another theory is that babies, being born naked, were referred to as "litle bare ones," which over time was transformed into the shorter term "bairns." It's odd that BLT would use a Scottish term. Perhaps this hints at an earlier Scottish ancestry.

"Why did he give me up? Why did he hide me the way he did, throw me out to find my own way in the world?"

BLT was silent for a moment before she answered. "I knew him as well as any. I was his servant many a year. He was a dark soul and an angry one. The only time I ever saw him smile was when he found her."

"My mother?"

"She changed him in many ways. When she died birthing you, it broke him. At first I thought he would kill you, though you were just an innocent little thing." BLT's eyes were distant, remembering that long-ago night. "In the end, he told us to take you and hide you away. He couldn't look at you any longer. Why he hid you among Humans, I don't know. We just did as he asked."

He wished he could have met his mother. By all accounts, she'd been wonderful. His father sounded like a total nightmare. The decisions Briach Morn had made fourteen years ago had brought his son to this derelict building, this cellar, and this moment.

"Hey! Are ye comin'?" Finbar called impatiently. Brendan hurried as quickly as he dared toward the yellow spill of lamplight.

He emerged from the rubbish to find himself in a clearing. Looming against one wall was a massive, ancient hulk of a furnace. A cot was drawn up alongside it, neatly made with a thick down comforter covering it. Beside it was a rickety card table and a folding chair with a small stack of books on it. A lamp stood in the centre of the table casting its rich, steady glow. A cheap dresser completed the furnishings of Finbar's little den.

Finbar was bent over the dresser, rummaging in the top drawer. He sighed and lifted out a small bundle, carrying it over to the table. The outer covering was a beautiful green piece of cloth. No. It wasn't exclusively green, but green with a shimmering of all the other colours dancing through its weave. Brendan gasped at the beauty of it. He moved closer and laid his hand on the fabric. It was softer than silk. Never had his fingers touched anything so pleasing. He tried to lift the bundle but Finbar's hand fell on his wrist.

"This is the blanket you were wrapped in when you arrived at St. Bart's. I knew just looking at it, it were of Faerie design." He looked into Brendan's eyes. "Remember now, we have a bargain. Ye won't be grabbin' this token and runnin' off. We have a deal."

Brendan nodded his assent. Finbar removed his hand. With trembling fingers, he undid the bundle of cloth. BLT leaned forward on his shoulder as the token was revealed.

The amulet glimmered warmly in the honey-coloured light. The intricate gold chain shimmered softly, thin links spread across the cloth like a golden string. The amulet was a circular golden medallion filled with swirling gold lettering that spelled his name in old-fashioned script: BREANDAN. The Faerie spelling, Brendan noted. Four gemstones studded the letters in no discernible pattern he could make out.

Brendan reached out and traced the letters with his fingertip. Surprisingly, the gold was warm, almost like a living thing. In spite of that, Brendan shivered. He felt a current of energy, a sympathetic vibration thrumming through his skin at the point of contact. He was meant to have the amulet. Nothing in his life had ever seemed more certain to him. He opened his hand to grasp it.

"Before you take yon bauble, My Prince"—Finbar's

voice was firm. Brendan looked up into the pale blue eyes—"remember your pledge to me. You will give me what I desire."

"I remember." Brendan nodded. He turned his eyes back to the amulet. He swallowed loudly and reached for it, closing his fingers around it.

Nothing happened. There was no burst of energy. No sudden understanding dawned in his mind. He had no epiphany, nor did he gain super-strength. He was still Brendan Clair, only now, he held a finely crafted piece of personalized jewellery in his hand.

Brendan was slightly disappointed. He'd expected something to happen. "Is that it?"

BLT shrugged. "It's just a piece of jewellery until you are initiated. Looks nice though, don't you think?"

Brendan raised the amulet, spreading the chain and dropping it over his head. It slid beneath his shirt and lay against his skin, warm and heavy.

"So," Brendan said. "I have what I came for and I thank you, Finbar. Now I have to go back to the Swan to be initiated. Tell me what you want from me."

Finbar's eyes suddenly filled with tears. "I want to go back!" he said, his voice cracking with emotion.

"Go back?" Brendan was shaken by the man's tears. "I don't understand. Go back where?"

Finbar stepped close to Brendan, his eyes filled with need. "I want to go back and live among the Fair Folk again. I want to go back home."

"I still don't get it," Brendan said. "You're Human. You aren't a Faerie."

"Oh," Finbar moaned, "you're wrong, lad." He tore open his shirt and revealed a terrible puckered scar on his chest. The mark was in the shape of a circle with a strange symbol burned into its centre.

"Aaaah!" BLT sighed. "Now I understand!"

"Well, could you fill me in?" Brendan was getting annoyed.

BLT hovered between them and explained. "He bears the mark of an Exile. When a Faerie transgresses against the Truce, he stands the chance of being sentenced to Exile in the Human world. A great and fearsome magic is worked upon the criminal, stripping him of all of his Faerie Gifts, save long life. Then he is cast out and ostracized by the Faerie World. None may reveal themselves to him on pain of Exile themselves. He is doomed to know of the Faerie World and long for it but never be a part of it again. It explains how he was able to take the amulet from you. He was once a Faerie."

Brendan looked at the abject misery in Finbar's eyes. "How horrible," Brendan said. "Why? What did you do?"

Finbar hung his head. "I fell in love with a Human woman." When he looked up, his eyes shone with tears. "She was beautiful. I couldn't help but love her. I wanted her to know everything about me. I told her of the secret world, the world she couldn't see, and I took her for my wife."

"I don't understand," Brendan said. "What was your crime?"

"Unions between Humans and Faeries are forbidden," BLT said. "The punishment is Exile."

"I've been so lonely, wandering the world trying to forget the woman I'd loved and the world I'd lost," Finbar sobbed. "When you arrived here, I saw my chance. I stole the amulet and waited for you to return for it. Then I would strike my bargain with ye."

Brendan shook his head in disbelief. He looked at the misery in Finbar's face and felt he couldn't be angry for the pain the old man had put him through. How could anyone be so cruel as to punish someone for falling in love? The more he thought about Finbar's case, the more outraged he felt. What if he were to fall in love with Marina Kaprillian? Or rather, what if she fell in love with him (highly unlikely but he was just imagining)? Would that mean he would be Exiled, too? It was ridiculous!

"How can the Exile be reversed?" Brendan demanded. "What do I have to do?"

BLT's face went blank. "There's nothing anyone can do. Exile is irreversible."

"There must be something," Brendan said, looking at Finbar's stricken face.

BLT shook her head with a look of genuine sadness. Finbar sobbed and sat down on his cot. The old man hid his face in his hands and wept bitterly. Brendan sat down beside him.

"I'm sorry," Brendan said softly. "I don't know what I can do. Why would you even want to come back if you love her so much? How could you bear to leave her behind?"

Finbar wiped his eyes on the sleeve of his coat and looked at Brendan. "She's been dead nigh on two centuries. My Aislinn died of fever during the Famine in 1832. We were forced to stay on a ship off the coast until the fever took those it infected. The survivors were put ashore in this new land and I was among them. Now, I'm doomed to live without her."

Brendan couldn't imagine how it might be to live with that kind of sadness forever. He would want to come back to the people he knew and seek solace. What if his parents turned him away when he needed them most? He couldn't imagine a worse loneliness. He laid a hand on the amulet nestled warmly against his chest. There must be something he could do.

"I made you a promise, Finbar," Brendan said firmly. "I will do my best to honour it. I will do everything I can to have your Exile lifted."

"Oh my." The icy tone was all too familiar now. Brendan looked up to see Orcadia sauntering into the lamplight. "Such authority as befits a prince of your standing, Breandan. Making promises you can't possibly keep."

Brendan stood up to face her. He tried to put on a brave face despite the terror that was flooding through him. BLT fluttered to rest on his shoulder. "I've found my token. I will be initiated. I won't let you stop me. Step aside."

"I don't think so." Orcadia smiled sweetly. "You've led me on a winding path, young nephew, and managed quite well considering you had no idea what you were doing. You certainly made me look foolish back there at the hospital. That's all over now. Greenleaf and D'Anaan and Ariel"—she spat the names as if they were poison on her tongue—"they cannot help you now. I'll give you one more chance. You must come with me and join my cause, make war on the Humans and be my right hand." The smile left her face. "Or you will die."

FAMILY

Brendan concentrated with all his might and said, slowly and clearly, "Leave me alone!"

Orcadia laughed, waving a scolding finger playfully at him. "Not this time! You caught me off guard once. Now I know what you're capable of and I won't be Compelled a second time." She glared at him. "So much power and so raw! Let me teach you how to harness your strength! Together, we will make the Humans bow to us. The Fair Folk will rule the Earth again, as they were always meant to!"

Brendan shook his head. "I won't join you. I've lived among Humans my whole life. I know they aren't perfect. They can be selfish. They can be cruel. They don't always do what's best …" His mind was full of the trip through the lake with Oona. "Maybe they don't know how lucky they are to have such a beautiful world to call their own, but they are my people even though I'm not Human myself. My parents took me in and loved me, tried to make sure I was a good person. My friends helped me when I needed them and asked for nothing in return." As he spoke, Brendan's voice became stronger, more sure. "Humans made a mess of the Earth, it's true. I won't give up on them, though. They just need to be shown how to change."

Orcadia listened to his speech with a smirk on her face. When he was done, she shook her head in mock sadness. "What a little fool you are. You can't see the big picture. I think you need help to focus your mind." Orcadia raised a pale hand and beckoned to the shadows behind her.

"No!" Brendan cried as his sister, Delia, stepped into the light. Orcadia must have grabbed her on her way to school. She was dressed in her uniform and her feet were caked in muck, but she didn't seem to notice. The blank expression on her face made it obvious to Brendan that she was under Orcadia's power.

"Let her go," Brendan said through gritted teeth. "Now."

"I don't think I will." Orcadia tapped her chin in a mockery of contemplation. "No. I won't do it. Unless, of course, you join me."

"Never," Brendan said. "If you harm her in any way, I will make you pay for it."

"Oh, that is truly funny. You will make me pay. You haven't got a chance, Breandan. No one can help you! You're uninitiated. The only friends you have are Humans, a sawed-off pipsqueak of a Lesser Faerie, and a miserable Exile. Oh, no, no, no, my dear foolish nephew. I can do whatever I want and you can't stop me." Orcadia turned to Delia. "Sweetheart, pick up those garden shears, will you?"

Obediently, Delia reached out and plucked a pair of shears out of a barrel nearby. She held them up. The rusty blades gleamed dully in the lamplight.

Brendan's mouth went dry. "Don't …" he whispered.

"Now, Delia dear, put the blade to your throat."

Without hesitation, Delia raised the blades and pressed the sharp edge upward under her chin.

"Stop it!" Brendan could barely speak he was so terrified.

Orcadia turned her attention back to Brendan. "Now, Brendan. I will give you one last opportunity to see the error of your ways. Pledge yourself to me and I will let her live. Refuse, and I'll order her to cut her own throat."

Brendan was completely helpless. He knew he couldn't let his sister die. She had been the bane of his existence for as long as he could remember, teasing him, playing tricks on him, insulting him. He'd always thought that he couldn't stand her. Now, when she was about to be taken away from him forever, he knew that despite all the crap she put him through, he loved her.

With that realization, Brendan suddenly felt a surge of strength. His worry and his fear were overwhelmed by another emotion so powerful it flooded his heart and ignited his mind. He looked at Orcadia's smug face, smirking back at him, and the fire in his heart intensified to an almost painful degree. The emotion that possessed him was anger.

Orcadia seemed to sense the change in him. Her smirk slipped slightly. She took a step backward as he raised his hand and pointed at her. He channelled all his rage into one word.

"*No!*"

The effect was immediate. Orcadia was hurled backward as if a giant fist had smashed her in the chest. She flew through stacks of rubbish on her way across the cluttered cellar. Brendan heard, rather than saw, her hit the far wall.

Delia dropped the shears and fell into a heap on the concrete floor like a marionette whose strings had been severed.

"Oh-ho!" BLT crowed, pumping her fist in triumph. "You nailed her good. A *Shout!*[81] I wouldn't have believed it unless I'd seen it!" She capered in mid-air in a bizarre hovering victory dance.

Brendan rushed to Delia's side. She was breathing easily, almost as if she was in a deep sleep. Finbar came up behind him.

"She's all right, lad," the old man assured him. "Just in a deep sleep."

A searing blast of energy sailed over their heads and smashed into the furnace. The cot was set alight.

"Get her out of here," Brendan demanded. Finbar gathered Delia into his arms as Brendan stood to face Orcadia.

She walked toward him, blasting stacks of junk out of her way to clear a path. "You dare strike me, whelp?"

"I told you before," Brendan said firmly with a bravado he didn't feel. "I don't like it when you call me names."

"I'll do worse than that." She raised her hands, and a ball of bristling purple energy coalesced between her palms. "Die!" She flung the ball toward him.

Brendan's intention was to duck out of the way. In his panic, he willed himself to move aside. As soon as he framed the desperate thought, a strange thing happened.

The world seemed to slow down. It was as if some divine being had pressed "Slow" on the DVD of the

---

81 A *Shout* is a telekinetic attack generated by a Faerie's voice, capable of physically damaging opponents. The power of the Shout is directly linked to the concentrating and will of the Shouter. It only works for Faeries. Don't try Shouting at people to knock them down. You'll only get a sore throat and a few weird looks.

universe. He saw the ball approaching, and he had all the time in the world. He watched, fascinated, as the energy tumbled toward him, plumes of force erupting and dying back into the orb like tiny solar flares on the surface of a miniature sun. He turned his head and saw BLT hovering in space, her face frozen in wide-eyed fright. Her tiny wings, usually a blur of movement impossible for the naked eye to follow, flapped in slow and languid strokes.

Brendan looked the other way and saw Finbar with Delia in his arms moving toward the stairs with infinite slowness.

I'm warping! Like that Bartender Saskia. They called her a Warp Warrior. I've speeded up. It's awesome!

In the time he'd been marvelling at the Warp phenomenon, the energy ball had moved closer by a couple of metres. Brendan looked around and his eyes settled on a baseball bat sticking out of a barrel.

"That'll do nicely," he said.

First, he grabbed the handle of the bat and pulled it out of the box. Next, he dashed across the cellar, ducking under the ball of energy on his way. He stopped directly in front of Orcadia and studied her snarling face, full of rage and hatred. Brendan's own rage welled up inside him. He cocked the bat preparing to smack the helpless Faerie in the side of the skull.

Instead, he paused. *Despite all the trouble she's caused I couldn't just smash her like that. It's too ... too much like her.* Walking over to the ball of energy inching through the air, he stood in its path and slightly to the side. He took up a batter stance, waggling the tip of the bat in the air. He'd never been good at sports. He'd always been clumsy, uncoordinated. Now, though, he had all the time in the world. He felt completely in control. Being a Faerie had brought him a lot of pain, discomfort, and terror, but there was an upside. Taking careful aim, he swung the bat and connected with the ball of energy.

Time returned to normal.

The impact shivered up through his forearms. The bat shattered in his hands. The wood scorched. The ball of energy went sailing like a rocket, up into the wooden beams overhead. The wood exploded, and the upper floor fell in a cascade of rubble onto the surprised Orcadia, who disappeared under an avalanche of debris.

"Home run," Brendan said with grim satisfaction. The warping seemed to have drained his strength. He staggered, his limbs quivering and his arms aching from the swing of the bat.

A piece of stray wood tumbled through the air and struck the oil lamp on the table. The lamp shattered, sending burning oil scattering across the piles of rubbish. Immediately, the rubbish began to burn.

"By the Wild Hunt! You're a Warp Warrior!" BLT cried. "This is totally incredible."

Brendan didn't hear her. He didn't hear the crackle of the flames or Finbar's cries for him to get out of the cellar. He was completely focused on Orcadia lying in the rubble at his feet.

She moaned and tried to rise, but Brendan wouldn't let her. He placed his foot on her shoulder and pushed her back to the floor, pinning her down. Blood, red but tinged with a hint of purple, glistened in her pale hair where a stray piece of falling debris had struck her in the scalp. She looked up at him with hatred in her eyes.

"Well," she rasped. "What are you waiting for? You have to kill me. If you don't, I'll find a way to kill you."

Brendan sneered, "You really are pathetic. I'd be doing the world a favour."

"Then do it!"

He still held the stump of the bat in his hand. He looked at it and made a decision.

"I won't be like you," he said. He tossed the bat aside. Flames licked the walls all around them now. The smoke was growing thick. "I won't be a killer. My parents taught me right from wrong. My Human parents, that is."

"Fool," Orcadia snarled. She struggled to rise. "If my brother could see what you've become, he'd be disgusted."

"Don't be so quick to put words in my mouth, Orcadia." The voice was deep and strong. Brendan turned to see where it was coming from. In the centre of the flames raging in the cellar, a shadow appeared. Brendan backed away toward the stairs as a tall Faerie stepped out of the heart of the flames. "I think he is an exceptional child."

Brendan looked into the face of the newcomer. His skin was white as milk and his lips a thin bloodless line. He had pale blond hair and violet eyes.

"Hello, Breandan," Briach Morn said. "I am your father."

Brendan didn't know what to say. He stared at the tall stranger with wonder in his eyes. "You … you're supposed to be …"

"On the Other Side? I was, and I will be again soon." Briach Morn smiled gently.

"They told me no one could ever come back from there."

"So I believed as well." Morn nodded. "But, like all Faerie power, will plays an important part. I willed myself here because I wanted to see you. My wish was sincere enough to grant me a short reprieve. I doubt that I will be able to do it again."

"Brother"—Orcadia struggled to her feet—"stay! I need you! Together we can take this world back."

Morn's face hardened. "You are wrong, Orcadia. I have had many years to contemplate what I've done. We will never rule here again. We have had our time. We must accept that."

Orcadia's face turned into a snarling mask of fury. "Weakling! You may have lost your nerve but I haven't. I will do it without you. There are others who will rally to my flag …"

"Oh, dear sister, do shut up, will you," Briach Morn said wearily. He flicked his wrist and Orcadia was jerked from her feet. She sailed across the cellar toward the shadow in the heart of the raging flames.

"Noooooooooooo!" she cried as she fell into the heart of the fire and disappeared.

"That's better," Briach said, smiling. "Sisters, eh? No end of trouble."

Brendan laughed in spite of himself. "I know." He looked at the fire. "What will happen to her? Is she …?"

Morn shook his head. "Not dead. She'll be waiting for me on the Other Side. There'll be hell to pay but no matter. I have an eternity to smooth things over with her."

The fire was spreading, consuming every bit of dry rubbish it could find. The heat and the smoke didn't affect Brendan, though. Morn seemed to have cast a protective ring about them.

His Faerie father reached out and took Brendan's face in his long, elegant hands. The skin felt cool on Brendan's cheeks. Briach Morn looked into his son's face and smiled a sad smile. "You look so much like her. Your smile especially."

Brendan felt like crying but he swallowed his tears. "What was my mother like?"

His father's eyes clouded as if he were looking into another time. "She was fair and kind. Such a generous heart. Her people couldn't understand why she would give herself to me. I understood. She was a Healer, you see, and I was sick. I was sick in my very soul. She gave me a reason to think the world might be a wonderful place. She gave me you." He smiled down at his son, and this time Brendan did begin to cry. "I didn't understand what a wonderful gift that was until now."

"Why did you leave me, then? Why did you go to the Other Side and leave me alone in the world?"

Briach's fingers brushed away Brendan's tears. "I am truly sorry for that now. I couldn't bear to live in a world where your mother didn't exist, just as I couldn't bear to look in your face and see her there. I chose to take myself away. I didn't want to leave you under the influence of my sister, and your mother's people hated me. They blamed me for her death. So I left you in the care of Humans because I believed that was what your mother would have wanted. She thought that our future in the world lay with Faeries and Humans coming to an understanding and accepting one another. I tried to make it start with her own child."

The fire surrounded them. Even through Briach's magical barrier, Brendan began to feel the heat. His father's tone became urgent. "I haven't much time. You have found your token. Do you wish me to initiate you into your birthright?"

Brendan gaped. "You could do that?"

His father nodded.

Brendan thought quickly. He wanted to be a part of the Faerie World but he didn't want to abandon his Human family. He loved them. He thought about the mother he'd never known and what she would have wanted him to do. He made a decision. "Yes. Do it!"

Briach smiled and closed his eyes. He laid a hand on Brendan's chest, resting his palm on the amulet.

"Welcome," Briach Morn said softly. "Welcome, Breandan."

Brendan felt a shock of tingling warmth spread through his chest. The warmth raced outward from Briach Morn's hand and radiated quickly through Brendan's entire body. For an endless instant, he was aglow. Then the sensation dissipated, leaving a slight tingling in its wake.

His father held him close then and whispered a single word into Brendan's ear: his secret name. Brendan's eyes opened wide and he smiled.

"Keep it safe," his father said. Morn dropped his hand. "It is done. You must go now and so must I."

Brendan blinked away tears. "Can't you stay? Please? Just a little longer?"

Briach Morn smiled sadly and shook his head. "I've stayed too long as it is. Even my will has its limits. The Other Side would have me back. I love you, my dear Breandan. I will think of you always."

With a final wave, Briach Morn turned away and stepped into the heart of the flames. He disappeared from sight.

The heat and roar of the flames immediately assaulted Brendan. He put his hand over his mouth and staggered for the stairs. His feet weighed a ton. He was completely exhausted. Through slitted lids he tried to find his way, feeling along the wall as he climbed the rickety staircase.

He emerged onto the ground floor to find the smoke completely surrounding him. He staggered a few steps in the direction he thought the door might be. He ran into a wall. Panicking, he realized he was completely disoriented. He had no idea how to get out. He could hardly breathe.

You make it this far so you can die in a house fire? What a rip-off!

He felt a tug on his sleeve. He squinted through the smoke and was delighted to see BLT pulling him by the arm.

"C'mon, use your Sight." She coughed. "You can do it!" Brendan wiped his tearing eyes and tried to concentrate. Forcing aside his panic and fatigue, he imagined that the smoke was no longer there. He blinked and it seemed as though he could focus. He saw BLT fluttering ahead of him. Beyond her, clear as day, he saw a patch of light ahead. He dashed toward it and emerged into the sun.

He staggered through the mud until he reached the fence. Finbar grabbed Brendan by the collar and hauled him through.

"We have to get away from here." He heard Greenleaf's urgent voice. "The fire crews will be coming soon."

Titi spiralled around him and gave BLT a high five. Greenleaf's Lesser Faeries winked at Brendan and said "Well done!"

Brendan raised his head to see the old brick building engulfed in flames. *I got out of there? It's a miracle*, he thought. Then he passed out.

ARRANGEMENTS

Brendan opened his eyes to find that BLT seemed to have grown to Human-sized proportions. Then he realized she was straddling the end of his nose.

"Hallo, Breandan!" She smiled, raising a tiny cup. "*Sláinte!*"[82]

"Cheers," Brendan answered. "What is that?"

"Hot chocolate," she said, grinning. "With marshmallows." BLT's wings whirred, and she rose into the air to hover above him.

Brendan looked past her at what appeared to be a tangle of vines. He didn't know where he was. *Did I fall asleep under a tree?* He looked at the vines more closely and realized they were not alive. Rather they were carved in loving detail out of wood.

"You're awake," Kim said. Brendan turned his head to find her leaning against the wall in a chair by the side of his bed, her tattooed arms crossed over her chest. She was dressed in jeans and a T-shirt. Her field hockey stick

---

[82] *Sláinte* is a common Irish toast meaning, as most toasts do in any language, "to your health." The exception is the Ulikwe Tribe of Central Africa who say *Ututu*, which, roughly translated, means "I will strangle you in your sleep." Needless to say, few people drink with the Ulikwe Tribe if they can avoid it.

leaned against the wall within easy reach. "You were really out of it."

Brendan pushed himself up onto his elbows and looked around. He was in a snug room that contained little in the way of furniture. Besides the bed and the chair, there was a compact, ornately carved wooden bedside table and a full-length mirror hanging on the back of the door. The walls were panelled in wood, polished to a warm glow. A fire burned in the tiny fireplace, making the room comfortably cozy.

"Where am I?" Brendan asked, groggily. He snapped fully awake. "Delia!"

Kim laid a hand on his shoulder, calming him. "She's fine. Greenleaf took her home and Compelled her to forget. She'll be fine."

Brendan relaxed. "Where are we?"

"The Swan," Kim said. "Greenleaf brought you back. You were a little the worse for wear. The Healers worked on you and you slept through the night."

"Through the night?"

"And the day," BLT piped, her high voice filled with excitement. She fluttered down to rest on Brendan's shoulder.

"Like I said, you were out of it," Kim repeated.

Brendan stretched. "I don't feel so bad now."

"We heal quickly," Kim said in an offhand way. "One of the benefits of being one of us."

He reached for the amulet. It was gone.

"It's inside of you now," Kim said, seeing his confusion. "You are initiated. No one knows how you managed it, but you're one of us."

Brendan was about to tell her of his encounter with his

father but he caught himself. That experience belonged to him and he was reluctant to share it. "I didn't have much choice in the end."

Kim snorted. "You act like that's a bad thing."

Brendan thought about it for a moment before saying, "It isn't good or bad. It's just who I am. I'm going to try to make the best of things."

Kim, her face a picture of seriousness, considered his words for a moment. "That's a remarkably mature attitude for a total dumbwad." Then she cracked her familiar smirk.

They both laughed. Kim tossed him a bundle of clothes. "These should fit. Get dressed. Everyone is waiting for you downstairs." She grabbed the field hockey stick and slung it over her shoulder. "I'm glad you're okay." She winked and left him to dress.

"Hurry up!" BLT shouted, buzzing once around his head before zipping out the door.

Ten minutes later, Brendan stood in front of the mirror examining the changes his initiation had wrought.

His skin glowed with health. All evidence of adolescent acne was erased. He ran his fingers over his cheek and marvelled at the smoothness. His hair was lustrous and thick, streaked with hints of purple and gold. Holding his hands out in front of his face, he wiggled his fingers and was amazed at their elegance. He bounced on the balls of his feet. He felt as light as a feather. On an impulse, he dashed at the wall, ran up it, and somersaulted to a graceful landing. He couldn't help but laugh out loud.

"This is totally sick," he said joyously.

The most amazing change was not cosmetic. His sight was so acute he could pick out minute details of his environment. He could see the almost invisible marks of the carver's chisel in the vines on the ceiling. He could see the pores of his skin. For a person who'd always worn glasses, the ability to actually see, without artificial aid, was truly marvellous.

Yes, being a Faerie had its upside, to be sure. Now he had to face the downside. His Human family and his Human life were in jeopardy. He steeled himself for the coming confrontation. Opening the door, he left the room.

He found himself at the top of the stairs he'd seen when he first came to the Swan. The room he'd slept in opened onto a hallway, facing into the pub below. The buzz of conversation almost drowned out the musicians and the DJ. Almost, but not quite. Brendan stood at the top of the stairs and looked down at the pub floor.

Every seat was taken, and many more Faeries were jammed into the bar. The crowd was so huge he suddenly felt nervous. *Could they all be here just to see me?*

He had his answer an instant later.

"There he is!" Og's voice roared. "Prince Breandan himself."

The burly Artificer stood up at the corner booth and raised a foaming pint of ale. Everyone in the room joined him, raising glasses with a mighty shout.

He made his way down the stairs and waded into the crowd. His back was slapped. His hand was pumped. His cheeks were pinched. He was kissed and hugged and crushed. Finally, Leonard pushed his way to Brendan's side and grabbed the boy's arm. "Give 'im some room, mon!" The massive shoulders served as a battering ram, forcing a clear path to the corner booth. Brendan gratefully scooted along behind him.

Sitting in the booth were Ariel, Kim, Deirdre, and Greenleaf. BLT sat on the edge of a bowl full of olives gnawing on a grape that looked like a pumpkin in her tiny hands.

"I'm trying to cut back," BLT joked, juice dripping down her chin. "One step at a time, eh?"

Og stood up and offered Brendan his seat on the bench beside Kim. "Ye did it, nephew!" Og was beaming with delight. "Look at you. What a fine figure of a Faerie ye are, as well."

The rest of the crowd went back to their conversations, dancing, and drinking. They were keenly aware that the gathering at the table was a family affair.

Ariel smiled his sad smile. "Well done, indeed, Breandan. You found a way to survive Orcadia and somehow initiate yourself." The grey eyes became shrewd. "I'd love to hear how you managed it. What became of Orcadia?"

Brendan felt those ancient eyes boring into his soul. "I don't know. Things are kind of hazy. I guess she was trapped in the fire."

Ariel nodded but said nothing. Brendan was sure he could see right through him. "As for the amulet, I picked it up and put it on ... after that, I blacked out."

"Good thing I found you." BLT sprayed bits of grape onto the table. "I saved your life, ya know. At least I gave you a few pointers, right?"

Brendan laughed. "Yes, you did. Thanks, BLT." He shot a smile at Og and said, "And thank you for lending her to me."

"I'm glad she could help." Og shrugged. "I knew ye'd see the value in her. I had faith in ye!"

Deirdre reached a hand across the table and caressed Brendan's cheek. "Now I can see my sister in you. It's in the shape of your face." Her eyes teared up. "I'm so glad you're among us now."

"We must start your training at once. There's so much you have to learn," Ariel said. "You can stay here for now until you get settled. I trust that the room was comfortable?"

"About that ..." Brendan frowned. He'd made a decision in the burning cellar, and he was determined to follow it through. "I want to go home."

"Home?" Deirdre said, confused. "You're home right now."

"I mean to my Human parents," Brendan said firmly. "I'm not leaving them."

Kim laughed. She turned and held out a hand to Og. "Ha! I told you! Pay up!" Og grumbled and fished some coins out of his pocket and dropped them into her palm.

"No," Deirdre snapped. "That is not possible. You cannot go back. You are one of the Fair Folk! Your place is here with us. We are your family."

"Yes," Brendan agreed. "You are my family. I know that, but so are the people who raised me and loved me and did all the hard work of making me into the person I am. I won't abandon them now. Nothing you can say will change my mind."

Deirdre was about to protest, but Greenleaf spoke instead. "I think we have to respect Breandan's wishes in this."

"It is highly unusual," Ariel said. "In fact, I don't think I've ever heard of it happening before."

"Breandan is unusual, to say the least." Greenleaf smiled at Brendan before continuing. "He has displayed aptitude in at least three of the Disciplines of the Art. He has the Power of Command, Compulsion, Summoning, and Binding, and from what BLT has told us, he's a Warp Warrior to boot. I've never heard of anyone having such a broad range of Talents."

"And there's the prophecy," Og said pointedly. "Ow!" He hopped on one leg as he rubbed his shin. Glaring at Kim, he growled, "That's twice now."

Kim smirked.

"Will someone finally tell me about the prophecy?"

Ariel held up his hand. "It is conjecture, as are all prophecies. Long ago, when the Truce was struck between the Fair Folk and the People of Metal, an oracle declared that a time would come when the two tribes would be reconciled once again. A prince would come who was of both worlds. Many people believe that prince is you, Breandan."

"What am I prince of?" Brendan said. "Do I have my own kingdom? Or a castle or something?"

Og laughed, "Sadly no. These titles are ancient ones, from the time when Faeries ruled the world. Now, they're just titles."

"Perhaps not," Greenleaf said. "Who knows what is in a name? I believe in the power of words. A name is a powerful word indeed."

"I have a little gifty for ye, nephew. Consider it an initiation gift," Og rumbled. He held out a massive paw. Resting in his palm was a wristwatch. Examining it closely, Brendan discovered that the face was carved out of grey stone and the band was some sort of hide. "I made it meself. Your glamour is embedded in it. While ye have it on, you'll appear Human. It's just temporary, until ye learn to cast the glamours yer own self." Og winked. "And it's also waterproof to a thousand metres and it gets Wi-Fi."

Brendan took the watch and strapped it on. He looked up at Og and grinned. "That's Uncle Og."

"Ye hear that?" Og laughed. "He called me Uncle Og!"

"Speaking of gifts," Greenleaf interjected, "I would like to take it upon myself to give Breandan his instruction … if there are no objections?"

Ariel nodded. "I guess we have no choice, Breandan. You may return to your Human family, and we will make provisions for your instruction as far as the Disciplines go. Greenleaf will stay on at your school to watch over you."

Brendan stood. "Thank you. I know this is weird for you. It's doubly weird for me, believe me. But I can't help it. I'm doing the right thing."

"I hope you are right," Ariel sighed. "You've chosen a difficult road, Breandan. One world is hard enough. Two worlds may be more than anyone can handle."

"I'll be okay," Brendan said. "Oh, and by the way, my name is Brendan. No extra 'a' from now on." Somehow, it was important to Brendan to retain that little bit of his old self. "Brendan."

"As you wish." Ariel chuckled.

"I'd better be going," Brendan said. "My mum and dad will be worried sick."

"Call them on the way home," Og said, tossing him a small flat block of wood. Brendan caught it easily. His old clumsiness was a thing of the past.

He walked out through the crowd. Well-wishers slapped his back and made sure he knew they were glad he'd come through the Quest unscathed. As he approached the door, someone grabbed him by the arm. He was spun around to find himself looking into the face of Finbar. The old man smiled.

"Finbar! I'd forgotten. Are you all right?"

"Sure, I'm fine. Never better."

"Are you going to be reinstated?"

The old man shook his head. "Nay, not yet anyway. They're discussin' my case." Finbar cracked a smile. "But since I gave you a hand, they're lookin' at me with a kinder eye. I have ye to thank fer that." The old man offered his calloused hand and Brendan shook it gladly.

"Thank you," Brendan said sincerely.

"Thank me? Fer what? If I hadn't lifted yer token, ye would never have had all this trouble."

"Well, you saved Delia and I owe you a lot. I'll lobby for you."

Finbar winked and let go of Brendan's hand.

Brendan turned and walked the rest of the way to the door. He reached the door of the Swan and looked back at his newfound friends and family.

Og, Kim, Deirdre, and Greenleaf smiled and waved. Brendan couldn't help but feel excited about the possibilities his new life presented. Finbar ducked his head meekly and waved. Brendan waved back. Though he was desperate to get back to his Human family, he suddenly was reluctant to leave.

Then he caught sight of Ariel. The ancient Faerie sat unnaturally still, watching him with those inscrutable eyes, an enigmatic expression on his pale face. Brendan sensed that Ariel was a dangerous person for all of his benign, grandfatherly demeanour. He looked at Brendan as if he could pry open his mind and examine the boy's inner thoughts.

Brendan looked at that face and realized he couldn't get out of the Swan soon enough.

"Good luck, mon," Leonard said, laying a massive arm around Brendan's shoulders. "You've chosen a difficult path but I tink you be up to de task."

Brendan looked up into the smiling dark face and smiled back. "I think it's going to be okay, Leonard."

"You be careful," a feminine voice growled. Saskia, the bartender with the yellow, wolfish eyes, sidled up and took Leonard's arm. "If you need anything, you be sure and let us know. I would be happy to help you with your Warp training."

"Cool! Thanks a lot. I was really wiped out after I warped."

"Everyone is after their first time. It gets better with practice."

With one last look around at the bizarre and beautiful menagerie of Faerie patrons, he stepped out the door of the Swan of Liir and into the cool, crisp November evening.

The sun was already setting. He was standing in the grass behind the Ward's Island Community Centre. A man came around the side of the building rolling an empty beer keg through the wet grass.

"Whoa!" the man said. "You scared the crap outta me. I didn't know anyone else was back here."

"Sorry," Brendan said. He looked back at the wall of the Community Centre. The door to the Swan was clearly visible. He decided to try a little test. He pointed at the door. "Can you see that?"

The man looked at the door and his shoulders fell. "I know. I really gotta paint that wall. It's peeling something fierce. There's just no dough, my son."

Brendan set off in the direction of the public ferry terminal. He would have gone to the Faerie Terminal but he still didn't have any noble metal. The thought of the bargain he'd struck with the Ferryman sent a shiver down his spine. He was sure that bird would come home to roost one day. He went to the ferry operator and wove a tale about how his wallet and phone had been stolen. He promised to repay the man if he let him take the ferry back to the city. Though dubious, the operator agreed.

Later, dozing on the ferry, he was woken by the buzz of wings. A light pressure on his shoulder heralded BLT's arrival.

"Hey, Brendan," BLT said softly. "Don't let me wake you."

"What are you doing here?"

"I'm with you now," she said proudly. "I've decided that you're gonna be where the action is and that's where I wanna be." The Lesser Faerie pulled a single skittle from inside her vest and held it up to him. "To adventure!"

"Adventure?" Brendan snorted. "You haven't been to high school, have you? It's more like prison."

"*Eeeew!*" A little girl across the aisle from Brendan pointed at his shoulder and made a face. "Look at that huge fly!"

Brendan smiled and patted BLT on the head. "She's my friend!"

The girl buried her face in her mother's side. The mother glared at Brendan. He laughed and turned away, looking out the window. He gasped.

"Holy …" He couldn't believe his eyes. Seeing the city with his new Faerie Sight was a shock.

The ferry was approaching the docks. The skyline was nothing like he remembered. No, that wasn't exactly true. The familiar buildings were there: bank towers, condos, and office buildings. There were simply more, as if another skyline had been laid overtop the one he knew. Jagged pieces stuck out of the familiar bank buildings. Towers and lights and strangely shaped buildings rose where no buildings were supposed to be. Most notably, the CN Tower, normally a long pointed stick with a bulge near the top like an olive on a toothpick, now had two bulges, a smaller one above the one he had known all his life.

There was a whole other city he had never known existed until his eyes had been opened by his initiation.

"Thanks, Dad," Brendan said softly and he wondered if Briach Morn, on the Other Side, might hear him.

"This is so crazy!" Brendan laughed out loud.

BLT's laughter tinkled in his ear. "Oh, my dear Prince Brendan. You have a lot to learn!"

Epilogue

Brendan was terrified of what his parents' reaction would be. He expected them to be absolutely furious. He'd been rehearsing excuses for his disappearance on the walk home. BLT had tried to be helpful but she really didn't have any experience with angry parents. Her suggestions were hardly workable: erase their minds, set a fire to distract them, etc.

So he was quite shocked when his parents weren't angry at all. They were so delighted to see him on the doorstep that he didn't even have to explain. They blamed themselves, sure that their revelation of his adoption had been the motivation for his running away. They didn't care where he'd been. They were just glad to have him back.

Of course, Delia was annoyed.

"If I'd run away, you guys would have grounded me for, like, a decade," she said sullenly.

The last time Brendan had seen Delia, Orcadia had been threatening her life. Brendan was so happy to see her safe he couldn't help himself. He threw his arms around her and held her as she thrashed.

"Gross! What's wrong with you? Get off me, you creep!"

But he wouldn't let go, despite her protests. He hugged her close and smiled at his parents over her shoulder. He was home.

The next day, he went back to school. BLT rode along in his knapsack as he walked through Queen's Park. The squirrels chirped, "Hello? Hello? Food?" Brendan tossed them some bread he'd brought along for just such an occasion. Lord Chitter's voice shouted at his back, "What? No jam? Bring a muffin next time, you big punk!"

Brendan smiled but didn't look back.

In homeroom, Harold and Dmitri were delighted to see him. For Brendan, the reunion was bittersweet. They didn't mention any of their shared adventure so Brendan had to assume that his Compulsion had worked. He was relieved but a little sad that they couldn't share his happiness. From now on, there would be a distance between him and his close friends.

"We were so worried," Dmitri exclaimed.

"Yeah," Harold said. He looked at Brendan strangely, and for an instant, Brendan worried that his Compulsion hadn't worked on the chubby boy but after a second, Harold smiled, saying, "We thought you'd gone nuts like Chester."

Brendan frowned. "What do you mean, nuts like Chester?"

"Didn't you hear?" Harold was full of glee. "He ran off all of a sudden. He just lost it and started running. They finally picked him up outside of Niagara Falls trying to run across the bridge into New York State. All he would say is, 'I gotta get lost! I gotta get lost!' over and over again."

"They have him sedated in Sick Kids Hospital," Dmitri added. He wasn't quite so ecstatic at Chester's misfortune but he couldn't help a small grin.

"If ever a guy deserved a little bad luck, it'd be Chester." Kim's voice cut into the conversation. "He's a jerk."

Kim walked into the classroom and plunked down in her customary seat without so much as a glance at Brendan's surprised expression. Her glamours were up, but Brendan could see a ghost of her Faerie features shimmering beneath her Human façade. She dropped her knapsack at her feet, the field hockey stick poking out. Before Brendan could say anything, the bell rang to start the day.

Walking to English class, Brendan managed to get a word with Kim as Harold and Dmitri walked ahead.

"I didn't think you'd be back," Brendan said.

Kim shrugged. "Somebody has to keep you from hurting yourself. You've got a lot to learn and until you do, I'll be watching over you. Besides," she smiled, hauling the field hockey stick out of the knapsack and brandishing it in front of her, "All-City Championships are next month."

Brendan laughed as they entered class.

"No weapons in the classroom please, Kim!" Mr. Greenleaf's clear, crisp voice called out. The Faerie stood in his impeccable green suit and yellow vest at the front of the class. He had just finished writing his name on the blackboard in his elegant, flowing handwriting. He smiled at Brendan and gestured for him to take a seat. Kim rolled her eyes and replaced the stick in her bag.

Shaking his head but smiling, Brendan took his customary desk.

"I am Mr. Greenleaf," the substitute teacher began. "I'm sure you all will be delighted to hear that Mr. Bowley will be back today. Though he won a tidy sum in the lottery, he felt it was still his duty to bring the glory of chemistry to young minds." The announcement was greeted by a universal groan. Greenleaf laughed. "The good news, for me, is that your English teacher, Ms. Hewlett, is going to be away on maternity leave for the rest of the year so I will be replacing her as your teacher." This announcement brought a titter of excitement from the girls and an eye roll from Kim. "I am delighted to be given this opportunity to further your education." Greenleaf's eyes found Brendan's and lingered there. "Delighted." Brendan smiled back.

"Excellent." Greenleaf clapped his hands once. "English! The written word! Is there anything more noble or capable of transporting the heart? I think not. Let's begin with poetry."

Later on, in gym class, Brendan found himself standing on the sidelines as the Murderball game progressed. He had found it laughably easy to avoid the ball. All his former clumsiness was gone. He could have stayed in the game right until the end if he had wanted to but in the second round, he'd let the ball strike him. People would wonder if he suddenly changed too much. Besides, there was no real glory in winning when the game was so easy. He wasn't a bully like Chester.

The thought of Chester sedated in the hospital gave him a stab of guilt. He had to do something about that.

"Hey." A feminine voice intruded on his thoughts. He looked up into the beautiful face of Marina Kaprillian. "I'm Marina Kaprillian."

He'd thought she'd been lovely before when he had only had Human sight. Now, with his Faerie Sight, she positively glowed. Her hair was filled with streaks of light. Her blue eyes sparkled. Her skin was smooth and free of blemish. Brendan felt weak.

As for Brendan himself, he still wore his glasses because he couldn't think of a plausible excuse for losing them. He would have to replace the lenses with plain glass or risk constant headaches. He'd been vain enough that when he called upon the wristwatch Og had given him to raise his glamour, he'd left out the pimples that had been the plague of his life before his Initiation. Now he looked at this perfect creature and felt that he didn't have to be afraid or self-conscious. He was secure and happy with who and what he was.

"Hi," he said. "I'm Brendan Clair."

"I know who *you* are." With that, she just smiled and walked away to rejoin her friends, who tittered behind their hands. Marina was absorbed into the embrace of that fortress of girlie giggling with only a single backward glance that skewered Brendan's heart effortlessly.

He was delirious, weightless, afire. He'd thought that there could be no greater change in his life than learning his true nature but the attention of the most beautiful girl in Robertson Davies Academy had trumped even that. He leaned back against the wall of the gym and smiled.

Kim caught his eye. She stood across the gym and glared at him. She frowned and shook her head slightly. Brendan glared back, refusing to let her glower ruin this moment. He recalled Finbar's Exile and the pain the old man had gone through. He cast his eye back to Marina. She flashed him a shy smile.

Brendan smiled back. *Exile would be worth it.*

Everyone was going for a slice after school but Brendan begged off. He had something to do.

He knew that Chester was in the psychiatric wing at Sick Kids. Brendan managed to find the room, and without resorting to any Compulsion, he managed to talk his way in to see his former nemesis.

Brendan entered the private room to find Chester lying in a bed, propped up by pillows. The boy was secured to the bed by padded restraining straps on his wrists, his ankles, and across his chest. Chester was sedated, but he still thrashed weakly in his sleep, straining against the straps and mumbling over and over, "Gotta get lost! Gotta get lost!"

Brendan moved into the room to the bedside. He looked down on his handiwork, and even though he hadn't been in control himself when he Compelled Chester, he felt ashamed of himself.

"Oh!" A woman's voice caused Brendan to turn toward the door. A short woman in faded jeans and a sweatshirt and carrying a cup of coffee stood there. Her face was tired. She looked surprised to see anyone in the room. "Who are you?"

"I'm Brendan Clair," Brendan said quickly. "I'm a friend of Chester's. From school. I thought I'd come and see how he was doing."

The woman smiled then. It was a weary smile. "That's so nice," she said. "I'm Chester's mum." She walked to the bed and stood beside Brendan to look down on her son. "They don't know what's wrong with him. His father died suddenly last year and he has taken it hard. He used to be a straight-A student, but he's been failing this year. He's been getting into trouble, and I don't know what to do."

She smiled up at Brendan, and he saw the dark circles under her eyes. "I'm so glad you came. It's nice to know he has some friends … besides the ones that he gets into trouble with."

Brendan didn't trust himself to speak. He turned to Chester. The boy's eyes darted back and forth under the purple lids. Sweat drenched the sheets. Brendan leaned over and brought his mouth close to the sleeping boy's ear.

"Chester," he said softly, firmly, pitching his voice so that Chester's mother couldn't hear. "This is Brendan. I know you can hear me." Chester's thrashing lessened slightly. "Listen to what I say. You don't have to get lost any more. You can come home now."

The effect was immediate. Chester relaxed completely. He smiled in his sleep. In a moment, he was breathing deeply and easily.

Brendan stood up and smiled. Chester's mother gasped. "I don't believe it." She beamed at Brendan, her face full of relief. "What did you do?"

Brendan smiled and ducked his head shyly. "I told him you needed him to come back."

Chester's mum burst into tears. She dropped her coffee with a splash and crushed her face into Brendan's chest. For a moment, Brendan was mortified but he quickly recovered. Very gently, awkwardly, he patted the woman on the back as she cried.

"Everything's going to be okay," Brendan said softly. And he believed it.

Epi-Epilogue

When Harold got home from school, he went up to his room right away. He wanted to look at the sketchbook again.

He'd hidden it under the mattress in his room. His mother didn't change the sheets until the weekend so he knew it would be safe there.

He flopped onto his bed and flipped the book open to the first page. He'd obviously drawn this sketch. He recognized his style, but he couldn't for the life of him remember ever having drawn it.

The sketch depicted his friend Brendan, only Brendan was strangely transformed. He was surrounded by an aura of energy. His eyes shone with an inner light. Over Brendan's shoulder, a tiny winged woman fluttered.

A bizarre picture. Why had he drawn it? When had he drawn it? He couldn't remember. He flipped through the sketch pad. There were more pictures of winged people, weird dog-things, a frightening woman with wild eyes radiating waves of power.

Harold had no idea what to make of it. Sitting on his bed in the gathering dusk, he decided he wouldn't rest until he figured out the mystery.

"Harold! Dinner!"

"Coming, Ma!"

He stuffed the sketchbook back under the mattress and hurried down to dinner.

Acknowledgments

I would like to thank Jennifer Notman, my editor, and all the good people at Penguin Canada. I would also like to thank Lorne, Morgan, Beth, Zoe, Robbie, and Kim for reading the early drafts. Finally, thank you to all the librarians who have embraced my books. They are the secret heroes and heroines of reading.